A SECOND CHANCE AT LOVE

As the two girls walked to the other side of the buggy to chat, Nettie followed their progress. The tenderness on her face as she watched her daughter and Esther together kickstarted Stephen's heart.

"*Danke*," Nettie said in a soft, breathy voice. "Katie has spent the whole school year being lonely. She brings a book and sits far from the other children during recess. I'm glad she has a friend."

She glanced up at him, her eyes glimmering with tears and gratitude. The air whooshed from Stephen's lungs, and he couldn't take his eyes off her.

Nettie melted under Stephen's caring look. Her heart expanded until it pressed against her ribs. The sky turned bluer; the grass, greener. The whole world took on shimmery hues.

She'd never felt this way before . . .

Books by Rachel J. Good

HIS UNEXPECTED AMISH TWINS

HIS PRETEND AMISH BRIDE

HIS ACCIDENTAL AMISH FAMILY

AN UNEXPECTED AMISH PROPOSAL

AN UNEXPECTED AMISH COURTSHIP

AN UNEXPECTED AMISH CHRISTMAS

AN AMISH MARRIAGE OF CONVENIENCE

Published by Kensington Publishing Corp.

An AMISH
MARRIAGE *of*
CONVENIENCE

RACHEL J. GOOD

ZEBRA BOOKS
Kensington Publishing Corp.
www.kensingtonbooks.com

ZEBRA BOOKS are published by

Kensington Publishing Corp.
119 West 40th Street
New York, NY 10018

All Kensington titles, imprints, and distributed lines are available at special quantity discounts for bulk purchases for sales promotion, premiums, fund-raising, educational, or institutional use.

Special book excerpts or customized printings can also be created to fit specific needs. For details, write or phone the office of the Kensington Sales Manager: Attn.: Sales Department. Kensington Publishing Corp., 119 West 40th Street, New York, NY 10018. Phone: 1-800-221-2647.

Zebra and the Z logo Reg. U.S. Pat. & TM Off.
BOUQUET Reg. U.S. Pat. & TM Off.

First Printing: September 2022
ISBN-13: 978-1-4201-5462-7
ISBN-13: 978-1-4201-5463-4 (eBook)

10 9 8 7 6 5 4 3 2 1

Printed in the United States of America

Chapter One

Strong winds rattled the sides of the buggy as Stephen Lapp pulled into the Green Valley Farmer's Market. Beside him, his twelve-year-old daughter, Joline, clung tightly to one of her younger twin sisters, who squirmed on her lap. The other three children huddled in the back seat, their eyes wide, as gusts swept across the deserted parking lot. Each blast shook the buggy, but the horse kept his head bent and plodded forward.

The sun hadn't peeked over the horizon yet, and in the morning grayness, an immense dark shadow loomed near the top of the market building, twisting and writhing in the air. Stephen sucked in a breath.

The huge wooden signboard had come loose on one end. It dangled precariously while winds whipped it back and forth, clapping it against the building with loud bangs. If the other chain snapped, the sign would plummet to the ground.

The wood cracked hard against the cement block building, and Joline jumped. "Daed, will it crash into us?"

Even the horse grew skittish. Stephen steered in a wide circle away from the noise and danger. He parked the buggy on the opposite side of the building. They'd be safe over here. While he tied up the horse, Joline helped her siblings out.

Stephen handed her his key to the employee entrance. "Take everyone inside and start putting out the meats." He could trust her to look after her brothers and sisters. Although he wished he didn't have to do it, he often depended on her to take her *mamm*'s place.

"What are you going to do?" Joline's voice quavered.

"I have to fix that sign."

Joline's face creased with concern. "*Neh*, Daed, you can't do that."

She'd spoken Stephen's doubts aloud, but something had to be done before the sign fell and hurt someone. Or splintered into pieces.

His son Matt piped up. "Can't Martin do it?"

The maintenance man usually pulled in before anyone else to unlock the employee doors. Although Stephen and his children had only been working at the market for a week, Matt had already taken a shine to Martin and liked to follow the maintenance man as he made his rounds. This morning, though, Stephen had arrived extra early. Martin wouldn't get there for at least thirty minutes. They couldn't wait that long.

"You all go in and set up while I figure out what to do." If his children were watching, Stephen couldn't act brave enough to fool them. Better not to have them around.

Joline herded the others ahead of her, but after she unlocked the door, she peeked over her shoulder with concerned eyes.

Stephen pasted on a sickly smile. "Let's trust God for this." He needed to reassure himself as much as her.

She studied him closely and then nodded. "I'll pray for you."

"*Danke*." He needed all the Divine help he could get.

After his children had gone inside, he entered the maintenance shed attached to the side of the building. One part of him prayed Martin had left the door unlocked. The other part hoped he hadn't. Then Stephen would have an excuse for avoiding the sign.

His fingers closed over the doorknob. *Please, Lord . . .*

He trailed off, unsure of which outcome to request. The knob rotated, and the latch clicked open. Gulping back his disappointment and his growing fear, Stephen pushed open the door. He waited a few moments for his eyes to adjust to the dimness.

Tiny emergency lights gave off enough light so he could make out several ladders leaning against the far wall. They ranged from a short stepladder to a tall expandable extension ladder.

Could he wait a half hour? Maybe he could stand in the parking lot and direct people away from that side of the building until Martin fixed the sign. But what if it fell?

The feisty ninety-two-year-old woman who owned this market had mentioned her dad had hand-carved that sign. If it got destroyed, she'd be devastated.

Stephen couldn't let his fears stop him from doing what was right.

As he reached for the extension ladder, words from Corinthians flashed through his mind: *My grace is sufficient for thee: for My strength is made perfect in weakness.*

"You have plenty of weakness to work with here, Lord," he whispered.

He maneuvered the ladder out of the shed and fought the wind to carry it around the building. He leaned it against the wall close to where the sign banged back and forth. So far, it hadn't pulled loose.

As he tugged on the rope to expand the ladder and the rungs went higher and higher, his stomach sank lower and lower. How could he ever climb up there?

Steadying the ladder as well as his nerves, Stephen drew in a deep breath. *Lord, I need your strength.*

He mounted the first few rungs. It was still an easy jump to the ground. Then, palms slick with sweat, he pulled himself up higher.

Don't look down, he chanted on each rung. But dark clouds from the past enveloped him, and old memories overwhelmed him. In his mind, he plummeted, free-falling through the air with nothing to support him, nothing to catch him. Stephen clenched the ladder rails. His stomach knotted, and his chest constricted. Forcing himself to breathe, he pushed away the nightmare and lifted his foot to the next rung. And the next.

Gusts of wind lifted the wooden sign, smacking it into the building and jarring the ladder. Stephen froze. His heart banged in time to the wood crashing overhead.

Horses' hooves clip-clopped below. Car engines growled into the parking lot. If the sign ripped loose, someone down there could be badly hurt. He'd never let that happen if he could prevent it. Never.

Gripping the rails so tightly they bit into his hands, he closed his eyes and felt for the next few rungs. But now he had to loosen his clenched fingers to grab the sign.

He hadn't thought about having to hold on with only one hand. His trembling legs jiggled the ladder.

Please help me, Lord.

The sign blew in his direction. He reached out and snatched it one-handed. Only Divine intervention could have allowed him to capture it on the first try.

Thank you, Jesus.

Stephen twisted his head toward the hook on his right. He'd placed the ladder near the sign so he could catch it. But he hadn't thought about hanging it afterward. Now he'd have to lean far over to attach the chain. What if the ladder tipped?

His imagination painted a vivid picture of him clinging to the sign as the ladder toppled. Then the sign giving way . . .

Nettie Hartzler stared up at the man clutching the market sign. The ladder shook as he reached out. What was he thinking?

As he fumbled to hang the chain over the hook, one foot of the ladder rose slightly. He was going to fall.

She dragged her horse to a stop, slid open the buggy door, and without even bothering to tie up her horse, raced over. Praying for strength, she gripped the ladder and threw her body toward the opposite side to counterbalance him.

"Stand up straight," she screamed.

She couldn't hold his weight and the ladder's. Overhead, chain clinked against metal. Had he hooked up the sign? She couldn't waste energy by looking up. She pitted every ounce of her strength against the tilt of the ladder.

She couldn't believe this man. Who climbed a ladder in a windstorm? And didn't even tie it off?

The ladder tilted a quarter inch toward her, then a bit more until both legs rested on the asphalt. The pressure against her shoulders and arms eased slightly. He must have followed her instructions.

She glanced up to see the sign hanging properly. Good. Now she'd keep holding the ladder until he descended.

But he stood there, frozen. What was he doing?

"Are you coming down?" she asked.

"I–in a minute."

His breathless answer and his white-knuckled grip on the ladder revealed how frightened he'd been about falling. Maybe he needed a moment to catch his breath.

"Don't worry. I'll keep holding the ladder until you get down."

"*Danke*." His response came out choked.

Nettie couldn't blame him. She knew firsthand how perilous falls from heights could be. Her stomach curdled. She needed to get him down from there. Before all her horrible memories intruded.

"You can come down now," she called to him, but he didn't move. "Please?" she added when he remained motionless.

"I can't," he croaked.

"Of course you can. Just lower one foot after the other. You'll be down before you know it."

"I–I've never climbed down a ladder."

What? He had to be kidding. As an Amish man, surely he'd helped with barn raisings. Maybe almost falling had addled his brain.

She didn't have time to wait. She'd come in early to make salads because they'd run out yesterday before closing. Friday market hours ran late, so she hadn't been able to do it last night. But if this stranger didn't come down soon, the market would open, and they'd have no salads ready to sell today.

He still hadn't budged. He must be telling the truth. She'd have to help him.

"Lift one foot and lower it. Feel around until you touch the rung below."

She waited while he did what she'd suggested. He didn't loosen his grip as he descended.

"You'll have to slide your hands down as you go." She had a sudden vision of him letting go with both hands. "One hand at a time," she corrected.

Slowly, painstakingly, he shuffled from one rung to the next. At this snail's pace, she'd be too late to make salads. If Fern made them instead of her . . .

Nettie closed her mind to that possibility. She needed to make sure Gideon thought she was more valuable than Fern. Nettie couldn't afford to let Gideon's budding attraction to Fern bloom. She had to protect her children.

The minute the stranger set both feet on the ground, she blasted him. "What were you thinking? You didn't even tie off the ladder or make sure the feet were level." She gestured to several large eyebolts anchored in the concrete blocks at various places around the building.

"I—I . . ."

She didn't wait to hear any excuses. "Nobody climbs a ladder in this weather."

"But the sign." The man's chest heaved. "I didn't want . . . anyone to get hurt."

He sounded as out of breath as she was.

"Did you even care that you might have endangered

lives if that ladder fell on someone? Why don't you think about others before doing something like that?"

Behind her, a sarcastic voice said, "I could say the same about a careless person who lets a horse run loose in the market parking lot."

She whirled around. "My horse." She'd forgotten all about her buggy.

Nick Green laughed and waggled his eyebrows. "You're lucky your brother-in-law arrived to save the day."

"I-I'm sorry." She hadn't meant to cause trouble.

Her pulse slowed as she spied Gideon leading her horse around the building to the shelter. His sister Caroline followed in his buggy. Several cars waited behind them to turn into the parking lot.

Heat splashed across her cheeks.

"Seems to me," Nick drawled, "you'd take the log out of your own eye first."

Ooo. Nettie's fingers curled into fists. Nick loved to taunt her. She longed to say something cutting in return, but she had to work at the same stand.

Her brother-in-law Gideon had opened the end of his stand to two people who'd gotten pushed out of their market stalls by the previous owner. Because of that, Nettie had two irritants to deal with every day—Nick and the bakery owner, Fern. Both of them made her life miserable.

Nettie settled for a haughty comeback. "I didn't know you knew any Bible verses, Nick."

"Fern's a good teacher." His smirk made it clear he'd been trying to get under her skin. And he'd succeeded.

"Humph." Nettie tried to keep her expression neutral.

She didn't want Nick to know how much the taunt hurt. "I hope you learn something."

She turned to leave before Nick could jab her again. But she'd forgotten about the man on the ladder. Despite her own mistake in leaving her horse unattended, someone needed to make sure this stranger didn't do anything that dangerous again.

She faced him. "And I hope you learned your lesson. You could have been"—her next word came out strangled—"killed."

Tears stung her eyes. She spun around and ran into the building before they fell.

Chapter Two

Stephen stared after her. She'd saved his life, and he'd been too shaky and tongue-tied to thank her.

He relived the moment the ladder leg lifted from the ground. The whole ladder listed to the right, and he'd have tipped over if she hadn't arrived. She'd hung on to the ladder with all her might until both ladder legs ended up flat on the ground. Then she'd talked him down.

What a fool he'd made of himself! Confessing he'd never climbed a ladder before. Needing to be coaxed down step by step like a baby learning to walk. How humiliating!

"I think she likes you." Nick's eyes gleamed with mischief.

"*Jah*, right." Stephen shook his head. He'd watched Nick provoke that woman until her eyes filled with tears and she ran away. Or maybe she'd been running from his embarrassing ladder experience.

"I mean it," Nick insisted. "I've never seen her talk that much to anyone before."

"She wasn't talking. She was scolding."

"Scolding is Nettie's love language."

Maybe it was time to do what Nettie had done and flee. Nick seemed to enjoy taking personal digs. Somehow, he'd already found one of Stephen's sore spots.

"Oh, wait." Nick did a double take. "You have a beard so you must be married."

"You think?" Stephen parroted the *Englisch* teens who'd worked in his market stand in New York State.

Nick heaved a huge sigh. "Too bad. I thought you might be the answer to Fern's prayers. All of us agree that Gideon should marry Fern. Even Mrs. Vandenberg."

Huh? Nick's conversation was getting more and more confusing. Stephen didn't know any of these people.

Seeing his blank expression, Nick tried to clarify. "Gideon is Nettie's brother-in-law, and Mrs. Vandenberg owns the market."

"I see." Stephen did recall his brother talking about the lady in her nineties who meddled in people's lives and the one whose sign he'd just fixed, but he couldn't follow Nick's story.

"Anyway, the only one standing in the way of Fern's happiness is Nettie."

For some reason, Stephen couldn't picture the woman who'd taken the time to talk him down from the ladder being mean enough to interfere in someone else's relationship. And after she'd saved his life, he didn't want to listen to Nick's bad-mouthing.

But Nick kept talking. "I keep hoping someone will come along to distract Nettie and—"

All Stephen wanted to do was return to the stand and get away from all this gossip. And he should find Nettie's stand so he could thank her. If he asked Nick where she worked, though, Nick would find it suspicious.

As politely as he could, Stephen said, "Nice meeting you, Nick. I don't want to keep you from your stand, and I'd better get this ladder down."

Before Stephen could lower the ladder, Martin headed over. "Sorry I'm a bit late. I'll take care of that. I heard you fixed the sign. Thanks so much."

Somehow getting praised for his cowardly behavior made Stephen more humiliated than he'd been when Nettie talked him down.

He swallowed the sour taste in his mouth. "It was nothing. Thanks for getting the ladder."

"It's my job." Martin grasped the rope and smacked a palm on one of the rungs. The top half of the ladder slid down smoothly.

Stephen turned to find Nick waiting for him. He suppressed a sigh.

Nick fell into step beside Stephen. "So, if you know someone we can match Nettie up with, let me know. Although she'd never say it, I'm sure Fern would like Nettie out of the way."

What could Stephen say to that? *Out of the way* sounded like Fern might hurt Nettie. Why did Nick see Nettie as such a problem? Stephen tried to reconcile Nick's picture of Nettie with the woman who'd rushed to help him.

"But Fern thinks Nettie has first dibs."

Was this some kind of a contest? None of it made sense to Stephen. "I thought you said Nettie is his sister-in-law."

"She is. But Gideon's been taking care of her ever since his brother died. We all think Nettie's hoping to be Gideon's next wife."

Nettie was a widow? Stephen understood that pain. He'd lived with it for seven years now.

Nettie rushed into the chicken barbecue stand, out of breath and out of sorts. She'd lost the opportunity to show Gideon how invaluable she could be. Not only had Fern set out her own baked goods, she'd also made the salads and prepped some lunch trays for later. Now she and Gideon had their heads together as she helped him fill the display cases with side dishes.

Normally, the scent of the chicken roasting on the spits filled Nettie with contentment. Today, it roiled her stomach. What would she do if Gideon married Fern? Nettie—and even more worrisome, her children—would no longer be a part of his life.

"There you are." Caroline smiled at her. "We were scared to see your horse loose and nobody driving the buggy."

Nettie shriveled inside. She'd already been overshadowed by Fern. Did Caroline have to add to that?

"We were so afraid something happened to you. But then we saw you helping someone fix the sign. That was so kind of you."

"I didn't have much choice. It was either steady the ladder or watch him fall."

Caroline shook her head. "Only you would see it that way."

Nettie bristled. What did Caroline mean by that? Did Nettie even want to know? Smoothing down her apron, she asked Gideon in a mild voice, "What do you need me to do?"

He peeled his eyes from Fern. "The salads are made, but you could help Fern finish prepping lunch trays."

Her teeth gritted, Nettie joined Fern at the back counter. Fern had been the one who'd come up with the idea of putting plastic silverware, napkin packs, and condiments on lunch trays to save time during the noontime rush.

Struggling to keep her voice civil, Nettie answered, "Sure. And by the way, thank you for taking care of my horse and buggy this morning." Under Fern's watchful glance, Nettie tempered the smile she longed to give to Gideon.

"Of course." Gideon's sunny smile lifted Nettie's spirits for the first time that morning. "It was good of you to help that man with the sign. He looked like he was having a rough time."

He had been, but for some reason, Nettie didn't want Gideon to criticize the man—a bit ironic after she'd lit into him herself.

She worked in silence beside Fern until they'd created several towering stacks of trays. With Saturday being their busiest day, Nettie hoped they'd prepared enough. Nick and Fern stayed too busy on the weekend to assist much with barbecued chicken sales. Which meant Nettie had more time alone with Gideon. Except that they were usually so rushed, she had no time to appreciate it.

Once the morning customers flooded in, many of them flocked to Fern's baked goods. The barbecued chicken part of the stand didn't get busy until ten, so Nettie had some time to talk to Gideon.

"Mamm's going to bring the children over later if that's all right," she told him.

"Of course. They're always welcome."

Nettie smiled. Gideon loved her four children as if they were his own. When her husband died, Gideon had agreed to take care of them, and he'd kept his promise for the past two years.

What would her children do if Gideon got married? They couldn't stay at the house. How would she care for them? She'd come to depend on him for so much.

Gideon nudged her. "Looks like Fern could use some help. Since we're not busy yet, maybe you could go down there."

Nettie bit back a sigh. Not only would she have to work with her rival, but she'd also have to leave Gideon's side. But she trudged over and did her duty.

Once she began serving customers, Nettie relaxed, and her smile became genuine. Except each time she accidentally bumped into Fern. Luckily, Nick had long lines at his candy counter, so he didn't have time to bother them. At least not for the first ten minutes.

Between customers, Nick announced, "Nettie, I tried to match you up with the man you helped this morning so Fern could have a clear shot at Gideon." Oblivious to the two shocked gasps that followed his statement, Nick continued, "Too bad, though. Stephen's married."

"The beard didn't give it away?" Nettie couldn't keep the sarcasm from her tone.

Fern shot an apologetic sideways glance Nettie's way, and then said, "That was so kind of him to fix the sign."

Fern's graciousness made Nettie's comment seem surly. Somehow, without even trying, Fern always managed to put Nettie in an unfavorable light. And now Nick had humiliated her in front of all the customers, who were staring at her curiously. He'd made her sound needy and desperate for a husband.

To get away from Nick, Stephen offered to help Martin carry the ladder to the maintenance shed. Martin's eyebrows rose. Obviously, he could handle it himself. After all, Stephen had managed it alone. But Martin glanced from Stephen's burning face to the man standing next to him.

Understanding dawned in Martin's eyes. "Sure. I'd be happy for some assistance."

Although Stephen would prefer to never go near a ladder again, he picked up the opposite end, grateful to be moving away from Nick.

After they'd rounded the building, Martin laughed. "I can carry it from here. I expect Nick's gone now. You wanted to get away from him, right?"

Stephen would rather not admit that. He'd only worked here a few days, and he didn't want to criticize anyone. "I, well . . ."

Martin waved a hand in the air. "Never mind. Didn't mean to put you on the spot. Nick's known for needling people." With a practiced heft, Martin angled the ladder to slide it into the maintenance shed.

Stephen waited until Martin closed the door. "I hope it was all right to take that out. The shed was unlocked."

"Yeah, that was fine. I need to remember to check the door before I go home at night. Don't tell Russell. He'd fire me on the spot."

"Of course not." It hadn't occurred to Stephen to mention it to anyone.

Martin clapped Stephen on the shoulder. "Thanks for staying mum and for putting that sign back up. I owe you."

"Happy to help." Stephen could say that now that he stood on firm ground. "I'd better go."

"Yeah." Martin gave him a teasing smile. "Don't worry. I'm sure Nick's gone."

With a nod, Stephen turned to leave. He had one more thing to do before he went to the meat stand. He'd never forget being up on that tipping ladder. Or the woman who saved him.

She deserved a major *danke*. He had to find her before the market opened.

But when he reached the doors, people were already streaming into the market. He hadn't realized it was so late. How would he find her with these crowds? And would she even have time to talk?

Maybe he should wait. But if he did, he might get too busy to take a break. Besides, he should have thanked her right away. He needed to make up for his earlier lapse in manners.

Weaving around people, he scanned each stand he passed. When he reached the middle of the market, he approached a small eating area with café tables and chairs. The scent of roasting chicken wafted from a nearby stand.

Stephen did a double take. Nick stood at one end of Hartzler's Chicken Barbecue, wearing a striped apron. He bent down to talk to a small girl and waited while she screwed up her face and deliberated about which candy to buy. None of the impatience or sarcasm from earlier showed on his face, but Stephen wanted to get away before Nick looked over and saw him.

He started to hurry away, but stopped. The chicken barbecue stand, one of the largest in the market, had glass display cases filled with salads and side dishes. Overhead, a large menu advertised chicken, fries, salads, and full meals. The far end held Nick's candy business and a small bakery, with a press of people lined up.

Two women waited on the bakery customers, and one of them was the woman he was looking for. He almost didn't recognize her at first, because unlike the frown she'd directed his way as she held the ladder, she greeted each person with a smile.

He sucked in a breath. Earlier, he'd been too shaky to appreciate her prettiness. With her face relaxed into sweetness, she had caring eyes. But Stephen could detect deep sadness in their depths. A sadness he shared.

He shook himself. He couldn't stand here staring. Nettie wouldn't have much time to speak to him, but he got into line. He'd buy cinnamon rolls for his children and thank her. He hoped Nick would stay too busy to notice him.

As Stephen approached the counter, Nick spotted him. His eyebrows rose, and he smirked. When he turned his attention to a small group of boys choosing whistle lollipops, Stephen released a pent-up breath. He'd been expecting a sarcastic comment.

Maybe Nick would be too busy to come up with any barbs. But Stephen had underestimated the man's talent for annoying people.

"Whoa, that was fast." Nick's derisive tone set Stephen's teeth on edge. "Watch out for that guy, Nettie." Nick shook his head. "A married man preying on a helpless widow."

"I'm not . . ." Stephen strangled off the words as Nettie

looked up at him. He directed his next comments to her. "I came to thank you for helping me this morning."

Her lips pinched together as if she wanted to give him another lecture. A lecture he deserved. He should have tied off the ladder. He'd seen his brothers and his friends do that during barn raisings. If he hadn't been so gripped by fear, he would have made more logical decisions.

"I, well,"—he swallowed hard—"I might not be alive if it hadn't been for you."

Nettie's eyes shimmered with tears. She lowered her head and busied her hands with folding a bakery box.

Had her husband's death been recent? Stephen hadn't meant to make her cry. "I'm sorry."

She kept her head bowed. "For what?"

For making you cry. But Stephen couldn't say that. "For, um, for being so foolish."

Her head popped up. The pain in the depths of her eyes made Stephen's chest contract. He'd felt that same grief mingled with guilt. Did she blame herself for her husband's death? He wanted to reach out and take the soft, pretty hand tucking white cardboard flaps into slots to form a small box.

As if she'd read his mind, she set the box on the counter and tucked her hands behind her back. Then she focused her gaze on the counter between them. "May I help you with anything?"

Stephen started. He'd been holding up the line. "I'm sorry," he said again, then wished he hadn't. "I mean for holding up the line. I'll take six cinnamon rolls." That would be enough for the children and his brother Amos. If he ordered seven, Nettie would have to make a larger box. He didn't want to put her to the trouble.

When she didn't respond, he repeated his order. Then he felt foolish. She must have heard him the first time. She'd only been waiting for the other woman to slide the glass door into place so she could get into the other side.

While Nettie slid out the metal tray of cinnamon rolls, Stephen examined the other woman. She was petite and pretty, but her looks couldn't compare with Nettie's large brown eyes that held such depths of emotion. Or the smiles she'd given the younger customers. She obviously loved children. Stephen found so many things about her far too appealing. He caught himself. He didn't need any more distractions. Not right now.

Nettie could barely concentrate on filling the order. Each time she looked at the man in front of her, her heart raced. Adrenaline burned through her bloodstream. She relived the scene of the ladder tipping. Her fear. And all the old memories of watching her husband plummet to his death. While she stood frozen in place, too far away to save him. His screams and her shrieks echoed in her head.

Today, she'd bitten down hard on her tongue to prevent a scream from escaping. And she'd managed to rescue this stranger despite being overwhelmed by the old powerlessness and helplessness.

That reminded her of Nick's comment. *Helpless widow.* His words burned into her. Is that how people saw her? It made her sound like a user. And a loser. Was that how Gideon viewed her too? And now Nick had shamed her in front of this newcomer.

Her face flushed with heat. Had Nick been repeating market gossip? Did everyone talk about her that way? And he'd said it in front of Fern.

Fern who right now was patiently waiting for Nettie to slide the tray back in so she could get into the bakery case. Flustered, Nettie gave the metal tray such a hard shove it banged into the tray next to it. All eyes turned in the direction of the loud clatter, flaming her face even more.

"I'm sorry," she said automatically, then wished she hadn't. It reminded her of the man waiting for this box. He'd apologized for the ladder incident. And for . . .

She thrust the box in his direction. "Can I get you anything else?"

He shifted from one foot to the other as if undecided. His glance strayed to Fern, who was counting out cookies for a woman with three small children. A frisson of jealousy shot through Nettie. Even strangers preferred Fern.

Lord, please take these feelings from me, Nettie pleaded.

"Could I get another cinnamon roll?" he asked, jolting her back to the market stand.

Nettie bit back a sigh. Why hadn't he asked for seven in the first place? Now she'd have to make a new box and discard the smaller one. They couldn't reuse a bakery box someone had touched.

She reached out for the box he held, but he drew it back, and she stared at him, confused.

"I don't need a box or a bag. If you could just wrap it up in that"—he gestured toward the bakery paper Fern was using to lift bear claws into a box—"I'm going to eat it."

"I see." Nettie wished her words hadn't come out so clipped. They sounded judgmental.

She waited for Fern to finish. This time she slid the tray in and out gently. For some reason, she didn't want this stranger to think of her as bad-tempered. She'd scolded him about the ladder. Then he'd seen her crash the trays together. He must be contrasting her surliness with Fern's sweet tones as she spoke to her customer. He probably wished he'd gotten into Fern's line.

Neh, he'd picked her line so he could apologize.

She handed the wrapped cinnamon roll to the man without meeting his eyes. His fingers brushed hers, sending shock waves through her. Nettie pulled her hand back so quickly he almost dropped the roll. With a quick grab, he caught it. But he'd squashed it, and the icing smeared across the paper.

Humiliated, Nettie offered, "Let me get you another one."

He shook his head. "It'll taste fine, and that's what counts."

"Are you sure?"

"I'm positive."

His response sounded so firm, so sure. He sounded like a man used to making the best of any situation.

"I, um, never introduced myself. I'm Stephen Lapp. I'm working with my brother Amos at Lapp's Pastured Pork. I just moved from New York." He spoke so fast his words almost ran together.

The man behind him cleared his throat.

Stephen's cheeks went ruddy. "I didn't mean to hold up the line. I just wanted to thank you for what you did this morning."

At the admiration glowing in his eyes, Nettie shifted from one foot to another. "It was nothing."

"Nothing? You saved my life."

"*Jah*, well, anyone else would have done the same. I just happened to be the first one there."

"I'm glad you were and that you acted so quickly."

The man behind Stephen glowered. Nettie had to get Stephen to stop talking and leave. She'd be glad to get away from his praise. It made her too uncomfortable. At the same time, she didn't want him to go.

Fern butted in. "*Jah*, Nettie, you were amazing. I don't think I could have held the ladder like that."

Stephen turned a brilliant smile in her direction.

Nettie's teeth clenched. One more person had fallen under Fern's spell. Nettie forced herself to take a deep breath. She had to get control of this envy.

Anyway, why did she care what Stephen thought? A man foolish enough to climb a ladder without securing it most likely would be careless in everything he did. His wife must worry about him all the time. Being married to a man like that would lead to heartbreak.

Chapter Three

"Where's your *daed*?" Onkel Amos asked Joline.

"I don't know." She hoped he was all right. She hadn't seen her *daed* since he'd spotted that wooden sign dangling near the top of the building, and he'd gone to fix it.

"I won't be long," he'd promised.

That happened a lot. Daed always wanted to help. And Joline often watched the four younger ones. She'd been five when Mamm died. By the time Joline had turned seven, she'd taken over most of the cooking, cleaning, and childcare. Ever since then, they'd all helped Daed in their meat stand in Mayville, New York. Until that farmer's market closed. She missed it there.

Onkel Amos had invited Daed to work at Dawdi's market stand in Ephrata, Pennsylvania. They'd only been here a few days, but Joline had already memorized Amos's layout. Earlier, she'd directed her brother and sisters as they put the pork in the display cases and wiped fingerprints from the front glass. By the time Amos arrived, everything sparkled.

"Done already?" he'd asked. "Looks like you got everything in the correct places."

Joline beamed. At home and in the market, she did a great job. Daed always said he couldn't take care of things without her. He made her feel competent—unlike at school. That had only gotten worse since they'd moved here.

But what had happened to Daed? He hadn't returned. It had been more than an hour. Had he fallen?

If he had, one of the stand owners would have seen him crumpled on the ground. She shivered at that picture. Daed always warned her not to let her imagination run wild.

But she couldn't help it. Her *daed* always avoided climbing. Why had he decided to do it now?

"I'll go look for him."

Amos smiled at her. "*Danke*. Hurry back. I might need your help soon."

Joline headed outside. No, Daed. The sign hung in its usual place, so he must have managed it. And no blood or bodies lay on the ground under it, so he'd gone up and down the ladder safely. But if he'd finished, why hadn't he returned?

Had he gone to get something to eat? Following her *onkel*'s order to hurry, she scurried through the market, dodging people and checking food stands. She skidded to a stop near a small café table. Daed stood a short distance from Hartzler's Chicken Barbecue.

In one hand, he held a white bakery box. In the other, he gripped a squished pastry. As he nibbled it, he watched a woman working in the stand.

Why is Daed staring at that woman?

The caring, concerned look in his eyes and the thoughtful expression on his face worried Joline. She didn't know the woman's name yet, but from the first day they'd started working at Dawdi's meat stand, Joline had labeled the ladies who worked at the chicken barbecue stand *Smiley*, *Dreamy*, and *Sourpuss*.

Since then, she'd learned *Smiley*'s name was Fern. And *Dreamy* was Caroline. But Joline hadn't found out *Sourpuss*'s name. And she didn't want to.

Joline headed over and tugged at Daed's sleeve. "Amos needs help." She tried to make it sound urgent.

"What?" Reluctantly, her *daed* pulled his eyes away from Sourpuss. "Amos can't handle the customers?"

Guilt niggled at Joline. Her *onkel* hadn't said he needed her *daed*. But something about the look in Daed's eyes as he studied the woman in this stand made Joline's stomach jumpy. She lowered her gaze and focused on the small swirly patterns in the concrete floor.

"We're busy." Although she was pretty sure that was true, they could probably manage without Daed. At least for a while. She and her siblings could help Amos handle the lines. And Amos had only asked *her* to come back. Her fib added queasiness to her jittery stomach.

"Tell Amos I'll be right there." Daed turned to look at the woman one more time.

"But what are you doing?"

"Trying to figure something out. I won't be long." He held out the bakery box. "Here. Take this back for everyone."

The tang of cinnamon rose from the package. Daed must have gotten sweet rolls for all of them. *Yum*.

She couldn't wait to eat hers. Instead of scampering back to the stand, though, Joline stayed beside her *daed*. She didn't want him to get distracted. "Aren't you coming back with me? Amos wanted me to find you."

A faint smile crossed Sourpuss's face. Then her face drooped into its usual worry lines.

Daed shifted to walk away and almost bumped into Joline. He glanced down at her in surprise. "If the stand is busy, why didn't you rush back?"

"I, um . . ."

But Daed race-walked toward the stand, leaving her behind. Joline rushed to keep up with him.

"Daed, how come you were staring at *Sour*—that, um, woman?"

"Did you see the deep sadness in her eyes? I feel like God is calling me to comfort her."

The only thing Joline saw was grumpiness. But if she said that, Daed would remind her not to be critical.

Always look for the best, he'd say.

Joline usually tried to be cheerful, but moving so far away from home to live in this new town, attending a different school without the friends she'd grown up with, and dealing with a busy and stressed *daed* had proved to be too much. The last thing they needed was for him to get interested in some woman.

That would be a disaster.

Chapter Four

"Stephen, wait," a wavering voice called after them.

Who was calling him? He hadn't met many people here yet. He turned to find an elderly *Englisch* woman hobbling toward him. Even with her cane, she looked about ready to fall over.

"You go on back to the stand, Joline," Stephen told his daughter. "I'll be there as soon as I talk to this lady."

Joline huffed. Now that she was twelve, she seemed to be developing an attitude, but she always obeyed.

Then he hurried toward the woman so she wouldn't totter much farther. He reached out a hand to catch her if she toppled.

"You were calling me?" Now that he'd approached her, he wondered if she might have been calling someone else, but her sparkling eyes focused on him.

"I certainly was." She sounded winded.

Stephen hoped she hadn't been chasing him for a while. He waited while she caught her breath.

"You don't know me, but I'm Mrs. Vandenberg."

The owner of the market. *Jah*, he'd heard of her. For

a woman in her nineties, she seemed spry and lively, although her balance was shaky.

"I understand I owe you a thank-you. My father started this market and carved the wooden sign out front. You kept it from being destroyed."

"It's a well-made sign. It would be a shame for it to break."

Mrs. Vandenberg studied him for a long moment. "You see the value in protecting things. I bet you take in strays, don't you?"

He nodded. They'd only been living in Lancaster County for a week, and already they'd fed and adopted a too-skinny barn cat and a mangy hound with its ribs showing. They added those strays to the two rescued kittens and one puppy they'd brought from Mayville. How had she guessed that?

She beamed. "Don't look so surprised. I have good instincts about character, but I also depend on God to give me nudges."

Stephen smiled back, wondering how he could slip off politely. He didn't want to hurt this lonely elderly lady's feelings, but Joline said they needed him at the stand.

Mrs. Vandenberg appeared to be settling in for a long talk. "Anyone who takes in strays is bound to care about helping people, too."

"Of course."

"Wonderful." She pursed her lips for a moment. "Not everyone does."

As far as Stephen knew, everyone in the Amish community went out of their way to help others. Too bad she'd experienced unkind people.

Her voice dropped so low he could barely hear her.

He was uncertain if she was talking to him until he heard her words. "Thanks, Lord, I think he'll be perfect."

Perfect for what? She'd only just met him. How did she know that? Unless she planned to ask him to donate to a charity. Then he'd gladly give as much as he could.

She wobbled again, and Stephen reached out to steady her.

"Would you prefer to sit down?" He motioned to the nearby café tables. He'd rather not see her take a tumble.

"Thank you. That might be wise. I'm not as stable on my feet as I used to be."

Stephen took her arm and assisted her to the closest table. After he helped her into a chair, he stood facing her, hoping to hint that he needed to head off.

"Sit down. Sit down." She patted the table across from her.

He edged back a bit. "I really should go. I'm needed at the stand."

"It's all right. I prayed God would save the large crowds until you're back behind your meat counter. You do believe God can work miracles, don't you?"

"Of course." But did adjusting the flow of customers count as a miracle? In his heart, he had no doubt God could do that. But would He?

Mrs. Vandenberg spoke as if she trusted God implicitly for everything and anything. Stephen had been raised to have that same faith, but sometimes he wrestled with doubt.

"I heard hanging that sign was a hair-raising experience."

Stephen drew circles on the tabletop with his finger to

avoid her piercing gaze. "Well, I'm not used to climbing ladders."

Her brows drew together in a puzzled frown. "I figured you'd do a lot of that."

"I, um . . ."

As if sensing his discomfort, she cut him off. "Interesting. You don't like heights, yet you risked your life to hang that sign during this windstorm."

Heat crept up Stephen's chest and burned his cheeks. He hadn't said he feared heights. How had she guessed?

"My goodness, you're even more perfect than I expected. You'll do. Yes, indeedy." She turned her eyes heavenward with a beatific smile. "Lord, you've done it again."

Her prayer confused Stephen. What had God done? And what did Mrs. Vandenberg mean about him being perfect?

She pinned him with another searching glance. One that seemed to see deep into his soul. "Good thing Nettie came to the rescue, eh?" Mrs. Vandenberg raised her voice almost as if she wanted Nettie to overhear.

He couldn't resist looking in Nettie's direction. She frowned a bit and acted unaware of their attention, but the way she straightened her shoulders showed she was at least a little pleased with the recognition.

Mrs. Vandenberg startled him back to the table. "I'm sure you already thanked her."

"I did." He hoped he hadn't given her—or Nettie—the wrong impression by staring.

"Good." Mrs. Vandenberg's voice fell to a whisper. "Nettie needs someone to look out for her. She's had a rough time of it."

Stephen nodded. Being widowed wasn't easy.

"I'm so glad you agree. I figured with you taking in strays, you'd be the kind who'd also care about widows and orphans."

He *rutsched* in his seat. This conversation seemed to be heading in an uncomfortable direction. He recalled Nick's suggestion that someone needed to distract Nettie so Fern and Gideon could date. Hadn't Nick said Mrs. Vandenberg agreed with that?

Stop it, Stephen. She might want to ask me to contribute money or build something for Nettie or do some chores or . . .

But deep inside, he suspected that wasn't the case. After all, Nettie's family and the church would take care of those things. They wouldn't ask a random stranger to help. Maybe, with Mrs. Vandenberg being *Englisch*, she didn't realize that.

"So"—Mrs. Vandenberg leaned forward—"are you willing to take this on?"

The intensity of her expression made Stephen draw back in his seat. "Take what on?"

"Nettie."

"What do you mean?" Although he asked the question, he had a dreadful feeling he already knew the answer. And he wouldn't like it.

"For right now, she needs a little time and attention. You could take her out and give her a chance to have some fun."

Stephen groaned inside. Mrs. Vandenberg had no idea that spending time like that with a widow in the Amish community pretty much meant you planned to marry her. How could he get out of this gracefully?

"It can just be casual for now," she went on.

"Actually," Stephen interrupted, "that's hard to do. If I take her places, people might assume I plan to marry her." And Nettie might too.

Mrs. Vandenberg brushed aside his protest. "Nothing wrong with that."

Jah, there was. He didn't even know Nettie. You didn't jump into a relationship with someone you'd met only once. He also wasn't ready to risk opening his heart to a woman again. Losing his wife had been too painful. And he had too much going on in his life right now to be dating.

"I'm counting on you. I'm sure you'll think of a way."

Earlier, Stephen had wondered if he could find a way to erase the sadness in Nettie's eyes. But this wasn't how he'd intended to do it. Nettie needed time to heal from her loss. The last thing she needed was the false hope of a relationship. Especially one that might end in a broken heart. For one or both of them.

Nettie kept glancing at the couple sitting at the café table near the chicken barbecue stand. She'd finished helping Fern because Gideon needed her. Normally, she'd take advantage of the time she spent with him to focus his attention on her and the children.

But the ladder climber and Mrs. Vandenberg kept throwing glances in Nettie's direction. They must be talking about her. What were they saying? She wished she could read lips.

She kept filling orders, but their conversation distracted her. Although she warned herself not to look, she couldn't help it. After Stephen assisted Mrs. Vandenberg to her feet and she hobbled off, he sat back down at the table, looking thoughtful.

From time to time, he'd glance in her direction. Her eyes skittered away. She didn't want him to think she'd been looking at him.

"Nettie?"

Gideon's voice snapped her back to the customers lined up in front of him. He held a tray with four chicken legs and two bags of fries. The woman must have ordered a salad or side dish.

"Sorry, I didn't hear the order."

Gideon's eyebrows rose. "Two garden salads. One broccoli-bacon salad. And a quart of potato salad to go."

Nettie shriveled inside. So much for proving she was invaluable to him and the business. The customer's chicken would be cold before Nettie doled out the salads.

"I'm sorry," she repeated, this time to the customer, and hurried to fill the order.

A scoop of broccoli salad splattered onto the floor as she reached over to plop it on the paper plate. A mayonnaise-covered blob of broccoli slithered across Gideon's shoe.

Nettie ducked her head and slid an apologetic glance in Gideon's direction. He was busy filling a foil-lined to-go bag with chicken pieces, so he hadn't noticed.

She pointed to the mess. "Be careful. I'll clean it up as soon as I—"

Before she could finish, Gideon took a step forward and slid. He waved his arms to keep his balance. *Smack!* The bag of chicken hit her in the face.

"*Ach*, Nettie!" Gideon grabbed the edge of the counter with one hand to catch his balance. He turned to examine her. "Are you all right?"

A corner of the bag had poked her in the eye, and tears spurted out. She blinked to stop the sting and the tears. She'd always longed for Gideon to pay more attention to her. Now she cringed. Of all the times to get her wish. Right after she'd made a fool of herself.

"I'm fine." Her embarrassment made her words come out brusque. She pinched her lips together. She sounded nasty and unkind.

"You sure?" He stared at the tears streaming down her cheeks.

Nettie tried to modulate her voice this time. "It's nothing. The bag caught the corner of my eye."

Gideon's gaze dropped to her hands. Nettie wanted to sink into the floor. She still held the tray he'd handed her a while ago with the order unfilled.

He turned to the customer. "Those fries must be cold by now. We'll replace them." He called over his shoulder to his sister, who was draining fries, "Caroline, two fries, please."

While Gideon handed the bagged chicken to an *Englischer* and made change, Nettie hurried to put the salads on the plate and fill a quart container with potato salad. She had the tray ready when Caroline brought the fries.

"Let's replace the chicken, too." Gideon lifted the four legs with tongs and set them in a small warming pan they used for discards. Those often served as their lunch. Keeping his feet planted, he leaned over and pulled out replacement chicken pieces.

Feeling sick inside, Nettie tossed the cold fries into the trash bin. They all abhorred waste because it cut into the business's slim profit margin. And she'd watched Gideon, head in hands, struggle to balance the books in his home office. Her carelessness had caused him to lose a whole meal. She'd also slowed the line of customers.

Now she'd cause even more of a backlog. "Caroline, can you take over the salads while I clean that up?" Nettie pointed to the salad splashed on the floor and Gideon's shoes.

"Sure." Caroline took Nettie's place instead of waiting on customers.

Nettie grumbled to herself as she grabbed a cleaning rag. Why couldn't anything ever go right? All she wanted to do was prove her worth to Gideon. Instead, she spent most of her time making mistakes.

She knelt and cleaned up the floor so Caroline wouldn't slip too. Then she rinsed out the rag and returned to wipe Gideon's shoes. Her face burned as she asked him to lift his foot so she could also clean off his sole. If only she could hide out for the rest of the afternoon.

As she hung the rag on the rack to dry, her gaze met Stephen Lapp's. He was still at the table studying her. He must have seen the whole fiasco. The heat in Nettie's cheeks increased one hundredfold.

She tried to tell herself she didn't care what he thought of her. But embarrassment coursed through her for her clumsiness.

Stephen sat at the table after Mrs. Vandenberg departed, deciding what to do. He'd already been trying to think of ways to cheer Nettie up, but he definitely couldn't do what Mrs. Vandenberg had suggested. He'd never want to give Nettie the wrong idea.

From time to time, his eyes were drawn to her. When she dropped a blob of something on the floor, she'd become flustered. She'd hung her head and looked as if she was waiting for a scolding.

Gideon didn't appear to have a bad temper. But with the way Nettie shrank back, Stephen almost charged over to the stand to protect her. He eyed Gideon closely to monitor his reaction, but the man seemed calm and unconcerned. Obviously, it wasn't Gideon she feared. Unless he acted different in public than in private.

Stephen shook his head. He sized up people pretty well—not as well as Mrs. Vandenberg, of course—but he'd seen no signs that Gideon had gotten riled. Had Nettie's husband been abusive?

The thought made Stephen sick. He hoped not. Maybe she needed to get over more than her husband's death.

As her eyes met his, Stephen noticed desperation in her face. Then she flushed a pretty shade of pink, making her look even more attractive.

Before he could tear his gaze away, she ducked to clean up the spill. He wondered if her hasty action had been partly to break eye contact. When she stood and walked to the sink to rinse off the cloth, she avoided glancing in his direction.

That gave him another reason why Mrs. Vandenberg's request wouldn't work. Even if he'd agreed to take Nettie out, she'd made it clear she wanted nothing to do with him. That let him off the hook.

Yet her expression called him to do something to ease her sorrow. But what could he do to help?

Pushing the question from his mind, Stephen hopped up from the table. He had to get back to the stand. After meeting Mrs. Vandenberg, he'd completely forgotten about Joline's urgent request. He race-walked down the aisle. His brother was probably swamped.

Stephen arrived at the stand to find a large group of people waiting. Amos, Joline, and Matthew were rushing around taking orders and slicing, and the younger children were tearing butcher paper, wrapping meats, and making change. Stephen moved to the far end of the counter to start a new line. For the next hour, they were all rushed off their feet.

When they finally had a brief lull, Stephen drew in a breath and turned to his brother. "Sorry I didn't get back earlier to handle these crowds."

Amos mopped his forehead. "No problem. Your kids and I easily took care of it. Actually, this is the first rush of customers we've had this morning."

Was his brother trying to ease his guilt? Stephen froze in place. Or . . . had Mrs. Vandenberg's prayers really worked a miracle?

Before Stephen could come up with an answer, another flood of customers gathered at the counter. All morning and afternoon, they were rushed off their feet. Every time they stopped for a breather, another influx began.

What had Mrs. Vandenberg said? She'd prayed God would wait until he was back at the stand to send large crowds. The Lord had certainly done that. Was it possible . . . ?

As clearly as if she'd been standing beside him, Mrs. Vandenberg's words echoed in his ears. *You do believe God can work miracles, don't you?*

Stephen did believe that, but had Mrs. Vandenberg's prayers brought in these customers?

Chapter Five

Stephen slipped out of the stand right before the market opened on Tuesday morning. "I'll be right back." He hurried down the aisle before his brother could stop him.

"Wait!" Amos called after him. "The stand rent's due today. I need to catch Russell."

Not if Stephen got to him first. "I won't be long." He jogged toward the far end of the building, where Russell usually started opening up. A loud jingle of keys told him he'd chosen the right direction.

"Russell?" Stephen projected his voice, and the man turned with a scowl. He obviously didn't like to be interrupted.

The man rubbed Stephen the wrong way. He had a bad temper, but Stephen detected something else underneath the meanness. The only word that came to mind was *evil*.

Stephen shook his head. He had no business judging anyone. And he should never label anyone with a terrible word like that. But his instincts warned him Russell couldn't be trusted.

Stephen reached into his pocket and pulled out the check. Russell's glower switched to a smarmy smile. He almost snatched the check from Stephen's fingers. The market manager's gloating expression left no doubt of his greed.

He glanced down at the check, and his eyes held a calculating look. "You're paying your half of your brother's monthly stand rent?"

Half? Monthly? Biting back a nasty retort, Stephen steeled himself for an argument. He prayed for patience and kindness. "That's my brother's stand rent for a full year. Twelve months' rent."

Disappointment slithered across Russell's face. Had he actually been hoping to collect a year's rent every month?

"When Amos comes to pay, you can let him know I've taken care of everything." His brother had no idea Stephen planned to pay. He hadn't told Amos because his brother never would have agreed. But now, Amos could open a stand in the new market in downtown Lancaster.

Stephen had sold his hog farm in New York for an excellent price. He could afford to help his brother reach his dreams. Expanding Dawdi's business to another market would have made both Daed and Dawdi happy.

The crafty look in Russell's eyes unnerved Stephen. Would Russell try to say he'd only paid one month's rent?

"I'd like a receipt for that check."

The way Russell's eyes narrowed, Stephen suspected he'd been right to worry.

"I can't do it now. I have to unlock the market." Russell scurried off.

Stephen followed him. "Why don't I take the check back? I can bring it up to your office later and get a receipt."

Russell slid the check in his pocket and walked even

faster. "If you come up to my office at the end of the day, I'll write one out."

Other than following Russell and haranguing him or wrestling him to the ground and taking the check back, what choice did Stephen have? He'd have to trust the man. But only until closing time.

As Russell unlocked another door, Stephen rushed back to the stand, doubt troubling him.

"Where have you been?" Amos asked when Stephen arrived at the stand. "I told you I needed to pay the stand rent."

"*Neh*, you don't." Stephen didn't want to tell his brother what he'd done and start an argument. Not when customers had already started streaming into the market.

But Amos ignored him and headed for the door at the back of the market. By the time he returned, the stand had gotten busy. They had no time to talk. But Amos's usual worried frown didn't mar his brow. Stephen smiled to himself, glad he could lift one burden from his younger brother's shoulders.

When Joline arrived after school and ushered her brothers and sisters into the stand, Stephen decided to collect his receipt from Russell. No point in waiting until the end of the day. "I'm heading out for a bit. I won't be long."

"Where are you going?" Joline demanded.

"I have a little business to take care of." Stephen was glad his brother had accepted the payment without complaints or disagreement, but he'd rather not stir things up by mentioning Russell.

"I'm going with you," Joline announced.

Lately, his daughter had been shadowing him everywhere. Was she having trouble adjusting to living in

Lancaster County? He needed to talk with her about it, but he didn't want to do it now. He'd rather not take her with him to Russell's office. He didn't want to expose her to the creepy feeling he got around Russell.

"Stay here and help Amos. He'll need you while I'm gone."

"Why are you leaving when we just got here. Don't you want to hear about school?" *Oops*, she didn't want to talk about that. But maybe her brothers did.

"Of course, I want to hear about everyone's day as soon as I get back."

"Why can't I go with you?" A whine crept into Joline's voice. "I like spending time with you."

"And I like being with all of you. Don't worry. I won't be gone long."

Joline's eyes narrowed. "You'd better not be."

He raised an eyebrow at her, and she lowered her gaze.

"I mean," she mumbled, "we need you here. Sometimes we don't have enough people to wait on everyone."

Stephen needed to sit down with her and have a talk about her attitude. Now, though, he had to hurry. Joline was right about them getting overwhelmed with customers. He planned to be back in a few minutes.

As he passed Hartzler's, he couldn't help searching for Nettie. Guilt niggled at him. He hadn't exactly promised Mrs. Vandenberg he'd help Nettie, had he? Or had he?

So far, no ideas had come to mind. He should try to think of something.

Nettie glanced in his direction. Stephen gave her his sunniest smile. Her eyes widened. But instead of smiling back, she dropped her gaze and turned away. Had she misread his intentions?

If she hadn't already made it clear that she thought him a fool for not tying off the ladder in a windstorm, she'd just proved she had no interest in him. His heart lightened. If Mrs. Vandenberg pressed him about a relationship, he had a good excuse.

With a spring in his step, Stephen headed to the staircase and climbed the steps two at a time to Russell's office, feeling freer than he had since Mrs. Vandenberg had made her request.

Russell's office door stood open a crack. Feet on the desk, he leaned back in his chair while he talked on the phone. Russell hadn't spotted him. Stephen stepped back, not wanting to disturb the market manager.

But Russell's loud voice boomed into the hallway, and Stephen couldn't help overhearing the conversation.

"That's right. I need to get rid of that kid."

A *kid*? Stephen tensed. What did Russell plan to do?

"He's a juvie, and I want him out of this market ASAP. He needs to be behind bars, where he belongs."

Stephen's jaw clenched. Who was Russell talking about?

Russell stayed silent for a while as loud squawking came from the phone. Stephen couldn't make out the words, but the man on the other end sounded furious.

"I told you. I'll pay you for that job along with this one. You know I'm good for the money. It's just that things are a little tight right now."

Stephen found it hard to believe Russell was hurting for money. All the stand owners paid their rent today, and Stephen had given Russell a full year's rent.

"Just get it done," Russell growled. "I'll pay you when I see results." He slammed down the phone.

After sending up a brief prayer that God would help

him find a way to protect the kid Russell planned to make trouble for, Stephen rapped on the doorjamb. In his annoyance, he hit the frame extra hard, and the door squeaked open a few more inches.

"Why are you skulking outside my office door?" Russell's face, suffused with red, hardened. His feet crashed to the ground, and he leapt up, hands knotted into fists. "You eavesdropping?"

Stephen took a step back. He had no intention of getting into a fight. But he wouldn't let Russell intimidate him. If the manager had wanted privacy, he should have shut his office door and talked quietly.

His gaze steady, Stephen stared at Russell until the other man simmered down.

"Well," Russell barked, "what did you want?"

"I came for my receipt."

"I told you to come after closing. You have no business interrupting me during the work day."

"I thought part of a manager's job was giving receipts for rent they've collected."

The crimson of Russell's face darkened almost to purple. "First of all, I'm not just the manager, I'm the *owner*," he practically screeched. "And, second of all, we operate on the honor system here. I never give out receipts."

Stephen held his ground. "You promised me one. Since you believe in the honor system, I'm sure you never break your promises."

Russell looked about to explode. He obviously didn't like to have the tables turned on him. His eyes narrowed in a wicked glare. "No one else in the market is this suspicious."

Maybe they should be. Stephen kept that thought to himself. No point in riling the market *owner* further.

While Russell yanked open a desk drawer, Stephen tried to piece together the information he'd heard since he began working last week. Amos had told him Mrs. Vandenberg owned the market, but Russell had just claimed that title. Who really was in charge?

Russell's pen slashed a few numbers on the sheet of paper in front of him. Then he held up the receipt, dangling it between two fingers as if it were a piece of smelly trash.

Stephen took it from him. On the preprinted form with the market logo at the top, Russell had jotted the date and the amount Stephen had paid.

"This won't do." Stephen set it back down on the desk and pointed to the memo line. "It needs to say, *Twelve months rent paid in full*. And I'd like your signature on it."

"There's no need for that. We both know what it's for."

"That may be, but I want it on there so other people know."

"They can tell from the paper."

This morning Russell had acted like Stephen's check had been for half the stand rent. Without written proof, Russell could claim they owed him money next month or the month after that. Stephen wouldn't take that chance. The more time he spent around Russell, the less he trusted him.

"I'd like it written on the paper to be sure there's no mistake." Stephen kept his voice firm and gestured again to the memo line.

When Russell realized Stephen wouldn't back down, he huffed and wrote what Stephen had dictated.

"Your signature too." Stephen wanted this document to be as official as possible.

"I thought you Amish believed in handshakes to seal bargains and didn't get into signing all this contract stuff."

Did Russell rely on that to cheat Amish stand owners? Stephen had no problem with verbal contracts, but only with people he trusted. And this man was not one of them.

Russell scribbled his name and shoved the paper across the desk. "I've always heard New Yorkers are suspicious."

Outsiders sometimes accused New Yorkers of being distrustful and unfriendly, but they were referring to people from New York City. Stephen came from New York State. He'd never understood why New Yorkers had that reputation. All Stephen's customers from Long Island and Manhattan had been nice.

As he picked up the receipt, Russell continued, "You're going to have a lot of trouble getting along around here if you're so hard-nosed. You'll find people don't take kindly to these antics."

So far, Stephen hadn't met anyone other than Russell he'd consider untrustworthy. He folded the receipt and slid it into his pocket. He had a feeling he might need this sometime as proof.

Joline worried as her *daed* headed off in the direction of Hartzler's stand. Was he going to talk to Sourpuss again? How could she stop him?

The longer he was gone, the more upset she became. What did he see in that woman?

Her stomach twisted as she thought about having a grump for a mother. If her *daed* picked anyone, Sourpuss would be the last person she'd want. But the truth was, she didn't want anyone.

Daed had shown no interest in women in Mayville. He'd spent all his time with the family. And Joline liked being in charge of the household responsibilities and telling everyone what to do. Since they'd moved in with Amos, she still handled many of those jobs. Except when his fiancée, Betty, came over.

It was hard enough feeling pushed aside when Betty cooked meals, but if Daed married someone, their new *mamm* would take over the kitchen and the house. Joline didn't want to be bossed around, especially not by Sourpuss.

As she waited on customers, Joline tried not to think about that possibility.

Each time the second hand swept around the clock, her teeth clenched tighter. Ten minutes passed. Then fifteen.

Daed had been gone too long. She needed to go after him.

She slipped past her brother Matthew, who was cutting the end from a rack of spareribs. Maybe she could sneak out without Amos noticing.

"Joline?" Her *onkel*'s voice stopped her escape.

"*Jah?*" She tried to sound innocent.

"What are you doing?"

"I want to find Daed and tell him we need him."

Amos's sideways glance revealed he didn't quite believe her. "I'm sure your *daed* will be back soon. Why don't you stay here and help?"

"I won't be long." Feeling guilty about ignoring her *onkel*, Joline dashed off before he could call her back.

Once she'd ducked into the center aisle, she slowed. If

Daed had started heading back to the stand, she didn't want to miss him. She tried to keep an eye on the aisles on either side just in case.

The farther she walked, the more her stomach churned. He didn't know anyone else at the market well yet, and it was too early for a snack. He must be with Sourpuss. She reached the middle of the market and spied him weaving through the tables and chairs in the food court.

As she'd feared, he must have been at Hartzler's Chicken Barbecue. She felt sick. What had he been doing here all this time?

When he turned to look in Sourpuss's direction, Joline raced toward him. "Daed," she yelled. She had to distract him from that woman.

A young girl's screech startled Nettie. Nearby, a cute, dark-haired girl of about twelve ran toward the café tables, waving wildly. She flung herself into a man's arms. The collision almost knocked him over.

Stephen Lapp. The crazy man who'd almost fallen from the ladder. The married man who'd just given her a flirtatious smile.

"Whoa, Joline," he said. "Easy there. What's the matter?"

"We didn't know where you were. You took so long." Joline shot a suspicious look at Nettie.

The girl seemed to be blaming Nettie for something. *Hmm* . . . Had the girl's mother sent her daughter to find her wayward husband? Amish men believed in being faithful, but maybe this man cheated on his wife.

She wished she could reassure the girl. Nettie had no interest in stealing her father. Even if Stephen Lapp were single, he'd hold no appeal. *Jah*, he was handsome, but the inside counted so much more.

And Nettie pitied anyone in a relationship with a man who endangered his life. She'd never want to go through the pain of losing a husband again.

Squeezing her eyes shut, she tried to block out the picture of Thomas . . .

"Nettie, are you all right?" Gideon asked softly.

Her eyes flew open. How could she have forgotten where she was? "I—I had a bad memory." Her words came out strangled.

The pity on Gideon's face made her uncomfortable, but the sympathy in his eyes quickly turned to guilt. He still blamed himself for Thomas's accident, although she'd reassured him many times it hadn't been his fault.

For the second time that morning, she turned away from a man's smile. The first had been bright, the second sad. Both had pierced her heart in different ways.

Nettie wished she could have switched Stephen's warm smile to Gideon's face. Instead, she'd reminded Gideon of the painful past.

"I'm sorry." She meant that two ways—sorry for bringing up a hurtful topic and for missing the customer's order. "What salads did they want?" Nettie made her voice brisk and businesslike, hoping to dispel the gloom that had descended.

Gideon repeated the list, and Nettie filled the tray as fast as she could. But as she passed the lunch tray to him, she couldn't help noticing Stephen still stood in the same place. This time, though, he wasn't looking in her direction.

He held his daughter's hand as he leaned down to listen

to her torrent of words. Nettie couldn't hear what the girl was saying, but her face reflected deep distress. Stephen concentrated on the child, his face full of empathy.

He might not be a faithful husband, but he seemed to be a good father.

Chapter Six

Joline had to impress on Daed how upsetting his leaving had been. She wanted him to think twice before running off to Hartzler's stand.

She threw her arms around him. "Where have you been all this time?"

"I had some business to take care of."

Business? Did Daed consider getting them a new *mamm* a job? Too bad Sourpuss hadn't heard that.

"I—we missed you." Keeping her head against Daed's chest, she poked her fingers in her eyes to create some teardrops. Once they started dripping down her cheeks, she pulled back to be sure Daed saw them.

"You're crying?" He looked astonished. And concerned.

Gut. He should be paying more attention to his children than to some strange, grumpy woman.

Daed reached for the silver holder in the center of the nearest café table and pulled out a brown napkin. It would be rougher than a tissue, but he handed it to her to mop up her tears.

Gulping as if holding back more tears, Joline wiped

her face. "I-I'm sorry. I didn't mean to cry. It's just— Well, you were gone so long, and I didn't know—"

Oops. Gone so long? How long had it been? Fifteen minutes? She didn't want to overdo it, or Daed might realize . . .

"I didn't think I took that much time."

"But—but we didn't know where you were." She tried to bawl again, but no liquid came out. Crying turned out to be harder than she'd imagined. Joline pressed the dampest part of the napkin against her eyes to hide the lack of tears.

"I only ran an errand in the market. I promised I'd be right back."

She sniffled. "But you didn't . . . come for the longest time."

"Joline, don't you think you're making too much of this?"

An *Englisch* neighbor in Mayville had once called Joline a drama queen. Daed had laughed about that after the lady left, and he sometimes teased Joline about it. She had to be careful not to sound like that.

Daed squatted down and put his hands on her shoulders. "What's this really about?"

She hung her head and used the napkin to hide her now dry eyes.

Maybe tears hadn't been the best idea. They seemed to make Daed suspicious. Could he tell they were fake?

Maybe not. He'd given her that napkin, and he leaned close as if he cared a lot about her feelings.

She choked out her words. "I worry whenever you leave us that you might not come back."

"I left you in charge many times at the stand in Mayville. You never had a problem with it before."

"But you didn't do dangerous things there. Like climbing ladders and—and—" Joline snapped her mouth shut before she added *getting friendly with Sourpuss*.

"Is that what's upsetting you? I promise I won't climb any more ladders. It probably frightened me even more than it did you."

"What if something happens to you here, and we don't know it?"

"That's not likely. With all the crowds in the market, people would come to my rescue. And someone would tell you right away."

"But what if they didn't?" Joline peeked over one corner of the napkin to see if her arguments were working.

Daed was studying her intently. She raised the napkin edge so it covered her eye again. "I don't want to lose you." She tried to make her voice sound lost and lonely.

"I don't think you will. But if God chooses to take me, Amos and Betty will take you in. You have nothing to fear."

But I do. She didn't really worry about Daed getting hurt. He'd had a bad accident as a boy, so he was always extra careful. Except for when he'd climbed the ladder the other day.

She couldn't tell Daed her real fear.

And she couldn't keep crying. If she did it too often, he'd know it wasn't real.

Asking to go with him hadn't worked. And chasing after him gave him too much time with Sourpuss. Joline had to find a better plan to keep Daed away from Hartzler's.

* * *

His daughter's sudden burst of tears surprised Stephen. Joline rarely cried, and only over tragedies, such as her mother's death. Yet, genuine tears had trickled down her cheeks, and her words had grown incoherent.

Something about the waterworks seemed off, though—almost as if she were putting on a show. But why?

He found it hard to believe his daughter would be that devious. And what had she hoped to achieve?

As he stood, he couldn't help noticing Nettie watching them with sympathy. When he met her gaze, her eyes grew cold. Then she turned away abruptly with a look of disgust. He wished he knew what he'd done to make her dislike him so much. Was she really that upset about the ladder incident?

Stephen didn't have time to worry about that now. They needed to get back to the stand.

He reached for Joline's hand. "Let's get back. This last hour before closing is always the busiest. You should have stayed to help Amos."

"You should have too," his daughter pointed out.

She seemed almost angry at him, but he didn't think it had anything to do with waiting on customers. He had to figure out what was going on in her mind. She'd mentioned school. Perhaps something exciting had happened that she wanted to share and he'd cut her off.

"So how was school today?"

Her shoulders slumped, and she didn't answer for a few seconds. Then she brightened. "Matthew's team won the baseball game at recess, and everyone says he's the best player they've ever seen, and they all want him to be on their side tomorrow, and—" She paused for breath.

As she rattled on, Stephen stared down at her. Reporting on her brother's accomplishments was unlike Joline. She always preferred to be the star. Stephen had never heard her brag about anyone else's wins before. And she'd avoided mentioning anything about herself.

"And how did you do in the game?"

Her face twitched. "I, um, didn't play today. I had other things to do."

"Oh? Like what?" He'd never known her to turn down a chance to beat Matthew at baseball.

She turned her head away so he couldn't see her eyes. "Just things. Nothing interesting." Then in an animated voice, she added, "But you know what Abby did?"

They'd reached the stand, and Joline's voice held an *I-can't-wait-to-tattle* note. Stephen stopped her. "Why don't you let Abby tell me?"

He hoped Abby would confess whatever she'd done without Joline's interference. But he had his doubts. Joline and Abby had proved to be his two troublemakers, and they rarely repented. He'd often prayed about their tendency to lie and cover up their misdeeds.

"Tell you what?" Abby asked as they entered the stand.

Joline pranced into the stand with a gloating expression. "About what you did at school today?"

"Joline . . ." Stephen warned.

Seven-year-old Abby glared at her older sister. "Did you tell Daed what you—?"

Stephen held up a hand. "Girls, that's enough. You know the rules. No tattling." The usual late-afternoon shoppers had gathered to pick up something to cook for dinner on their way home from work. "Let's pay attention to the customers. We can talk tonight at supper." He had a feeling he wouldn't like what he'd be hearing.

Nettie tried to push Stephen Lapp from her mind. Seeing him reminded her of the ladder, and the ladder reminded her of falling, and falling reminded her of her husband's accident. And the accident reminded her of his death. So now each time Stephen appeared, her memories cycled rapidly from Stephen to ladder—falling—accident—death.

She tried to push those pictures aside to concentrate on filling orders, but images whirled behind her eyes. She blinked several times to clear them and missed another salad order. Gideon had to repeat it.

If she didn't get this right, she might not have a job. And that led to another loop. Without the job, she wouldn't spend time around Gideon, Fern would have a clear field, Fern and Gideon would fall in love and marry, leaving Nettie and her children with no support and no home. If Gideon fell for Fern, Nettie's life would head into a downward spiral. No job—No Gideon—No future.

These gloomy predictions trapped Nettie in darkness, so it took a while before it penetrated that someone kept calling her name.

"Nettie? Yoo-hoo, Nettie."

Not Gideon this time. Mrs. Vandenberg.

"May I help you?" Nettie moved down the stand to where the elderly woman stood by the refrigerated cases containing salads.

"I hope so, dear." Mrs. Vandenberg looked apologetic. "I'm sorry for taking your time when you're so busy"— she waved toward the long line of customers that Nettie had been ignoring—"but you looked as if you had a bit of time to talk."

Leave it to Mrs. Vandenberg to find a nice way to point out Nettie had been lost in thought and not paying attention to her job.

Her face burned. "I should be helping Gideon."

"I know, but I won't keep you more than a minute. Can you stay for a short while after closing? I have a favor to ask."

Nettie usually hurried home to help her mother-in-law fix supper, and she needed to get the children ready for bed, and—

"This won't take long. I promise." Under her breath, it sounded as if Mrs. Vandenberg mumbled, "Not tonight anyway."

Sensing Nettie's hesitation, the elderly woman added, "If you came in Gideon's buggy this morning, I'd be happy to give you a ride."

"It's not that. It's . . ." Nettie hesitated. After all Mrs. Vandenberg had done for them after the accident, Nettie couldn't say *neh*. "All right. I'll meet with you."

"Great." The old lady's megawatt smile almost lit up the whole market. "Perfect, in fact. Let's meet right there." When she waved her cane toward a café table, she wobbled. Grasping the top of the counter with a gnarled hand, she managed to stay on her feet.

Nettie held her breath until Mrs. Vandenberg had safely propped herself on her cane again. "I'll see you there as soon as I'm done."

She returned to help Gideon as Mrs. Vandenberg thumped off, her cane beating a jaunty, but uneven rhythm.

What in the world had made the woman so joyful? Something about Mrs. Vandenberg's excitement made Nettie nervous. She hoped agreeing to meet hadn't been a mistake.

Joline's stomach lurched the closer they got to closing. Once they'd cleaned up and headed home, Daed would question them about school. She could count on Matthew to keep her secret, but what if one of the others let it slip?

Glowering at Abby would keep her quiet. Esther, Abby's twin, never tattled because she barely talked. And Ben didn't pay much attention to anything besides baseball, dogs, and food.

But what would Joline say if Daed asked her directly? She didn't like to lie.

Her conscience pricked her. Wasn't fake crying after chasing Daed kind of like lying? So was making up excuses about why she worried about him leaving the stand.

Joline shoved that uneasiness aside. She had her brothers and sisters to take care of. They wouldn't want a grouchy, sour-faced *mamm*. It was her job to protect them.

Besides, their family was perfect just the way they were. They didn't need anyone else.

"Time to clean up," Amos announced, jolting Joline from her reverie. "Your *daed* and I can take care of the last customers while you wash up and put things away."

Maybe if she slow-walked the jobs, it would delay facing Daed's questions. Joline dragged her feet. But her siblings, eager to get home for supper, hustled around, covering some of Joline's jobs too.

"Stephen, could I talk to you?" a wrinkled, old woman with white hair called to her *daed*.

He held up a hand. "Be right there." He ripped off a piece of butcher paper and set the loin roast on it. "Joline, can you dip out a quart of barbecue?" He wrapped up the pork and took the payment.

While Ben made change, Joline filled a white plastic container and gave it to her *daed*. He smiled at the *Englisch* lady as he handed her the purchases along with some bills and coins.

After she left, he turned to Joline. "Why don't you take my place here while I talk to Mrs. Vandenberg?" He scooted down the counter and leaned on the top to get closer to the old lady.

Joline wished she could get near enough to hear, but she waited on customers until Daed returned. "What did she want?"

"She wants me to stay for a while after the market closes to talk to her." He sighed.

"Why didn't you tell her *neh*?"

Daed peered at her closely. "How do you know what I told her? Were you listening in?"

Joline shook her head. "You did this." She huffed out a breath. "That's what you do every time you have to do something you don't like."

He laughed. "You're good at figuring out people, Joline. Make sure you use it for good, not harm."

"I could use some help with customers," Amos called.

They didn't have time to talk until everyone had been served and Russell locked the market doors. Then Daed let out a huge sigh, glanced at Joline, and laughed. She giggled because they shared a secret.

He turned to Amos. "Can you take the kids home with you? Mrs. Vandenberg wants to talk to me after we finish cleaning."

"Mrs. Vandenberg, huh? What did you do that the market owner needs to talk to you?"

Daed frowned. "I don't know. You think there's a problem?" But something in her *daed*'s expression showed he already knew what this Mrs. Vandenberg wanted, and he didn't like it.

"I'm sure it's nothing to worry about." Amos carried the money bag over to where Ben was counting coins. "You do know, though, that Mrs. Vandenberg has quite a reputation as a matchmaker?"

Matchmaker? Joline's fingers slipped. The metal pan of barbecue she'd held clanged on the cement floor. Tomato sauce and shredded pork splattered everywhere.

Would that old lady pick somebody for Daed to date? If she was the market owner, did she get to boss Daed around? She couldn't make him get married, could she?

Joline grabbed a rag and squatted down. It would take forever to clean up this mess. But Mrs. Vandenberg might create an even bigger mess. One Joline could never fix.

Chapter Seven

When Stephen arrived at the café, Nettie sat at one of the tables. He nodded to her and headed toward a different one.

"Stephen?" Mrs. Vandenberg's wavery, but authoritative, command stopped him. "Over here please." She gestured to Nettie's table.

He'd been afraid Mrs. Vandenberg planned to talk to him again about helping Nettie. He hadn't expected her to bring the two of them together. Even worse, his brother's teasing remark about matchmaking flitted through Stephen's mind. If Mrs. Vandenberg believed he and Nettie would make a good couple, her instincts must be off.

Although Stephen hadn't gotten to know Nettie well, he'd seen her facial expressions. They revealed one truth for sure—Nettie disliked him, maybe even despised him. You couldn't have a match when one person loathed the other. Some of the tension inside him unraveled.

By the time he crossed the floor, Mrs. Vandenberg had lowered herself into a chair beside Nettie. Stephen had a choice of the two remaining seats—beside Nettie or across from her. He chose across, then regretted it. He'd be right in the firing line of her fiery or dismissive looks.

He shrugged inwardly. The one good thing about this meeting is that Nettie would make her preferences clear, letting him off the hook.

Mrs. Vandenberg surprised both of them by fishing into her huge pocketbook and pulling out an expensive leather folder. "I want to tell you about a new project I've been working on."

Nettie caught Stephen's raised eyebrows and returned a puzzled glance followed by a shrug. So far, that had been Stephen's most positive interaction with her.

They both focused on the stack of papers she'd extracted. Mrs. Vandenberg unfolded and spread out a floor plan that covered most of the table. "Several months ago, I bought a large conference center that was going out of business. It's in downtown Lancaster within walking distance of a few of my low-income housing units and group homes for runaway teens."

Stephen's confusion increased. He doubted she'd called them here to brag about her charitable contributions, but what did all this have to do with him? Or with Nettie?

Mrs. Vandenberg continued, "At present, the area is considered the most crime-ridden spot in the city. I intend to change that."

Tapping a spot on the diagram, she indicated the entrance. "Right now, the streets around here are an eyesore, but I've been buying up abandoned and boarded-up buildings to fix up for the Transitions Project."

Despite his not understanding his purpose in being here, the plans intrigued Stephen. "What's that?"

"Affordable housing for homeless families to help get them back on their feet."

This woman had such a generous heart, Stephen vowed to help her however he could, even if it meant doing something for Nettie, who was leaning forward, engrossed in the plans.

"Is this a community center?" Nettie pointed to rooms labeled *Gym*, *Weightlifting*, *Homework Helpers*, *Mentors*, *Theater*, *Computer Center*, *Library*, *Art*, and *Childcare*.

Stephen followed her dainty finger as it traced a trail across the page. *Counseling*, *Career Center*, *College Counseling*, *Health Center*. She stopped at *Dining Room*, a huge room with tables and serving counters marked.

"It looks more like a school."

He agreed, except for the many rooms Nettie hadn't reached yet—*Life Skills*, *Literacy Classes*, *Game Room*, *Video Gaming*, *Pool Hall*. Stephen raised startled eyes and met Mrs. Vandenberg's twinkling ones.

"I see you've reached the fun spots. I'm hoping this will bring in kids off the streets. I want to attract all ages, build their self-esteem, keep them in school, give them opportunities."

Stephen still failed to see how he could play a part in all this, except to support it financially.

"They have a high truancy rate in this part of the city. I aim to reverse that."

Nettie leaned forward, her face alight. "It'll take more than a community center to change that. Many of those kids need food, clothes, or shoes. They often don't have coats or shoes to wear."

How did Nettie know so much about this? Stephen admired her passion.

"You're exactly right, Nettie." Mrs. Vandenberg pointed to a spot marked *Clothes Closet*. "I've lined up donations of clothing, shoes, coats, and other garments. Some churches will collect used items, but I've also lined up newer, fashionable clothes direct from corporate donors. Everything will be free."

"*Ach*, how wonderful!" Nettie's eyes shone.

Stephen marveled at the transformation. With her face and eyes glowing, she radiated beauty. He couldn't keep his eyes off her.

Just then, Amos ushered the children down the aisle. Joline stopped and looked from Stephen to Nettie and back again with a puckered brow. He hoped Nettie hadn't noticed.

The other children had already reached the front door. Amos came back for Joline. When he set a hand on her shoulder to urge her forward, she planted her feet and resisted. Stephen motioned for her to go with Amos. She didn't move.

"Joline, obey your *onkel*." He kept his warning low and stern.

Nettie and Mrs. Vandenberg glanced from Stephen to Joline and Amos.

"You . . . you . . ." Joline sputtered. "Don't—" Each word was anguished.

Don't do what? Help Mrs. Vandenberg? Stephen frowned. What was wrong with his daughter? Her eyes looked damp. Tears twice in one day?

"Sometimes change isn't as bad as we fear, Joline." Mrs. Vandenberg spoke to his daughter as if she were an adult. "Often, it brings new blessings."

"Sometimes it's worse," Joline mumbled.

Stephen had never heard her talk back to an elder. "You will apologize to Mrs. Vandenberg now."

"I'm sorry," Joline mumbled, keeping her eyes fixed on the ground.

He had to have a talk with her as soon as possible. They had to deal with her attitude.

This time when Amos guided her to the door, Joline went, although she dragged her feet the whole way. She stopped in the doorway, spun around, and squinted at everyone at the table.

Grateful that Mrs. Vandenberg and Nettie had returned to the plans, Stephen lowered his brows to signal his disapproval. Joline rushed out the door. Concern over how to handle her misbehavior filled his thoughts, so he barely heard the discussion around him.

Mrs. Vandenberg patted his arm. "Whether she realizes it or not, that girl is at an age where she needs mothering."

Stephen winced. Those words were a direct hit to the heart.

"Don't worry." Mrs. Vandenberg favored him with a cheerful grin. "All in good time. God will provide."

Wasn't it enough for a father to love his daughter dearly? What if he wasn't ready for a wife? Had Mrs. Vandenberg already begun hatching plans? He didn't want to be a target of her matchmaking.

Yet his gaze strayed to Nettie, and the excitement on her face touched him.

For the first time ever, Nettie's soul bubbled over with enthusiasm. Since childhood, she'd been dragged around by circumstances out of her control. Now, she had the power to change someone else's life.

"Some children can't go to school because they need to stay home to care for younger brothers and sisters or a sick family member while their parents work." Nettie wanted Mrs. Vandenberg to understand the many difficulties these children faced.

"Great idea," Mrs. Vandenberg mused. "We can hire health aides and childcare workers." She took out a pen, hovered it over the diagram a moment, then jotted *In-Home Care* on one of the blank rooms. "Let me make a quick call."

Nettie sat there amazed as Mrs. Vandenberg put those plans in motion. How wonderful it must be to have the power to change people's worlds. Nettie often railed at her own powerlessness.

Mrs. Vandenberg smiled at Nettie. "Thank you for that idea. I'd already planned for childcare here at the center for teen moms."

Nettie's whole body grew ice cold. She crossed her arms and pressed them against the pain shooting through her stomach. She tried to keep her face neutral, but inside, a swirling mass of emotions blocked everything the others said. Her throat clogged.

"Nettie? Are you all right?"

The concern in Mrs. Vandenberg's voice tugged Nettie back from the dark place. "I'm fine," she croaked. It wasn't a total lie. The past was over. Except she had to live with the consequences.

Stephen flashed her a sympathetic glance and an understanding smile. Would he look at her that way if he knew the truth?

She tried to tune in to what Mrs. Vandenberg was saying.

"We have tutors for homework help along with a library and computers. To encourage teens to stay in school, I'm offering full scholarships to college or trade school for those who keep their grades up."

Nettie and Stephen exchanged a look. Neither of them believed in higher education, but *Englischers* looked at things differently.

Mrs. Vandenberg's knobby finger tapped a large empty space in the middle of the paper marked *Chapel*. "Most of all, I want to tend to their spiritual growth. We'll have church services, Bible classes, and a full-time pastor."

"But children can't listen or learn when they're hungry." Nettie pressed the back of her hand against her lips. Why had she blurted that out? She didn't want them to know she had firsthand knowledge.

"Exactly." Mrs. Vandenberg beamed at her and then included Stephen in her smile. "That's why I wanted to talk to both of you. With schools letting out in a few weeks, we've applied to be a government-funded summer meal site, but I don't want to see anyone go hungry."

Nettie squeezed her eyes shut as hunger pangs gnawed at her stomach. She never wanted any child to experience that hollow emptiness, that gut-wrenching anguish. She'd clung to Gideon's promise to prevent her own children from going hungry. Although she'd been with the Amish church long enough now to know they took care of their own, she'd never let go of that fear and desperation.

Mrs. Vandenberg reached over and squeezed Nettie's hand. "I'm sorry if this is distressing you."

Nettie's eyes popped open. Had she given herself away? "I—I just don't want children to go hungry."

"I understand." Mrs. Vandenberg's searching gaze indicated she knew all about Nettie's past.

But how could she?

Gnarled fingers tightened over Nettie's. "I chose you because I knew you'd care."

Across the table, Stephen's furrowed brow revealed his puzzlement, yet his eyes shone with admiration and caring. "You really feel strongly about this, don't you?"

"You would too, if you'd ever gone hungry." The minute she said the words, Nettie wished she could take them back.

Stephen turned to her with startled eyes. Nettie's lips curved into a sad smile. He'd have no idea how an Amish child would suffer from hunger. And she wasn't about to tell him.

The lingering sorrow in Nettie's expression roused Stephen's curiosity. He'd never heard of an Amish community that didn't take care of those in need. Although he'd like to find out more, her guarded expression shut down questions.

"So," Mrs. Vandenberg continued, "I hoped the two of you would be willing to collect donations from the food stands after we close on Saturdays. Often fruits, veggies, baked goods, and meats won't last until we reopen on Tuesdays. A lot of that ends up wasted."

Stephen usually cooked older pork roasts for barbeque or froze those meats for the family to use later, but if Mrs. Vandenberg could use it, he'd gladly donate it.

"My charity will pay whatever the stand owners want for their leftovers."

"You don't have to pay me." He'd give whatever he could each week, even some of his newer meats if it would help people.

"It's not on the diagram yet, but a refrigeration company will be installing supermarket-type freezers with glass doors, and we'll have various display cases for produce, baked goods, and such."

It didn't make sense to him to collect food about to spoil. "Won't the food go stale or rot?"

"*Neh.*" The word exploded from Nettie's lips. She leaned across the table toward him. "If people know about it, everything will be snapped up by Saturday night or Sunday morning."

"I believe Nettie's right." Mrs. Vandenberg turned to him. "If we have any leftover food, you're welcome to it for your pigs."

Pigs might eat almost everything, but most people didn't realize sugar, pastries, or too much fruit would be bad for them. Same with certain vegetables.

"I guarantee you'll run out." Nettie sounded dead certain.

"Don't poor *Englischers* use welfare?" He hadn't meant to challenge her.

Nettie's color heightened, and she leaned forward emphasizing each word. "Many people run out of benefits before the end of the month. Have you ever tried to live on welfare?"

"*Neh*, I haven't." The Amish didn't believe in using welfare. That's why they helped others.

He still must have looked unconvinced, because Nettie

glared at him. "People who haven't lived in poverty have no idea how hard it is."

Jah, they'd had lean years, especially after he'd first started pig farming in Mayville, but they'd never gone hungry. Between the garden and the pigs, they'd always had something to eat. His heart went out to those who didn't.

Nettie kept going. "Besides, not everyone who's poor goes on welfare. Some refuse to take government handouts. Others don't qualify. Some parents sell their groceries for drugs, and their spouses and children go hungry."

Mrs. Vandenberg sighed. "SNAP was supposed to help with that. Unfortunately, people still find ways to cheat."

"And innocent children pay the price." Nettie's voice rose.

"That's why I've started this center."

Nettie flashed Mrs. Vandenberg a blinding smile. "I'm so happy you're doing this. I wish we could do it all over the country."

"Once this is up and running, I plan to add centers in York and Harrisburg."

"Harrisburg?"

Nettie's choked voice and downcast eyes made Stephen long to comfort her. Why had that town name upset her?

With compassion in her eyes, Mrs. Vandenberg reached out and patted Nettie's hand. "Yes, dear. And I hope you'll assist in planning that one."

Stephen couldn't help being curious. It sounded as if Nettie had some connection to the capital city, but as far as he knew, no Amish lived there.

"I'm hoping to expand to Pittsburgh and Philly next

year. But your suggestion of going national gives me an idea." Mrs. Vandenberg pulled out her phone and made another brief call. "Janine, about our STAR center opening, see about getting some national coverage. I'll prep an additional press release with steps to replicate our program."

After she hung up, Mrs. Vandenberg pinned each of them with a searching glance. "What do you say? Are you willing to be a part of this?"

Nettie pressed both hands to her heart. "I'll do anything and everything I can to help."

Stephen planned to do the same. "I'd be glad to join you."

"I knew I could count on both of you. And I'm so glad you're willing to work together." Mrs. Vandenberg stressed the last word. The glimmer in her eyes signaled more than just a thank-you.

Chapter Eight

As Nettie moved her chair back to follow Mrs. Vandenberg, Stephen stopped her. "Nettie, wait."

"I really need to get home." The children were waiting, and she'd left her mother-in-law to fix supper alone.

Besides, she didn't want to hang around here with a married man. Not one whose glances sometimes made her uncomfortable. She'd told Mrs. Vandenberg she'd do anything, but that didn't include getting cozy with Stephen Lapp.

As she scraped her chair farther back so she could escape, he said, "I'm sorry Mrs. Vandenberg asked us to work together on this."

Ouch! She'd been thinking the same thing, but she never would have said it aloud and hurt his feelings like he'd just hurt hers.

"It's just that I've noticed you don't seem to like being around me. I don't want to upset you."

Nettie blinked. Once again, she'd mistaken someone's meaning with her bad habit of looking for the negative. She owed him an apology. "It's not you. I mean, it is, but not in the way you think."

"I see." His shoulders slumped.

That hadn't come out right. Despite how often blunt remarks spilled from her mouth, she never intended to be mean. She often had difficulty phrasing things tactfully. Her awkwardness around people troubled her.

"You don't understand." Nettie squeezed her eyes shut. She'd just done it again. That sounded accusatory.

Stephen's mild "I'd like to try" made it even worse. His politeness highlighted her rudeness.

"I didn't mean that the way it sounded. My words and meaning get tangled up sometimes."

His steadfast gaze held no judgment. His patient waiting gave her a chance to gather her scattered thoughts.

"I meant because you're new here, you don't know about my past. I—my husband died a little over two years ago."

"I heard that. And I'm sorry."

She examined his face. His words seemed genuine and heartfelt. Why could she never take people's comments at face value? She wished she were more like Stephen with his open, trusting manner. But unlike him, she'd never ignore her marriage vows and spend time with someone else.

Once again, the judgmental part of her had condemned him. *You have no right to cast the first stone.* She'd only intended to tell Stephen why she preferred to avoid him.

Taking a deep breath, she tried to explain. "Did you hear how my husband died?" Her tone came out much too harsh.

He shook his head.

She stared down at the table. "He fell off the roof

and . . . I saw it all. But I couldn't reach him in time to help." Her hands clenched.

Stephen covered her fists with a large warm hand. "I'm so sorry. I can see why the ladder tipping upset you."

A shiver ran through her at his touch—so kind and comforting. But he was married. She snatched her fingers away and tucked them into her lap. Did he think he could take liberties with her because she was a widow?

"I didn't mean to— I, well, I only wanted to—" His cheeks blazed crimson. "I'm sorry you lost your husband. I know that pain and loneliness." His Adam's apple bobbed up and down. "My wife died seven years ago."

A widower? She'd misjudged him. And his smile. But that didn't change anything.

After Stephen told Nettie about his wife, her eyes softened for a moment. When she lost that wary, worried look, her prettiness took his breath away.

Then, as if someone pulled down blinds to block the view, her eyes went blank and shuttered. She blocked off her thoughts and emotions.

He wondered what had made her so guarded. He'd love to ask her more about that and about how she knew so much about poverty, but he didn't want to offend her. Better to stick to business.

"How do you want to divide up the responsibilities?"

She blinked and didn't answer.

That had been an abrupt change of topic from talking about their losses. Stephen wished he'd eased into it.

Nettie ducked her head. "I'm not very good at talking to people."

"Do you want me to ask everyone? I can do that, although I don't know many of the stand owners yet." She probably knew everyone, but he couldn't ask her to accompany him even if it would make it easier. A widow and widower walking together through the market would definitely stir up gossip.

She *rutsched* in her chair. "It doesn't seem fair for you to do all the work. And I really want to do whatever I can for this project."

"I don't mind asking people for their leftover food. It'll be a good way for me to meet everyone in the market."

"I could make a list of the owners. That way, you'd know who to talk to at each stand."

"Great idea." His face relaxed into a smile. "A list would help a lot."

Right away, she drew back into herself. Had she misread his facial expression?

He put on a neutral expression and kept his tone businesslike. "After I find out who wants to participate, we can divide up the Saturday food collection. Will that work?"

She nodded, her expression still distant as if she needed or wanted to block him off. Then she stood. "I should get home. Everyone will be wondering where I am."

Stephen stared after her as she hurried toward the employee exit. If they had to work together, he needed to find a way to get beneath Nettie's prickly exterior to the woman he'd had glimpses of today—the passionate defender of the poor, the caring volunteer who wanted to help, the compassionate woman who'd shown sympathy for his loss. What had made her so closed up, so afraid to let people get to know her, so afraid to reveal her real self?

Nettie rushed out to the parking lot, eager to get away. Being around Stephen frightened her. His friendliness and openness made her want to confide in him. But they were strangers. Even Gideon, who knew more about her than anyone, only knew part of the truth.

The brisk wind made her shiver. Or perhaps those tremors came from the chill around her heart. Nettie wrapped her arms around herself to keep warm and searched the growing darkness for Mrs. Vandenberg's car.

Footsteps sounded behind her. Stephen. She'd hoped to get away before . . . Before what?

"Do you need a ride, Nettie?"

His deep, caring voice poured over her like a soothing balm. It slid past all her defenses, soothing her, lulling her. She hardened her inner barriers. She had to protect herself.

"*Neh*, Mrs. Vandenberg is driving me home." Hadn't Mrs. Vandenberg said that?

"I can't leave you out here alone. I'll wait with you until she arrives."

"No need for that. I'll be fine." *Go away, please*. Nettie willed him to heed her inner message.

"It's no problem."

"You need to get home to your daughter and—" She'd almost said *your wife*. After believing he was married, she found it hard to readjust her picture of him to a widower.

"*Jah*, I do. I don't know what got into her today. Joline's always been a bit hard to handle, but I've never seen her so defiant."

Nettie suspected Mrs. Vandenberg's assessment that Joline needed mothering might be true, but from the girl's venomous glares, the last thing Joline wanted was to share her *daed* with another woman. She couldn't tell Stephen that.

He sighed. "It's not easy parenting alone."

"*Neh*, it isn't." She had to be honest, though. "Gideon has been a big help." He'd stepped into a father's role, especially for her boys. "I couldn't have done it without him."

Something flared in Stephen's eyes but quickly died. "It's great to have someone like that in your life. I've had some assistance from the church and now from my brother and his fiancée, but it's still a lot of responsibility."

Nettie pictured single women flocking around the handsome widower, offering meals and childcare. "And you haven't remarried?" She pressed her hand to her mouth. Why had she let that inner thought slip out? "Sorry. I didn't mean to pry."

"It's all right." He stared off into the distance with a rueful smile on his lips. "I really haven't had time between the business and parenting."

And in those seven years you never met anyone? Nettie pinched her lips together to keep that question from escaping.

Instead, she said primly, "I see."

He shifted from one foot to the other, clearly as uncomfortable with the topic as she was. "I need to hitch up the horse, but if Mrs. Vandenberg hasn't arrived by then, I'll take you home."

"*Neh.* What would she think if she comes and I'm not here?"

"I can't drive away and leave you standing here. Didn't you say you had to get home?"

She did, but not with him. The last thing she needed was to be cramped inside a carriage together. Every instinct warned her to flee. She could start walking home once he'd gone behind the building, but what if she missed Mrs. Vandenberg? And doing the ten-mile walk in the dark meant she'd arrive home long after supper. Who'd put the children to bed?

Nettie was still standing there undecided when Stephen pulled around the building.

He reached across and slid open the passenger door. "It doesn't look like Mrs. Vandenberg's coming."

"She always keeps her promises." But had Nettie heard her correctly?

"What if she can't make it for some reason? We could both be waiting all night."

"No need for you to wait." Had that sounded rude? Nettie wished she could rephrase it politely.

"I'm not leaving you alone here at night."

"I'll be fine. I'm sure she won't be long."

"Nettie, please get in. We both need to go home."

She tried her earlier excuse. "What if Mrs. Vandenberg comes and I'm gone?"

"I'm sure she'll realize I took you home. She probably needs to lock up anyway. I turned the doorknob lock, but I couldn't do the rest."

Stephen gave her an imploring glance. Nettie couldn't ask him to wait here when he had a daughter at home who needed him. And her own children should be put to bed.

Suppressing a sigh, she climbed into the passenger seat. All she'd wanted to do was get away from him. Instead, she was stuck inside a tight space with him, so close their arms would brush against each other if she moved. She huddled against the door to prevent that.

Stephen shifted in the driver's seat. At his nearness, her heart hammered uneven rhythms. She struggled to draw in a breath.

Strong, well-shaped hands took a firm grip on the reins. Stephen appeared to be sure of himself, a man in control of his life.

A man like that would never understand her chaotic past. She tried so hard to hide those old mistakes, to bury the old fears. But deep inside, she was too flawed for any man.

What in the world was she thinking? She had no interest in Stephen. She found it hard enough to be around him because she always pictured him on that falling ladder. But if he knew the truth about her, he probably wouldn't want to associate with her, even as friends.

For the past two years, Nettie had clung to Gideon as a lifeline. Gideon was the only one who knew some of her past. If he stopped supporting her and the children, she'd have to depend on charity from the church. Never again could she head down that dark road.

"Nettie?" Stephen's gentle question nudged her from the old terror closing over her.

Her *jah* came out shaky.

"Are you all right?"

She swallowed back a sarcastic laugh. Had she ever been all right? Not as long as she could remember. What would Stephen say if she told the truth? She could never take that risk.

She had to deflect him, so she did what she always did—went on the defense. "What makes you think I'm not?"

"You're so quiet and—" He snapped his mouth shut.

"And what?"

"Well, you look sad."

Most people said she appeared grumpy, not sad. She had to stay away from Stephen. He was much too perceptive.

When she didn't answer, he said softly, "It can be lonely sometimes."

"You have no idea," she murmured. But of course, he did. He may not have been through everything she had, but he'd lost his wife. "I'm sorry. I'm sure it's been hard for you too."

"It has, but we learn to mask our sadness. Sometimes I think hiding our feelings is living a lie."

Had he read her mind? "That's always bothered me."

"You don't have to worry. You have a very expressive face. I don't think anyone could accuse you of being dishonest."

Nettie laughed shakily. "I hope I haven't given too much away." How much had he seen? He couldn't read her past in her expressions, only her present.

"You're too young to have any deep, dark secrets."

A sharp pain shot through her. He'd never know how far his teasing words fell from the mark.

* * *

When Nettie retreated into herself, Stephen regretted his lighthearted joke. If they were going to be working together, he had to stop offending her.

She'd made it clear she didn't like personal remarks. They sent her scurrying into her shell.

Her brow furrowed. Then she squeezed her eyes shut as if warding off pain. He wanted to reach out and smooth the anguished lines from her face.

Is she remembering her husband's fall? If only my presence didn't remind her of that terrible day.

When she opened her eyes, he wanted to reassure her. "Nettie, I wish I didn't remind you of your loss, but if it helps, I promise I'll never climb a ladder again."

"Glad to hear it." Her flippant remark held a cynical note. She didn't believe him.

How could he convince her? "I've been scared of heights since I was six. That day you helped me was the first time—and it'll be the last time I'll ever do anything like that again."

She glanced up at him, surprise on every line of her face. "You never climbed a ladder before?"

He slowed his horse as they approached a stop sign. When they reached it, he lowered his gaze. Grateful the darkness concealed his heated cheeks, he nodded. He'd never confessed this to anyone before.

In Mayville, everyone in the community had known about the incident and never asked him to do anything that involved heights. Even at barn raisings, he worked on the ground.

"You didn't know about tying it off?"

Stephen was embarrassed to admit his ignorance. "I

stay as far away from ladders, hills, and balconies as I can, so *neh*, I didn't."

"Good thing I arrived when I did."

"That's for sure. You saved my life." He still trembled inside at the possibility he'd have crashed to the ground.

"I've never met an Amish man who had a fear of heights. Most boys scramble into haylofts, climb trees, help their *daeds* fix roofs, and —"

"I did too—until the summer I turned six. Up to that point, I had no fear."

He flicked the reins to make the horse move again. Then he plunged into his story. He wanted her to understand. "I always followed my older brothers around. They didn't want me to come that day, but I tagged along." If only he'd stayed home.

"They were taking turns on a tire swing suspended high over the creek. I wanted a turn too." Pictures scrolled before him, blurring the road in front of him.

"You're too little." Ezekiel held the swing high over Stephen's head.

"Aww, let him." Mark, his oldest brother, motioned for Ezekiel to give Stephen a chance.

The rubbery smell filled his nostrils as he crawled into the black circle. His heart pounded as Mark pulled the tire high in the air.

"Hold on tight," he called as he let go.

His other brothers lined up to give the swing an extra shove as it passed.

Wind rushed past Stephen's face, chilling his body. His stomach somersaulted as he whooshed through the air.

Below, the creek turned into a tiny ribbon. His mouth dry, he clenched his teeth to hold back screams.

Creeeak . . .

Stephen shook himself from the past. The cracking noise that followed that creak still haunted him in his nightmares. He pushed back the rising terror and swallowed hard. "As the swing flew over the creek, the branch"—he took a deep breath—"broke."

"*Ach*, Stephen." Nettie's sympathetic glance softened her face, reminding him of the gentle side she kept hidden.

But it couldn't stop the flood of memories.

For a moment, he hung suspended. His heart and breathing stopped. Then down, down, down . . . he plummeted, his stomach dropping faster than his body. His ears rang with his brothers' shrieks.

"*Curl into a ball,*" *Mark shouted.* "*Tuck your head in.*"

But frozen in terror, Stephen couldn't react.

Mark yelled again.

Stephen barely had time to pull his knees up and tuck his head before he splashed down bottom first. Icy water closed around him. Jagged rocks tore into his back, slashed his arms. The tire hit next, cushioning his head, keeping his face above water.

"*Run, get Daed,*" *Mark commanded as he waded into the knee-deep water.* "*Tell him to call an ambulance.*"

Those were the last words Stephen heard that day.

"Stephen?" Her face creased with tension, Nettie repeated his name, "Stephen?"

Dragging himself back from the blackness, he focused on her sweet face to swim back to the present. "Sorry. I try not to revisit that trauma."

"What happened?"

He tried to clear his head. Did she mean about him blanking out just now or about the accident? He didn't want to dwell on either.

"I broke a bunch of bones, had a lot of stitches, and spent several weeks in the hospital."

"You survived, and that's what matters." As she said that, her face crumpled as if she were visualizing a tragedy. Not his, but her own.

Why had he brought this up? Instead of reassuring her, he'd only reminded her of her own loss.

As she'd listened to Stephen's story, Nettie's mind drew parallels to her husband's accident. She'd experienced that same body freeze as Thomas slipped over the edge.

She needed to run to him, but couldn't move. Not that she could have broken his fall from the barn roof, but every time her mind replayed the scene, she'd somehow saved him.

"I didn't mean to upset you." Stephen looked distressed.

She wanted to wipe the guilt from his face. "It's not your fault. We have to remember both accidents were God's will." While Nettie parroted what she'd been taught, her heart refused to believe it.

"That doesn't mean they don't still cause pain."

"True. And doubt."

He nodded.

"I know I shouldn't question God's will, but when I look at things from my past, I can't help it." Sometimes as she lay in bed at night reviewing all the heartbreak she'd faced in her life, Nettie couldn't help asking, *Why, Lord? Why did all this happen to me?*

"Not everything in life is easy to accept." Stephen's sympathetic answer made it clear he understood.

Nettie had never voiced her doubts aloud before, and Stephen's words comforted her. She'd been afraid her in-laws and people in the Amish community would judge her. Maybe Stephen would too, once he thought it over.

She hadn't meant for this conversation to get so personal. What had she been thinking to confide so much about her private life to a perfect stranger?

When they stopped at the next stop sign, a fancy car pulled out of a nearby parking lot heading toward them. Mrs. Vandenberg's Bentley. No lights shone in the building where the car had been. Why had the driver parked there?

A back window rolled down, and Mrs. Vandenberg waved. Her car pulled beside the buggy, and Nettie slid her door open so they could talk. And to make it easier to escape. She'd told Stephen way too many things she wished she could take back. Now all she wanted to do was get away.

"Oh, good, I see you got a ride home, Nettie." A smile played on Mrs. Vandenberg's lips. "I was hoping you would. We're headed to the market to lock up."

Stephen leaned over so he could speak to Mrs. Vandenberg, and his nearness set Nettie's pulse drumming faster.

"I worried about that. I did turn the doorknob lock, but the deadbolt's still undone."

"Thank you. It's nice to know you're responsible and can be trusted to care about others." She shot Nettie a *don't-you-agree?* look.

Even if Nettie agreed, she'd never say so aloud.

"Well, I know you're in good hands, Nettie. Enjoy your ride, you two."

Nettie had intended to leave the buggy and ride in the car. Mrs. Vandenberg's comment killed that hope. She was stuck in the buggy with Stephen.

Now that she'd spilled so many of her inner thoughts, the rest of the ride home would be uncomfortable. She wished she'd held her tongue.

As the elderly lady gave them both a cheery wave and her mouth curved into a secretive grin, a vague suspicion flitted through Nettie's mind. Mrs. Vandenberg loved to be a matchmaker. Had she planned this ride home? And was Stephen in on it?

Chapter Nine

The whole way home from the market, Joline steamed. She couldn't believe what she'd seen. She relived walking past the café tables and freezing in place.

Neh, neh, neh!! Joline had squinched her eyes shut. When she opened them, she prayed the woman sitting across from her *daed* had disappeared. But she hadn't.

Joline couldn't stand it. Not Sourpuss. Why was Daed with her?

Swallowing back the sickness sloshing in her stomach, Joline had to find a way to protect Daed. And her siblings. If Mrs. What's-Her-Name planned to match Daed with Sourpuss, she was making a BIG mistake.

All the relief that had coursed through Joline when she learned Daed would be late getting home evaporated. She'd hoped to avoid his questions about school. But even telling him about getting in trouble with Teacher Emily wouldn't be as bad as him spending time with that woman. What was she going to do?

Daed didn't return until after they'd all gone to bed. Joline had lain awake waiting for his buggy to rattle down the driveway. What had he and that woman been talking about all this time?

She fell asleep plotting ways to keep her *daed* away from Sourpuss. When she woke, none of her plans seemed like they'd work. She stewed over them at breakfast and couldn't concentrate on her schoolwork. Once again, Teacher Emily scolded her for not paying attention in class. But it was more important to prevent Daed from making a terrible, horrible mistake.

At recess, for the first time since she'd started at this school, Teacher Emily didn't make Joline sit inside writing sentences or finishing up work she should have done in class. She skipped out the door, grateful for her freedom.

Instead of joining the other scholars for baseball, which she loved, she skittered around the side of the *schulhaus* to think in private.

Joline climbed a small hill, where she could look down on everyone and be alone. In her old school, everyone would be running around looking for her and begging her to come and play. They wouldn't have started any games without her.

Here, nobody even cared. They didn't even notice her missing.

Below her, Katie Hartzler, clutching a book in her hand, headed for a big oak tree.

Last week, after Teacher Emily announced Katie's *onkel* would be donating chicken barbecue and all salads, drinks, and desserts for their school picnic to celebrate the end of the school year in two weeks, Joline had stopped at Katie's desk.

"Does your *mamm* work at Hartzler's?" Joline demanded.

Katie's wide eyes revealed her fear. "*J-Jah.*"

"Is her name Fern or Caroline?"

"*Neh,* her name's Nettie." Katie's voice shook.

"Joline? What are you doing out of your seat?" Teacher Emily snapped. She'd been busy with the younger group of scholars, but now she frowned at Joline.

Instead of answering, Joline turned back to Katie. "Tell her to stay away from my *daed.*"

Her eyes shimmering with tears, Katie pressed her back against her chair.

"Joline Lapp, return to your seat this instant." Teacher Emily's voice cracked like a whip.

Joline scurried to her seat. She'd wanted to keep Sourpuss away from Daed, but she hadn't meant to scare Katie that much.

Teacher Emily dismissed the scholars she'd been working with and called Joline to her desk. Despite the teacher's admonition for everyone to concentrate on their work, the other scholars sneaked peeks while Teacher Emily scolded Joline.

She'd never gotten in trouble at school before and never had a teacher call her up to the front of the room. To keep her lips from quivering, Joline pinched them into a tight line. An expression Teacher Emily mistook for defiance. Joline fought back tears.

She lost two days of recess for misbehavior and defiance. The first day, Teacher Emily made her write Proverbs 28:13. Joline's hand cramped as she jotted the verse one hundred times: *He that covereth his sins shall not prosper: but whoso confesseth and forsaketh them shall have mercy.*

The second day, she scribbled the required apology letter to Katie after copying the first part of Proverbs 17:17—*A friend loveth at all times*—one hundred times. Teacher Emily peeked in from time to time, and whenever she did, Joline hid the other note she intended to give Katie. A message about keeping her *mamm* away from Joline's *daed*. Like Joline, Katie had no control over her parent. But maybe Katie could say or do things to make her *mamm* hesitate.

After handing over the extra message, Joline regretted it. In Mayville, she'd always looked out for the younger scholars. Even though she wanted to protect Daed from Sourpuss, she shouldn't have been mean to Katie. That note probably wouldn't work anyway.

Stephen had started the morning with a spring to his step. Not only was he excited about participating in Mrs. Vandenberg's project, but he'd get to meet all the other stand owners in the market.

And, although he didn't want to admit it, after last night's conversation, he looked forward to working on this project with Nettie. He loved her enthusiasm for helping children in poverty. And he hoped she'd overcome some of her negative feelings about him.

"You're really cheerful today," Amos remarked as they organized the display cases before the market opened.

"Well, you were already in bed last night when I got home, so I didn't get to tell you what we discussed last

Rachel J. Good

night." And Stephen had overslept this morning and had to rush through his usual jobs of caring for the pigs.

Bubbling with enthusiasm, he described Mrs. Vandenberg's plan. As he finished, Caroline Hartzler approached the stand.

She held out a paper covered with pretty, dainty handwriting. "Nettie asked me to give you this list."

Some of Stephen's excitement leaked out. She couldn't even face him to turn over the list?

After their talk the night before, he thought they'd made a good start to their working relationship. But he must have pried too deeply, forcing her to retreat.

He should give her the benefit of the doubt. Maybe she'd stayed home because of illness.

Stephen reached for the paper. "I hope she's all right. Not sick or anything."

Caroline blinked. "You mean Nettie? No, she's her usual *mürrisch* self. Maybe even grumpier than usual." With an apologetic smile, Caroline covered her mouth. "Sorry, I shouldn't have said that."

He hoped he hadn't been responsible for her grouchiness. But he suspected he had. Perhaps, though, she had too much work to do. "Sometimes work can be overwhelming."

Caroline's sarcastic smile indicated she didn't believe that reason. "We all have the same amount of work, and you don't see me running around with a hangdog expression."

You haven't lost a husband, he longed to say. He settled for a milder comment. "Sometimes others carry burdens we can't see."

"*Jah.*" Caroline's face flushed. "Forget I said that.

Nettie's been through some hard times. And this thing with Fern and Gideon hasn't made it any easier." She sighed.

Nick had mentioned that. Last night, Nettie had claimed Gideon helped her with child-rearing. Stephen had no idea how old Nettie's child was, but children took a lot of work. He hated to think of her losing support. And if she loved Gideon . . .

"Sorry." Caroline clapped her hand over her mouth again. "Seems I'm a fount of gossip this morning."

Stephen didn't mind. He'd like to know more, but it wouldn't be polite to ask. He worried Nettie might end up with another heartbreak.

"I'd better go before my tongue gets me in any more trouble." Caroline gave him a guilty grin. "As my brother often reminds me, *the tongue is a fire*, and mine has lit some pretty large blazes."

Stephen smiled, but he had to admit he probably agreed with her brother. Still, he couldn't help liking Caroline's directness. She seemed the kind to overshare information—quite the opposite of Nettie.

"Please thank Nettie for the list." *Even if she didn't want to give it to me herself.*

"Will do." Caroline waggled her fingers before rushing off.

Amos stared after her. "Gideon has his hands full keeping her out of trouble."

"What do you mean?" His brother's willingness to say something negative about Caroline surprised Stephen.

"You know I don't like repeating rumors, but if even half of what I've heard about Caroline's new boyfriend is true, she should be staying away from that trouble. And if Gideon weren't so distracted by Fern, he'd put a stop to it."

Gideon and Fern. Everyone kept linking their names. Stephen's heart went out to Nettie. She was in for another rough time. If only he could find a way to keep her from getting hurt.

With a sigh, he read the list she'd created. Stephen admired the precise, loopy letters that decorated the page. Nettie had the soul of an artist. And the precision of an accountant. She'd listed each stand in order starting from Ridley's Organic Meats & Produce, the huge business at the front of the market. Stephen ran his finger down each aisle.

Amos moved closer to peer over Stephen's shoulder. "What's that you've got there?"

"A list of all the stand owners. I agreed to ask everyone to donate leftover foods to Mrs. Vandenberg's project."

"Want some help? When we're not busy, I can do the stands to the left of ours, and you can do the right."

"That'd be great." Stephen had hoped to share this job with Nettie, but her shyness had gotten in the way.

Maybe that shyness had also prevented her from giving him this list. That might be some of it. What he'd learned of Nettie's personality last night made him suspect she'd avoided him out of embarrassment. How could he let her know he didn't think of her any differently after everything she'd confided?

Actually, that wasn't true. He did look at her in a new light. He'd seen a gentler, more vulnerable side of her, and he'd come to like and admire her.

Only as a friend, of course.

* * *

Nettie waited for Caroline to return. "Was Stephen there? Did you give him the list?"

Caroline laughed. "Of course. If you were so worried about it, why didn't you give it to him yourself?"

"I had to prepare the trays." Heat crept into Nettie's cheeks. She wished she didn't sound so defensive.

"I had work to do too." Caroline's smile made Nettie feel small.

Her sister-in-law hadn't tried to do that. She just oozed self-confidence. Talking to people came naturally to her. Maybe Nettie would have an easy, outgoing temperament if she'd been raised in a family like Caroline's and Gideon's where their parents shared their love and faith. When you grew up in a home like that, it would make it easier to trust people.

"Do you need any help?" a soft voice said behind her.

Nettie had been so lost in thought she hadn't heard Fern approaching. "*Neh*, I'm almost done." Nettie disliked the edge in her voice every time she spoke to Fern.

Gideon gave Fern an *I'm-so-glad-you're-here* smile. A warmer greeting than he'd ever given Nettie. In Nettie's mind, that spelled trouble for her children. She wanted them to grow up in the safe, caring household they'd lived in since her husband died. Gideon falling for Fern would ruin those plans.

"Fern, I could use some help putting salads into the display case." Gideon patted the counter beside him.

"I can do that." Nettie hurried over before Fern could reach Gideon's side. She slid open the door, and then realized she'd have to go back to the refrigerator to get the containers of salad. She'd been so intent on keeping the two of them apart, she hadn't considered she had nothing to put in there.

She'd made a fool of herself—again. And everyone had probably guessed her motive.

As usual, Fern had a kind and thoughtful response. "Would you like me to bring you the salads from the refrigerator?"

"*Danke.*" Nettie managed not to sound too ungracious.

Fern's suggestion earned her an adoring look from Gideon.

Nettie's stomach sank. With every day that passed, more and more she feared Gideon would break his promise to take care of her and the children.

Stephen and Amos took turns visiting other stands whenever business slowed. When his children arrived after school, Stephen took advantage of the extra help to slip out of the stand. Amos, realizing where Stephen was heading, gave him a nod.

"*Daed!*" Joline's shrill yell stopped him. She came running after him. "Where are you going?"

"To talk to other stand owners about a program Mrs. Vandenberg's starting."

"I want to come with you."

"Amos needs you at the stand. This time of day is always hectic." People dropped in after work to pick up quick meals for the evening or food for the weekend.

"Then why are you leaving now?"

"Because we need to get a list of donations so Mrs.

Vandenberg can get everything set up. She has workers coming in early Monday morning to install everything. I wouldn't normally leave Amos alone in the late afternoons."

Rather than returning, Joline walked beside him to the next stand. "I want to help you."

"If you really want to help, go back and wait on customers."

"Please let me go with you."

"You can come to two stands, and then you need to get back to work."

His daughter stuck so close to him, he bumped her with his elbow each time he jotted notes. After hc checked two owners off Nettie's list, he gestured toward Amos's stand. "All right, now you've seen what I'm doing. Time to assist with customers." He headed for another stand.

Joline headed in the direction he'd pointed, but when he turned to face the next counter, he caught a flurry of motion out of the corner of his eye. His daughter had ducked behind a support pole. What in the world was she doing?

He didn't have time to figure out Joline's antics. Saturdays were their busiest days, so Stephen wouldn't be able to do this tomorrow. He needed to visit as many stands as he could before they closed tonight. After they got home, they'd talk about her disobedience. He still needed to discuss last night's behavior with her. He'd add tailing him around the market to that list.

She'd been upset when she'd seen him with Nettie. Maybe Joline was checking to see if he'd spend more time at Hartzler's. Mrs. Vandenberg had mentioned Joline needed a *mamm*. Was his daughter hoping for one deep down? Or did she want to prevent him from finding a wife?

He could set Joline's mind at rest over that. He'd never met anyone yet he'd like to court. And Mrs. Vandenberg's matchmaking abilities seemed to be off target with him. Nettie would never be interested in him. He reminded her of one of the most painful memories of her life. Who would want to live with that?

Besides, she'd made it clear she was interested in someone else. Someone who seemed to prefer another woman. Stephen's heart went out to her. She'd had a lot of pain already. He understood the agony of losing a spouse, and he hated to think she might also be facing a broken heart.

Stephen finished another aisle and checked those owners off. Only one more row to finish. Next to each name, he marked the donations they'd agreed to give. He also promised to buy produce too wilted for the center to use. As long as it wasn't spoiled, he could feed it to their pigs.

He should check to be sure Amos didn't need assistance. Pivoting quickly to head back, he surprised Joline. She ducked behind a large potted plant in the Plant Palace, but not quickly enough to evade detection.

With a sigh, Stephen marched over and stood with his hands on his hips. Sheepishly, she slipped out to face him.

"Didn't I tell you to go back to the stand?"

"*Jah.*" Joline scuffed the toe of her shoe on the cement. "But I want to be with you. I miss you when you're gone."

He hardened his resolve against her pleading eyes. "When I tell you to do something, I expect you to do it. Go back to the stand now. We'll talk more about this after we get home tonight."

The way she dawdled as she obeyed bothered Stephen. He hoped he wasn't witnessing the birth of teenage rebelliousness. If so, he needed to nip it off now before it went any further. The last thing he needed was for her to influence her younger brothers and sisters to follow her example.

Chapter Ten

Stephen's plans to deal with Joline's defiance that evening came to a screeching halt when he returned to the stand.

"Glad you're back." Amos wiped his sweating forehead. "We've been swamped."

"Sorry." Stephen frowned at Joline to remind her she should have been here working. Then he stepped up to the counter to take an order. They were rushed off their feet until closing time.

As they waited on their final customer, Mrs. Vandenberg came tottering over to the stand. "Do you have a minute, Stephen?"

Throwing an apologetic glance his brother's way, Stephen went to talk to her. Instead of cleaning up, Joline followed him.

"Go do your job." He made his tone stern.

Her head jerked up, and she stared at him, startled. Then, a hurt expression crossed her face, and she whirled around and left. To do her chores, he hoped.

"Sorry about that," he said to Mrs. Vandenberg.

"No need to apologize. Children should always be parents' first priority. After God, of course."

Stephen nodded, but her observation troubled him. Had he been putting his children's needs first since they moved here? If he were honest, selling the New York farm and getting established here in the Lancaster area had taken most of his time.

Joline seemed to be begging for his attention. Had he neglected her and his other children? Maybe getting involved with Mrs. Vandenberg's program wasn't a good idea.

"Could you possibly meet again tonight?" Mrs. Vandenberg asked. "Nettie went home early, but she said you had the lists."

"Not tonight." He gestured to Joline, who'd edged close enough to listen. "I need to talk to my daughter and spend time with my children."

"It's all right, Daed." Joline straightened her shoulders. "We can talk another time."

That was odd. After all her fussing about wanting to be around him, now she didn't care if he didn't come home? Or was she trying to avoid a lecture and possible punishment?

Looking angelic, she volunteered, "I can pray with everyone and make sure they go to bed on time."

Mrs. Vandenberg studied Joline. "I bet you do a lot to take care of your brothers and sisters, don't you?"

Joline puffed up with pride. "*Jah*, and I do the cooking and cleaning and—"

Stephen waved a hand to halt Joline's bragging. She snapped her mouth shut, but she glowed under Mrs. Vandenberg's admiring look.

"That's wonderful. I imagine your father couldn't run the house without you."

His daughter threw back her shoulders and started to answer, then glanced over at him. He shook his head. "Joline does what needs doing."

He didn't want her to be prideful about the tasks she'd taken on. At the same time, he hadn't really considered all the responsibilities she'd been handling since her *mamm* died. She'd been doing most of it since she was around seven.

For the first few years, his sister had stayed with them. When she left to get married, Joline took care of it all. And she'd been doing it ever since.

Mrs. Vandenberg smiled at his daughter. "That's amazing, Joline. I'm glad you don't mind me stealing your dad for a while tonight." She faced Stephen again. "I'll see you at the café tables whenever you're done. Please be sure to bring the list."

As he carried a container to the sink for her to wash, Stephen puzzled over Joline's change of heart. "So, you don't want me to come home with you tonight?"

"I didn't say that." Rather than looking up at him, she concentrated on scrubbing a serving spoon that looked clean.

"Last night you were upset when I went to talk to Mrs. Vandenberg. And you acted rude to her because of it."

"I'm sorry." Joline clattered a metal container into the sink.

"We still have to talk about that. And I'm not the one who deserves the apology."

"I'll tell her," she mumbled.

"*Jah*, you will. But what I want to know is why after following me around all day, insisting you wanted to be with me, you suddenly don't mind me going to a meeting."

His daughter shrugged. "I don't know. Maybe watching you made me realize how important this is?"

She didn't sound too sure of her answer. Something more lay beneath her willingness to let him go without protest. His instinct told him something was wrong, but he wouldn't get a response out of Joline here, and he didn't want to keep Mrs. Vandenberg waiting.

He whispered a prayer for wisdom to deal with his daughter and her rapidly changing moods. He had a feeling living through her teenage years would require plenty more prayers.

When her *daed* finally moved off to do other cleaning, Joline let out the breath she'd been holding. She hoped she'd sounded convincing.

Mrs. Vandenberg had provided the perfect excuse. As long as Sourpuss wouldn't be there, Daed could go to a meeting every night. At least until school let out.

Joline had crumpled the note from Teacher Emily and stuck it under the caked food and juices she'd poured into the garbage. She couldn't help feeling relieved as the liquid soaked through the envelope. That should make it unreadable. Then she'd buried the wet letter under meat scraps and other discards.

On the way to the market, Joline had peeked inside the envelope. Teacher Emily had listed several times Joline had misbehaved. No way could she give this note to her father.

Maybe he'd be so distracted with Mrs. Vandenberg's center, he'd forget to ask about school. At least Joline hoped he would. And even better, he wouldn't spend this evening with Sourpuss. Joline had little control over events the next day, though. Two delivery drivers came with Mrs. Vandenberg to discuss the list with Daed. Joline hadn't been paying much attention as they finalized sizes of heated and refrigerated trucks.

Before they left, Mrs. Vandenberg called to Daed, "I hope you and Nettie will come to look over the center tonight to see if everything looks good for the grand opening. We're still adding a few things, but maybe the two of you might have some suggestions. You're welcome to ride with me."

"I want to go too," Joline blurted out.

Daed's eyebrows rose.

She tried to come up with a reason. "I didn't get to be with you last night."

"Yesterday you said you were fine with me spending as much time as I needed with Mrs. Vandenberg."

Why had she suggested that?

"That was before I missed you at bedtime." Joline averted her eyes so Daed couldn't see she was fibbing. She'd purposely gone to bed before he got home so she wouldn't have to talk about her behavior or about school.

"I see." Daed sounded puzzled and a bit exasperated.

Mrs. Vandenberg chimed in, "I think it's a fine idea. It might be good for Joline to see what life is like for some of these children. And I have enough room in my car for all three of you."

"That's kind of you." Daed nudged Joline. "I think you have something to say."

"I'm sorry I was rude to you the other day." She made

herself act contrite, but to her surprise, she really did feel bad.

Mrs. Vandenberg seemed like a nice, understanding lady. It wasn't her fault that Joline worried about Daed getting interested in Sourpuss. Well, maybe it was a little. After all, Mrs. Vandenberg liked to be a matchmaker. And she had brought Daed and that woman together.

"You know, Joline, things aren't always what they seem."

Had Mrs. Vandenberg realized the apology had been fake? Or did she mean something else?

Nettie refilled the large container with potato salad and hurried back to slide it into the refrigerated display case.

"Yoo-hoo, Nettie, can I talk to you for a minute?" Mrs. Vandenberg stood at the far end of the display case, away from the lines of customers.

"Go ahead," Gideon encouraged her. "Caroline and I can handle things until you get back."

With a quick sideways glance to be sure Fern remained at the far end of the counter, Nettie headed over to talk to Mrs. Vandenberg.

"I just came from Lapp's, and we worked out all the details for picking up the food next Saturday. Thank you for all your help."

Nettie hadn't done anything yet. "But I thought Stephen and I would be collecting the donations." She planned to do more than her share then to make up for not asking people to give.

"I didn't mean to disappoint you." The sly look on Mrs. Vandenberg's face added extra meaning to her words.

"It's not that. I didn't do much." Nettie regretted handing over the list. "Stephen did all the work."

"He couldn't have done it without your list. Don't look so disappointed. You can spend time with him tonight. I'd like both of you to come to the center for a tour and to give any last-minute ideas."

"I—I couldn't." The last thing she wanted was to spend time around Stephen. "I have to put the children to bed and—"

Gideon sidled past her to get more trays. A job she should be doing.

"What's the matter, Nettie?"

Had her distress been that obvious?

Mrs. Vandenberg answered for her. "I'd like Nettie to look around the STAR center tonight."

"I can't," Nettie repeated. "The children—"

"I can take care of putting them to bed," Gideon volunteered. "Mamm won't mind helping if we need her. It's good for you to get out sometimes."

"But—but . . ." Everyone ignored her spluttering.

"Thank you, Gideon. That's settled then." Mrs. Vandenberg pulled out a tablet and checked off an item on her list. "I do need to talk to Aidan if you can spare him for a few minutes, Gideon."

"Of course. Caroline can watch the fries if Nettie comes back to wait on people."

"Perfect. I'll see you tonight after closing, Nettie. My car will be near the front door."

Gideon maneuvered past Nettie with the trays. "I'll send Aidan down here. And congratulations on the center,

Mrs. V. Nettie told me some of what you'll be doing. It sounds fascinating."

"*Danke*, Gideon. I'm excited to see what the Lord does with this venture. He always takes these projects in the most interesting directions."

"Well, I'll be praying God blesses this one." Gideon set the trays down and went to talk to Aidan and Caroline. "If it gets too busy, we can ask Fern to help."

"She's way too busy." Nettie determined to handle every customer in the chicken barbecue lines, even it killed her. Anything to keep Fern down in the bakery end where she belonged and away from Gideon.

Aidan brushed past Nettie and went to talk to Mrs. Vandenberg.

Despite being overwhelmed with customers, Nettie overheard their conversation.

"Me?" Aidan's voice cracked as it rose. "You want me to help inner city kids? What can I teach them? According to Russell, I hang around with juvies."

Nettie ground her teeth. Russell, the market manager, picked on Aidan every chance he got. She had to admit, Aidan played the part with his tattoos, nose ring, and wild hair. But they'd all discovered the teen had a heart of gold.

What in the world did Mrs. Vandenberg expect Aidan to do? He wasn't exactly a stellar role model.

"My goal is to keep kids out of gangs." Her face earnest, Mrs. Vandenberg leaned on the counter. "You know how to play video games and pool, right?"

"Ya think?" Then as if regretting his flippant attitude, he apologized. "You want me to teach kids to play video games and pool? You're serious?"

"I certainly am. Anything to get kids off the streets

and into a safe space. Once they're in the center, we'll try to teach them about God, making good decisions, and encourage them to stay in school."

Aidan groaned. "I hope you don't expect me to set an example."

"Actually, I'm counting on you to do exactly that."

"I don't know." He sounded doubtful, but he straightened his shoulders. "I guess I could give it a try."

"I'm so glad, Aidan. I hope you'll come along with us to the center tonight. We're preparing for the grand opening next week."

Aidan's face scrunched up. "On a Saturday night?"

Nettie imagined Aidan had plenty of plans that didn't include showing young kids how to stay out of trouble.

"I can give you a ride," Mrs. Vandenberg offered.

"In the Bentley? Um, no offense, but that's not my style. Maybe I'll buzz by later if I get a chance. But I'll definitely come next week."

"We'll be open until ten thirty." She handed him a business card with the address.

"I'll see." Aidan hesitated. "Okay to bring some friends along to the opening?"

"Sure, the more the merrier."

Aidan wandered back to the fryer muttering. "Not sure they'll want to go."

Ten thirty? Nettie never stayed out that late. She missed the next customer's salad order.

Surely, Mrs. Vandenberg wouldn't expect her to be there that long. The children would miss her at supper and bedtime, and they'd be asleep for hours before she returned. Nettie had one other concern. Would she be expected to spend all that time with Stephen?

Worry about all of those carried her through until closing time. When Mrs. Vandenberg arrived, Gideon waved Nettie off.

"We can take care of it from here," he assured her. "And the children will be in good hands."

Nettie had no doubt of that. She trusted him to take care of them. "*Danke* for watching them."

"I'm always happy to do it."

"Let's go, Nettie," Mrs. Vandenberg called. Then she added, "Aidan, I'm looking forward to seeing you over there."

"Yeah, Mrs. V." He gave her a cheery wave. Only Nettie heard him mumble, "If the homies'll go."

"All right, let's go, Nettie."

"I'm not ready—" As she left the stand, she ran a hand over her hair, hoping to smooth down any wayward strands that might have escaped. She checked that her *kapp* was on straight.

"You look lovely as always. Doesn't she, Stephen?"

"Of—of course."

Nettie could have died. She hadn't realized he'd been coming up behind them. She never would have preened if she'd known that.

And Stephen wasn't alone. His petulant daughter appeared glued to his side. The girl's glare sliced through Nettie.

"Everyone ready to go?' Mrs. Vandenberg beckoned for them all to follow her.

Nettie swallowed hard. She wasn't ready. Leaving her children alone for the night made her antsy. Were they all right? Were they missing her? She'd never gone off and left them like this before, without even saying good night or goodbye.

She longed to be home, cuddling her children, telling them bedtime stories. She preferred her familiar routine. And she dreaded spending long hours with Stephen and his bodyguard. At least that's how she thought of his daughter.

When they got to the Bentley, the driver opened the back door, and Joline slipped past Nettie to get in first.

"Joline!" Stephen's warning didn't stop her.

She scrambled inside with a quick "Sorry."

"Smart move, little lady," the driver said. "Your legs are shorter so you'll fit better there. Of course, this model has a third row of seats under the trunk floor. They're best for smaller people, so I can give you your own row if you'd like."

"*Neh*, thank you," Joline said primly, scooting over to the center of the seat. "I'm fine here."

Stephen shook his head. She'd gone from rude to ultra-polite in ten seconds flat. Maybe the luxury of the Bentley had subdued her.

He regretted that they still hadn't had their talk. The longer he let her get away with this behavior, the more likely she was to believe her attitude was acceptable. They'd be at the center tonight, and tomorrow they had church. He didn't want to wait until Sunday evening, but he might have no choice.

He leaned over and, keeping his voice low, warned, "I expect you to be polite and respectful." He added, "To everyone and at all times."

The brief up-and-down bob of her head didn't ease his concerns.

"I mean it. And tomorrow after church, we're going to have a talk."

She swallowed hard and averted her eyes.

When the driver pulled in front of the building that took up a whole city block, Stephen marveled at the huge neon star on the top of the building. Over the entrance, a smaller star shone. Above it, letters in blue and red spelled out, *Be a STAR*.

As they moved around the center, Joline's tense expression warmed into wonder. "Wow!" she exclaimed as they toured all the rooms.

Even Stephen, who'd seen most of the plans, was impressed. Mrs. Vandenberg had added more areas than the original plan had shown. Kids and teens would certainly flock to this building. Some of the new additions included a dance studio and a gardening center where children could grow container gardens to take home.

Beside him, Nettie had tears in her eyes. She kept shaking her head as they went from room to room. "Mrs. V, this is wonderful," she choked out. "All the neighborhood children will want to hang out here."

"I hope so." Mrs. Vandenberg's face softened as she watched Nettie's excitement.

"I wish . . ." Nettie didn't finish.

"I know, dear. You inspired this."

Joline broke in. "What's this room?"

"When it's finished, it'll be a science lab. I can't believe all the volunteers we have who are willing to teach and supervise in each of the areas. I've had to hire several new staff members to handle background checks and clearances."

When they finished the tour, Mrs. Vandenberg led them to a small conference room. "Have a seat." She pulled out a notebook. "Now, I'd like any suggestions you have for improvement."

Stephen couldn't think of anything he'd change. "I think children will love it." He deferred to Nettie, and she totally surprised him.

"Having glass windows in the front isn't a good idea."

"You're right," Mrs. Vandenberg conceded. "But I like how they let in natural light. Plus, they allow kids to see inside. I hope it will make them want to enter."

Nettie shook her head. "You'd be better off without them. Are they bulletproof glass? You should put bars or metal mesh over them."

"I appreciate what you're saying, Nettie, but I believe in trusting God."

"Trust in God doesn't always stop bullets," Nettie murmured so low Stephen could hardly hear her.

What an odd thing for an Amish woman to say! Stephen agreed with Mrs. Vandenberg. In Mayville and here, he never locked the doors, and he left his safety up to God. "Whatever happens is God's will." He tried to say it gently so he didn't come off as judgmental.

Nettie turned to him. "So I should have just let you fall from that ladder?"

"*Neh*, I'm glad you saved me." But hadn't God brought her there to rescue him?

"I know neither of you understand, but those streets out there are dangerous." Passion lit her face. "They may not be as bad as other cities in this state, but there are gangs here too."

"You're right." Mrs. Vandenberg tapped her pen on a notebook page. "I did talk to the police. Kids as young as ten get into gangs."

Joline's eyes widened. Up until now, she'd listened silently. *Ten?* she mouthed to him.

Stephen frowned. Not at his daughter, but at the thought. "Why would children get involved in gangs at that young age?"

"They want to imitate the teens," Nettie said, her face sad. "If you can encourage them to come here, you might save some of the younger ones from a life of crime."

Nettie's insight into city life amazed Stephen. "How do you know so much about all this? Did you work at an inner-city mission or something?"

"*Neh.*" Nettie snapped out an answer that cut off conversation.

Her closed-down expression offered no clues. She obviously didn't want to talk about it. He regretted asking the question.

Nettie shifted in her chair, uncomfortable under Stephen's curious gaze. What would he think if knew how she'd acquired all this information? Better for him not to know.

A bit embarrassed to be doing all the talking, Nettie raised an eyebrow signaling for Stephen to jump in with comments. So far, he'd only praised the center. Beside him, Joline glared at her.

When Nettie first learned Stephen was a widower, she'd

wondered why he'd gone seven years without remarrying, but now she suspected she might have the answer. He didn't seem to be aware of his daughter's actions, but women who'd been interested in him probably faced Joline's hostility.

"Anything else?" Mrs. Vandenberg directed the question to Nettie.

She disliked being the only one to bring up things to fix. But she wanted this center to be safe for the children who'd come here.

"You need bright lights in the alley on that side." Nettie pointed to her left. "The darkness makes it easy to do drug deals. And it would be easy to hide behind the dumpster to commit crimes."

"I'll get on it right away." Mrs. Vandenberg dialed her phone. "Martin, how soon could we get lights installed on the west side of the building?" She waited. "I'll hang on while you check."

"Anything else you can think of, Nettie, while I have Martin on the phone?"

"Do you have any security guards? Any way to screen people coming in?" If Mrs. Vandenberg didn't, she'd have drug deals going on in the restrooms. Or maybe even out in plain sight.

"I'd rather not keep anyone out."

Nettie bit back a sigh and explained about drug deals, child traffickers, turf wars, gang violence, and drive-by shootings. "You need to protect the children in this building."

Stephen's expression flickered between fascination at her knowledge and amazement at the fact she knew it. He must be wondering why an Amish woman would know about these things. She'd rather not see his face if he discovered how she'd learned all this.

Mrs. Vandenberg broke into her thoughts. "I've financed a lot of projects in this city, and we've had some problems from time to time, but so far God has been good."

"How many of those programs involve young children?"

"Just the daycare centers."

"But they don't let people in off the streets. People have to ring and be admitted to a front office, right?"

"True." Mrs. Vandenberg jotted some notes in her notebook. "You're right. More needs to be done to make this a safe haven."

She stopped and listened to the phone she'd tucked against her shoulder. "I guess we don't have much choice. Tell them to install them as soon as they can."

That didn't sound good. Nettie waited for Mrs. Vandenberg to hang up the phone.

"We won't have the lights for opening day, but they'll get them up a few days later."

"I wish you had them now. You have a side door to that alley. With the darkness back there, it's also easier to break into the building."

"I'll ask the police to make frequent checks until we're open."

Nettie still hadn't finished. "What about winos? The druggies? The street people? They may come inside to get out of the summer heat or to warm up in winter."

"I've built some shelters nearby."

Nettie beamed. "Perfect. But you'll need someone to direct them or take them there."

Mrs. Vandenberg picked up her pen again. "I'll see about hiring some security—"

"Not with uniforms." Nettie hadn't meant to interrupt her. "You'll scare off kids whose families are avoiding cops or immigration."

"I had thought of that."

She should have kept her mouth shut. She'd talked way too much. Stephen's admiring gaze had bobbed back and forth between her and Mrs. Vandenberg like he was watching a Ping-Pong match.

"Ping-Pong," she said suddenly.

Mrs. Vandenberg laughed. "I had planned for that, but the tables haven't been delivered yet. Nettie, you're amazing."

"I agree." Stephen's enthusiastic response followed Mrs. Vandenberg's comment.

Unaware of Joline's scowl, he smiled at Nettie. But the admiration in his eyes would die quickly if she revealed the truth about her past.

Chapter Eleven

By the time Nettie arrived home, all four of her children were sound asleep. Though she tried not to think about Stephen's look, it warmed her heart as she lay in bed that night, making it difficult to drift off. His kindness and friendliness had increased her loneliness.

And seeing Gideon's buggy missing from the barn brought back Nettie's fears about the future. What would she and the children do and where would they go if he married Fern?

Mrs. Vandenberg's words echoed in Nettie's mind: *I believe in trusting God.* Stephen had added, *Whatever happens is God's will.* Nettie wished she had their simple faith. She doubted either of them had ever worried about whether or not they'd have a roof over their heads or where their next meal would come from or if someone might do them harm.

Nettie told herself God would take care of her and the children. But she'd spent so much of her life scrambling she found it hard to relax. As she drifted off to sleep, her head told her one thing; her heart told her another.

When the sun rose on Sunday morning, she struggled

to rouse herself from her dreams. She'd been basking in Stephen's smile. Shaking off the dream, she hurried to the kitchen to make breakfast. The last thing she needed was to get interested in a man she couldn't be honest with.

Her daughters entered the room, and Katie helped start breakfast so Nettie could fix Sadie's hair.

"Did you thank Gideon for putting you to bed?" Nettie asked as she combed Sadie. After twisting the sides tightly, she secured her daughter's fine hair into a bob.

Katie stirred the oatmeal. "He didn't put us to bed."

Sadie lifted her head an inch from the table. "Fern did."

"Stay still." Nettie's sharpness came more from learning Fern had been at the house than annoyance at her daughter. Nettie yanked the netting into place.

She'd assumed Gideon would take care of the children. She never would have gone if she'd known anyone other than her mother-in-law would help him. Nettie went from a slow simmer to a raging boil as she pictured Fern sitting at the dinner table and then tucking the girls into bed.

"She's really nice." Katie turned off the heat and put a lid on the oatmeal pot.

"*Jah*, she is." Sadie wriggled down from the chair. "She told us a story."

"And she hugged and kissed us like you do, Mamm. She said she didn't want us to feel lonely."

Nettie struggled to tamp down her temper. She should be grateful Fern had been so kind and loving to her daughters.

Lord, please take these old fears from me. Help me to trust You. And take away my jealousy of Fern.

When she opened her eyes, Katie was studying her. "But we missed you, Mamm."

Sadie turned around and hugged Nettie's legs, and her heart overflowed. These two precious girls and her two sons were gifts from God.

Gideon had promised to take care of them. If he couldn't, the church would help to care for them. She had to keep reminding herself she had a support system here in the Amish community, something her mother had never had. And in all of this, Nettie had to learn to trust God. Something she found hard to do.

Joline woke on Sunday morning filled with dread. Her life seemed to be crashing down around her. Last night, the admiration in Daed's eyes as he'd gazed at Sourpuss scared her. And Mrs. Vandenberg's satisfied smile showed she planned to keep up her matchmaking.

That wasn't the only thing worrying Joline. Last night, she'd dreamed Daed had found the note in the trash. The relief that flooded through her on awakening lasted only a few minutes.

Jah, they'd emptied the contents of that small garbage can into the dumpster. Joline had tied the black trash bag shut herself and, to everyone's surprise, she'd volunteered to cart it outside. It had landed inside the dumpster with a satisfying *thunk*. It might already be at the dump.

But what if someone mentioned the school problems to Daed when they were at church today? What if someone tattled? Someone like Katie Hartzler? Or her *mamm*?

One other thing bothered Joline. She'd been so upset about Daed and Sourpuss, she'd forgotten to go over her schoolwork with Matthew on Thursday night. When Teacher Emily called on Joline to read on Friday, she'd stumbled and stuttered her way through words that tangled before her eyes.

She'd messed up the first sentence so badly she dropped the book, clutched her forehead, and claimed to have a headache and an eye ache. She sank into her seat, laid her head on the desk, and couldn't lift her head to finish the rest of her schoolwork.

For the first time ever, Joline had rejoiced not to be going out for recess. She couldn't face everyone now that her secret had been exposed. She'd hoped to keep her reading problems hidden from her new teacher and class-mates.

In Mayville, Teacher Diane had known and understood. She'd let Matthew read quietly to Joline when she needed extra help. Although she and Matthew had come up with a plan to keep everyone here from finding out, Joline had missed one evening of practice.

For the rest of the school day, she'd shielded her eyes and barely participated in lessons. Whenever she peeped through her fingers, Teacher Emily was studying her thoughtfully. Next week, parents would meet with the teacher for end-of-the-year conferences. Joline dreaded Daed finding out all the things she'd done. What would he do?

She didn't want to go to church today. All the kids from her class would be there. Joline couldn't face another day of humiliation. And of being left out. Staying in at recess had kept her from making friends.

Today might be a good day to be sick. An upset stom-ach? A headache?

A little while later, Daed tapped on the door. "Joline?"

He peeked in, his face creased with worry. "You didn't start breakfast yet. Are you all right?"

"I'm feeling sick." She wasn't lying. Her stomach churned.

"Stay in bed. Matthew and Ben can help with your chores."

She hadn't realized she'd get out of feeding and inspecting the pigs. But the guilt swirling inside didn't let her enjoy skipping her jobs.

Her stomach growled as they all ate breakfast without her. Once everyone had gone out to the barn, Joline sneaked downstairs to grab a bite to eat.

She'd just finished pouring milk on a bowl of cereal when Daed banged into the kitchen. She almost spilled the milk.

Daed eyed her for a bit. "*Hmm*. Looks like you're feeling better. Hurry and get dressed for church."

She should have waited. Coming down here had been a huge mistake.

Stephen's gaze kept straying to the woman sitting across from him in church. He dragged his attention away from Nettie and to the minister's sermon. Stephen chastised himself when the service ended. He'd spent more time examining Nettie than listening to the Word of God.

During the meal, Amos introduced Stephen to many different men. He hoped he'd soon be able to remember everyone's names. He did know a few of the ones he'd spoken to at the market.

When they headed out to the barn to talk, Esther ran after him. He stopped and knelt down. His shy daughter never approached him with a crowd around. He wanted her to feel comfortable.

"Daed? Can my friend Katie come to visit after school tomorrow?"

Surprised, Stephen smiled at her. "Of course." His children normally didn't play with friends after school because they had chores, but for the first time ever, Esther had asked to have company. He didn't want to discourage her.

In Mayville, she'd been too nervous to talk to people. She depended on her outgoing twin to do all interacting. Abby had been Esther's only playmate since they'd been small.

"Can you ask her *mamm* for me?" Esther gazed up at him, her wide eyes filled with trust.

"Let's do it together." He wanted to encourage her to get more comfortable talking to people. "Do you know who her *mamm* is?"

"*Jah*, she's over there." Esther pointed out Nettie.

Stephen stopped. "Maybe we should wait until they're ready to leave before we ask her."

"I want to do it now."

Stephen didn't. He already had to avoid giving the wrong impression at the market. He didn't need to stir up speculation here at church.

"I have an idea. Why don't you play with your friend until it's time for her to go? Then I'll ask her *mamm*. Or you could have Katie ask her *mamm*."

The excitement in Esther's eyes dimmed. "I want you to do it."

"I promise I'll ask her. Come and get me when it's time."

Esther skipped off, leaving Stephen to dread departure

time. Even if he talked to Nettie at her buggy, rumors could fly. But he'd made a promise, and he'd see it through.

Later, when Esther came to get him, he followed her over to Nettie's buggy and issued the invitation.

"If it's all right with you, Katie can ride her scooter home with the girls tomorrow after school." He hoped that would work because he and Amos had scheduled a barn cleaning since it was a non-market day.

Nettie appeared startled. "Katie does chores after school."

Stephen should have anticipated that. Visiting friends after school might be unusual, but he really wanted to encourage his daughter's first friendship. He lowered his voice so Esther, who was talking to Katie, didn't hear. "Esther's very shy, and she's never had a friend before. I was hoping maybe . . ."

"I see." Nettie's lips slid up into an attractive smile. "I'm sure Katie will enjoy that. She really likes Esther."

When Stephen announced it to the girls, his daughter's face filled with sunshine.

Oddly, Katie looked a bit wary. Maybe she was as shy as Esther and visiting a new place made her frightened. Esther probably would be overwhelmed if she'd been invited to Katie's house.

Stephen tried to make Katie feel welcome. "We'll look forward to having you tomorrow, Katie. All of Esther's brothers and sisters like having friends over."

If anything, Katie appeared even more scared. Poor girl. Tomorrow, he'd do his best to make her feel at home. Once she arrived, she'd probably relax.

As the two girls walked to the other side of the buggy to chat, Nettie followed their progress. The tenderness on her face as she watched her daughter and Esther together kickstarted Stephen's heart.

"*Danke*," Nettie said in a soft, breathy voice. "Katie has spent the whole school year being lonely. She brings a book and sits far from the other children during recess. I'm glad she has a friend."

She glanced up at him, her eyes glimmering with tears and gratitude. The air whooshed from Stephen's lungs, and he couldn't take his eyes off her.

Nettie melted under Stephen's caring look. Her heart expanded until it pressed against her ribs. The sky turned bluer; the grass, greener. The whole world took on shimmery hues.

She'd never felt this way before. If only this moment could last forever.

Behind her, someone coughed. "Excuse me, could we get by?"

Abruptly, Nettie broke their gaze. What had she been thinking? Everyone getting into their buggies must have seen them. What a fool she'd been!

She stepped aside so Anna and Levi King could shepherd all their adopted and foster children into their buggy. Radiating happiness as her husband pushed her wheelchair, Anna held her bouncy baby, Ciara, in her arms and sent Nettie a knowing smile. A woman-to-woman vibe that celebrated the joy of love.

For a moment, Nettie responded, letting all her innermost emotions bubble to the surface again. Then, she lowered her eyelids to break that connection and return herself to sanity.

"I need to go." She made herself say the words. She did need to get out of here and get far, far away from the topsy-turvy feelings threatening to derail her life.

"I'm sorry." Stephen backed up. "I didn't mean to cause any problems. I only wanted to invite Katie to—"

She left his apology hanging as she climbed into the driver's seat and slid her door shut. Nettie berated herself. Why had she done that? She'd cut him off mid-sentence. Could she have been any ruder?

The fears welling up inside were no excuse for insulting him. To make up for it, she tilted the corners of her mouth up into a half-hearted smile and gave a cheery wave. She detected surprise mixed with hurt in his eyes before she turned to be sure Katie had gone to collect her siblings.

Five minutes later, Katie climbed in and sat beside Nettie, lips pinched together and jaw set.

"What's wrong?" Guilt flooded Nettie. She'd been so wrapped up in her own emotions, she hadn't paid attention to her children.

"I don't want to go to Esther's house." Katie's voice quavered. "She has too many sisters."

That puzzled Nettie. "She only has two."

"But they're bigger and . . . and meaner."

"Have they been teasing you?"

Katie's only answer was a sharp indrawn breath. She pressed her lips together into an even tighter line and refused to answer.

If either of Stephen's girls had been unkind to Katie while they'd been playing after church, someone would have noticed and stopped them. And Nettie would have heard about it. Katie had been within Nettie's sight most of the time. In fact, Katie had hovered near Nettie since church ended.

She never wanted to put her children in unsafe situations. She'd had her own traumas over that. But having someone teasing her daughter didn't compare with the dangers Nettie had faced. Maybe she protected Katie too much. Her daughter needed to learn to ignore bullying or—as Nettie had learned through painful experience— to stand up for herself.

After she heard Daed's plans to talk to Nettie, Joline trailed him and Esther. She secreted herself on the other side of the Kings' buggy, close enough to hear the conversation. But before they finished talking, three of the Kings' adopted children raced toward her. As usual, Assad held his younger brother's and sister's hands.

Curiosity brightened Taban's face. "What are you doing?"

"Um . . ." Joline tried to look nonchalant. "Looking for my *daed*."

"He's right over there." Assad pointed toward the other side of their buggy.

"*Jah, danke.*" She slipped toward a nearby tree within hearing distance of Nettie's buggy.

"You're going the wrong way," Taban called out. "Over there." His loud voice carried.

Joline hoped Daed stayed too engrossed in the conversation to pay attention. *Neh*, wait. She didn't want him to do that.

Once she collected the details she needed, including

what time Nettie planned to pick up Katie, she hightailed it out of there.

Abby came after her. "Daed says it's time to go."

Joline hung back, taking as much time as she dared to reach the buggy. She'd rather not head home because that meant facing Daed.

Her stomach clenched as they turned down the lane to Amos's house. How much could she hide from Daed? He'd find out most or all of it at the parent-teacher conference, but for now, she'd have enough to deal with if Dad scolded her for her attitude and for disobeying.

By the time they pulled into the driveway, she'd chewed her lip so hard it bled. Daed's discipline wasn't harsh, but she disliked disappointing him. Even a lecture made her heart hurt.

As she hopped out of the buggy, she pulled the seat forward so her sisters and brothers could get out. Then she planned to skedaddle to the house and escape. Maybe Daed wouldn't remember about the lecture.

"Joline?" he said. "I'd like you to stay here and help me with the horse."

She gulped. He hadn't forgotten. She fidgeted while he unhitched the horse.

"Why don't you rub down the horse while we talk?" he suggested.

Actually, she appreciated having something to do. Maybe it would distract Daed. Unfortunately, it didn't.

He cleared his throat—his preliminary to a lecture.

Before he could start listing all her misbehaviors, she jumped in. "I'm sorry, Daed. I don't mean to be so much trouble. It's just that I miss Mayville and all my friends."

And I'm having problems in school. And I'm scared you might like Nettie. And . . .

Sympathy flashed in Daed's eyes. "I think we all miss New York, but this will be our new home from now on. We need to accept that. And when we feel upset, we shouldn't take it out on others."

Daed launched into his expectations—no disobedience, backtalk, eye-rolling, or disrespect. Joline nodded as he outlined what he expected her to do and how she needed to respond.

Her apology and promise to do better seemed to satisfy him. Then he moved on. She tried to pay attention to the Scripture verses and words of wisdom he shared, but her mind drifted to that woman. What could Joline do if Daed and Sourpuss started to like each other and—?

"Do you understand?" Daed finished.

Joline nodded, although she'd heard little of his talk.

"So, what do you think you should do?"

About what? "Um . . ." *What had he said?*

If she answered wrong, he'd know she hadn't listened. She took a stab at the answer. "Apologize?"

"That would be a good first step, but I want you to think of other things to do. Think of ways to show you really mean it."

But what if she didn't? She didn't mind adding to her apology to Mrs. Vandenberg. But what about Sourpuss?

Sunday evenings Gideon and Fern went to the youth group singing, so Nettie bathed Sadie and the boys without help. It was becoming more and more apparent, she had to get used to caring for the children alone.

Nettie tucked Sadie into bed, then went in to tell the boys a bedtime story. Whenever Gideon took charge, he told them Bible stories every night. The boys had gotten used to that, so Nettie carried on the tradition even on days when she drooped from exhaustion, like today.

Last night, she'd gotten home well past her usual bed-time, and then images of Stephen's words and expressions had derailed her sleep for hours. Along with concerns about her children's future.

"Katie," Nettie called downstairs, "finish cleaning up that game. It's time for your bath."

A short while later, Katie hurried upstairs and slammed the bathroom door. Nettie settled on the bed beside Lenny.

David thrust out his lower lip. "How come you don't sit with me?"

Inwardly, Nettie sighed. "I'll sit on your bed tomorrow night."

Lenny snuggled close to her. "Gideon tells me to move over. Then we all smush together so David fits too."

Of course, everything Gideon did was perfect. At least according to her boys.

Nettie scooted Lenny over and patted the bed beside her. David's huge smile warmed her heart. She hurried through "Jonah and the Whale," pointed out the lesson that it was important to listen to God's direction, nudged the boys to say their prayers, and settled them both in bed.

David's pout had returned. "Gideon tells us longer stories, and he plays games with us before we go to sleep."

"He can take more time because he's only putting two

of you to bed. I have to take care of all four of you when he's not here."

"I wish he didn't go out with Fern at our bedtime." David had rolled over, and the pillow muffled his grumpy voice.

"Me too." Lenny scrunched his pillow into a ball and hugged it to his chest.

I do too. But Nettie kept her complaints—and her fears about the future—to herself.

Chapter Twelve

Joline gritted her teeth as Esther danced around the kitchen on Monday morning.

"Katie's coming to play today," her little sister sang over and over.

If it had been anyone else coming, Joline would have been thrilled for Esther. For the first time ever, her little sister had made a friend. But why did that friend have to be Sourpuss's daughter? Even worse, Katie's *mamm* planned to pick her up after running some errands.

Joline had two goals today. First, she had to make sure Katie never wanted to come to their house again. It was much too dangerous for Daed to see Sourpuss outside the market. The look in his eyes after church yesterday as he stared at her had warned of major danger.

He never seemed to notice Nettie's usual grumpy expression. She'd make a terrible *mamm*. Joline had to protect her brothers and sisters from that.

Besides, they don't need a mamm. *They have me.*

Her second goal was to prevent Daed and Sourpuss from meeting when she came to pick up Katie. Joline had a good idea of how to do that. Daed and Amos would be power washing the barn today. All she had to do was prevent Nettie's buggy from coming up the driveway. If Daed didn't hear it, he'd stay in the barn working until Sourpuss had driven off.

Coming up with a plan to do that had been brilliant. Except for one thing. She'd figured it out during the math lesson and gotten in trouble with Teacher Emily again.

Joline didn't mind missing recess, though. She had more important things on her mind. She whipped through her math problems, so she had quiet time to plan a way to keep Katie from visiting their house again.

In the afternoon, Teacher Emily kept a close watch on Joline. She and Matthew had practiced today's lessons ahead of time, so Joline recited everything flawlessly. But near the end of the day, while the other scholars read and printed answers to workbook questions, the teacher called Joline up front.

Joline approached the desk with trepidation. What had she done now? Had the teacher figured out what she'd done during recess?

"Sit down, Joline." Teacher Emily patted a chair right beside her desk with its back to the room. Her friendly smile put Joline on guard.

"I'd like you to read this for me." The teacher handed Joline a book—an eighth-grade reader.

"I'm only in sixth grade," Joline protested.

"That's all right. I don't expect you to know all the words in the story. Just try to sound out any words you don't know."

Joline gulped. She couldn't even read many words she did know. Taking the book with shaky hands, Joline took a deep breath and read the first two words, "*In the . . .*"

Ackk! Then it happened again. The words did their usual dances and jumps. Joline handed the book back. "I can't do this."

Teacher Emily refused to take the book. She bent close and whispered so nobody else could hear. "Read whatever you see."

Starting in the middle of a random sentence, Joline read, "*the dirb wnet*." That wasn't right. Now everything blurred, and a sharp ache started in her temple. She rubbed her eyes. "I can't see the words."

"How do you do your lessons? You read perfectly almost every day."

Joline didn't want to share her secret. "Matthew helps me."

"You memorize things?"

Ducking her head, Joline confessed, "*Jah*."

"How did you do your schoolwork in New York?"

"Teacher Diane let Matthew read to me quietly."

"I see. And when I asked you to write the sentences during recess, you weren't mixing up the words on purpose?"

"*Neh*."

"I'm sorry I scolded you for that. Sometimes scholars who are having trouble act up. I wonder if that could be what's been happening here?"

The gentleness in Teacher Emily's voice made Joline want to cry. Almost. Maybe some of her bad behavior was because of schoolwork, but most of it came from being lonely and left out and worrying about Daed. Joline couldn't tell the teacher any of those things.

She had to be strong and not cry. Her brothers and sisters and Daed depended on her. In Mayville, she never got in trouble. Everybody liked her. She had lots of friends. And every day, she knew what she needed to do, where to go, what to take care of.

Here, everything had changed. She didn't know anyone. When she walked around the market, nobody knew her name. Amos arranged his display cases differently than Daed had, so she often went to the wrong places to get meats. Market days and times weren't the same.

Even at home, things were different. In Mayville, she'd shared a room with her sisters. Amos's house had a lot more rooms, so she had her own room. But that was lonely. Even the routines were different—cooking, cleaning, shopping. Sometimes she cooked; sometimes Betty did. Joline had to get used to the ways Betty and Amos cleaned and find where they stored groceries and supplies.

"Joline?" Teacher Emily jolted Joline from her thoughts.

"You'll get used to it here. I know it can be hard to adjust. We only have a few days left. Why don't you keep doing your schoolwork the way you have been? Next year, we can figure out ways to make it easier for you."

"*Danke.*" Joline wasn't sure if that was the right response, but she appreciated Teacher Emily's understanding.

As she returned to her seat, Joline's eyes burned with unshed tears. Maybe by next school year, she'd have friends. And she'd be getting good grades. And Daed would have forgotten Sourpuss.

The talk with Teacher Emily had softened Joline's heart. A little. Maybe she shouldn't be mean to Katie. But how else could she save her family from getting a new *mamm*?

* * *

After school, they all waited for Katie. She dragged her feet when she went to get her scooter, and seeing the fear in her eyes as she joined them, Joline debated about canceling her plans.

"Come on." Esther beckoned to Katie to join her.

Joline always made the twins and Ben ride in front of her to make sure they were okay. If any danger came, like a swerving car, Joline would get them off the road to protect them.

But Katie lagged so far behind, Joline let Esther trail them. Joline prayed they wouldn't get hurt. Her neck ached from swiveling to watch the two of them behind her, then Ben and Abby in front. At least they didn't have far to go.

Less than a mile later, they turned in to the driveway. Joline let out a sigh. They were safe.

Daed had asked them to call him when Katie arrived, so Joline headed to the barn. She knew better than to stick her head inside when they were power washing the walls.

She stood outside the door and yelled over the noise of the gasoline engine and rapid-fire spray, "We're home, Daed."

"Be right out." A few minutes later, some of the racket quieted, and he stuck his head out the door. He smiled at Katie and Esther as they parked their scooters. "Welcome, Katie. Have fun playing with Esther."

She gave him a shy smile and a barely audible *danke*.

"We're almost done here. Joline, can you fix everyone a snack?"

Joline always did that after school. Why did Daed think he had to tell her to do it? She squashed her irritation because she wanted Daed to believe her side of the story later. If she acted sweet now, he'd be more likely to doubt Katie's accounts of what happened. "I will, Daed." She flashed him her brightest, most angelic smile. "And I'll take care of everyone."

"I know you will." The tender, trusting look he gave her made her squirm inside.

She turned so her guilt wouldn't show. Then she waited until he went inside the barn to shoo everyone into the house.

Joline reached into her lunch box for the apple slices she'd packed that morning. They'd browned from sitting all day, but the pigs wouldn't care. They gobbled down anything.

She caught up with Katie and put on her sweetest smile. "Do you like pigs, Katie?"

Katie stared at her uncertainly. Then she shrugged.

"We have some cute baby piglets." Joline kept her voice gentle and friendly. "Would you like to see them before we have a snack?"

After a quick glance at Esther, who nodded, Katie squeaked out a hesitant *jah*.

"Come on then." Joline beckoned to the two younger girls. "Right this way." She led them out to the pigpen.

The pigs grunted and pressed against the fence when they smelled the apple slices. Katie hung back, staring with frightened eyes at the huge noses sticking through the fence.

"Here." Joline handed Katie most of the apple pieces. Then she positioned herself near the gate latch. "Oh, look over there." Pointing behind Katie and Esther, she said, "Is that a new kitty?"

When they turned to look, Joline undid the gate and let one pig charge out. "*Ach*," she yelled, as she pressed against the gate to keep the other pigs inside.

The loose pig raced straight for Katie, who screamed and ran along the outside of the fence. The pig, who matched Katie's height, trotted after her, snuffling for the apples.

"Don't run, Katie," Esther called after her. "Throw the pig some apples."

But Katie was too terrified and hysterical to do what Esther said. Katie ran faster, and the pig galloped faster. She hit a patch of mud. Her feet slid. With an ear-shattering wail, she plopped into the mud with a huge splash.

Surprised, the pig squealed as brown glop splattered everywhere. Then, it waded into the mud and loomed over Katie, who thrashed in the muck, trying to scrabble away.

"Drop the apples," Esther yelled.

Katie only clutched them tighter. The pig, eyes glittering, opened its mouth, grunted, and bent its head, going for the apples.

"He's going to eat me," she shrieked.

Chapter Thirteen

Terrified screams rent the air. Stephen dropped the wand of his pressure washer and rushed outside.

Joline had her whole body smushed against the gate of the pigpen, trying to keep the pigs from escaping. Nearby, Katie was writhing in the mud, a pig wallowing happily beside her, intent on snatching what looked like apple slices.

Stephen raced over, scooped her into his arms, and held her close, despite the mud dripping from her clothes and soaking into his shirt. With two fingers, he gently pried her hand open, so the squashed apple bits tumbled to the ground.

While the pig nibbled the treat, Stephen backed away and held Katie high enough her legs didn't dangle near the pig. Joline shoved the gate into place and clicked the latch. He eyed his daughter. "Joline, how did that pig get out?"

She didn't meet his eyes. "Katie didn't know she shouldn't undo the latch."

A muffled protest or apology came from Katie, whose face remained pressed against his shirt front.

"It's all right, Katie. We all make mistakes."

She shook her head back and forth vigorously, spreading more stains onto his shirt front, but she didn't say a word.

He shot Joline a stern look. If she'd paid attention, Katie never would have opened the gate. Stephen didn't want to make their little visitor even more uncomfortable than she already was, so he dropped the subject. "Get that pig back in the pen," he told Joline.

Stephen held Katie close until Joline shut the pig behind the gate. Then he set her on the ground. "You'll be all right now." *Well, except for her clothes.*

Esther appeared about ready to burst into tears as she studied Katie. Her chin wobbled. "I'm sorry, Katie."

Katie kept her gaze fixed on the ground, and Stephen guessed she was close to tears. "Why don't you hose Katie down?"

A gleam lit Joline's eyes.

Hmm . . . A loose pig. A mischievous grin. Stephen didn't like to accuse his children without proof. Yet, somehow this all seemed suspicious.

Katie wrapped her arms around herself, smearing mud onto the clean parts of her dress. The late afternoon sunshine had warmed the air, but Katie might be a bit too chilly. Especially after they rinsed off her clothes. Ordinarily, he'd have put Joline in charge of this cleanup, but the bothersome doubts made him hesitate.

"Abby, run in and get two towels for Katie. Esther, you're in charge of the garden hose. Do it gently."

"I can do it," Joline volunteered.

"You'll each have a job. I'd like you to wash Katie's dress and hang it on the line." Stephen didn't know if it would dry before Nettie came to pick up her daughter, but at least Katie's clothes would be clean. "And Esther, lend Katie one of your dresses."

The girls scurried off to do his bidding. All except Joline.

As she started off after the younger girls, he stopped her. "I'd like to hear more about the accident. I'm sure Nettie will want details."

With a trapped look, Joline said, "I'd better get some wash ready. It doesn't make sense to run the washer for only one dress."

She scooted off before he could suggest using the laundry tub to clean the dress. The way she avoided him made him sure she'd had something to do with Katie's fright. But why? Joline had always gone out of her way to be kind to Abby's Mayville friends. He told himself she wouldn't do anything mean or hurtful.

Joline stopped on the back porch as Daed headed toward the garden hose Esther was unwinding.

"I'll need to rinse myself off too," he said.

"I'm sorry." Katie turned teary eyes to him.

"It's all right." The smile Daed gave her upset Joline. He had the same soft *I-care-about-you* look he gave Joline.

Maybe her plan had backfired. She didn't want him to start thinking of Katie as part of their family.

Nothing had gone right today. Joline had only meant to let the pig snuffle Katie's hands for the apple. Then Joline would have herded it back into the pen. She tried to tell herself it wasn't her fault Katie panicked and ran.

And Joline hadn't made Katie slip and fall in the mud. Or had she?

With a sickish feeling, Joline admitted that Katie never would have been running in the first place if the pig had stayed in the pen. So, *jah*, all the blame sat squarely on Joline's shoulders.

She rushed into the house, gathered up dirty clothes, and loaded Mammi's wringer washer in Amos's basement. Abby bounded down the stairs with Katie's sopping wet dress, and Joline did the laundry. She ended up stuck down in the basement or hanging clothes on the line most of the time Katie was there. As Joline hung the final piece of clothing outside, Abby tagged after her.

"Esther and Katie aren't playing with me," Abby whined. "Esther's my twin, not Katie's."

"We should make sure Katie doesn't want to come back here again." Joline picked up the laundry basket to carry it into the house.

Abby trailed her. "How?"

"We'll have to think of something." Joline racked her brain as they walked down the hall to Abby and Esther's room.

With Joline to back her up, Abby stepped into the bedroom she shared with Esther. Katie sat next to Esther on the floor, playing with one of their adopted stray kittens. Katie cringed as her eyes flicked from Abby's irritated face to Joline standing behind her. Small for her age, Katie swam in the dress she'd borrowed from Esther, making her appear tiny, fragile, and helpless.

Esther's pleading *please-don't-hurt-my-friend* look sent a pang through Joline. She didn't want to destroy her sister's first friendship. But why couldn't Esther have chosen someone other than Sourpuss's daughter?

After glaring at Katie for a few minutes, Abby swooped down to grab the kitten. "That's my cat."

Her sudden movements startled the kitten. With a yowl, the tiny cat fought itself free, clawed her way up to Katie's shoulder, and scooted from the room.

Katie howled louder than the cat. The too-big dress hung off one shoulder, exposing bleeding scratches. Teardrops trickled down Katie's cheeks.

Esther's eyes welled with tears. "*Ach*, Katie. I'm so sorry. I'll be right back." She jumped to her feet, raced from the room, and returned with a clean, damp rag. Kneeling beside Katie, she wiped at the blood, smearing it.

Joline squatted beside Esther. "Here, let me. A soft patting motion would work better."

Katie squealed and backed away.

"Don't touch her." Esther had never used that steely tone before.

As Joline backed away, she tamped down her guilt. Once again, she hadn't meant for Katie to get hurt. She'd only wanted to frighten her away. Those scratches were Abby's fault.

Still, Joline couldn't escape the blame for that. She'd played a part in upsetting the two sniveling girls on the floor. She'd been wrong to go after Katie when all she really wanted was to prevent Sourpuss from being around Daed.

Speaking of that, Sourpuss would be here soon. Joline needed to put that part of her plan in action.

"Katie, I'm sorry you got hurt." Joline kept her words gentle, the way she did with her younger brothers and sisters. "Your *mamm* will be here soon. You might want to go outside to watch for her."

The wariness in Katie's expression faded into relief. "Will you go out with me?" she asked Esther.

Esther hopped up and extended a hand to help Katie to her feet.

"Maybe you should straighten your dress," Joline suggested.

Abby swallowed hard as Katie covered the scratches. "I didn't mean to hurt you. I just wanted my kitty."

Katie, who was trying to hide her shoulder, didn't answer. A quick bob of her head might have been an acknowledgment of Abby's apology.

As Katie headed for the door, the dress billowed around her, making her look like a frail doll dressed in oversized clothing. Joline's remorse increased. She shouldn't have been so mean. From now on, she'd concentrate only on separating Daed and Sourpuss.

When Esther reached the door, she whirled around. "I don't want you to follow us," she said to Abby and Joline.

"I know." Joline hoped her contrite expression might soften Esther's fierce, protective expression. "Abby and I are both sorry. Why don't we all play four square on the driveway? I'll get the chalk."

Esther cocked her head to one side and studied Joline. "I don't want you to hurt Katie."

"I promise I won't." And this time she meant it. Joline intended to be nice to make up for what she'd done.

"You'd better not." Esther put an arm around Katie's shoulders and shepherded her toward the staircase. "If you aren't nice, I'll tell Daed."

Joline hurried to get the chalk. She wanted to have the four-square blocks laid out before Sourpuss arrived.

Abby stared after Esther and Katie as they descended the steps, Esther's arm still around Katie's shoulders.

"Don't worry." Joline hugged Abby. "Katie will be going home soon, and Esther is still your twin. She loves you and will want to play with you."

"You think so? Maybe she'll be mad at me for hurting Katie."

"She'll forgive you. And let's be nice to Katie until she goes home." Joline hoped that would help. It might make Joline feel less guilty.

Earlier, she'd sketched four large squares at the end of the driveway closest to the street. The game would block Katie's *mamm* from driving up to the garage and barn. That way, Daed wouldn't hear the buggy come in. If he stayed in the barn until Nettie drove away, everything would be perfect.

By the time Katie's second turn to serve arrived, she'd relaxed enough to give a fleeting smile. Joline released a long, slow sigh.

A buggy started to turn into the driveway, but the driver spotted them playing and drew alongside the front lawn instead.

"Mamm," Katie screamed, and dropped the ball. She dashed into her mother's arms.

Sourpuss wrapped her arms around her daughter. A lump rose in Joline's throat. She'd been younger than Katie when Mamm died. Daed hugged her, but Joline missed the softness and sweetness of Mamm's hugs.

Joline's eyes watered. She brushed away the moisture with the back of her hand.

Placing one hand on Katie's shoulder, Sourpuss— whose usual grumpy look had transformed into a loving smile—held her daughter away from her and studied her outfit. "What's this you're wearing?"

"Esther's dress. Mine got all muddy when I fell because a pig chased me and—" Katie spoke so quickly her words all ran into each other.

Joline prayed Katie's *mamm* wouldn't question everything that happened. She stepped up. Although it pained her to talk to the woman, Joline would do whatever she could to keep Sourpuss and Daed from meeting. "I washed Katie's dress and hung it out to dry. I'll go get it."

"No need. I want to thank your *daed* for having Katie." Sourpuss handed the reins to Katie. "Hold on to these. I'll be right back." Then she marched up the driveway.

Other than tackling her, Joline had no way to stop Sourpuss. She'd failed at the most important part of her plan.

Stephen emerged from the house in fresh clothes. He and Amos had finished pressure washing the barn, and they were both glad to get out of their sweaty clothes. And Stephen's dirty clothes still had mud stains despite hosing himself down.

He'd washed up first because Nettie would be arriving soon. He'd rather not be a stinking mess when he met her—especially because he owed her an apology. Poor Katie!

Maybe he should have supervised the children more closely. Normally, he could count on Joline, but lately, he'd begun to wonder.

He shook his head. Joline couldn't be expected to catch everything her siblings and Katie did. He'd piled a lot of responsibility on her young shoulders. Mrs. Vandenberg might be right. Joline needed a *mamm*.

The screen door slammed behind him, and Amos caught up to him.

"Are you heading to Betty's tonight?" Stephen asked.

His brother's lips curved into a contented smile. "*Jah.* Is Joline all right with fixing supper?"

Stephen nodded. Joline never complained about doing that. In fact, she seemed to prefer it when Betty didn't come over here to cook. Which reminded him, he needed to get started on house hunting.

He turned to Amos. "I should try to find a place to buy near here. Any suggestions?"

"No farms on the market that I know of. Wish I could let you have this house. Betty and her family want us to live closer to them after we marry." Amos sighed. "If only I could do that and also afford to start a stand in the downtown market."

"I can pay you for this house if you want to buy one near Betty's parents. What does the stand cost?" Stephen could help with the extra.

"A little more than Green Valley. Even with the discount Russell gave me, I can't manage both payments."

"Discount? What do you mean?"

"Well, when I went to pay my rent this month, Russell

told me that starting next month, he was cutting the bill by fifty dollars."

"What?" Stephen's question shot out of his mouth so loud and sharp, Amos jumped back.

"Sorry." Then lowering his volume, Stephen enunciated each word. "You paid Russell this month?"

"Of course, I always give him the rent check on the first."

His temperature rising, Stephen asked, "And Russell accepted it?"

"Snatched it out of my hand the way he normally does."

Stephen had gone to Russell first. Amos had been upset that he'd had to wait to pay Russell. So that meant Russell already had Stephen's payment when Amos caught up with the market manager. That scoundrel!

"I can't believe he did that. He took my money and yours. When you came back after talking to Russell, you were grinning. I assumed it was because you'd found out I paid."

Amos frowned. "So, you're the reason he lowered the monthly payment?"

Lowered the payment? Stephen clenched his fists and his teeth. He yanked off his rubber gloves. "Wait here a minute. I'll be right back."

He rushed into the house and dashed upstairs. In the bedroom, he slid open a desk drawer and pulled out the receipt. *Thank heavens, I asked for this paper. If I hadn't, I'd have no proof, and Russell would keep collecting rent from both of us.*

When Stephen returned to the yard, he handed the paper to his brother.

Amos stared at it, his bushy brows meeting in the center of his forehead. "What is this?"

Fuming at Russell's deception, Stephen gestured to the receipt. "That's how much I paid Russell for a year's stand rent."

"You did what?" Amos's voice rose. "I'm not some charity case. I can afford to pay my own bills."

"I know that." Stephen stared down at the ground in front of him. "I wanted to pay my fair share. I have five kids, so that makes six of us and one of you. I should pay a lot more."

"As for kids, I'll soon catch up to you," Amos boasted.

Stephen gave his brother a playful punch. "Don't put the cart before the horse."

"What? I can't believe you said that." Amos's furious words echoed through the yard. "I'd never have children before I get married. Betty and I would never do anything that sinful."

Over his brother's shoulder, Stephen glimpsed Nettie rounding the corner. She stopped dead. Shock flickered in her eyes. Then her face crumpled. Her shoulders hunched, and she lowered her gaze.

The same shame and embarrassment sent waves of heat sweeping up Stephen's neck. His face probably matched the brick wall behind him. "I'm sorry." He wasn't sure who he meant it for. His brother or Nettie. Or maybe both.

"You should be." Amos stalked off.

Stephen couldn't believe he'd fought with his brother in front of Nettie. Even worse the subject of their conversation wasn't something to talk about in front of women, particularly a woman he barely knew.

Without looking at him, Nettie said stiffly, "Thank you for having Katie."

Stephen nodded, but Nettie had already turned and fled. He didn't go after her. What did you say after a humiliating experience like that? He hoped she'd forget it by the next time he saw her.

Chapter Fourteen

Nettie sat in the buggy, shaking. Hot flashes of pain flooding over her. Had Amos said that on purpose where she could hear? And what about Stephen's comment? *Don't put the cart before the horse*. That cut deep into her soul. And his brother's voice had carried loud and clear, condemning those who disobeyed God's Word.

She'd thought she'd put everything behind her, but Stephen's words had ripped open old scars. She couldn't face him. Not now. Not ever.

Katie slid open the passenger door and hopped in after a brief wave to one of the twins who stood watching with sad eyes.

Nettie pushed aside her own upset to focus on her daughter. "Katie? Is something wrong?"

Her daughter hung her head and bit her lip. "I don't like pig farms."

The vehemence of her daughter's exclamation startled Nettie. She didn't like pig farms either. At least not this one. She turned the buggy around and flicked the reins to hurry the horse. She couldn't wait to get out of here.

"Wait!" Joline screamed. She dashed after the buggy, wet cloth flapping in her arms.

Katie's dress. Nettie pulled the horse to a stop.

After a quick glance at Nettie, Joline rounded the buggy to Katie's side. Instead of opening the door, Katie scooted closer to Nettie's side. Her daughter had called Esther's sisters mean.

"She can't bully you now," Nettie assured her daughter.

Katie lifted surprised eyes to Nettie's face. "How did you know?" she whispered.

"You told me earlier, remember? Just open the door and get your dress, so we can leave."

Panting, Joline held out the damp fabric. "I'm sorry." Her eyes flitted from Katie to Nettie.

An up-and-down tilt of her chin was Katie's only acknowledgment. She grasped the dress, her fingers far from Joline's, and tugged it to her. After a sharp look from Nettie, Katie mumbled a *danke*.

When Katie slid the door shut, Nettie's relief matched her daughter's. She eased her horse back onto the road and encouraged him into a trot. Like Katie, Nettie couldn't wait to get away from this place.

Not only were the Lapp girls mean, but she also couldn't face their father. If she didn't have the STAR center project, Nettie would avoid him completely.

Picking up Katie had made them late for supper. Gideon's *mamm* had heated tomato soup and made grilled cheese sandwiches. Nettie wished she'd been here earlier. She tried to cook all the meals she could to make up for her in-laws housing her and the children.

"Sorry I wasn't here." Nettie headed to the sink to

wash up. "Why don't you sit at the table, and I'll finish getting everything ready?"

She guided her mother-in-law to the table, where everyone but Gideon waited. No one had set a place for him, so he must be out with Fern tonight. Nettie schooled her face to hide her disappointment.

Another night she'd have to put all four children to bed by herself. And another night she'd spend worrying about Gideon falling for Fern. And another night sharp pangs would shoot through Nettie's stomach as she worried about her children's future.

After the boys and Sadie had their baths, Nettie sent Katie in for hers.

Katie wrapped her arms protectively around herself, wrinkling the excess material of Esther's dress into tight folds across her belly. "I don't need a bath. I got hosed down at Esther's house."

"A rinse under a hose doesn't count. Get into the tub."

Her back rigid, Katie didn't move. "I will when nobody's in here."

With a sigh, Nettie trudged down the hall. Katie seemed much too young to already need privacy. She tucked Sadie into bed and kissed her.

Sadie wriggled to a sitting position. "I'm thirsty."

"Only a little sip at bedtime." At three, Sadie sometimes wet the bed at night. Nettie picked up the cup from the bedside table and headed into the bathroom.

"Mamm!" Katie shrieked when Nettie opened the door.

"I just need a little water for—" Nettie stopped. "Katie, what's on your shoulder?"

"*Neh*, don't look." She turned her back.

Nettie ignored Katie's plea and rushed over. "Turn

around and let me see." When her daughter didn't obey, Nettie crossed her arms and tapped her foot. Her daughter understood the signal: *Do it now or else.*

Slowly, Katie turned around. Scratch marks covered her shoulder. A big red bruise colored her skin on the opposite hip.

"What happened?" Nettie pointed to the scratches. "These look fresh. What did they come from?" She examined the bruise more closely.

Katie whimpered.

"*Liebchen,*" Nettie said as softly and gently as she could, "it's all right. You aren't in trouble."

"*Jah,* I am."

Her daughter's strangled words tore at Nettie's old wounds. "*Neh,* you are not. I won't let anyone hurt you again."

Katie shook her head. "You . . . can't . . . stop . . . them."

But Katie was wrong. Nettie would do whatever it took to end the bullying.

It took time to wring the full story from Katie. Gideon had returned and put the boys to bed before Nettie established that not only had Joline let out a pig that had chased Katie, but Katie also had fallen in a mud puddle and slammed her hip on a rock. Later, the Lapps' cat had gouged Katie's shoulder.

Teary-eyed, Katie recounted earlier bullying. Joline had said mean things in school.

"You should have told me."

"*Neh.*" Katie pressed her lips together for a moment as if deciding whether or not to confess the rest. "I think the pig chasing me was because Esther told Teacher Emily."

"Your teacher knew?"

"*Jah*, she made Joline stay inside for recess."

Had the teacher informed Stephen? She certainly should have. But if he knew, why had he let it happen again at his farm?

Nettie had vowed to always keep her children safe and secure, something her own *mamm* had never done. Nettie couldn't believe this had happened without her having any clue.

"The next time I see Stephen, I'm going to talk to him."

"Don't, Mamm. Stephen's really nice. He saved me from the pig, and he held me close even when I messed up his shirt with mud."

Nettie swallowed hard at the picture that painted in her mind—Stephen cuddling her daughter. Worse yet, her pulse fluttered as she recalled the warmth of his hand over hers and imagined being cradled against his broad chest, hearing the firm thump of his heartbeats.

She slammed a steel door down in her mind to block her wayward thoughts. She needed to concentrate on protecting Katie. "I can't let those girls keep bullying you. Maybe I should also speak to Joline."

Her daughter sucked in a sharp breath. "*Neh*." Tears brimmed in her eyes. "She'll do something worse."

"I promise I'll keep you safe." Nettie would do whatever it took to defend her child. And her first step would be to confront Stephen.

* * *

The children had off school on Friday because of conferences, and Joline had begged to spend the long weekend with their cousins in Big Valley. At first, Stephen demurred. Amos could use the help, especially on Friday when Stephen went to the conference.

Amos only laughed. "I handled everything alone before you arrived. People will just have to wait."

"But you said you were losing customers who went to a less busy stand."

"That may be. But you won't be gone long. Let the kids have some fun."

Stephen had relented, and on Thursday evening, he hired a car to take all five of his children to Big Valley.

The house seemed hollow and empty when he returned. Amos had gone to bed. Stephen tried to tell himself the kids would only be gone until Sunday evening. But he missed them terribly. They hadn't been separated since his wife died.

With loneliness pressing down on him, Stephen trudged upstairs. Mrs. Vandenberg's statement about Joline needing a *mamm* came back to him. He'd thought about that again a few days ago. For some reason, Mrs. Vandenberg's pick for a wife floated through his mind. And all that night, Nettie Hartzler drifted through his dreams.

She remained on his mind when he woke the next morning. Despite reminding himself multiple times that Nettie had feelings for Gideon and also that she'd fled after hearing the conversation with Amos, he couldn't get her out of his head. Thoughts of her stayed with him as he left the market for the parent-teacher conference.

He arrived early, hoping to get back in time to help

Amos with the suppertime rush. Two other buggies were parked in the lot. One was empty, but Nettie sat with Gideon in the other.

Stephen mentally shook himself. So much for his day-dreams.

Katie hopped out of the back of their buggy and started across the playground.

"Hi, Katie," Stephen called as he got out to tie his horse to a hitching post.

She whirled around and stared at him. With a half-hearted wave, she craned her head to see into the buggy.

"The girls aren't with me. I'm sorry. They went to visit their *aenti*."

As soon as he said that, Katie smiled, gave him a much friendlier wave, and skipped off toward the swings.

Nearby, a buggy door rattled open. Nettie sailed toward him like a ship on a collision course. Judging by her expression, the ship was about to explode.

Without any greeting or even an attempt at a smile, she said flatly, "We need to talk." From the look on her face, something had distressed her.

Stephen hoped nothing had gone wrong with Mrs. Vandenberg's plans. He finished securing his horse. "Sure. What is it?"

Gideon stared over at Nettie, his face surprised and curious. Evidently, he had no idea what was going on. He studied Nettie with concern. Stephen tried to judge if his worry meant he cared about Nettie as a special friend and future wife or if it was the same concern Stephen felt for his sisters and sisters-in-law.

Before he could decide, Nettie's face darkened. "I

trusted you to keep an eye on my daughter when she visited your farm."

Stephen held up a hand to defend himself. Maybe he shouldn't have invited her when he was power washing the barn. But Katie had seemed fine whenever he first checked on the girls. A little wary, always hanging back, but Esther often did that too.

"I'm so sorry. I don't know how that pig escaped."

"I do."

He stared at her. "You do?" He hadn't mentioned that Katie had accidentally released it. In fact, he hadn't mentioned it at all because he didn't want to embarrass her. But Katie must have confessed to her *mamm.*

"I certainly do." She took a deep breath. "Your daughter did it. She's been bullying Katie."

Stephen knew in his heart Esther would never hurt anyone. Nettie was mistaken. Maybe Katie had lied to cover up what she'd done. He had to defend Esther. "I've never known Esther to do anything unkind."

"Esther?" Nettie stepped back. "Not Esther. She's been a good friend to Katie. Esther's a lovely little girl."

Stephen agreed, but he couldn't praise his daughter. Still, Nettie's response left him confused. If Esther hadn't let the pig out, it must have been—

"The pig isn't the only thing that upsets me. Katie didn't even want to show me the scratches on her shoulder."

"Scratches?" How did that happen? He'd never known his girls to be that cruel. Could Katie have gotten them somewhere else and blamed his daughters?

"The scratches came from a cat, but the girls provoked the kitten."

Accusing his daughters of goading a cat convinced Stephen that Katie had made up a story. She didn't seem to be the type to tease a cat, but maybe she'd upset one of the kittens by accident. None of his children ever mistreated an animal. They all loved strays as much as he did.

Nettie hadn't finished. "Joline also bothered Katie at school." Nettie sounded close to tears.

Stephen struggled to picture Joline doing that. He'd never known her to hurt anyone. All the parents in Mayville asked her to watch their children. She loved the little ones, and they loved her. And she took care of her brothers and sisters like a little mother. All four of them adored her.

"Katie wouldn't even come with me to the market today."

"I'm sorry Joline isn't around so we can get to the bottom of this. I'll talk to her and her sisters as soon as they get home."

Teacher Emily opened the door to the *schulhaus* and ushered out a young couple.

His face burning, Stephen stepped back. He hoped people didn't misunderstand the intensity of his conversation with Nettie.

"Our conference is next." Her bright pink cheeks revealed her embarrassment.

Gideon climbed from the buggy and joined her. Stephen paced the parking lot while they were inside talking to the teacher. Katie swung listlessly. Stephen was tempted to talk to her, but he should discuss this with his children rather than questioning Nettie's daughter.

He hadn't come up with a satisfactory solution before Teacher Emily opened the *schulhaus* door. His heart heavy, Stephen headed toward her, but he kept an eye on Nettie as she called Katie and got into the buggy with Gideon.

Stephen tried to push aside his worries about the girls as he went into the building. Teacher Emily gestured for him to sit on the opposite side of a table that held a stack of folders. Once they'd both settled into their seats, she slid the top five folders from the pile and spread them out in front of her.

"I know moving to a different area and attending a new school can be hard on children." Teacher Emily gave him an understanding smile. "Although I try to teach my scholars to be friendly to newcomers, they've grown up together, so they tend to stick with certain favorite friends."

Stephen nodded.

"Because it's only two weeks until the end of the school year, the children have routines, preferences, baseball team rotations . . ." She lifted both hands in a *what-can-you-do?* shrug.

Why hadn't he waited until the school year ended to uproot his children? They would have had the summer to make friends at church. Then they'd have fit in better. But the buyer of his New York farm had wanted to move in right away.

"Your sons are pretty evenly matched, so they'll balance out the baseball teams as long as I rotate them onto different teams." She smiled. "I think, though, everyone will want Matthew playing on their team."

Stephen's eyebrows drew together. "What about Joline?"

His daughter was even more skilled at baseball than Matthew.

Teacher Emily's lipped thinned. "I'll get to that in a minute. The boys are doing fine in their lessons."

But Stephen didn't want to wait. Maybe Lancaster had different rules than Mayville. "Girls can play on the baseball teams?"

Teacher Emily stared at him. "Of course."

Then why hadn't Joline been put on one of the teams?

Teacher Emily nattered on as if nervous. So far, she hadn't mentioned any of his daughters.

Teacher Emily rustled a manila folder, drawing Stephen's attention back to the conference.

She opened it and ran a finger down a list pinned to the left side. "Matthew's work is always excellent, and he finishes every subject well before the rest of the scholars." She handed him a small stack of papers. "Here are some samples of his best work."

She moved on to the next folders, flipping through them rather rapidly, and sliding papers across the table as she spoke. "Ben is quiet, but well-liked by everyone. I can count on him to listen and work hard. And the twins are doing fine with their schoolwork. I'm a little concerned that they don't seem to be making friends."

"Well, Esther has always been a bit shy, but Abby—"

"*Jah*, as I explained, I'm not sure Abby following Joline's lead is such a good idea."

When had the teacher said that? He must have missed it.

"I hope you've had a chance to talk to her about it."

"Not yet." They hadn't even finished the conference.

Teacher Emily frowned. "I realize we only have a few

days of school left, but I hope you'll encourage Abby to make friends with scholars who pay attention to their schoolwork."

Did the teacher mean Joline didn't? Stephen hoped his daughter's recent behavior hadn't carried over to school.

"So . . ." Teacher Emily drew in a breath. "Now we come to the girls. Let's start with Esther. She's timid and rarely answers questions. The work she turns in is neat and shows she understands what's she's learning. Abby, on the other hand—"

Stephen hid a smile. Abby's teacher in Mayville had labeled her distractable. But when Abby wanted something, not even a tornado could stand in her way.

"If she took her time, I'm sure her handwriting could be neat."

He didn't agree. First of all, getting Abby to slow down proved harder than dragging a stubborn mule to plow. Neither would cooperate. But Abby had always been sloppy and messy and impatient.

"She does fine with her oral lessons, but sometimes I can't read her written work."

"I'll talk to her about that."

"*Danke*, I'd appreciate it. We don't have much time left, but maybe she could practice over the summer."

Somehow, Stephen had trouble imagining that. But he'd try to encourage her.

"And I guess that leads us straight to Joline." Teacher Emily heaved a huge sigh. "First of all, I have some concerns about her schoolwork. The first week, she read perfectly and finished her work before the other scholars. She's a bright girl."

Stephen relaxed. He'd heard the same praise at every school conference in Mayville. "*Jah*, Joline likes to learn. She brings books home every night."

"She does?" Teacher Emily leaned forward. "I've never given any homework."

That surprised Stephen. "I thought teaching must be different here in Lancaster. The Mayville school never assigned homework." Amish schools usually didn't, but he didn't want to insult the teacher.

"I don't ever give homework either. Except to memorize parts for school plays or—"

Stephen tuned out. Why would Joline fake having to do schoolwork? She had been behaving differently, but pretending to have homework when she didn't seemed odd.

He furrowed his brow. Joline and Matthew had spent every evening with schoolbooks spread in front of them at the kitchen table while he got the younger ones ready for bed. Stephen hadn't paid much attention to what the older two were doing. Sometimes he'd hear the drone of their voices, especially his son's.

"I don't understand. Joline has always done well in school. Maybe she and Matthew were behind your other scholars? Perhaps they were trying to catch up?"

"That might be so. Although something happened last week that might explain the extra work. As I mentioned, since she arrived, Joline always read perfectly and did all her schoolwork."

Stephen relaxed back. He knew what was coming next—a repeat of every parent-teacher conference he'd ever had for Joline. *She's a wonderful student. Always hands in her work early. Rarely makes a mistake.*

Teacher Emily continued, "Last week, Joline seemed a bit distracted so I asked her to stand up and read a page aloud. She stumbled over the words and made several mistakes. She stopped reading mid-sentence, sat down, and refused to finish, claiming she had a headache."

Joline had disobeyed the teacher? He'd assumed her attitude had extended only to him, although she had been rude to Nettie and Mrs. Vandenberg. And based on what Nettie had told him, she'd also been mean to Katie. What was happening to his daughter?

That upset Stephen so much he hadn't paid attention to the teacher. He tuned back in to the end of her sentence.

". . . made me wonder if Joline has dyslexia."

"What?" Teacher Emily had blindsided him. *Dyslexia?* That caused children to have trouble reading because letters or words appear mixed up or backward. Stephen struggled to make sense of this. If Teacher Emily was right, how had Joline reached sixth grade without anyone ever being aware of it?

"I wish I'd known this when she first started. I should have figured it out when Joline wrote her sentences. I thought she was being defiant by switching some of the words and letters." Teacher Emily lowered her eyes. "I'm afraid I scolded her for carelessness."

Wouldn't he have known if his daughter had a reading problem? Now that he thought about it, whenever Joline needed to read anything, Matthew jumped in. Sometimes, he snatched it from her and teased her as he read. Other times, he pretended he wanted to read it first. Had he been covering for his sister?

Teacher Emily studied Stephen. "It seems as if this surprises you. Her teacher in Mayville never mentioned it?"

"*Neh*."

"Perhaps she had ways to help Joline?"

But why wouldn't Teacher Diane have said anything to him about it?

"It might be a good idea to get Joline tested."

One more concern to add to his growing list, but Teacher Emily hadn't finished. "That brings me to Joline's misbehavior."

Ach, Joline had been acting up at school as well as home? If only this conference would end. Stephen didn't want to hear any more. He'd been slammed with negatives about Joline since he arrived on the school grounds.

Teacher Emily fiddled with the edges of a new folder and appeared reluctant to speak.

"Has Joline gotten into trouble at school?"

The teacher lifted her head, her eyebrows raised. "You didn't get my note?"

"Note?" He'd made it to the conference at the right time, hadn't he? That was the only note he'd gotten.

"I sent a letter home with Joline last Friday."

"A letter?" Joline hadn't given him any letter. "I'm sorry. I didn't get it."

Lips pursed, Teacher Emily stayed silent for several seconds. "I see."

Stephen's spirits sank lower and lower as she detailed all the times Joline stayed in for recess.

As the teacher went on, Stephen set his elbows on the table and rubbed his forehead. What next? He couldn't believe all this. First Nettie, now Teacher Emily. Had Joline been acting up everywhere?

Until they'd moved here, he'd heard only praise of his daughter. These descriptions of what she'd done sounded as if they were done by a totally different person. And why hadn't he noticed how much she'd changed since they'd moved? *Jah*, he'd been concerned about her attitude, but how had he missed all this?

Chapter Fifteen

"*Ach!*" Amos stopped waiting on a customer to stare at Stephen. "I thought you went to a school conference. Did your horse go lame on the way back?"

Stephen waved toward the long line of customers. "Tell you later." *After he'd had some time to process it himself.*

He bared his teeth in what he hoped passed for a smile and filled orders by rote. But his mind whirled. What had happened to his helpful, dependable daughter?

He needed to talk to her right away, but she was two hours away. She'd been the one who'd begged to go to Big Valley. Had she planned that on purpose, knowing the report her teacher planned to give him and that he'd find out about the letter she'd never delivered?

As Amos passed, he clapped Stephen on the back. "If you need to take some time off, go ahead. We've slowed down a bit."

Stephen shook his head, then thought better of it. "Maybe fifteen or twenty minutes?"

"Sure. Go ahead. I hope when you get back, you'll tell me what's bothering you."

"I will." Stephen slipped from behind the counter and headed for the pay phone.

He pulled a slip of paper from his wallet and fished around in his pocket for change. The phone rang several times with no answer. Finally, Cornelius picked up.

"Stephen Lapp here. Any chance you could pick my children up early?"

"I'm doing an out-of-town overnight. I could leave at noon tomorrow."

He'd been hoping to get them right away. He could call another driver, but he'd already prepaid Cornelius for both ways. Getting Joline back here around four or five tomorrow would have to do. "*Danke*. I'd appreciate it if you could drop them at the market."

"Will do."

Cornelius's cheerful goodbye lifted Stephen's mood. Too bad his next errand would plunge him down again.

Stephen trudged toward Hartzler's Chicken Barbecue. The smell of roasting chicken tantalized him. Maybe he could pick up dinner for himself and Amos. Stephen had already gotten in line when he realized Nettie wasn't working. So much for his plan to apologize to her.

He'd hoped to get that over with. After what Teacher Emily had told him, Stephen owed her and Katie both an apology for his daughter's behavior and for doubting their accounts of Joline's actions.

He'd have to save that admission for tomorrow. It might be too much to ask, but perhaps Nettie could suggest some ways for dealing with preteen girls. He had no experience with that.

He returned to the stand and handed the chicken and fries to Amos. "Why don't you take a break? You probably didn't get any lunch."

"You're right." Amos patted his stomach. "It's been growling most of the afternoon. *Danke*."

"Save some for me."

"Of course. And I want to hear about the conference and whatever caused you to look so glum."

Unfortunately, they were the same thing. But Amos would find out soon enough.

Because the market stayed open until seven on Fridays, Stephen had no time to talk until they began cleaning up. Then he spilled the whole story to Amos.

"Joline?" Amos stared at him, incredulous. "You sure you heard right? Maybe the teacher mistook her for someone else."

"That's what I thought at first, except Nettie told me similar stories." Stephen recounted those. "So, Joline's been bullying the poor little girl."

Amos stroked his chin. "Something doesn't sound right to me. Joline's always been the opposite of what both these women described."

"I know." A dark cloud descended over Stephen. "I blame myself for some of it. I've been so busy getting settled here and helping Mrs. Vandenberg, I've neglected Joline."

"That doesn't explain the way she's acting."

"Do you think she misbehaved on purpose? If she had to stay inside at recess, she wouldn't be lonely and left out on the playground." Joline was smart enough to think of that.

"Could be," Amos agreed.

"But that doesn't explain her meanness to Katie."

"Guess you'll know more when they get back tomorrow."

"*Jah.*" But Stephen wasn't looking forward to cross-examining his daughter. And although he told himself he kept thinking of Nettie because of Katie's problems, he had to admit she kept popping into his mind for other reasons too.

Nettie woke early on Saturday morning, so she lay in bed, enjoying the misty land between dreams and reality. She'd prefer to stay in this half-waking state where she relived Stephen holding her hands. The warmth of his touch flooded through her.

Sadie pattered into the bedroom and shook her. "*Mamm?*"

With a sigh, Nettie rolled over and released the last traces of the fantasy world. But the memories tantalized her as she helped the children get ready for the day. Her mother-in-law planned to take them to an auction later that morning.

"Have fun," she said, wishing she could go with them rather than to work. "I'll miss you."

Her days always went better when the children came to the market. Life seemed a little less lonely. And it didn't give her as much time to concentrate on every interaction between Gideon and Fern.

By the time Nettie reached the buggy, Caroline had

climbed into the back seat. That meant Nettie sat beside Gideon on the drive to market.

For some reason, Nettie kept comparing images of Stephen to Gideon, and Stephen—at least the dream version of him—seemed more appealing. The matchup revealed her brotherly feelings for Gideon didn't hold a candle to the attraction that flared when she thought about Stephen.

Nettie tried telling herself a real person could never measure up to a daydream. That evaluation was unfair. Besides, what did she know of Stephen, other than the few times she'd spent with him?

She had to admit, though, the two times he touched her hands, she'd shivered. Gideon had often laid his hand over hers to comfort her in her grief, and she'd never experienced that same spark.

And when she rode to work with Gideon, she didn't end up breathless, the way she had with Stephen. If that tingly feeling Nettie had around Stephen matched what Gideon felt around Fern, she could understand its lure.

Nettie hadn't felt that thrill with Thomas either. She'd grabbed on to the first Amish young man who seemed to offer security. She'd behaved foolishly because she wanted to marry someone who'd help her leave her past behind.

Thomas had been planning to take over his *daed*'s barbecue stand. To her, he appeared rich and stable—the main attributes she'd looked for in a husband. That, and faithfulness. He'd given her that too. But he'd never given her one other thing she'd craved—love.

A tear trickled down her cheek. Fern and Gideon shared

that bond. A bond Nettie had never had. She hated to interfere with their special relationship, but she wanted her children to have a secure home. If Fern moved in, Nettie and her children would need to leave.

And as Nettie had discovered, the business she'd once believed held the key to unlimited riches struggled to balance income with expenses. Gideon couldn't afford to keep supporting her and the children if he married. She could handle poverty, but she never, ever wanted her children to endure it.

"Are you all right, Nettie?" Caroline asked.

"Of course." Nettie dashed the tear from her cheek and pasted on a smile. Her usual half-happy, half-sad smile. The smile that represented her world.

During the rest of the morning, she focused on Fern and Gideon, checking their connection. Each time they looked at each other, sparks flew between them, kindling flames. Those flames flared so hot, the blaze they ignited consumed Nettie's future, turning it to ash.

"Can you help Fern?" Gideon asked Nettie that afternoon as she slid coleslaw and potato salad onto a tray piled with chicken pieces and fries.

Nettie bit back a sigh. Her awkwardness, her somberness, and her pasted-on smile always contrasted poorly with Fern's loveliness, her kindness, her gorgeous smile. But Nettie plodded to the other end of the stand.

The only thing that brightened Nettie's day was Aidan. He loved to tease her, and after a few minutes, her face relaxed into a genuine smile. Who would think a teen with a nose ring and tattoos could charm an Amish woman into forgetting her troubles?

In many ways, Nettie felt more comfortable around Aidan than she did anyone in the Amish community. She hadn't grown up around the people in her church like everyone else. Aidan reminded her of her past, and she'd learned to tell people with good hearts despite their exterior appearances. He fit that category.

Nettie wasn't so sure about the group of rough-looking teens who clomped up to the candy counter, chains clanking. Most of the customers at the bakery and the candy counter swerved away.

A tall, skinny guy with a scruffy beard and a snake tattoo curling up his neck and onto his face smacked a hand on the counter. "Hey, dude. Where you been?"

Aidan lifted his chin. "Working. I took over my old man's candy shop."

"Here? Thought he was at the other end of the building." Scruffy Beard jerked a thumb over his shoulder.

After Aidan explained that someone put his dad out of business, his friends protested.

"You oughta make them pay," Scruffy Beard exploded. With his hot-headed temper, he volunteered to help do that.

Aidan rejected his offer, but Scruffy Beard was determined to put a scare into whoever had taken over the stand.

By then, Nettie had evaluated most of the guys. Some were definitely trouble. She'd guess Scruffy Beard had seen the inside of juvie hall at least once. So had two of his friends.

While Aidan argued with Scruffy Beard, Nettie sized up one of the younger hangers-on. He was trying too hard to act tough, but she could read the fear in his eyes. He'd end up hurt.

She still had Mrs. Vandenberg's card for the center. She slipped around the counter. Palming the card, she tucked it into his hand. He turned startled eyes in her direction.

"What's this?" he barked.

"It's opening tonight," she whispered in a low, urgent voice. "It'll save you from getting killed."

His face puckered in confusion. "You don't know nuttin'."

"You think not? Meet me at that building tonight, and I'll best you in a knife fight."

He looked her up and down, then threw back his head and roared with laughter. "You?"

But when her dead-serious eyes bored into his, the sniggers ended.

"Wow, mama, you tough. Okay, it's a date."

The dude standing beside him stared. "You and her?" He snickered.

Nettie gave him the same piercing stare. He blinked first.

"Don't mess with him or me," she warned. "Unless you're sure you can win a knife fight."

"With you?" He sneered. "One hand behind my back."

"You'll need both of them to handle me."

"Whoa. I'll be the one doing the handling."

"Prove it." Nettie pointed to the card. "I'll be there tonight. And I'll take you both on. Separately or together."

He waggled his eyebrows. "Sounds like fun."

Scruffy Beard and the others tromped toward the front of the market. The two teens Nettie had been sparring with traipsed after them.

"Don't," Aidan called after them. "I mean it."

"Fern?" Desperation in his voice, Aidan asked, "Could you watch my stand? I gotta stop them. When they get going—" He tore off the candy-striped apron and sprinted down the aisle.

As Aidan disappeared, Gideon rushed over. "What's going on? Where did Aidan go?"

"Aidan went chasing after his friends." Fern looked frightened.

Gideon dashed from the stand, and Fern followed. Most shoppers streamed toward the shouting and chanting, but Nettie remained rooted to the spot. She'd learned the hard way not to get involved in fights.

Instead, she prayed nobody would get hurt. In case the riot spread to the stand, she started closing down for the night. They wouldn't have any more customers. Everyone had either fled out the door or rushed to gawk.

As she moved the salads to the main refrigerator, she smiled to herself. If those two younger teens didn't get arrested now, she'd talked them into coming to the STAR center. Perhaps she'd just saved two kids from a life of crime.

Lord, please keep them safe and bring them to STAR tonight.

Nettie also hoped her knife skills hadn't gotten too rusty.

A gang of bikers, their faces furious, tramped past Stephen's stand. Customers plastered themselves against the display cases to get out of the way.

"Whew." Amos pretended to wipe sweat from his

forehead after they'd gone. "Wouldn't want to be the one they're after."

"Me either," a woman squeaked. "Can you give me that pork roast fast? I'm getting out of here."

As screaming and chanting came from the front of the market, the other customers headed for the nearest exit.

A loud voice drowned out the others. "You had no right to take this dude's stand."

Eyes wide, Amos glanced at Stephen. "What's that?"

"I don't know, but it doesn't sound good."

People scurried past their stand, either heading toward the commotion or running the opposite way.

"Maybe we should close down." Stephen opened a meat case and started transporting food to their refrigerator.

Amos headed for the cash box. "Might be best to skip cleanup. Let's just get the money and store the meats."

Stephen agreed. He'd been upset not to have the kids back today, but now it seemed like a blessing.

Russell came stomping down the stairs, screaming. "What's going on?" He charged to the front of the market. A few minutes later, he outshouted all the other noises. "YOU HOOLIGANS! GET OUT OF HERE NOW! OR I'M CALLING THE POLICE."

"Call away, old man," a teenager yelled. "You the owner of this joint?"

"Yeah, he is," someone responded.

A jumble of unintelligible voices and high-pitched screams rose and fell as Stephen and Amos hustled to empty the cases.

A few words stood out among the cacophony. *Jail. He don't scare me. Cops. Put that away.*

Stephen prayed that last phrase didn't refer to a gun. He tossed sheets over the empty cases. "Ready when you are."

"SEND THE POLICE," Russell shrieked. "There's a riot here. Green Valley Market."

He must be calling nine-one-one. Stephen squeezed out the low, narrow exit door after Amos. They were getting out just in time. Stephen turned to slide the bolt into place.

"I don't think that'll be much help." Amos motioned for Stephen to hurry.

He shrugged. "Might slow them down a little." Probably not much. It'd be easy to boost someone over the low, swinging door.

Together, they sprinted for the nearest exit. As he passed Hartzler's, Stephen slowed. The top edge of a prayer *kapp* peeked over the center worktable.

Amos nudged him. "Get a move on."

But Stephen screeched to a halt. "You go ahead. It looks like someone's hiding in that stand. I'll just check on them."

His brother stopped too. "I'll stay with you."

"*Neh*, go on. You've got the money. Get out safely." The last thing they needed was for Amos to get jumped for the cash he carried. "Watch out when you cross the parking lot."

Stephen pushed on Hartzler's swinging half door. They hadn't locked it. He hurried through the stand to where he'd seen the *kapp*.

"Caroline? Fern? Nettie?" he called. It had to be one of them.

Two eyes peered over the worktable. *Nettie*.

"I'll help you." Stephen rushed toward her with his hand extended. He had to rescue her and get her out of here.

Nettie stood. "Great. Can you hand me the rest of the salads in the case behind you? I've cleared some room in the refrigerator."

What? Stephen stared at her in shock. She'd been arranging the refrigerator while a riot teemed and boiled on the other side of the staircase?

"Are you going to help or not?" Nettie asked when Stephen froze in place.

"Um, *jah*, but I meant help you get out of here."

"I can't do that unless I've put everything in the refrigerator. If you can hand me the salads and chickens, it'll save a lot of time. That way, I don't have to walk around the counter each time."

As if in a daze, Stephen handed her a few salad containers. When the clamor swelled in volume, his face creased in distress. "We should probably go. It isn't worth losing your life over a few salads."

"Don't worry. Those kids will scatter soon," Nettie assured him.

"Kids? More like bikers. No telling what they might do. I don't want you to get hurt."

Nettie took the trays he held out. He sounded as if he really did worry about what happened to her. "I can take care of myself. But if you're worried, you don't have to stay."

"I want to protect you." No man had ever looked at her

like that—as if she were fragile and delicate. The tenderness in his eyes made her tremble.

"Look." He pointed to her hands. "You're shaking."

Nettie held back a laugh. "Not because of that." She flipped a hand in the direction of the uproar. "It's because—" She broke off before she confessed the truth. Heat coursed through her, warming her cheeks to glowing furnaces. She couldn't tell him he'd made her quiver.

Lowering her eyes, she managed to keep her voice even. "Could you take the chickens off the rotisserie?"

"Please, Nettie, let's go. Leave the chickens. If they go bad, I'll pay for all of them. Your life is worth more than that."

She'd never had anyone want to safeguard her this way. Her heart swelled with a strange emotion she couldn't identify. At the same time, she wished she could calm him. "Stephen, we'll be fine."

"I trust God too. But I also believe He gave us common sense to keep us out of danger."

"Common sense tells me that with the cops on the way, those teens will scatter. I saw all of them, and most of them, in spite of their piercings and tattoos, are cowards pretending to be macho."

"You saw them?"

"*Jah.* They came to the candy stand first." She motioned toward the other end of the stand. "I was down there helping Fern."

"Where are Fern and Caroline? They didn't hurt them, did they?"

"*Neh.*" His worry over Fern stabbed through Nettie. Maybe she hadn't been special to him after all. He'd probably have given Fern and Caroline the same looks. He cared about people. All people. Not just her.

Nettie sighed. She'd been foolish to get her hopes up. She chided herself. That crazy dream last night had put her in a romantic mood, and she'd turned Stephen's neighborly concern into a fantasy.

Screams, shouts, swearing, and crashes all grew louder as the rioting crescendoed.

"It's getting worse." Stephen came around the counter and took her hand. "Please, come now."

She squeezed her eyes shut, and the dream washed over her again. The press of his fingers against hers. The warmth. The gentleness. The—

Ach! What is wrong with me?

Her eyes flew open. She had to get herself under control. Gently, she disengaged her hand. That would help. At least a little.

Think about something else.

Maybe she could calm his fears. "Brawls like this build to a peak. That's what's happening now. The police will be here any minute."

"I know. That's why I want to get you away from here."

"*Jah*, I planned to leave before they secure the building and turn us into witnesses. And, if we're smart enough to avoid the cops, so are those teens. Fighting with Russell isn't worth getting nabbed. Believe me, they know that."

Stephen stared at her, his mouth hanging open. She could read the question in his eyes. *How do you know so much about this?* The same question he'd asked when she'd given Mrs. Vandenberg suggestions to improve the center. And the answer would be the same to both.

* * *

Stephen snapped his mouth shut. His jaw had dropped at Nettie's calm assessment of the chaos. Even more surprising, it seemed she'd been right.

Outside a pack of motorcycles revved up. Then, one by one, they zoomed off in different directions.

"How did you know they'd leave?"

She shrugged. "Common sense?"

He could tell from the evasiveness in her eyes that she was concealing a secret. He let it drop for now. "How soon will the police arrive?"

A slow, enticing smile slid across Nettie's face. "Not too long now. Can we get the chickens done?"

Stephen hustled to the rotisserie, slid off the top spit, and carried it to Nettie, who slid the chickens off and wrapped them up. He brought her the others.

Sirens sounded in the distance.

"Time to go now," Nettie announced. "But I need to collect the money from all three businesses. Could you toss the sheets over the counters?"

"Sure." Stephen flipped one sheet after the other to cover the display cases. They finished at the same time.

Nettie's broad *we-did-it* smile lit a smoldering fuse inside him.

"I just need to leave a note so everyone knows I have their money."

Stephen shuffled impatiently while she printed a large sign in her dainty handwriting and taped it to the swinging door.

Then she clasped the money bags to her, and together, they sprinted to the buggy shelter.

After they reached it, she stood as if lost and undecided.

"Is your buggy here?"

"*Neh*. I rode with Gideon this morning."

"He'll be tied up talking to the police. That might last for hours, right?" Since she seemed to know so much about things like this, perhaps she'd know about those procedures too.

"Could be. I can wait in the buggy until he's done. Thanks for your help."

She appeared to want to say something more. He waited, but when no words came, he offered to take her home. She demurred, but he persisted until she agreed.

Her relaxed demeanor didn't reflect the frenzy of whirring sirens blasting in the upper parking lot. The lot where she'd rescued him a few weeks ago. Had he ever thanked her for that? And he'd been meaning to apologize both for himself and Joline. He still expected his daughter to ask forgiveness and do a kind deed.

"Nettie, I—"

"Stephen, could we leave first and talk later? Unless you want to be grilled by the cops."

Again, she'd chosen right. Stephen pulled out of the lower lot, and the horse trotted down the road. They hadn't gone far, when a police cruiser circled the parking lot, checking the buggy shelter and shining lights into the dark gaps between the outdoor storage lockers and refrigerators.

"You timed that perfectly." He still couldn't get over how unfazed she'd acted.

"*Jah.*" Her tone changed to soft and faraway.

Stephen wondered where she'd gone. Wherever she'd slipped off to, sadness pooled in her eyes. With every fiber of his being, he wanted to erase that pain.

Chapter Sixteen

Stephen had only driven a few blocks when a thought hit him. "*Ach!*" He pulled on the reins to turn the buggy into the nearest parking lot. In all the excitement, he'd forgotten Cornelius planned to bring the children to the market between four and five.

"What's the matter?" Nettie looked as alarmed as he felt.

"The driver's dropping my children off at the market. They might even be there now." Would Cornelius use the front entrance? What would he do if he saw the police?

"Do you know which way he's coming? Perhaps you can meet him before he gets here."

"*Neh*, I don't." And he didn't want to return to the parking lot and risk getting drawn into the chaos.

"What about pulling into the parking area on the other side of the auction building? You can watch the road to the front entrance, and I'll keep an eye on the back."

"I can't ask you to do that. You need to get home."

"Taking care of your children is more important. Besides, I don't have any way to get home unless Gideon's done. And—oh, no—"

Alarmed, Stephen slowed the horse. "What?"

"*Neh, neh*. Keep going. I just remembered tonight's the grand opening, and Mrs. Vandenberg planned to pick us up after work."

With his worries over Joline and the biker bedlam, Stephen had totally forgotten. "Do you think she's arrived yet?"

"I hope not." Nettie's face scrunched up. "I don't want to think about her caught in that mob or being questioned by the police. She's a tough lady, but still . . ."

"We'd better watch for her too." Stephen drove into the parking lot behind the auction house.

They hadn't been waiting long when Nettie pointed to the Bentley approaching them, heading toward the market. "There's Mrs. Vandenberg." She hopped out of the buggy and waved.

The driver pulled in beside her. Mrs. Vandenberg's window slid down. Stephen, who was tying up the horse, couldn't hear Nettie's explanation, but in a few minutes, she returned.

"Mrs. Vandenberg wants the number to call your driver. You can direct him here."

Stephen hurried over and took out the slip of paper. Mrs. Vandenberg dialed and handed him the phone.

"Cornelius? How close are you?" Stephen breathed a sigh of relief to hear they were still ten minutes away. "Good. There's been a problem at the market, so we're waiting in the back lot behind the auction house."

He returned the phone to Mrs. Vandenberg. "*Danke*. They'll be here in ten minutes."

"I'm going up to see if they've settled the protest. I assume you'll need to take your children home, Stephen?

Why don't you take Nettie with you, and I'll pick you both up in an hour? Unless you need to get home to take care of your children, Nettie?"

"My mother-in-law took them to an auction today, and they'll be going to Yoder's for supper."

"Perfect." Mrs. Vandenberg leaned back against the seat with a satisfied smile. She turned to her driver. "We'd better check what's happening in the upper lot."

"I hope she'll be all right," Stephen said as they pulled away.

"She's tougher than she looks." Her eyes filled with admiration, Nettie watched the market owner leave. "Knowing Mrs. V, she'll whip everyone into shape, even the cops."

Stephen laughed as they headed back to the buggy. "You're probably right." The woman was a dynamo. "I hope the launch goes well for her tonight."

"If she gets a few of the younger gang members in there, word will spread. But she needs some tough undercover security to keep out drugs and violence."

Stephen longed to ask again how she'd figured all this out. But she'd rebuffed him the last time. He waited until they both settled in the buggy to ask, "You think she'll have success with gangs?"

"Maybe with some wannabes, but she also may stir up some turf wars. It looked like she had some solid research, though, so she might already have plans in place."

"Wish I had a way to help. I guess she can't count on us to recruit gang members." He laughed, but Nettie's mouth pinched shut. Had he offended her with his teasing?

* * *

Once again, Stephen had zinged her. How did she respond to his comment? Taking a deep breath, she said, "I did invite two of Aidan's friends to come to the grand opening tonight." She didn't mention her challenge or her promise.

Stephen's head jerked back. "You did what? You mean the ones who started the ruckus?"

Nettie didn't like the way Stephen was staring at her as if she were a strange creature. She should have kept this to herself. "Not the leader. He'd never come."

"What makes you think that?"

She shrugged. "He's too busy being tough. But the two I invited will probably show up."

Stephen studied her. "Weren't you scared to talk to them?"

Scared of two punks? Nettie swallowed back a snicker. "*Neh.*"

"You're amazing."

At his appreciative glance, Nettie's heart flip-flopped. She lowered her gaze so he couldn't read her reaction. She needed to get the conversation back to neutral ground. "I hope they'll bring others with them. If we can get the hangers-on like them, Mrs. V will have her best chance."

A car drove into the lot. Joline tumbled out of the car before it came to a full stop. Her face a darkening thundercloud, she raced toward Stephen as he walked over to speak to Cornelius.

"What's she doing in our buggy? Where am I going to sit?"

Her words carried to Nettie. *I wish I'd thought about*

this. Nettie didn't want to cause trouble. She'd get out and walk home.

"Joline." The sharp note in Stephen's voice halted his daughter in her tracks. "What did I tell you about being disrespectful?"

When Stephen glanced in Nettie's direction, she pretended to be engrossed in studying the auction building.

"If Nettie heard you, you might have hurt her feelings."

Nettie watched the unfolding scene from the corner of her eye. Joline pouted.

"You will be polite." Stephen set a hand on her shoulder and steered her toward the buggy.

"But how will we all fit?"

Nettie slid the door open and stepped out. "I can walk home so you have more room."

"*Neh*." His tone firm and flat, he quelled Joline's protests with a stern look. "The boys can ride back here." He indicated the rear of the buggy. "You three girls get in the back seat."

"But I always ride up front." Joline appeared as if she planned to start a mutiny.

Nettie longed to take off. That would settle this disagreement. But Stephen's next words prevented her from leaving.

"We should give our guests the best seats. And Nettie is a special guest tonight."

Special? No one had ever called her that.

Stephen pulled the seat forward and motioned for the girls to get in. Joline, her expression sullen, crawled in first.

Great. Joline had positioned herself behind Stephen,

so she could glare at Nettie the whole way home without him seeing.

As much as Nettie longed to leave, she didn't want to interfere with Stephen's discipline.

He pushed the seat back into place and waited for Nettie to get in. "Thanks for being so patient."

"It didn't take long. Your girls are much faster at getting in than I'm used to." Sadie and Lenny both needed to be boosted up and helped onto the seat.

"I meant waiting for the driver to come."

"That was no problem. I enjoyed talking to you." *Ach!* She shouldn't have said that.

Joline's eyes rounded. Then her gaze bounced to her father.

"I liked that too. You always have interesting ideas."

He'd be shocked to find out most of her thoughts. Nettie doubted he'd call those *interesting*.

As they rode toward Stephen's house, they discussed the center and talked about ways the two of them could help. Nettie tried to ignore the impatient huffs and hostile looks being shot from the back seat.

When they arrived, Stephen took care of the horse and asked Matthew to take Nettie into the house. Amos came out onto the back porch to greet her.

Nettie recoiled inside. Amos had been adamant about his beliefs the last time she came. Even worse, he'd lived here when she joined the community, so he knew . . .

Her stomach roiled. Maybe he had as much reluctance to invite her in as she had to enter his house. If so, it didn't show in his welcoming smile.

"Didn't know you were coming." He stepped back and gestured for her to enter the kitchen.

Stephen's children crowded around Amos, hugging his legs and chattering about their trip. All except Joline. She stood apart and aloof. Whenever her gaze strayed to Nettie, her eyes flashed.

Amos led everyone into the living room. Joline, arms crossed, hung back and waited for Nettie to go through the doorway.

Stephen entered the kitchen and said Joline's name in a stern voice. She whirled to face him.

"I met with your teacher. We need to talk."

At the disappointment written on his features, Nettie turned away. She didn't want to intrude on their privacy.

"Not now, Daed," Joline pleaded. "We have company." She brushed past Nettie, accidentally bumping her.

Stephen rushed over and supported Nettie's elbow to steady her. Instead, he threw her more off balance. Heat sizzled through her at his touch. She caught herself before she swayed toward him.

Joline zeroed in on their contact, and she directed narrowed eyes toward Nettie, even after Nettie sat in a chair far from Stephen. Joline's scrutiny didn't let up until Mrs. Vandenberg arrived.

When Stephen and Nettie headed for the car, Joline rushed to the door. "I want to go too."

As he had the last time, Stephen struggled with indecision. He needed to confront his daughter's attitude and actions. Leaving her here without any consequences for what she'd done might embolden her. Letting her come along meant he could clamp down on bad behavior.

He fixed her with an uncertain frown. "If I let you come, I expect you to behave."

"I will." Her breezy promise did little to dispel his doubts.

Maybe once they got to the center and Joline spent time around needy children, it might encourage her to be grateful for what she had. He had to find a way to impress on her that she had to be polite. Her rudeness to Nettie upset him.

As they walked to the car, he spoke in a low voice, giving her his list of expectations. Perhaps she'd taken some of it to heart because she didn't push ahead of Nettie. Instead, Joline wriggled past him to sit in the center of the back seat.

They reached the center an hour before opening time. Lines of children already stood outside, some with their noses pressed against the glass, peering in. A few parents accompanied their little ones.

Visitors ranged from about three to preteen, but none of them seemed to be Mrs. Vandenberg's target—gang members. Stephen suspected that, seeing this crowd, gangs would avoid the building like a police station.

The Bentley pulled into the underground garage, and Mrs. Vandenberg led them to an elevator. They passed a few scattered cars.

Mrs. Vandenberg beamed and waved toward them. "Some of the teachers are already here."

When she was out of earshot, Stephen leaned close to Nettie and whispered, "From the line outside, it seems she'll have a good turnout. I hope she won't be too disappointed not to attract gang members."

"I'm sure she's thinking long-term here. All of these children, even the three-year-olds, could be potential gang members. By catching them now, she can steer them in a different direction."

"True." Stephen hadn't thought about that. How did Nettie have so much wisdom?

Joline wriggled closer to hear what they were saying.

Stephen lowered his voice. "What did I say about politeness."

"Sorry."

"Unless you change your attitude, I'll ask Mrs. Vandenberg's driver to take you home." He held his daughter's gaze until she squirmed.

"I'll be good."

He'd heard a similar promise earlier. She hadn't stuck to it. "You'd better be."

After the glass elevator ascended, she looked around in wonder. Her expression transformed to awe as they followed Mrs. Vandenberg from room to room, checking that all the equipment had been placed properly and the various teachers and mentors had arrived.

Stephen hoped Joline would stay too absorbed in the many activities to act up. They ended their circuit in another gymnasium, this one fitted with gymnastics equipment. A young woman in a leotard bounced on a trampoline and flipped in the air.

"If you watched TV, you might recognize her," Mrs. Vandenberg said. "She's quite a star. It's a real coup to get her and her coach here to teach the kids."

"That's wonderful." Nettie waved toward one side of the room. "I always loved that horse."

"Did you now?" Mrs. Vandenberg seemed pleased.

"Horse?" Joline moved forward and craned her neck to peer around them. "I don't see a horse."

Neither did Stephen.

Mrs. Vandenberg and Nettie both laughed.

Nettie pointed to a long leather-covered rectangle held up by metal bars. Two handles stuck up from the top. "That's a horse."

At Joline's incredulous expression, Mrs. Vandenberg explained, "If you'd watched the Olympics, you would have seen it. Maybe when Nettie used it, it was called a horse, but now it's called pommels."

"It doesn't look anything like a horse."

Stephen set a hand on her shoulder. "Manners," he whispered.

"Well, it doesn't." Joline dug in. She hadn't liked being laughed at, and now she was covering her embarrassment with stubbornness.

He gave her a warning with a quick squeeze of his fingers.

"Ouch!" she yelled.

"Stop the drama now." Stephen kept his warning quiet but firm. He turned to Nettie and Mrs. Vandenberg. He had to admit, he was as curious as Joline. "Where did you learn to use a horse?"

A mischievous smile crossed her face. "On our farm."

Stephen drew in a breath. With her worried expression gone and her eyes sparkling with teasing, she looked so appealing. He'd already forgotten what he'd asked her.

Behind Nettie, Mrs. Vandenberg winked. Stephen's face burned.

Joline stepped between them and said, "You didn't ride that kind of a horse on a farm." She jerked her thumb toward the equipment.

Stephen had had enough. He never liked to discipline his children in public, but Joline had been warned. "Excuse us a minute." He motioned with his head to a spot a few feet away.

For a moment, she appeared about to defy him. Then, she hung her head and walked to the place he'd indicated.

He squatted in front of her so he could meet her eyes. "Don't you ever speak that way to anyone again. If you have a question, ask it nicely or stay silent."

"You care more about her feelings than mine." Joline's voice rose.

People had already been staring at them because of their Plain clothes. Now it seemed every head had turned in their direction. He wished he'd chosen somewhere else to scold her.

Regardless, Stephen wouldn't let prying eyes—or his daughter's attempt to deflect the blame—stop him from correcting her misbehavior. "We're going back over there, and you will apologize. And I don't want you to speak again until you can do it properly."

She stayed by his side, but nudged him away from Nettie.

"I'm sorry." Joline didn't quite sound sincere, but catching his frown, she followed up with, "Will you forgive me?" That seemed a bit more genuine.

"Of course." Nettie smiled down at Joline, who lowered her gaze.

Then, Joline screwed up her face as if it was a hardship to be polite. "Where did you learn to use that kind of horse?" With a quick glance at Mrs. Vandenberg, she added, "Or pommels?"

To Stephen's relief, his daughter's question came out neutral. Not warm or friendly, but it had no undertones of snarkiness.

"In school."

Nettie's answer startled Stephen. Joline gaped.

Joline put her hands on her hips. "Amish schools don't have those."

"Joline Lapp," Stephen thundered.

"She isn't telling the truth." Joline burst into tears. "She's making fun of me." She whirled around and fled.

Stephen started to go after her, but Mrs. Vandenberg laid a hand on his arm. "Leave her alone for a while. Let her calm down. She's going through a rough time."

"*Neh*, you can't." Nettie turned and ran after Joline.

"Wait!" Stephen couldn't break Mrs. Vandenberg's grip, which had tightened on his forearm. For a tottery, old lady, she had tremendous strength in her fingers.

"Relax, Stephen," she counseled. "God has this under control. You do believe that, don't you?"

He'd just told Nettie that not long ago. "*Jah*, but I should do something. I'm her father."

"Actually, a woman's touch might be exactly what your daughter needs."

Mrs. Vandenberg had mentioned that before. She might

be right, but Stephen suspected Nettie would be the last woman Joline would want to see.

"I'd better go after them." He gently prised Mrs. Vandenberg's fingers from his arm.

"Don't be surprised if you can't find them," she called after him.

What in the world did she mean by that?

Chapter Seventeen

Joline dashed through the building, weaving through the crowds milling in the hallways, gawking in all the rooms. Guides frowned at her, but nobody stopped her.

She had to get away. If Daed came after her, he'd force her to go back there to apologize. Joline would never do that. Not when that Sourpuss woman had lied to all of them. Amish schools did not have those horse things.

Even worse, Daed had never, ever yelled at her like that. And not in front of a whole crowd of people. Joline couldn't go back in and face everyone, but he'd make her do it.

And when they got home tonight, he'd pile on punishments for acting rude and for destroying Teacher Emily's letter and for letting out the pig and for being mean to Katie and for getting in trouble at school and for . . .

The list went on and on. She'd get extra chores and be grounded all summer. Plus, he'd insist on making her apologize to Sourpuss.

Well, he couldn't do any of that if he couldn't find her. That gave Joline an idea. She'd run away.

Maybe if she went missing, Daed might be so frantic,

he'd forgive her for everything. All he'd care about was getting her back. And once he did—if he did—he'd be so happy he'd forget all about her disobedience.

And maybe, for once, her *daed* would pay more attention to her than to Nettie.

Panic clawed at Nettie's chest. Joline had grown up in the country. To most of the people outside these doors, an innocent like that would be shark bait.

Mrs. Vandenberg meant well, but she was too trusting, too naïve. She didn't have any idea of the horrible things that could happen in the city. For a well-educated woman, she made some foolish decisions. Especially about safety.

Nettie had to find Joline before the little girl ran into dangers.

I once knew another girl like her. It didn't go well.

Ahead of her, she caught a glimpse of Joline snaking through the crowds.

"Joline, wait!" Nettie's heart hammered in her chest as she ran faster. She had to catch up.

The young girl swiveled her head for a second. Spotting Nettie, she turned and ran faster.

"Don't go outside," Nettie screamed. "It's dangerous out there."

"Anything's better than in here." Joline sprinted past the front desk and banged out the door.

Outside the front window, Joline hesitated, glancing both ways. Noticing Nettie through the glass, Joline tore off in the opposite direction and disappeared from view.

Nettie slammed into a family entering the center. She'd

been so busy concentrating on Joline, she hadn't seen them.

The father grabbed her arm. "What are you doing? Leave my kids alone."

"I'm sorry." Her breathing came hard and fast. "A little girl." She pointed to the door. "A runaway." She jerked her arm free and skirted around all of them.

God, please keep Joline safe.

A group of laughing teens pushed their way through the door. Nettie's instincts told her they might cause a disturbance. But first, she had to find Joline.

Please hurry, she mentally begged the boys. She pinched her mouth shut and waited. Riling them up might lead to a confrontation. That was the last thing she needed.

Making disparaging remarks and mocking the younger children who raced around excitedly, the group made their way into the center. Nettie wanted to deal with them before they caused trouble.

But each second that passed was one more second Joline could get hurt.

Nettie did the only thing she could do as one teen after the other entered—prayed and prayed and prayed. She asked God to keep every one of these young men calm and out of trouble. And to let her reach Joline in time.

As soon as the last teen made it through the door, Nettie rushed out.

Frantic to get away, Joline plunged into a nearby alley. Maybe if she hid behind that dumpster, Sourpuss would run past without seeing her. Then Joline could sneak out of the dimly lit area and run the opposite way.

She couldn't let Sourpuss catch her, or her whole plan would be spoiled.

Joline slithered into the alley, staying close to the brick wall to hide in the shadows. She hadn't gone far when a man's silhouette emerged from behind the dumpster. He flicked an odd-looking cigarette butt into the air. The bright spark flew in an arc and landed near her feet.

She froze as the hulking figure sauntered toward her. In the dim light, Joline could make out the black skull and crossbones tattooed on his forehead. She panicked. He hadn't seen her yet. If she darted toward the street, would he come after her?

"Hey, li'l mama. Whatcha doin' out here? Don'tcha know any better than to run around alone this time of night?"

Like a frightened rabbit, Joline darted away. Combat boots thundered after her. Chains clanked. He was gaining on her. Joline's heart battered against her ribs. She zigzagged back and forth, hoping to escape.

She'd almost made it to the sidewalk when strong hands closed around her waist. *Neh!* She wiggled and squirmed trying to twist out of his grasp.

Blasts of laughter assaulted her ears. "A wildcat, huh? We gonna have ourselves some fun."

The spit dried in Joline's mouth. She opened her parched mouth to scream. Only a gurgle came out. He clapped a hand over her mouth and jerked on her bob to tug her head back. He yanked so hard, he wrenched some of her hair free from her bun. Strands flew around her face as she twisted in his grasp.

One hand released her bun. Joline tried to writhe away,

but the arm encircling her neck tightened, and the man dragged her back against him as he fumbled in his pocket.

Click! Something cold and metal pressed against her throat. When he switched hands, the knife grazed her skin. "One peep out of you and . . ." He wrapped his other hand around her waist and dragged her toward the alley.

She wanted to scream for help, but she gagged at his skunky breath.

His lips close to her ear hissed out a snakelike whisper. "Don't make a sound. And do what I say."

Was he going to kill her?

Nettie burst through the front door and dashed in the direction Joline had gone.

Farther down the sidewalk, Joline was trying to wriggle free from a stocky teen who'd grabbed her by the waist. He'd covered her mouth with one hand and was tugging her toward the dark alley at the side of the building. If only Mrs. Vandenberg had installed security lights.

One streetlight outside the alley shone faintly. Metal glinted in the hand pressed to Joline's neck. *Ach!* A knife. *Nooooo . . .*

Without a weapon, Nettie couldn't tangle with a knife. The only way to beat an assailant like that was with surprise. She prayed she wouldn't be too late.

"Call nine-one-one," she yelled as she sprinted back into the building, letting the heavy front door slam behind her. "Send police to the alley."

She raced to the side door. If she could slip out without

the teen hearing, she might be able to startle him. That was her only chance.

She eased the door open.

Dear Lord, please don't let it squeak.

One inch . . . two . . .

So far, no noise.

He glanced over his shoulder. Had he seen her?

Joline twisted and wriggled. He turned back and slid the knife under her chin.

Don't, Joline. You'll only get hurt.

Nettie wished she could warn Joline, but she dare not cry out. She didn't want to alert him.

While he was occupied getting Joline under control, Nettie slid the door open far enough to slip out. She closed it silently and ducked behind the dumpster.

"Stay still," the teen commanded, "or I'll slice ya." He dragged Joline farther back into the darkness of the alley.

They'd almost reached the dumpster. Nettie had to act now. She wished she had a knife of her own. With a switchblade, she could probably take him. But with him holding a knife against Joline's throat, Nettie couldn't take a chance of wrestling the switchblade away.

Legs trembling, she padded up behind him. She pitched her voice low and gruff. "Let her go now or I'll shoot." She pressed a finger into the small of his back.

If he figured out her ruse, she'd be dead. If the knife slipped, Joline would die.

He froze. She only had seconds before he realized she'd lied.

"Let go," she repeated. Had her voice wavered on the last word? *Please, please don't turn around.*

The teen's arm shook a little. Had she frightened him? What if he cut Joline by mistake?

Please, God, save her.

Motorcycles roared in the distance, getting louder, coming their way. What if he had backup? His friends would hurt or kill both her and Joline. Even worse, what if they were part of a rival gang? She and Joline might get caught in a turf war.

Two bikes rumbled into the alley, followed by four more. Headlights bounced off the bricks, illuminating the three of them frozen in place.

One teen hopped off the first bike. "What the—?" He gestured to someone behind him. "Snake, keep an eye on the bikes."

Nettie recognized that voice. *Aidan.*

Thank you, Lord.

"Aidan," she shrieked. "Grab Joline."

The teen holding Joline whipped his head around.

As hard as she could, Nettie karate-chopped his arm.

Combat boots pounded toward them.

The teen swore. Let go of Joline. Whirled around. Slashed with his knife. Sharp searing pain burned high on her left arm. Blood poured from the cut. She'd fought against tough odds before.

With one swift move, Aidan swooped Joline behind him. Using her right arm, Nettie hit out again at the attacker's wrist. The knife clattered to the cement.

The attacker screamed and grabbed his wrist. "You broke it," he snarled. "You gonna pay."

Before he could lash out at her, Aidan and another guy jumped the attacker and wrestled him to the ground.

Aidan pinned the attacker's hands behind his back and straddled him.

Sirens sounded in the distance.

"Cops," one of the bikers shouted. "Gotta get out of here."

Nettie wanted to help them. After what had happened at the market earlier today, the last thing these bikers needed was to run into the cops tonight.

"The center has an underground garage," Nettie yelled. "There's an elevator up to the main floor. You can hide out in the center."

Several engines revved. They took off like a shot, but one teen hopped off his bike. The teen she'd invited to the center.

"I'll take the little girl inside," he volunteered.

Joline had her back plastered against the brick wall. One hand pressed to her mouth, she shivered uncontrollably.

"Go with him, Joline. Find your *daed*."

"You have him?" the guy with Aidan asked.

"Yeah. Got anything ta tie him with?"

"*Nah*. I gotta go."

Nettie pressed her bleeding arm tight against her body, and with her other hand, fumbled for the ties holding her work apron.

She handed Aidan the apron. "Tie him with that."

Aidan stared at her in alarm. "You're bleeding." He whipped off his bandana with one hand and tossed it to her. "Use that."

When Aidan twisted the attacker's arms behind his back, he shrieked, "She broke my wrist." He tried to wriggle away, but Aidan held him tightly.

Someone burst from the door behind her. "Nettie?"

At Stephen's deep voice, her past and present collided. Everything hit at once. Nettie's knees buckled, and she crumpled to the ground.

"Listen, man," Aidan said to Stephen as he tied up the attacker. "Can you keep an eye on him? I gotta get out of here." Aidan beat it to his bike and gunned the engine. He squealed around the corner before the police cars arrived.

Stephen knelt beside Nettie. "Are you hurt? Where's Joline?"

"She's . . . safe . . . inside." Nettie's eyes fluttered shut. She didn't want Stephen to know how hearing his voice had affected her, to read her most intimate feelings, or to discover the secrets she'd hidden from the Amish community.

Stephen had combed the center for Joline. He'd been at the far end of the building when Nettie shouted to call nine-one-one. Panicked, everyone streamed in that direction. Swarms of people smashed Stephen against the wall or blocked his way as he struggled toward the sound.

Amidst the pandemonium in the lobby, he couldn't find Nettie or Joline. Had something happened to them? Why couldn't he see them?

Revving engines drowned out the buzz of the crowd. Something seemed to be happening outside the front door, but he'd never get through the throngs by the entrance.

A side door led to the alley. No one seemed to be in that hallway. He headed there. Maybe he could get outside and find Nettie.

Stephen banged open the door. On the ground in front

of him, a smaller teen was tying a larger one up with—
An apron? An Amish apron.

Standing off to one side, Nettie, her face pale, held a colored cloth to her arm. Was that blood?

When he called her name, she collapsed. He hurried to her side. Had she fainted? Stephen leaned closer. Her breathing seemed a little ragged. She must have been badly frightened. And she'd been hurt. Her arm was bleeding.

Before Nettie's eyes closed, she'd assured him Joline was safe. He hoped she was right. But what had happened out here?

Had there been a fight? Had Nettie gotten caught in it?

The teen on top looked familiar, but Stephen couldn't place him. After a quick command for Stephen to watch the trussed teen, the other kid hightailed it out of there before the police pulled up.

If Joline was all right, he needed to stay with Nettie. The cloth had dropped from her wound. Her dress sleeve had been slashed, and blood smeared her arm, so he couldn't tell how deep the cut had gone. He pressed the rag against the cut to stop the bleeding. Then he cradled her in his arms.

Her eyes flickered open. "Stephen?"

She seemed to be as dazed as he was. Holding her softness accelerated his pulse. He forced himself to concentrate on her needs and stopping the bleeding.

Between taking in small gasps of air, Nettie said, "There's . . . something . . . you should . . . know . . ."

Whirring sirens deafened him as police cruisers

screeched to a halt. Flashing lights blinded him. Car doors slammed.

"Back here," Stephen shouted, waving to get their attention. "We need an ambulance."

Nettie protested. "I'll be all right. I've had worse cuts."

One of the cars pulled into the alley. Its headlights shined on Stephen, Nettie, and the bound teen. Two officers, their guns drawn, approached. Others stood, blocking the entranceway.

"What's going on?" one demanded.

"I don't know. I just got here. Someone was tying up that kid." First, Stephen nodded in the direction of the apron-tied teen. Then, he tipped his chin toward Nettie. "She's cut."

He started to say his daughter was missing when the rotating blue and red flashers atop the car spotlighted a small figure who'd pushed open the back door and huddled in the shadows. "Joline?"

His daughter shivered, her eyes wide with terror, fixed on the teen on the ground. A paramedic arrived to check Nettie and freed her from Stephen's arms. He held them out to Joline.

She shook her head. "He might hurt me." Her voice quavered.

"Who?" Was she afraid of the police officers?

"That man." She pointed to the teen now being assisted to his feet by two other officers.

"He can't hurt you," Stephen assured her. This time when he opened his arms, she came running and buried her face against his chest.

"But he already did hurt me."

Stephen felt sick.

Nettie called out to the officers, "He grabbed and held this girl at knifepoint. And he's the one who slashed at my arm."

One of them snapped handcuffs on the teen's wrists. He yowled and screamed that he had a broken wrist.

"Let the paramedic check him out," the officer said.

A woman officer came over and squatted beside Joline. "Can you tell us what happened?"

Joline still clung tightly to Stephen with one arm as she pointed to the teen, who kept insisting he'd done nothing.

"I tried to get away, but he grabbed me and went like this." Joline pressed a hand over her mouth and pantomimed a knife against her throat. "He pulled me back here into the alley. Then old Sourpuss saved me."

"Old Sourpuss?" The officer glanced at Stephen, who gave him a blank look.

"Her." Joline pointed to Nettie, whose sliced arm was being examined.

Stephen raised his eyebrows. "You mean Nettie?" He looked up at the officer. "Nettie Hartzler."

Joline nodded, then hid her face against his shoulder again. "I thought I was going to die."

"The knife belongs to him?" The officer indicated the teen they were leading away.

Joline lifted her head. "*Jah*, it's his." She swallowed hard and squeezed her eyes shut. "He held it here." She touched her neck.

"Can you go through the story from the beginning?" the officer asked.

Shivering, Joline recounted the event, trembling harder each time she mentioned her captor. "Then Nettie came up behind us, but we didn't know it was her 'cause she sounded like a man. She said she'd shoot if he didn't let me go."

"Nettie had a gun?"

Biting her lip, Joline stared off into the distance. "I don't think so. Where would she get a gun?"

The officer made a note. "I guess we need to find that out."

Stephen didn't believe Nettie had a gun. Where would she keep it hidden? And why would she have one in the first place?

"Then the motorcycles came." Joline waved toward the spot where the police cars had gathered.

The officer glanced to where Joline had pointed, then at a nearby policeman who returned her quizzical expression.

"Motorcycles?" the officer asked. "I don't see any."

"That's 'cause they drove away fast when they heard the sirens."

"Were they friends of the young man who held you?"

"*Neh*, I don't think so. They helped Nettie. I think they knew her."

The officer leaned closer. "What makes you think that?"

"Nettie called out to Aidan to grab me. I've seen him in the market at the same stand as Nettie."

"Aidan Green?" The officer jotted down more information.

"I think so." Stephen hadn't formally met Aidan, but the boy's father was Nick Green.

She frowned. "That's odd. My brother had a disturbance at the Green Valley Farmer's Market this afternoon, and Aidan seemed to be the ringleader."

"I don't know much about that." Stephen and Amos

had packed up rapidly, and then Stephen had helped Nettie. None of them had gone to the front of the market.

Joline interrupted his thoughts. Once again, she vied to be the center of attention. "Aidan grabbed me and dragged me behind him."

Stephen hadn't heard this part of the account before. "Did he hurt you?"

His daughter rubbed her wrists. "*Jah*. Not as much as that—that—" Shivering, she turned and buried her face against Stephen's shirt.

It pained Stephen to see his little girl so scared and shaken. He rubbed a hand in circles on her back to soothe her.

The officer waited patiently until Joline lifted her head. "Then what happened?"

"That guy turned around and stabbed at Nettie."

Stephen sucked in a breath. A vivid picture of Nettie being attacked flashed through his mind. He wished he'd been there to rescue her.

Joline studied his face and frowned. She continued, "Nettie chopped at his arm, and he dropped the knife."

"What did she use?" the officer asked.

"Huh?" Joline stared at her with a puzzled frown.

"Did Nettie use a gun or another weapon to chop his arm?"

"*Neh*, just her hand. Like this." Joline mimicked a karate chop.

"So Nettie had nothing in either hand?"

Joline shook her head.

Stephen's chest constricted. She'd gone after a knife-wielding attacker? Why had she put herself in such danger? Why hadn't she run away?

"And then?" the officer prompted.

"Then he cut Nettie." Joline made a slashing motion on her left arm. "She twisted away real fast."

Thank the Lord. Stephen tried not to imagine what might have happened. What actually had occurred was upsetting enough.

"Then she and Aidan told Snake to take me inside. I didn't get to see what happened next." Joline seemed disappointed.

"Snake?" The officer's question echoed Stephen's thoughts.

Snake? His daughter had been brought into the building by someone named *Snake*?

"*Jah*, he's nice. He took me inside, and we looked around the building together. He really liked the room with the pool tables. When he wasn't looking, I sneaked out the back door."

"Thank you for all your help, Joline. If you think of anything more to tell me"—she handed Stephen her business card—"have your dad call me."

"I will." Joline leaned over to look at the card, and loose strands of hair fell into her eyes. She twisted them around her messy bun.

"The paramedics should examine your daughter," the officer suggested.

Stephen stood and took his daughter's hand.

"I don't have anything wrong with me," Joline protested.

"Let's just have them check you." Stephen led her over to the ambulance, where a woman was placing a bandage on Nettie's arm. Stephen winced as the paramedic pushed the sides of the cut together, but Nettie sat stoically.

Now that they'd cleaned up her arm, the long line from

just above her elbow to her shoulder showed as a scratch. It was amazing she'd escaped with a scrape and a small, deep cut. She could have been killed.

He stepped closer. "Will she be all right?"

The paramedic nodded. "She's one lucky lady. To tangle with a switchblade and end up with only a small cut? Somebody up there"—she pointed toward the sky—"was looking out for her."

Jah, God had taken care of Nettie and Joline. Stephen still couldn't believe Nettie had risked her life to rescue his daughter, but he was grateful she had. God had given her the courage to confront the attacker. If not for Nettie, Joline might have been badly hurt or worse.

Nettie had blinked back tears as the paramedic disinfected the cut on her arm.

"It stings, huh?" She gave Nettie a sympathetic look.

It did, but the antiseptic hadn't made Nettie's eyes burn. The gentle way Stephen had held her—as if he wanted to protect her from harm—had touched her deeply. It surpassed all her daydreams of holding his hand. This had been real. Her breath caught in her throat. If only she were worthy of that kind of love.

"Now that we've cleaned this up, it doesn't look so bad. From here to here"—the paramedic indicated the mark from above Nettie's elbow to her shoulder—"it's only a surface scrape."

Jah. Because she'd used good defensive moves. If she'd been a little faster, he wouldn't have jabbed her at all. Being out of practice meant her reflexes had been too slow. Of course, since she'd joined the Amish, Nettie no longer needed self-defense techniques. If she planned to spend time here at the center, though, she might have to brush up.

"We can close this now with this butterfly bandage." The paramedic pulled out some white strips.

"*Gut*." Nettie had no desire to head to the hospital. She'd had butterfly bandages before. Quick and easy. And the cuts healed fast.

As the paramedic pushed the cut closed, Nettie squeezed her eyes shut to capture the lingering feeling of being in Stephen's arms. She'd relaxed against him, feeling safer than she ever had in her life. So safe she'd almost blown it by confessing . . .

"All done." The paramedic's declaration interrupted a lovely daydream. "You can open your eyes now. I know people faint at the sight of blood, but you'll be fine."

The woman thought Nettie had been scared of blood? She'd never had that luxury. She'd had to deal with much worse than this.

Reluctantly, she opened her eyes, unwilling to let go of the memories of Stephen. But there he was, heading toward her with Joline clinging to his hand. Joline peeped at Nettie's arm, then stared at the ground.

When Stephen asked the paramedic if she'd be all right, Nettie almost swooned. He cared about her.

Then he bent closer. "*Danke* for saving Joline. I'm so sorry you got hurt."

"It's all right. Mainly a scratch." Nettie stood and waited for her wooziness to clear. Was it from standing too quickly, from being too close to Stephen, or from the past memories flooding through her mind? They gushed over her like a waterfall, submerging her. She sucked in air before the water closed over her head and suffocated her.

Stephen reached for her other elbow to support her. "Are you all right? Maybe you should stay seated for a while."

Joline's sharp-eyed look steeled Nettie's backbone. Although Nettie longed to lean against him, she slipped her arm from his grasp. One thing had become clear to her tonight—despite her longing and fantasies, she and Stephen had no future. For so many reasons. And a switchblade was only one of them.

Chapter Eighteen

Stephen hung back while the police interviewed Nettie. He'd heard Joline's version of the story, which made him sick. He should have kept a better eye on her. And even though she needed to be disciplined, he shouldn't have humiliated her in front of a roomful of people.

If he'd talked with Joline earlier . . . If he'd come down hard on her when she'd first started acting out . . . If he'd . . .

Stephen stopped himself. He could have done a better job parenting, but regretting the past wouldn't change what had happened. He needed to concentrate on the future. And his first action—after thanking Nettie— would be to spend more time with Joline. And to make his expectations clear.

Stephen couldn't help overhearing Nettie recounting the story. She said the same thing Joline had about the teen dragging Joline into the alley. Then she described sneaking out the back door to surprise him, pretending to have a gun.

What had she been thinking? Didn't she know how dangerous that was?

The male officer taking down Nettie's story gave her a skeptical look. "The kid believed you?"

Nettie lowered her head. "I, um, stuck a finger in his back."

The officer frowned. "Never a good idea to go after an attacker like that. He could have cut the girl."

"I had to take a chance. I couldn't let him hurt her. I figured if he didn't believe me, he'd turn around and go after me instead."

Joline pressed a hand against her mouth, and Stephen swallowed hard. Nettie would have sacrificed her life for his daughter?

"Next time, call the police and wait until we get here."

"Who knows what might have happened to her by then. And I did yell for someone to call nine-one-one as I ran to the side door. I hoped you'd be coming soon."

The officer's expression turned grim. "You could have taken some strong men out with you to overpower him, but you'd still have risked the little girl's life."

"I didn't want anyone else to get hurt."

A heavy sigh was the officer's only response.

Nettie went on with her story, repeating the same scene Joline had described, only she added one more detail. "If I'd been faster, he never would have slashed me."

The officer blew out an exasperated breath. "Unless you've been trained, it's not easy to evade a determined knifer."

"I could have done it. I should have done it." Nettie appeared frustrated.

Stephen couldn't believe she'd taken a chance like that. And to expect she could outmaneuver an experienced knife fighter? What was she thinking?

"Do you know how many times situations like this end in tragedy?" the officer scolded. "Next time don't take matters into your own hands."

Nettie ignored him and continued with her statement. "A group of bikers drove up and helped."

Joline also had mentioned the bikers. Stephen had believed her, but the woman who'd interviewed her had appeared dubious. This officer had the same disbelieving look.

"Where are they now?" he asked.

Nettie shrugged.

"She's lying," Joline said.

Stephen shushed her. He hoped the officer hadn't heard Joline's comment. He didn't want Nettie to get into trouble.

"You don't know?" the officer persisted.

Nettie stared down at the ground. "I, umm, suggested they go into the building for the grand opening."

Had she heard Joline? Or did she come clean on her own? Stephen edged closer to hear this part of the story. Joline had been inside when this happened.

"I don't know if they went inside or if they drove off." The evasive way Nettie said it, she seemed to be covering for the bikers.

"We can check the building. Would you recognize any of them?"

She hesitated. "Maybe."

"Maybe?" the officer echoed.

"I don't want to get any of them in trouble. Not after they helped capture the attacker."

"If they haven't broken the law, you have nothing to worry about."

Still, Nettie sat there, nibbling on her lower lip. Stephen wanted to tell her Joline had already named Aidan, so the police knew at least one of them.

"One of them took Joline into the building to keep her safe. Another one tackled the attacker. Then we tied him up."

"With your apron?"

"*Jah.* We didn't have anything else to use."

"Very clever." The officer's response sounded derisive. Stephen's hackles rose, but Joline giggled.

In a whisper, she repeated, "*With her apron.* Old Sour— I mean, Nettie—tied up that man with her apron?" Joline covered her mouth to stifle her snickers.

Stephen had to admit Nettie had been very resourceful. He'd come out of the building to see the teen trussed up, but he had no idea how it had happened. He couldn't get over Nettie's bravery. He owed her—and Aidan and Snake, whoever he was—a debt of gratitude.

Nettie went on. "Then Stephen, Joline's dad, came out the exit and kept an eye on the teen so Aidan—" Nettie clapped a hand over her mouth.

"Aidan?" the officer pounced on her slip.

She looked sick.

The officer who'd interviewed Joline was walking past. "Aidan Green. The gang of teens the Ephrata police were called out for this afternoon. The riot at Green Valley Farmer's Market."

"It wasn't a riot," Nettie burst out. "The teens only wanted to protest about one of the stand owners putting Aidan's *daed* out of business. Russell called the police. He shouldn't have. They were peaceful."

How did Nettie know that? She hadn't been at that

end of the market. When Stephen found her, she'd been calmly packing up the food in the display cases. She'd never seen what happened.

Nettie glanced up. Her eyes widened as they met his. "Tell them," she begged.

Stephen needed to break their connection, but he couldn't look away. He wanted to back her up, but he had no idea what had happened at the front of the market. He'd heard chanting and shouting, but he didn't know if the teens had been peaceful.

The officer who'd interviewed Joline jumped in. "My brother was on that call. The stand owner didn't press charges. The teens fled. I'm guessing they're the same ones that were here tonight. Not sure why they were so far from home."

"Because I invited them to the center." Nettie threw both officers a defiant glance.

For a moment, she reminded Stephen of Joline. When Nettie was young, had she been like his daughter? Maybe Mrs. Vandenberg was right. Nettie might be able to help him with Joline.

He'd like to get to know Nettie better. He had to admit she intrigued him. Maybe Mrs. Vandenberg had known what she was doing as a matchmaker.

Nettie couldn't help staring at Stephen. He had a gleam of admiration in his eyes that warmed her heart. If only she were worthy of it. She tore her gaze away.

She had to clear Aidan and his friends.

"We'll need to talk to this Aidan Green and anyone else with him."

"They didn't do anything wrong. If they hadn't come here when they did, this might have ended differently." Nettie was pretty confident she could have taken the teen, but Aidan had been a godsend. The Lord had definitely been watching over her and Joline.

"Don't worry," the woman officer said. "We just need their eyewitness accounts. Nobody's planning to lock them up or anything."

"Unless they have outstanding warrants on them or something," the other officer added darkly.

The way he talked made Nettie's insides clench. He hadn't even met Aidan and his friends yet, but he sounded as if he'd planned to cart them off to jail.

She couldn't let that happen. When the officers headed into the building, Nettie wanted to run inside and warn Aidan and his friends to flee, but she couldn't get up and leave the interview. She did the only thing she could do— pray that God would protect them as He'd protected her and Joline.

After Nettie finished her statement, Stephen ushered her and Joline back into the building. Nettie appeared so shaky, he wished he could support her. But she drew away from him. And though he had no right to touch her or hold her, he'd done both tonight, and it had stirred deep longings in his soul.

Mrs. Vandenberg greeted them as soon as they walked through the door. "I understand you're quite the heroine, Nettie."

Joline didn't display her usual disdain, but her face

pinched up a little. Stephen gave her a slight frown, and she smoothed out her expression.

"Aidan and his friends couldn't get over your self-defense skills. According to them, you'd pretty much subdued Joline's attacker before they arrived."

Nettie's cheeks pinkened, and she stared at the ground.

Stephen couldn't keep the amazement from his voice. "You did? You could have been killed."

"*Jah*, well, someone had to stop him."

"But you?"

"Nobody else was around." Nettie wished he'd stop admiring what she'd done. She'd responded on instinct. Nothing more.

"You could have called for people to help tackle him when you ran through the building." Stephen wished he'd been in the lobby then. He'd have followed her to protect her.

Nettie turned to Mrs. Vandenberg. "Did the police find Aidan?"

"Yes. I let them use my office to interview him and each of his friends. I'm a little worried about Aidan having two run-ins with the police today. He wasn't in trouble at the market, and I'm sure he didn't do anything wrong here either, but still . . ."

Nettie frowned. "It doesn't look good."

Mrs. Vandenberg nodded. Then she leaned down to get closer to Joline, and Stephen reached out to steady the older woman when she wobbled.

She smiled up at him. "You're such a good protector. Nettie here could use someone like you in her life. Especially if she plans to keep up her street-fighting career."

Stephen wasn't sure whose face burned the hottest—

his or Nettie's. But the truth was he longed to take care of Nettie. If only he could keep her from harm. He had no idea how he could do that, though, if she often dashed into danger.

Joline fumed as everyone gathered around Nettie and praised her courage. *I was brave too, but nobody notices that.*

She'd lost a little of her resentment toward Sourpuss. After all, the woman had saved her. And when Sourpuss smiled, like she'd been doing a lot tonight, she didn't look half bad. But Joline still didn't want Sourpuss as a *mamm*.

When Mrs. Vandenberg suggested Daed needed to protect Nettie and his eyes shone like he'd love to do that, Joline gritted her teeth.

Neh, neh, neh. Never, never, never.

Joline was grateful for the rescue, but she had no intention of giving up her *daed* to any woman. And definitely not to a grump.

Mrs. Vandenberg looked Joline in the eye, while Daed steadied the shaky, old lady. Joline hoped she wasn't in for a lecture. So far, whenever she ran into this woman, Mrs. Vandenberg gave her advice. Most of the time, Joline couldn't figure out what it meant.

A group of small children raced by, and a loose strand of hair blew in Joline's face. She twisted it around her finger nervously, waiting for Mrs. Vandenberg to speak.

Before she could, Daed gasped. "Joline, your hair."

Had he been so busy mooning over Sourpuss he hadn't even noticed her hair?

"How did that happen?" Daed stared at her in concern.

"That man grabbed me by the hair."

Daed's eyes widened. "You didn't tell the police that."

"I forgot." She hadn't meant for that to come out so defensively. She shuffled her feet and tried to decide how to make up for it. Daed had scolded her for being disrespectful.

That hadn't been more than an hour or two ago, but it seemed like a lifetime had passed. Joline had grown up some in that time. She wanted Daed to know it so he didn't frown at her or try to give her another talking-to.

He only gave her a warning look, and she nodded to let him know she understood. His lips curved up. But then he focused on her hair again.

"Would you like me to comb you, Joline?" Nettie asked in a sweet voice.

Neh almost burst from Joline's lips, but she pinched them shut to hold the word back.

Before she could find a polite way to say *neh*, Daed beamed at Nettie. "So kind of you."

Kind? She was probably doing it to make Daed think she was nice, but you could tell from her everyday face, she was a grouch.

"I can do it myself." Joline tried to say it without meanness.

Mrs. Vandenberg, who'd watched all this from her hunched-over position, stared directly into Joline's eyes. "You can do a lot of things yourself, can't you, Joline?"

Joline tossed her head, making other pieces of hair fly loose from where she'd twisted them around her bun. She probably looked like a mangy, stray dog. She brushed the pieces from her eyes and tried not to show her embarrassment.

She still hadn't answered Mrs. Vandenberg's question. The old lady's patience and her steady gaze unnerved Joline. If she said *jah*, she'd sound prideful. But if she replied *neh*, she'd seem incompetent.

"Any answer is all right, child."

The word *child* roused Joline's temper. "*Jah*, I can do many things." Her snappish response probably would earn her a scowl. She flicked her eyes in Daed's direction to check, but he stayed focused on supporting Mrs. Vandenberg.

"Competence is a good trait." Mrs. Vandenberg's words vibrated with approval. "Accepting help, though, is not always weakness. It can be a strength."

Huh? That didn't make sense.

"Do you like helping your younger brothers and sisters?"

"Of course." Here, Joline stood on firmer ground. Nobody would think her conceited for admitting that.

"Doesn't it make you feel good when you can do things for them?"

"*Jah*." Joline tried to work out where Mrs. Vandenberg planned to head with her argument. She'd started talking about Joline accepting help. Now she'd flipped it to Joline assisting others. Sometimes older people got addled.

"Don't you think people like doing things for you?"

How did Mrs. Vandenberg always manage to sting people? She did it in sneaky ways.

Joline squirmed. "I guess."

"Excellent." Mrs. Vandenberg pushed herself upright with Daed's help. "Then you'll be nice enough to let Nettie help you."

What could Joline say to that? If she refused, she'd

come off as ungracious. Without a word, she bowed her head to give Nettie access to the bun.

"Would you rather do it over here?" Nettie indicated a shadowy niche where they'd be out of the crowd.

When they reached the corner, Nettie positioned herself so no passersby could see Joline. It was nice of Nettie to think about their privacy. Joline had never had her hair fixed in public before. And she didn't want to go into the brightly lit restrooms where people might stare at them. She endured enough stares for her Plain clothes, especially here in the city.

"I don't have a comb, so I'll have to use my fingers," Nettie apologized. "I hope it won't hurt." She removed the hairpins so swiftly Joline didn't realize it until her hair cascaded down her back.

Gently, Nettie combed her fingers through Joline's waist-length hair. The tenderness brought tears to Joline's eyes.

She'd been doing her own hair for years. After Mamm died and her *aenti* married, Joline had managed to pull her hair back and flip it over her hand until she'd formed a somewhat messy bob. Sometimes, women from church would redo it for her, but they usually yanked when they combed her out.

But Nettie's touch reminded Joline of Mamm's caring hands. She wanted to jerk away. To stop the tears threatening to fall. But if she did, Nettie would see them.

Joline clamped her teeth on her lower lip and fought against the moisture stinging the back of her eyes. It had been so long since anyone had done something like this for her. She could do it herself, but it made her heart ache and swell with longing for someone to love her. To put down some of her burdens.

Those were foolish desires. To have them, she'd have to give up control. She'd have to give up her place in the family. She'd have to give up time with her *daed*. And she'd have to give up a lot of his love.

Too many sacrifices.

As Nettie smoothed back Joline's hair, twisted the sides, and secured it, Joline closed her eyes and imagined Nettie's hands were Mamm's hands. Joline battled the urge to relax back against Mamm.

When her bob had been fixed, Joline choked down the lump in her throat and blinked back the wetness under her eyelids. But some escaped and pooled on her cheeks.

Nettie set kind hands on Joline's shoulders. "All done." Nettie's gentle whisper arrowed into Joline's heart.

All the things she'd missed by not having a *mamm* welled up and filled her chest with a throbbing ache. All the years she'd longed for her *mamm*'s bedtime kiss. All the meals she'd wished to see Mamm sitting in her place at the table. All the tears she'd buried so she could comfort her brothers and sisters. All the chores she'd done to fill her family's emptiness so they wouldn't miss Mamm as much.

Joline resisted turning around. She didn't want Sourpuss to see her pain.

And then Nettie did the unthinkable. She spun Joline around and hugged her.

Although Joline stiffened, Nettie didn't notice. She reached down and brushed away the tears with a feather-light touch.

"You were so brave out there. I'm sorry if he hurt you."

"He didn't." Not much anyway. And that pain was nothing like this soul-searing agony.

* * *

Nettie swallowed hard. She wished she had a way to comfort this hurting little girl. The anguish deep inside Joline had nothing to do with the attacker. She needed a *mamm* but would never surrender being in charge of the household. Nettie had experienced similar misery. If only she could say something to ease Joline's suffering.

She could reassure her of one thing. She said in a low voice, "Joline, you don't have to worry about Mrs. Vandenberg's matchmaking. I'm not going to marry your *daed*."

Hope blossomed on Joline's face. "You promise?"

"I do." As much as Nettie found herself falling for Stephen, once he found out about her past, he'd realize she wouldn't make a suitable mother for his children.

Joline eyed her warily, and Nettie could read the question on the little girl's face—*How do I know I can trust you?*

"I know it's hard for you to believe that, but it's true."

With a tentative smile, Joline said words that sounded forced. "*Danke* for that. And for rescuing me."

"You're welcome. I hope we can be friends."

Joline didn't appear to totally accept that offer, but she gave a brief nod.

While they were having this heart-to-heart talk, Nettie had one more issue she wanted to raise. "I know you don't like me very much, but I'd appreciate it if you and your sisters wouldn't pick on Katie."

Joline lowered her head and didn't meet Nettie's

eyes. She hesitated for several seconds. Then she sighed. "All right."

Nettie hoped Joline would keep her word. "*Danke*."

Turning, Nettie faced out toward Stephen and Mrs. Vandenberg letting her back hide Joline. Nettie hesitated a bit to give Joline time to wipe her face and regain her composure.

"Ready?" she asked after a few minutes.

A relieved *jah* came from behind her. And Nettie wasn't sure, but there might also have been a whispered *danke*.

Before Nettie could step forward, Aidan came charging down the hall. His yell boomed around the lobby. "There she is."

The two kids Nettie had invited to the center jogged beside him. Scruffy Beard and a few of the kids who'd caused the ruckus at the market strode behind them, acting cool.

"Hey, Nettie, my man Diego here"—Aidan gave the young teen beside him a friendly push forward—"says you challenged him to a knife fight."

Why did Aidan have to say that in front of Stephen and Mrs. Vandenberg? They both stared at her.

She pretended to be nonchalant. "I wanted to get you to come here tonight."

"You didn't lie about your knife skills. We saw you out there." Aidan looked impressed. "You got some pretty slick moves."

Even Scruffy Beard looked impressed. "You quite a street fighter, mama."

Diego nodded. "Yeah, you saved that little girl."

"I'm not little. I'm twelve," Joline said indignantly.

From his lofty sixteen or seventeen years, Diego said, "Ya look like a shrimp to me."

Joline crossed her arms and huffed, but Diego had turned away. He faced Nettie. "You and me got us a promise. Let's throw down."

Nettie held up her hands. "I don't have anything to use." *Please go away, Diego.* She didn't want other people watching this interaction, especially not Stephen. What must he be thinking about her now?

Diego tossed a closed switchblade in Nettie's direction. She caught it easily one-handed.

His eyes lit up. "Yo, mama, you bad." He flicked his head toward Scruffy Beard. "Hey, Cogan, gimme yours."

The knife fitted Nettie's hand perfectly. The heft of the switchblade felt so familiar, so right. She only had to press the button, and the blade would shoot out. Her fingers itched to try it.

Instead, she handed it back. "I can't." *Not just can't, but won't.* Those days were over.

"Aww . . . Come on." Diego eyed her arm. "You gonna let a little scratch stop you."

Stephen wouldn't let Diego get away with bullying Nettie. He stepped between them. "A little scratch?"

Diego turned his small, mean eyes and challenging expression to Stephen. "She don't need you interfering."

"Leave her alone." Stephen deepened his tone in warning.

"Aww . . . ain't that sweet," one of the teens sneered.

Cogan laughed. "She don't need you. Your wife's a bad—"

Aidan elbowed him before he could finish. "They ain't married."

Diego's eyebrows rose. "You wanna fight me instead?" He held up the switchblade and made a few thrusts in Stephen's direction.

"Come on, Snake. Leave 'em alone." Aidan motioned for the other guys to come with him. "You don't want to fight, do you, Nettie?"

She shook her head. Then, she turned to Mrs. Vandenberg. "One thing I forgot to suggest—we need to forbid weapons in the building."

Mrs. Vandenberg had been eyeing the switchblade warily. "I'd already come to that conclusion. I'll get a sign posted."

Aidan caught Nettie's attention and shook his head as if the suggestion were crazy. "Not to be disrespectful, Mrs. V. A sign ain't gonna work."

Mrs. Vandenberg turned her head to look at him. "You think not, Aidan?"

"I know it won't."

Nettie backed him up. "Aidan's right."

"We can't frisk people coming into the center." Mrs. Vandenberg looked horrified.

Aidan flapped a hand like it was no big deal. "All the high schools around here use metal detectors. Kids are used to them."

His friends bobbed their heads.

Mrs. Vandenberg sighed. "I'll look into it. And I'd like you boys to keep those knives put away."

"Will do, Mrs. V." Aidan gave a cheery wave and

herded his friends toward the hallway. "Okay if we play some pool before we go?"

"Of course." She pinned each of them with a pointed glance. "I hope you'll all be willing to become mentors to some of the younger kids at the center."

Diego's eyes gleamed. "Ya mean teach 'em ta use a blade?"

"Definitely not. Besides, you'll be leaving them at home." Bestowing a beatific smile on him, she added, "If my plan works, nobody in this neighborhood will ever need to carry a knife again."

Several of the boys snickered.

Diego shook his head. "Keep dreamin', lady."

"I will. And I'll do plenty of praying for all of you. God can work miracles."

Stephen wasn't too sure about changing the gangs in the neighborhood, but he'd seen Mrs. Vandenberg's prayers at work. If he were those boys, he wouldn't be sneering.

Chapter Nineteen

Nettie was grateful her sleeve covered her scraped arm and the butterfly bandage. She didn't want Gideon or Caroline asking how she'd gotten the cut. And at the market on Tuesday morning, she tried not to wince as she fixed the salads and carried the heavy containers to the display cases.

Aidan breezed in as she washed broccoli and set it on the chopping board. "How you doing?" His gaze went to her left arm. "I can't believe you—"

Nettie held up her right hand to stop him. "Please," she whispered, "don't tell anyone."

His teasing tone showed he didn't plan to keep her secret. "You don't want everyone to know how skilled you are with a knife?"

Nettie brandished the knife she'd picked up to chop salad ingredients. "They already know my skills."

Aidan jumped back and held up his hands as if frightened. "Whoa. Don't go after me with that."

"She won't," Gideon said, "if you get to work."

Aidan laughed. "That's how you keep employees in line? You threaten them with Nettie's mad knife skills?"

She sent him a pleading glance.

He recovered quickly. "I mean look at how she's de-capitating that broccoli."

"*Jah*, she's *gut* at that." Gideon headed back to the rotisserie.

If Nettie hadn't been so nervous about Gideon discovering her real knifing abilities, she might have savored his compliment.

She found, though, Gideon's opinion of her didn't matter as much to her as Stephen's. How low would Stephen's evaluation of her sink if he ever found out the truth?

Nettie tried to push Stephen from her mind. As she'd told Joline on Saturday night, she and Stephen had no future together. Yet, no matter how hard she tried, Nettie struggled to keep her thoughts from straying to his touches and her dreams. If her past had been different, she could have remarried. But no Amish man would consider her for a wife if she told them about her life.

Even Gideon only knew parts of her past. She hadn't told his brother everything. Back then, she'd been young and foolish—doing what she had to do to survive and hiding any sordid, inconvenient details.

Unfortunately, even before Fern entered the picture, Nettie stood no chance. Not if she'd been completely honest. And now that she'd spent time with Stephen, she didn't want to settle for Gideon's brotherly love.

Outside, sirens split the air, startling Nettie back to the salad making. Everyone had been busy prepackaging individual salads for lunch. Aidan's head shot up.

"What's that?" His hands shook.

"Police cars? Sounds like it's out front."

Aidan danced from one foot to the other. Nettie's heart went out to him. Sirens still made her nervous.

The shrill noise died, to be followed by an ominous silence. Then someone pounded on the front door. Russell clattered downstairs to answer it.

"Look at what they did." His yelling echoed through the empty building.

Low murmuring came from the front of the market, interspersed with loud curses and complaints.

Most of the conversation remained garbled, until Russell shouted, "That's not all. Come upstairs."

Several pairs of boots and shoes clomped up the stairs.

"I should have pressed charges on Saturday." Russell's loud, indignant voice carried throughout the market.

Aidan froze. *Saturday?* he mouthed.

Fern tried to comfort him, and Nettie sent him a silent message. *Stay strong.* The police couldn't be here for him, could they? She hoped not. She trusted her instincts. If she was right, Aidan had to be innocent.

"What do you think happened?" Aidan's face creased into worry lines.

Gideon started out of the stand. "While they're upstairs, I'm going to see."

"I want to go with you." Aidan pressed a lid onto the container of applesauce he'd filled.

Caroline and Fern followed Gideon and Aidan. Nettie trailed behind. She wasn't sure she wanted to see what had brought the police to the market. An aisle away from Ridley's stand, they all stopped dead.

All his glass cases had been painted black. Red graffiti had been sprayed over the black. Red and black squiggles and swear words covered the walls behind the counter.

Grease had been smeared across the floor in front of the stand.

Aidan looked sick. "I shoulda told my friends about Bo not pressing charges."

Now that she'd met them, Nettie didn't like to think of Aidan's friends getting in trouble. When Gideon suggested they should get back to the stand, Nettie agreed. Aidan shouldn't be standing here looking guilty.

Before they could move, Russell stomped down the stairs with the police. Stabbing his finger at Aidan, Russell growled, "Arrest him. He's the culprit."

"You have any proof?" the policewoman asked.

"Look at his expression. That proves he's guilty."

"We can't arrest people based on their expressions. If we did . . ."

Aidan snorted. "Guess they'd have to lock you up."

Russell thrust his finger in Aidan's direction again. "He and his gangster friends did this."

"Do you know anything about this?" the officer asked Aidan.

Nettie had been about to protest, but Aidan, legs apart and arms akimbo, faced the officer with a defiant look. "I know my rights. You can't question me without my parents and a lawyer."

"Told ya he was a juvie," Russell spat out. "How many teenagers know to ask for a lawyer? And if he's innocent, why would he need a lawyer?"

Nettie muttered only loud enough for Aidan to hear, "He needs one so he's not railroaded into detention when he's innocent."

He shot her a grateful look as several other officers cordoned off the area with yellow caution tape.

That brought back some terrible memories. Nettie trembled inside for Aidan. She'd seen people convicted for crimes they didn't do. She prayed he wouldn't be one of them.

Police cars surrounded the front entrance when Stephen and Amos arrived at the market.

"I wonder what's going on." Stephen pulled around the lower end of the building and took the back way to the horse shelter.

"It doesn't look good." Amos tied up the horse. "Hope nobody's hurt."

"I don't see an ambulance." That brought back memories of the grand opening and Nettie getting hurt. He hoped she was all right. As soon as he could, he'd go down to check on her.

Once again, Stephen was grateful his children were in school instead of at the market. He hadn't expected a country market to be the scene of so much police activity.

He and Amos slipped through the employee entrance. Over on the other side of the front doors, a small crowd had gathered near Ridley's stand. Stephen felt sorry for whoever owned that business. They had a terrible mess to clean up.

Amos gasped. "Looks like Bo's been vandalized." He lowered his voice. "Do you think those teens from last weekend did it?"

"I hope not." Stephen wouldn't want to see Aidan and his friends get into trouble. Not after they'd helped rescue Joline. "Listen, Amos, I'm going to go by their stand to see if Aidan's all right. I won't be long."

Stephen didn't mention he had another reason for stopping by Hartzler's. First and foremost, he wanted to assure himself Nettie had suffered no ill effects. He'd prayed for her all weekend. And now Aidan had been added to that list.

A crowd had gathered around Hartzler's Chicken Barbecue. Many stand owners had come to find out what had happened, and quite a few of them studied Aidan with suspicion.

When Stephen caught Nettie's attention, her eyes lit up. His pulse sped up. Was she as glad to see him as he was to see her? His joy stretched his lips so wide his cheeks ached. Suddenly, her gaze grew shuttered.

Ach, he should have toned down his reaction. He'd frightened her back into her shell. But her initial response had been positive. He tucked that into his heart.

Are you all right? he mouthed. He tilted his head toward the sleeve covering the knife wound.

Alarm flashed across her face, and she sneaked looks to see if anyone had noticed their interaction. She sent off signals of desperation.

After checking again to be sure nobody was watching, she mouthed back, *Please, don't say anything*.

He nodded. Hadn't she told her family? Or did she mean she didn't want any customers to know?

I'm fine, she added.

Behind her, Aidan fiddled with the fryer and rotisserie. They wouldn't be cooking French fries this early, and Gideon usually waited to start the chickens until later in the morning. Aidan must be avoiding the gawkers. Poor kid.

Stephen couldn't get near enough to talk to Nettie or get Aidan's attention. Nettie kept sneaking peeks at him, so he tried asking one more silent question, *What about Aidan?*

He's innocent. Russell's trying to frame him.

That was so unfair. Stephen was well aware that Russell lied and cheated. In fact, he'd made up his mind to get Amos's rent money refunded this morning. Stephen had tucked his receipt in his pocket for proof. Too bad his brother hadn't insisted on a receipt as well.

Cheating stand owners was bad enough, but to accuse an innocent teen of a crime was low-down.

Let me know if I can help.

Nettie nodded and beamed at him. Then, she noticed one of the stand owners staring from him to her. She quickly turned her attention to the salads.

Stephen rushed back to his stand before the market opened. He didn't want anyone getting the wrong idea. Plus, he disliked sticking Amos with all the setup. He needed to be surc Nettie was okay, though.

Keys jangling, Russell brushed past Stephen.

Stephen hurried after him. "Hey, Russell, I need to talk to you a minute."

"No time. The cops are waiting for me at the other end of the market."

Ordinarily, Stephen would have written it off as Russell trying to get away from a possible confrontation. This time, though, the market manager probably was telling the truth.

"How're things?" Amos asked when Stephen entered the stand.

He told his brother about Nettie's message. "Aidan's a good kid. I'm sure he didn't do it." Although he didn't know Aidan's friends well, he hoped they hadn't either.

As the day went on, rumors flowed through the market like sewage from an exploding wastewater pipe, splattering Aidan's reputation. Stephen tried to combat the gossip by repeating that Aidan deserved to be considered innocent until he'd been charged. But the stories grew worse each time people repeated them. And Russell added to the smears by running around the market, loudly blaming Aidan.

When Russell went past their stand around noon, Stephen chased after him. Before he could catch up, Russell strode out the side door. By the time Stephen pushed the door open, Russell had his phone to his ear and was ducking behind the buggy shelter.

Few people came out to the shelter during the day, so it was secluded enough for a private conversation. But it did seem odd that Russell needed so much secrecy.

Not wanting to disturb Russell while he was talking, Stephen entered the shelter and petted his horse, intending to wait until the market manager walked past.

Russell's gruff voice penetrated the wooden walls. "I snapped a quick picture and texted it. It should be good enough to ID him. If it isn't clear enough, let me know."

After a long pause, Russell burst out in an exasperated whisper, "I already told you. I can't pay you until I get the insurance money."

Stephen's hand stilled. Had he just overheard something important? He tried putting a different spin on the words, but he kept coming back to Aidan. Should this conversation be reported? Stephen wasn't sure if his interpretation was right. He'd keep it to himself for now.

To be on the safe side, he stayed inside the shelter until

Russell returned to the market. Then he entered the market through a different door and headed Russell off.

"Hey, Russell, can I talk to you now?"

The market manager blew out an exasperated breath. "Can it wait until another time? Today's been hectic."

"It won't take long." Stephen wasn't going to allow Russell to put him off. "I just want you to return my brother's rent money for this month."

Russell frowned. "Don't know what you're talking about."

Stephen pulled the receipt out of his pocket and held it out. "Remember this? You also collected money from Amos."

"You have any proof of that?"

"We can get a copy of the canceled check from the bank if we need to. I'm sure Mrs. Vandenberg wouldn't be happy to hear about double charging on stand rent."

At that threat, Russell paled. "I can't get in my office until the crime-scene tape is gone. Sorry." He didn't sound the least bit sorry.

"I'm sure you have other sources of money."

"Not right now. Hold off a bit. And don't say anything to Mrs. Vandenberg until I see what I can do."

Stephen wanted to be fair, but he didn't want to let Russell get away with not paying Amos back. "I'll give you until Saturday. That's when I'll be seeing Mrs. Vandenberg."

Russell glared. "That doesn't give me much time."

"I'm sure the bank can issue you some emergency checks if the crime tape isn't down by then." The bank here in Ephrata had done that for Stephen when he'd opened an account after moving from New York.

Russell flapped a hand as if waving off a pesky fly. "Like I said, I'll see what I can do." He scurried off.

Stephen had a sinking feeling they might never see that money. He didn't trust Russell. He'd find a way to wriggle out of paying.

Engrossed in figuring out how to deal with Russell's possible excuses, Stephen ran right into Nettie. He reached out to steady her but stopped himself from grasping her upper arms. He gently held her forearms as he backed away.

"I'm sorry. I didn't hit your sore arm, did I?"

Nettie glanced around as if to be sure nobody had noticed their encounter. Then she lifted her head. When her eyes met his, Stephen was lost in their chocolatey depths. So lost he forgot to move his hands from her arms.

Nettie swallowed down the emotions overwhelming her. She didn't want Stephen to let go. His warm, strong fingers sent tingles through her. She could stay here forever, wrapped in the peace and comfort she always experienced in his presence.

An *Englischer* sidled past them, startling Nettie from the spell. What had she been thinking? They were in public with dozens of prying eyes fixed on them. She shook herself free.

"I'm sorry," Stephen repeated.

This time, he must mean for holding her. She was too

tongue-tied to reply. She should be sorry too, but she wasn't.

"I didn't want to hurt your arm," he explained.

"You didn't." She hoped he couldn't read the longing mixed with the ache that had caused her to flee the stand.

He glanced around as if checking to be sure he couldn't be overheard. "How is it?"

Nettie bit her lip. The scratch stung like crazy, and with all the moving she'd done today, the butterfly bandage pulled and burned. But none of it hurt as much as the events going on around her today.

She worried about Aidan as well as about her children. Every day, Fern and Gideon seemed to be falling more deeply in love. It was only a matter of time . . .

Stephen stood in front of her, waiting for an answer. Between her reaction to his touch and the way her mind had been racing in circles, Nettie couldn't remember what he'd asked. "What?"

"Your arm."

Nettie was pretty sure the itching and smarting meant the cut was getting better. "It's healing."

"*Gut. Danke* again for rescuing Joline. I just wish you hadn't gotten hurt."

The tenderness in his tone melted Nettie's insides. She forced herself to look elsewhere.

Stephen must have sensed her discomfort because he changed the subject. "How is Aidan?"

"He's scared Russell's going to get him sent to detention."

Stephen's long, deep sigh mirrored Nettie's frustration.

"If you see Mrs. Vandenberg before I do," he said, "can

you ask her to come talk to me? I heard something today that might help Aidan."

"Really? What?"

"I'd rather not say until I talk to her. I might have gotten it wrong."

Nettie suspected he'd gotten it right. The more she spent time around him, the more she'd seen his measured decisions. She'd changed her opinion of him since the first day she'd met him.

Thank God, she'd been able to stop that ladder from tipping. Back then, she'd yelled at him for taking risks. Even remembering the near fall, she tensed up as all the fear and other horrible memories came flooding back.

"Is something wrong?"

Stephen's worried expression brought her back to the present.

"I was just thinking about you on that ladder." Her voice shook.

"I'm sorry I frightened you." He studied the cement by his feet. "That had to be one of the scariest experiences of my life—after the tire swing and last Saturday night."

Last Saturday night had given Nettie nightmares. She reminded herself she'd saved Joline. She'd done what she had to do. But flashes of her previous life kept her awake. And now Gideon had added to that terror. She'd been so upset she'd fled the stand. And she hadn't paid attention to where she was going and ran into Stephen. Her unexpected attraction to him made her situation even more unbearable.

Stephen studied her. He seemed to see deep into her soul. Nettie wished she could hide her roiling emotions.

In a low, gentle voice, he said, "I wish we could both forget the pain from our pasts."

As much as Nettie wanted that to be true, only amnesia would allow her to forget all the failure, shame, and tragedy. And now she'd be starting that cycle all over again with her own children.

Chapter Twenty

After Nettie rushed off, Stephen couldn't get her out of his mind. Her sadness weighed on him. Mrs. Vandenberg had been right that Nettie needed someone to care for her, but what could he do?

Dating didn't seem to be the answer. Not when Joline was so opposed to Nettie. And right now, he had so much to do. Betty had helped Amos find a home and a market stand closer to her family. His brother would be moving in a few weeks. To replace the pigs Amos planned to take, Stephen had several auctions to attend. They were also spending evenings and days off fixing Amos's house. The house had been vacant for a while, so it needed a great deal of work. And the barn had to be rebuilt.

Then, he had the children to consider. They'd all be finished with school next week, so they'd be joining him in the stand. Having them would cover for losing Amos. And he'd talked to Joline about school and her negative attitude, but he needed to schedule her testing.

But excuses and commitments didn't lessen Stephen's guilt for not helping Nettie. They'd both agreed to work in the center on Saturday evenings and bring their children.

Maybe he could use that time to encourage her. With no other Amish families around, he didn't have to worry about people getting the wrong idea or starting gossip.

In the late afternoon, Mrs. Vandenberg stopped by. "Nettie mentioned you wanted to talk to me."

Amos's eyebrows rose. Stephen wished she hadn't said that. Now he'd face his brother's curiosity.

"Will you be all right alone if I talk to Mrs. Vandenberg for a few minutes?" At Amos's nod, Stephen stepped out of the stand. "Could we go outside where nobody can hear?"

"Now you have me wondering." She tottered along beside him, her cane tapping a jauntier rhythm than her shuffling steps.

Stephen reached for her arm as they stepped outside. She waved to her driver.

"Let's talk in the car. No one can eavesdrop."

A little guilt twisted inside Stephen. Eavesdropping was how he'd gotten this information. When they'd both settled inside the Bentley, he recounted what Russell had said on the phone.

"What time was that?"

"Right before noon."

"Interesting." Mrs. Vandenberg looked thoughtful. "I've hired a private investigator to look into this. He has contacts at the police station. I wonder who Russell called."

"It might be nothing," Stephen said, "but I wanted you to know.

"Then again, it might be significant." If Mrs. Vandenberg's crafty smile was any indication, he'd given her an important clue. "I'm convinced those teens are innocent, but we have to prove it."

If anyone could do it, Mrs. Vandenberg could. His spirits lighter, he returned to the stand. Amos kept giving Stephen sideways glances, but his brother waited until they had a lull in customers. "Something going on between you and Nettie?"

"*Neh*. Why?" Stephen went for a rag to clean up a small spill.

"She's giving people messages for you?"

"I bumped into her earlier after I talked to Russell." Stephen didn't mention the collision had been an actual one. "I told her if she saw Mrs. Vandenberg to send her to our stand."

Instead of pursuing more information about Nettie or Mrs. Vandenberg, Amos asked, "Russell?"

"*Jah*. I tried to get your money back. He says he can't get into his office. I gave him until Saturday."

"I don't expect to see that money again."

Stephen had already suspected that. It bothered him that Russell could get away with cheating. And with framing innocent teens.

On Thursday morning, Aidan didn't show up for work. Instead, Nick took his son's place.

Fern asked the question Nettie had been wondering. "Where's Aidan?"

Nettie edged nearer to catch the conversation.

"On probation. Thanks to that—" Nick bit off the next word. "That liar."

"They think Aidan's guilty?"

"What else could they think when Russell sends in three stoolies who pretended to be eyewitnesses?"

When Russell walked by, they lowered their voices, and Nettie couldn't hear anything until Gideon asked if Aidan had gone to jail.

"Nah, they don't usually do that to juveniles." Nick's face turned almost purple. "He's on probation. That dirty rat Russell also wanted to get a restraining order to forbid Aidan from coming on market property."

A restraining order? Probation? How could Russell do that to an innocent kid?

Nettie hoped whatever Stephen told Mrs. Vandenberg on Tuesday would help Aidan. And that the truth would come out.

They didn't have long to wait.

On Thursday, Mrs. Vandenberg insisted that Russell allow Aidan to work in the market, so Aidan was working on Saturday when Mrs. Vandenberg arrived. She'd gathered everyone around her to share some important news when two police officers burst through the back doors.

Aidan cowered behind his dad. "I didn't do anything wrong. You'll tell them that, Mrs. V, won't you?"

"Stop sniveling," Nick barked. "We'll fight this. I'm not letting you go to jail."

"Calm down." Leaning against the glass display case, Mrs. Vandenberg tapped the tip of her cane on the counter. "Russell's going to be shocked when these officers arrest the real culprit."

"It's not me." Aidan looked sick as the officers approached the counter, but they marched past the chicken barbecue stand and headed for the main staircase.

"Looks like they're going up to talk to Russell," Gideon said.

He stood so close to Fern, Nettie's breath constricted. If Gideon courted Fern . . .

Fern gave Gideon a sickeningly sweet smile before turning to Mrs. Vandenberg. "Are you sure they found out who did it?"

"I know they have, and I'm sure Russell will be down shortly. Then you'll all find out who vandalized the market. And they know it's not you, Aidan, so stop your shaking. Russell owes you a major apology."

When boots clomped downstairs, Russell's protests echoed through the market. "You've made a terrible mistake. It was that juvie, I tell you."

When they appeared, burly policemen flanked Russell, one on each side. And his hands were handcuffed behind his back.

"What?" Aidan shouted.

As he passed them, Russell tossed his head frantically in Aidan's direction. "That's the real criminal. That kid right there."

"Come along, Mr. Evans," one officer said.

"You have no evidence," Russell insisted.

Mrs. Vandenberg hobbled into their path. "I'm afraid they do, Russell. Lots of evidence."

Russell's face was livid. "You betrayed me?"

"No, you betrayed yourself."

The officers nodded to Mrs. Vandenberg, then dragged Russell around her.

Everyone in the stand stared after Russell, their mouths open. Customers stayed frozen in place until the officers escorted Russell out the door. Then buzzing started all around the market. Everyone circled Mrs. Vandenberg to find out what happened.

"Don't look so surprised," she said. "Russell is the logical suspect."

"I don't understand." Fern wrinkled her brow. "Why would Russell vandalize a brand-new market stand?"

"He collected insurance money for the vandalism, and he faked the robbery."

"But how did you find out?" Gideon asked.

"Most of what the investigator discovered needs to stay confidential until the trial." Mrs. Vandenberg's secretive smile left everyone curious.

"Can't you tell us anything?" Nick begged. He hadn't stopped grinning since Russell had gone past in hand-cuffs.

"First of all, I thought it curious that Russell didn't turn on the security cameras over the weekend."

Nettie had wondered about that too. "Very odd. Especially since he acted like the teens' protest last Saturday frightened him. Wouldn't he worry they'd come back?" She sent Aidan an apologetic look to reassure him she didn't believe he'd do anything like that.

"Exactly. And thanks to Stephen Lapp"—Mrs. Vandenberg gave Nettie a knowing look—"who overheard an interesting conversation, it led the investigator and the police to some additional incriminating evidence."

Nettie tried to hide her happiness. So Stephen had been able to help after all. Mrs. Vandenberg mentioned additional clues, and the others questioned Russell's motives, but Nettie remained focused on Stephen. She'd have to tell him he'd broken the case wide open.

She tuned back in as Mrs. Vandenberg finished summing up Russell's reasons.

"Most important, Russell wanted to blame someone who'd have a motive to hurt Bo."

"He set me up?" Aidan slammed his fist onto the counter, making the glass jars of candy rattle. "That dirty, low-down . . ."

"Weasel?" Mrs. Vandenberg suggested.

Nick chuckled, and everyone turned to stare. His whole body shook with deep belly laughs. "You have to admit"—he sniggered—"seeing Russell strong-armed outta here in handcuffs . . ."

Aidan smirked. "Yeah, that was the best."

Nettie agreed. Russell had it coming. And she rejoiced that at least once the system had worked in favor of an innocent teen who'd been framed. Now she couldn't wait to tell Stephen.

The only thing spoiling her joy stood a short distance from her. Fern and Gideon mooned over each other, while Mrs. Vandenberg grinned like a proud parent.

When Nettie came rushing over to their stand, her whole face aglow, and Daed smiled back with delight, Joline's fears kicked in. Nettie had made a promise. Could she be trusted?

Daed hurried over, ignoring the next customer. So unlike him.

"You did it!" she announced as if he'd won a prize or something.

Joline wasn't about to let this blossom into anything. She marched over. "Did what?"

Daed frowned at her demanding tone, but Joline didn't care. And Nettie appeared too thrilled to notice.

"Did you see the cops take Russell out in handcuffs?" she asked.

"*Jah*, we did." Joline earned herself a warning glare. She crossed her arms. Nettie had spoken loudly enough for everyone to hear, so why couldn't other people be part of the conversation too?

"Joline, you have a customer." Daed nodded to the *Englischer* standing near the ham loaf.

So not fair. Daed had walked away from the customer Amos was now waiting on. The *Englischer* could wait for Amos to finish. Joline didn't want to miss Nettie's news. And even more importantly, she didn't want Daed and Nettie to spend time alone together.

When Nettie fixed her hair last Saturday, Joline had seen how kind Nettie could be. What if she changed her mind about not marrying Daed and turned that sweetness on him? Joline tried to keep her ears tuned in to their discussion.

Daed leaned over the counter to be closer to Nettie. *Ach!*

"May I help you?" Joline forced herself to ask the customer. She could barely hear them.

"A ham loaf please." The woman pointed to the one in the front.

Joline snatched it out of the case and detoured around the cutting table to get a bag to wrap it.

"Mrs. Vandenberg said . . ."

With her lips parted and her eyes shining, Nettie looked like a woman in love. She had no intention of keeping her promise. Joline just knew it.

". . . the phone call you heard ended up being a clue."

"It did?" Daed's surprised look changed to a pleased one. "I'm so glad I could help."

"You saved Aidan from a life of crime."

Daed laughed. "I didn't do anything special."

Joline agreed Nettie had gone overboard.

"You don't understand." Nettie's expression grew serious. "Do you know how many kids end up going bad after a false arrest and conviction? Lots of teens get in with the wrong crowd and end up back in jail."

How did Nettie know so much about that? Maybe she learned knife fighting from one of those criminals. Joline would suggest that to Daed.

He just looked impressed at Nettie's facts.

"Joline?" Amos beckoned to her. "Your customer is waiting for that ham loaf. The bags are over here."

Oops! She hadn't meant to take so long. Joline scurried back, bagged up the ham loaf, and took the *Englischer's* money.

After her experience last weekend, Joline hadn't been planning to go to the center with Daed tonight. She'd changed her mind.

After supper that evening, Gideon surprised Nettie by offering to help with the dishes. Grateful to have their old partnership back, she relaxed. Maybe she'd read more into Gideon's and Fern's interactions, and everything would go back to normal. Then, she glimpsed his grim expression.

Perhaps if she reminded him of his connection to her children, it might soften his heart. "Before you start, Gideon, I have something I'd like to say." She swallowed hard. "The boys miss you when you aren't here at bedtime."

He reached for the glass she'd rinsed. "I've tried to be here for all of you."

"I'm grateful for that and for the way you tried so hard to rescue Thomas."

Gideon winced.

Maybe she shouldn't have brought up his brother. Gideon blamed himself for not rescuing Thomas. Nettie shared that guilt. That day, she'd remained frozen, unable to move.

When Gideon recounted his failure, she tried to reassure him. "You did your best."

She needed to get the conversation back on track. She'd only meant to inspire his deeper feelings for his nephews and nieces. Instead, she'd brought up their shared pain, plunging them both into gloom.

To relieve the tension, Nettie gave him her sunniest smile. "I also appreciate you taking care of us since then."

He didn't respond.

She lowered her head and fidgeted with the glass in her hands. "I guess things are going to be different."

"That's what I wanted to discuss." Gideon took a deep breath. "First of all, I want you to know I'll always support you and the children. That will never change."

Nettie scrubbed hard at a plate, wishing she could wash away what he planned to say.

"I'm not in a position to date anyone right now," Gideon continued, "but as soon as I am, I plan to ask—"

"Fern." Although Nettie attempted to say the name in a neutral tone, the word dripped with bitterness. Her shoulders slumped, she rinsed the plate and handed it to him.

As much as she wanted to protest, Nettie couldn't do that. Gideon deserved to go on with his life. He'd willingly taken on caring for his brother's children, but she and the children had weighed him down, preventing him from living his life.

Once Gideon started dating Fern, though, how long did she and the children have before they needed to find their own place to live? Where would they go?

He couldn't afford to keep up two households. Not once he had his own children.

Chapter Twenty-One

Nettie longed to run to the bedroom to be alone, but she'd promised Mrs. Vandenberg to come to the center and bring the children. For the past week, Nettie had been eager to spend time with Stephen. Even if she could never date him, she enjoyed his company, and the center gave her an opportunity to talk to him. An opportunity she'd never have otherwise.

"Mamm?" Katie came up behind Nettie, startling her. "Esther told me all the fun things they have at the center. I really want to go, but . . ."

"But what?" Nettie had a hard time concentrating on her daughter's whining about a small matter when she worried about whether they'd have a roof over their heads.

"Joline." Katie's face contorted in fear.

Nettie had forgotten about Stephen's children coming to the center too. "Wait until she picks an activity, and then you can find a different room."

"But what if she follows me?"

"Stephen and I will both be there. I'm sure you'll be fine." Actually, Nettie intended to keep a good eye on

Joline. After last Saturday, Nettie doubted Stephen's daughter would be foolish enough to go outside, but it would be better not to take any chances.

Katie gave her a skeptical look.

"I bet Joline will try gymnastics." She'd been fascinated by the girl practicing backflips on the trampoline. Until Stephen had scolded her. "Why don't you and Esther go to the art room or the library?"

"Maybe the library." Katie cheered up. "Joline can't read."

"What do you mean?"

"Teacher Emily asked Joline to stand up and read aloud. She made so many mistakes."

"Perhaps she was nervous." After all, they'd only just started in a new school.

"*Neh.* One day, the teacher asked Joline to sit by her desk and read. Joline couldn't do it."

Hmm. Could she be acting out because she struggled in school? And did Stephen know? The teacher would have told him, wouldn't she? Maybe she had trouble at her previous school.

"That's too bad." Nettie had endured teasing and laughter from her classmates. She and Joline had much in common. If Joline didn't have so much animosity, Nettie could have offered help.

Katie danced from the room, saying over her shoulder, "Esther will like the library too. And mean old Joline won't come in."

That reminded Nettie of Joline's promise last weekend. She'd agreed—reluctantly, it seemed—not to tease Katie. Would she keep her word?

* * *

As soon as Nettie slid into the large van Mrs. Vandenberg had sent to pick up both families, Stephen noticed Nettie's mood had plummeted. She'd been so happy and excited a few hours ago at the market. He'd never seen her that joyful. Now she looked as if her whole world had fallen apart. He wished he could do something to help, but what?

After she'd settled into a back seat with Katie clinging to her hand, Stephen turned around and mouthed, *Is everything all right?*

Nettie only shrugged and bent to help Katie fasten her seat belt.

What had plunged her into such despair? At the market, she'd bubbled over with excitement. First over the help he'd been to Aidan, then about bringing all four children to the center tonight. She'd said her sons and daughters had been eager to come. They all appeared enthusiastic. All except Katie.

He didn't blame her. Not after he'd heard how Joline had tormented the small girl.

When they got to the center, he made a point of sidling next to Katie to whisper, "I'll keep an eye on Joline. She won't hurt you."

Katie stared up at him with trusting and grateful eyes. He had to keep his promise.

Then he moved closer to Nettie. "Is there anything I can help you with?"

"*Neh*." She too turned to him with an appreciative gaze. "It's something I have to deal with alone, but *danke* for asking."

"If you want to talk about it later after the children are occupied . . ."

"I don't think so."

She'd made it clear she had no intention of sharing her burden with him, but Stephen didn't plan to give up. Even if she didn't want to confide in him, he could follow Mrs. Vandenberg's directive to cheer Nettie up. Maybe they could talk about Aidan.

Stephen had loved the passion in Nettie's expression when she spoke about keeping inner city kids out of trouble. Perhaps he could encourage her to talk about that. Mrs. Vandenberg might be able to use Nettie's ideas to add to the center or to start another one of the projects her center sponsored.

"I'd like to hear more about Aidan."

Her face relaxed into a fleeting smile. As it faded, Stephen missed its sunshine. If only she didn't carry such heavy burdens. He longed to lift them for her, to bring back the delight she'd shown earlier.

Several children, who looked to be around age ten, barged up to Joline and Abby, who'd been leading their siblings down the hall.

"You all in a play or somethin'?" one of the boys demanded while the others surged closer staring at both families' Plain clothes.

As the ragtag group surrounded them, Katie shrank back. Lenny and Sadie hid behind Nettie's skirt. Her face tightened and took on a guarded expression.

Joline stepped forward. "*Neh*, we're not."

An older boy laughed. "Neigh? You a horse?" The others snickered.

Stephen edged forward, hoping to stop her before she got in trouble.

Joline clenched her hands at her sides. She didn't like being laughed at, but she wouldn't let this boy intimidate her. "These are our everyday clothes because we're Amish."

He must have sensed she would get the better of him in a verbal battle. He gestured to her fists. "Wanna fight?"

Nettie set a hand on Joline's shoulder, and she glanced up, surprised.

"Fighting isn't the answer." Nettie kept her voice low.

Joline snorted. "You didn't think that last week when you got in the knife fight."

Everyone stared at Nettie. Even her own children had their mouths hanging open. She must not have told them.

Daed's voice, low and stern, cut through the stunned silence. "Joline!"

"Sorry," she muttered.

She hadn't meant to criticize Nettie. Not after what she'd done last Saturday. But if Nettie hadn't sounded so motherly, Joline never would have attacked her. Nettie's advice made Joline want to do the opposite. It also brought up some of Joline's soul-deep longings. She wanted a mother to love her—her own mother—not Nettie.

Every day since Nettie had combed her fingers through Joline's hair, Joline had ached for her *mamm*. That yearning had turned into a desperate need for an older woman to confide in.

In Mayville, Joline had been close to many older women in her church. She could go to them with questions. Here, Joline knew only one woman besides Nettie. But Amos's fiancée, Betty, acted too lighthearted and giggly. Joline couldn't imagine having a serious conversation with her.

And Nettie would never do. Joline could never trust her.

Joline had forgotten the kids around her. After her interest waned, the boy who'd challenged her shrugged and walked away. The others drifted after him.

Too bad. She itched for a fight. Anything to take her mind off not having a mother. She needed to run from these feelings she blamed Nettie for stirring up. "Can I go to the gym?"

Daed set a hand on Joline's shoulder to keep her in place. "Not until you apologize properly."

They'd talked about this in one of his many lectures this week. Daed insisted Joline look people in the eye and ask forgiveness. Not only was it the polite way to speak to people, but he also said others needed to see her regret. It also would make her think twice before saying something hurtful.

Joline didn't believe it would help. She always blurted things out before she thought. Even the Scripture verses Teacher Emily made Joline write hadn't changed her actions.

Just do it. Joline faced Nettie. "I'm sorry for what I said. Will you forgive me?"

Nettie had tears in her eyes. "Of course."

Katie tugged at her *mamm*'s skirt. "Were you really in a knife fight, or did Joline lie?"

"Katie." Nettie's tone held a warning note. "We'll talk later."

"But I want to know now."

"There's nothing much to tell."

"A bad guy grabbed me outside in the alley." Joline widened her eyes at Katie trying to convey the scariness. Something—maybe the huge ache inside as Nettie's hand moved to her daughter's shoulder—made Joline want to frighten Katie. At least a little. "Your *mamm* came out and made him drop the knife."

"Mamm?" Katie turned an *I-don't-believe-it* look in Nettie's direction.

"I'll explain more later."

"But Mamm . . ."

"I said later." Nettie's tone rang with finality. "Where do you want to go?" She started down the hall. "You can decide while we walk Joline to gymnastics."

How did Nettie know which gym Joline wanted? A tiny voice inside urged her to contradict Nettie. Joline could say she meant the basketball or volleyball gym just to be contrary. But she'd dreamed of doing those tricks the girl had done last week. Joline had even hidden her swimsuit under her dress so she'd look like she had on one of those leotards.

She also wanted to try that horse-thing Nettie had talked about. Joline could ride horses well. This might be a chance to show up Nettie. And she hoped she could make Nettie tell the truth about where she'd used that strange contraption. No way did Nettie learn it in school.

* * *

After they left Joline in the care of the gymnastics coach, Stephen waited for Abby. She trailed behind Esther and Katie, looking forlorn. "What would you like to do?"

"I don't know." She strained to hear what the other two girls were discussing.

Nettie leaned closer. "Do you like art, Abby?"

"I guess."

"*Jah*," Ben piped up, "she's a good draw-er."

"Hush, Ben." Abby acted annoyed, but her eyes lit up.

"Sadie would like to paint. Do you think you could watch her in the art room?"

"I guess," Abby said again, but she brightened a little.

Stephen smiled at Nettie. Abby always complained about being the youngest in the family. Nettie had made her feel grown-up by asking Abby to care for a little one. And she'd given Abby an activity that interested her and kept her from being left out.

"You're really good at this," Stephen said after they'd dropped off Sadie in Abby's care.

"At what?" Nettie seemed flustered, but pleased.

"At mothering." As he said it, a pang shot through Stephen. He ached for his children, who were going through life without a *mamm*.

Nettie flushed and turned away. "Esther, would you like to go to the library?"

His daughter ducked her head. "*Jah*," she answered softly.

"I already asked her, Mamm," Katie said.

Nettie smiled at both girls. "I thought so."

They reached the library entrance. "Wait here until we come back for you," Stephen told them.

They nodded, but their attention stayed fixed on shelves after shelves of books. Knowing Esther, she'd remain glued to a book all evening and have to be pried away when they left. How had Mrs. Vandenberg managed to stock a library in such a short time?

"Now," Nettie said, "what about you boys?" She looked to Matthew.

"I can watch the others," he offered, "if they want to play basketball."

"I figured we could count on you." Nettie favored him with a trusting smile, and he puffed out his chest. "Is that all right with the rest of you?" Nettie turned to check with Ben, David, and Lenny individually, but a chorus of enthusiastic *jah*s greeted her question.

Stephen couldn't get over the way she'd sensed what each of his children needed and handled them differently. It pointed up the gap in his children's lives and made Stephen's failings as a parent seem even more apparent. He tried, but he could never match Nettie's skills. Should he consider remarrying for his children's sakes?

Once all the children had been dropped off at their activities, Stephen and Nettie were alone.

Mrs. Vandenberg's cane clicked down the hallway. Her steps seemed livelier, although she still appeared shaky on her feet. "The children and their families seem to be enjoying themselves."

"They certainly do." Stephen matched her enthusiasm.

"You have a lot more people here this week than last week."

Despite the heavy weight she appeared to be carrying, Nettie seemed thrilled. "It's working. Kids are telling their friends."

"Did you see Aidan and his buddies arrived to help the preteens with pool and computer games?" Mrs. Vandenberg asked.

"That's wonderful." Nettie's slumped shoulders straightened, and her pinched lips curved upward. "It's great they're getting involved. I'm sure Aidan feels he owes you a lot."

Mrs. Vandenberg waved that away. "He owes me nothing. It was a joy to see truth prevail."

"That's true. It doesn't always." At that, Nettie looked downcast.

"You mentioned that before." Mrs. Vandenberg studied her. "Do you know of any other cases I should look into?"

"Not now. If only I'd known you years ago, you could have saved many teens from life in prison."

"Do you know some who could be rehabilitated?"

"It might be too late."

"Give me their names. I'll see what I can do. Perhaps we could work with the Innocence Project. I'd be happy to give them money and provide investigators to help."

"That would be wonderful." Nettie looked thoughtful. "You'll help some of the men and women who've been in prison for a while. But what about teens like Aidan who are getting framed? Or those who get sent to detention centers? Is there something we can do?"

"I know a few lawyers who'd be willing to work pro

bono. Why don't we set up a juvenile justice office here in the center? People can come in for free advice about their cases. Maybe we could staff it with some investigators too."

Nettie clasped her hands together, enraptured. "Mrs. V, you don't know how many lives you'll be saving."

She laughed. "I expect you'll tell me the statistics."

"I don't know exact numbers, but . . ."

Mrs. Vandenberg gave Nettie a tender, caring look. "God knew what He was doing when he directed me to ask you two to help with this project."

Stephen agreed that Nettie had been a huge asset to the center. Whenever she started talking about the needs of these city kids, she amazed him and left him feeling useless.

"Stephen, you've helped a lot too."

Had Mrs. Vandenberg read his mind?

"And you've been a real support on the other project I asked you to take on." After a sly glance at Nettie, Mrs. Vandenberg winked at him.

He could have died. Had Nettie caught that exchange? Would she guess what Mrs. Vandenberg meant? His collar felt so tight, it almost choked him. He ran a finger inside his neckline, but he couldn't stop the heat that swept from his chest to his cheeks.

Luckily, Nettie had stayed engrossed in her idea. She gave Mrs. Vandenberg a few more suggestions while Stephen struggled to regain his composure.

"Well, I'll get this idea set in motion." Mrs. Vandenberg turned to go. "Stephen, why don't you take Nettie into my office? You can have a private conversation there."

Leave it to Mrs. Vandenberg to put him in another tight spot. She had a way of boxing people in. If Stephen didn't take Nettie to the office, he'd come off as rude. But if he did take her, she might get the wrong idea.

Stephen suspected that's exactly what Mrs. Vandenberg had planned.

Chapter Twenty-Two

Being in the center made Nettie giddy with happiness at all the possibilities for the neighborhood children. At the same time, it couldn't heal all their hurts, reminding her of all her own inadequacies. And of why she shouldn't be spending time with Stephen, even though she enjoyed his company.

Mrs. Vandenberg kept throwing them together, hoping her matchmaking skills would light a spark. She'd lit an ember on Nettie's part, but cold, hard facts doused that tiny flicker before it could ignite. If Mrs. V kept fanning the flames, Nettie and Stephen could both end up burned.

Luckily, Stephen had no interest in her, but he took his obligations seriously, so he escorted her down the hall. Still, Nettie looked forward to discussing Aidan's narrow escape, Russell's arrest, and some of the new rooms and classes Mrs. V had added to the center.

After they'd entered the office, Stephen shut the door. "Nettie, I can't believe all the things you think of to help inner-city children. How do you—"

Once before, he'd asked her how she knew so much, and she'd cut him off. He stopped so abruptly now, he must have remembered that. Should she answer his question? He might not want to spend time around her if he learned the truth. Most likely, it would end their friendship. Nettie wasn't ready to do that. Not after Gideon's blow earlier tonight.

"I hope you don't mind me asking . . ." Stephen interrupted her downward spiral. "Something's bothering you. I'd be happy to listen if it would help." He motioned her to the comfiest chair and settled on a wooden, straightbacked one.

Did Mrs. Vandenberg use that for people she wanted to get rid of quickly? Nettie smiled to herself as she pictured Mrs. Vandenberg seating long-winded salesmen there.

"Want to share the joke?"

Stephen startled Nettie from her thoughts. How could he tell she'd been imagining something funny? Then she remembered the day he'd understood her mood perfectly. She might need to guard her feelings more around him.

She told him what she'd been thinking, and he laughed. "You're probably right. Although I'm not sure Mrs. Vandenberg needs an uncomfortable chair. She'd have no problem telling an unwanted visitor it's time to go."

"That's true."

The shared humor had eased some of the tension between them, but after Nettie stopped giggling, Stephen trained a thoughtful gaze on her again. "I'm not trying to pry, but this afternoon, you seemed so happy. Tonight, when you got in the car, you were upset."

Why did he have to be so perceptive? And honest?

"Sometimes talking about it helps." His caring expression invited her to share her problems.

Jah, but telling others often led to rejection.

"Nettie, whatever you say, I'd never tell anyone."

She believed him. But a lifetime of hurt cautioned her otherwise.

She wanted to shrug off his concern, but something in his face urged her to tell the truth. She didn't have to give him her whole history, just explain why she was upset tonight. "I got some bad news at suppertime. Gideon plans to date Fern."

"I'm sorry. It's not easy to lose someone you love."

What? Stephen thought she'd fallen in love with Gideon?

To be honest, she'd once hoped he'd marry her so she'd never have to fear for her children. And he was the only man who might accept her past. She could never tell anyone the whole truth, but Gideon knew more than anyone else. Deep inside, she'd always suspected she and Gideon had no future together, but tonight he'd confirmed it.

Slowly, she shook her head. "*Neh*, that's not it. I'm worried about my children."

Now it was Stephen's turn to look confused. Nettie could read the question in his eyes. He couldn't figure out what her children had to do with Fern and Gideon's relationship.

"Once Gideon marries, Fern will move into the house. The children and I will have no place to live. And after he and Fern start a family, my children will be too much of a burden."

"I see."

Did he? A homeless widow with four children struggling against poverty?

"Gideon became like a father to the children. They'll miss out on that." Nettie closed her eyes. How would David and Lenny handle no bedtime stories from their *onkel*? When she'd taken Gideon's place recently, her boys had complained she hadn't done as good a job as Gideon. Even more importantly, they needed a male role model.

That loss would be painful, but she had a deeper fear. "I also worry about my children going hungry."

"The church won't let that happen."

Stephen's reassurance didn't help. "I don't want charity. I tried never to be dependent on Gideon and his parents. I do most of the cooking and cleaning at the house, and I work at the market stand without pay to earn some of our keep."

"Getting help from the church isn't really charity. We're all doing things for each other. You can give back in other ways. I'm sure you help by taking meals to shut-ins or helping new mothers, hosting church and youth singings, donating goods to auctions, cooking for barn raisings and—"

Terror and panic flashed inside her.

Stephen must have noticed because he stopped abruptly. "I'm so sorry. I didn't mean to remind you . . ." Sympathy welled in his eyes. "I just wanted you to see you do plenty for the community."

Mamm had avoided charity of any kind. She'd refused government handouts or free church meals. Nettie had seen the effects poverty had on her mother. And Nettie had endured the pain as a child. She never wanted her own children to suffer.

But she had other deeper reasons. "That's not the only problem," she mumbled.

Stephen waited for Nettie to continue, but she only stared off into the distance. After the silence stretched between them, he prompted, "You were saying?"

Her curt "Never mind" tore at his heart. If only he could reach out and take that agony from her expression and her life. What could he do to get her to confide that sorrow?

He waited for a minute or two, before asking, "You'd rather not get help from the church?"

"I don't trust the church." She muttered so low he could barely hear her.

"Why?" He leaned forward, trying hard to understand.

Nettie couldn't meet his intense gaze. "You'll think I'm foolish."

"You're not foolish, Nettie. You're honest."

Fixing her attention on the plush carpet under their feet, Nettie shocked him with her next words. "When I needed help as a child, the Amish community turned their backs on us."

So far, Stephen had found everyone at church to be kind and generous. And he'd contributed to several recent fundraisers. His concern for Nettie overrode his disbelief. "I don't understand. You lived here in Lancaster County?"

"*Neh*, in Upper Dauphin."

"I don't know where that is, but I don't want to think any Amish community would neglect a child's needs."

"It happened so long ago. Forget I mentioned it."

Stephen couldn't let it drop. "I can't forget. Please tell

me, Nettie." He couldn't go back and erase the unkindness, but maybe talking about it might help her release some of her painful memories.

She hesitated, and he wanted to reach out and take her hands, assure her she'd be all right. Instead, he clutched his suspenders and gave her time to gather her thoughts.

Lord, if it will help her heal, please give her the strength to speak about it.

She started slowly and hesitantly. "My *daed* repaired boat motors for an *Englisch* company near where we lived. Over the years, he spent more time with the men at work than with church members and family. He came to prefer *Englisch* ways."

Stephen cautioned himself not to react, but he longed to comfort her. Her faraway look reflected her little-girl hurt and confusion.

"When I was eight, Daed left the Amish. And us."

"I'm sorry" seemed inadequate, but Stephen said it anyway. She'd gotten so lost in the past she didn't notice.

"Daed took a job in Harrisburg, and he loved living in the city. Because they were still married in the eyes of God and the church, Mamm followed him. The bishop advised her to stay in the community, but Mamm thought she could convince Daed to return."

Did she leave Nettie behind? Stephen tensed and sat forward.

"Mamm needed a job to support us, because Daed refused to give her any money."

At least, Nettie had been with her *mamm*. Stephen couldn't imagine how any man could abandon his wife and child. Nettie and her *mamm* must have felt lost in a city without him. No wonder Nettie understood so much about the needs of the children at this center.

"*Daed* wouldn't let us stay with him, so we got the cheapest apartment Mamm could find. The only job she could get was cleaning offices at night, so we lived in a bad area."

Stephen pictured an eight-year-old Amish farm girl in the slums alone at night. Nettie must have been petrified.

"Mamm's job barely covered the rent, so she took another one working weekends. Even so, we never had enough money."

"But didn't the church help?"

Nettie's face squinched. "Mamm worked most Sunday mornings. On the Sundays she didn't work, we had no way to get to an Amish church. Mamm took me to a nearby Mennonite church, and she joined. Our church—the Amish church, I mean—shunned Mamm along with Daed."

Shunning was supposed to bring people back to the church, but to a little girl without enough to eat, living in a dangerous area, it must appear the church had failed her. At the lost look in Nettie's eyes, Stephen again fought the urge to reach for her hand.

No wonder she didn't trust the church. She'd been abandoned by her father, left alone by her mother, and neglected by the church. He pictured his daughters being left by themselves in an unknown and unsafe place surrounded by strangers. Without enough to eat and with no support from the church, how would they have survived?

He swallowed hard. "I'm sorry that happened to you. I can't even imagine what your life was like. You must have been frightened."

For the first time, Nettie looked directly at him. "*Jah*. The first two years, I shivered through the nights. Sometimes from a lack of heat in winter, but mostly because . . ." She shrugged. "I'd rather not think about it."

He certainly understood that.

"After that," she continued, "I got protection."

"Your *daed*?" Maybe her father had returned, and that's how she ended up coming back to the Amish.

Nettie made a strange sound in her throat. "I never saw my *daed* again."

"Then how did you end up Amish?"

"A knife fight gone wrong. Someone died."

Stephen's blood ran cold. Had she—?

"*Neh*, I didn't do it, but"—she hung her head—"I could have. I made my escape before the cops arrived. Others weren't so lucky."

Were those some of the teens she'd mentioned to Mrs. Vandenberg?

"Lots of innocents got framed that night. Crooked cops, neighbors looking to get gangs off the streets, incompetent or overworked public defenders. It happens many times. If you don't have money, most likely you're going down."

Stephen struggled to picture Nettie as a street fighter. Her sweet features and her Amish dress made it impossible. But she'd lived the story she was recounting.

"The cops didn't get me that night, but I had a worse surprise waiting for me back at the apartment. Mamm had gotten off early. She had no idea what I'd been doing at night while she worked."

Nettie choked back tears. "I got sent off to her sister's house in Lancaster the next morning."

Stephen had wanted to learn the cause of the sorrow in her eyes. He'd never expected this.

"I wasn't trying to hurt Mamm. I just did what I needed to do to survive."

She'd had to join a gang at age ten? Learn to use a knife? How many lives—how many kids like Nettie—could they save at the center? This had made the mission here even more personal.

Once again, Nettie averted her eyes. "I've never told anyone about this."

Not even her husband? Perhaps not. She looked as if she regretted spilling her secrets.

"Please don't tell anyone," she begged.

"I promised you that before we started. I intend to keep my promise. No one will hear any of this from me."

She whispered a *danke* as the office door opened.

Mrs. Vandenberg peeked in. "Everything going okay?"

He and Nettie both nodded, and Mrs. Vandenberg pretended not to notice the wetness on Nettie's cheeks.

Now Stephen understood why Nettie had poured her heart into this center, and why she so often appeared tense and worried. For a little girl who'd lived with hunger and without the protection of the church, even the years of her marriage and living with her in-laws after her husband's death hadn't erased her old dread of her own children going hungry. And now she faced that same fate once Gideon married. Stephen's heart ached for her.

Mrs. Vandenberg tottered around her desk and lowered herself gingerly into the padded chair. "Poverty leaves deep scars."

Stephen started. Had Mrs. Vandenberg's comment been directed to him? She must have read his mind.

She turned to Nettie. "Do you think the feeding program will help these children grow up with fewer fears?"

Nettie stayed quiet for a long time. When she answered, she spoke slowly as if weighing each word. "I don't know. Having meals fills a huge need. But people who accept charity often feel shame."

Now Stephen understood her aversion to accepting help from the church. She associated it with the shame of her childhood.

"Anything we can do about that?" Mrs. Vandenberg asked.

A long pause ensued while Nettie tapped a knuckle against her lip.

Stephen wished she hadn't drawn his attention to their fullness. He had a sudden urge to trace that lovely bow curve at the top with a gentle finger. And then . . .

As if she'd read his thoughts, Mrs. Vandenberg studied him. She raised one eyebrow in a shrewd assessment. Stephen concentrated on the whorls in the carpet.

When Nettie broke the silence, she startled Stephen from his romantic reverie. *Gut*. Now he could channel his thoughts to something less risky than kissing.

"Nobody likes charity," Nettie said. "Well, almost no one. Some lazy people might. But most people prefer to earn their own way. It's hard when you can't do that."

Mrs. Vandenberg pursed her mouth for a moment. "It surprises me how many of our visitors come from families where one or both parents work. They don't make enough to pay for the basics."

"I know. My *mamm* worked long hours, but we still couldn't afford—" Nettie pressed a hand to her mouth as if to stop the words.

Had she gotten so comfortable talking to him she'd forgotten to guard herself around Mrs. Vandenberg? Stephen wanted to assure her neither of them looked down on her for her childhood.

"That's true for many people." Mrs. Vandenberg frowned. "Until we start paying workers decent wages, we'll be leaving families and children in poverty."

Nettie's eyes glistened with tears. "I never understood why cleaners who did hard physical labor like scrubbing floors on their hands and knees made less money than the office staff sitting at the desks. Somehow it didn't seem fair."

"A lot of things in life aren't fair." Mrs. Vandenberg had her usual brisk answer, followed by a solution. "I've been talking to politicians and business owners. It's up to us to do what we can to right those wrongs."

"*Danke*, Mrs. V."

Nettie's words overflowed with such gratitude Stephen's chest constricted. He, too, appreciated all Mrs. Vandenberg had done, but he had to admit he longed for Nettie to look at him like that.

"So back to the shame." Once again, Mrs. Vandenberg had turned into a savvy businesswoman. "What can we do to eliminate that? It's not the children's fault they're hungry or need clothes."

"*Jah*, but they still feel it. And they get mocked for being poor." Nettie's face crumpled.

Stephen wanted to wrap his arms around her and hold her close. She'd known that pain.

Then she brightened. "Earn. That's the key."

Mrs. Vandenberg leaned forward. "Tell me more."

"Earn to eat." Nettie's excitement infected all of them.

"Can the kids do jobs to earn their meals? What if you had a list of small things they could do? Like wash a window or clean a few toys in the babysitting room?"

Mrs. Vandenberg opened a desk drawer and removed a tablet. "We can make a list, and then we'll ask others to add to it."

They jotted down ideas, including everything from shelving library books to filing papers to answering phones to teaching other children skills to helping with homework. And they included plenty of cleaning chores.

"I would have done almost everything on that list," Nettie said, "to get a warm meal. Mamm would never accept charity from city churches or take government help. For me, anything would have been better than sneaking around to dig through dumpsters and cafeteria trash cans looking for discarded food."

Her words knifed through Stephen. How had he filled his own stomach and his children's when other children their age were that hungry? And now that he knew, what could he do about it?

Nettie had sworn him to secrecy, yet she suddenly seemed willing, even eager, to share details of her past with Mrs. Vandenberg.

Mrs. Vandenberg looked as sick as Stephen. "It's hard to believe children in this country have to do that. Programs like SNAP are supposed to take care of that. I know not all parents accept government assistance or even have access to it."

"And not all of them use it wisely."

This time, Stephen didn't wonder about Nettie's knowledge. She'd mentioned this before, but he hadn't known she'd lived through it herself. And she must have seen all of that with friends and neighbors too.

"We won't turn away anyone who's hungry," Mrs. Vandenberg said, "but we will encourage them to work. Actually, this might fit well with another idea I want to try."

Stephen couldn't get over her energy. Did this elderly woman ever take a break? She seemed to move from one project to the next.

"I've been reading about Homeboy Industries in Los Angeles. They offer job training and placement to gang members, and in some of the offshoot programs, the teens start their own businesses, making salad dressing, flavored popcorn, salsa, and other food products. Or they create artwork, T-shirts, and crafts. Some do solar panel installation, computer or HVAC repairs, or work in other service industries."

"That sounds wonderful." Then Nettie's joy dimmed. "But they'll never make as much as they do selling drugs."

"Some teens want to get out of gangs and need a way to make money legally, right?" Stephen asked.

Nettie smiled. "*Jah.* That's so."

Mrs. Vandenberg tapped her phone several times and passed it to Nettie. "Scroll down to see more information."

"I'd like to experiment with something like that and pay living wages." The excitement on Mrs. Vandenberg's wrinkled face made her look like a saint. "Maybe we'd encourage other businesses in the area to raise their wages, and it would lead to a decline in illegal activities."

Nettie took the phone and held it out so Stephen could see it at the same time. "Paying decent wages would be a good step. The way the center is set up now, it will attract younger kids and keep them out of trouble. This program could target actual gang members."

Stephen struggled to concentrate on the words and pictures with Nettie's soft hand so close to him. "It looks great." A deep longing swelled in his heart and soul to be a part of this mission—and to do it with Nettie.

Chapter Twenty-Three

Nettie's hand trembled as she clutched the phone—both because she would be fulfilling a lifelong dream and because of her nearness to Stephen. He'd scooted his chair beside hers so they could read the information at the same time. She wished she were worthy of a man like him.

She forced herself to keep her focus on reading the information. "One thing that concerns me is if we open this program at the center, will parents be afraid to send their children here? They won't want their young ones hanging around with gang members."

"Good point."

Stephen's congratulatory smile made her spirit soar. If only she deserved it. She'd once been one of those teens that parents ordered their young kids to avoid.

Mrs. Vandenberg clicked her pen against the paper for a few moments. "I'd been thinking of buying that abandoned warehouse across the alley. It's an eyesore, and I want the neighborhood around the center to be safe and appealing."

Stephen mirrored Nettie's excitement. "So you could start this new project in the warehouse?"

"It would be the perfect place for it." Mrs. Vandenberg reached for the phone on her desk. In a few minutes, she'd commanded someone to negotiate for the warehouse, and she'd made an appointment to work with an architect to redesign the interior.

Nettie wondered what it would be like to have enough money in the bank to buy buildings whenever you wanted, to start programs and pay for all the costs, to create whatever you dreamed of, and never worry about paying bills or getting put out in the street or going hungry.

Her eyes stung. Somehow it didn't seem fair that some people had it easy, while others always struggled to make ends meet, to fill their children's bellies, to scrape by. Yet, she didn't begrudge Mrs. Vandenberg her wealth. The elderly woman used her money to help everyone around her.

Stephen pointed out part of the description on the website. "They have a bakery, café, diner, farmer's market, and other businesses that employ teens. You'll be using the warehouse, but couldn't we also sell the products at Green Valley?"

"Brilliant." Mrs. Vandenberg beamed at him.

Nettie's heart swelled even more. "That's perfect." They smiled at each other while Mrs. Vandenberg made notes on her tablet.

When she finished, she lifted her head. "Gideon's been working on plans for me to enlarge the market. I'll have him include this in the expansion."

The name *Gideon* hit Nettie hard, reminding her of her dilemma and dimming her joy.

Stephen sent her a sympathetic glance. She tried to return his smile, but her lips refused to curve upward.

Mrs. Vandenberg looked alarmed. "Is everything all right, Nettie?"

Neh, it wasn't. But she shouldn't let future worries cloud this exciting new project for gang members. Mrs. Vandenberg deserved everyone's full participation.

Stephen must have recognized Nettie's struggle because he encouraged her with his *you-can-do-it* look. Knowing she had his unspoken support gave her the courage to forget her fears for now.

"I'm fine." She attempted to recapture the enthusiasm bubbling through her earlier.

Stephen leaned forward in his chair, and his eagerness bolstered Nettie's excitement. "Why don't we ask other stand owners if they'd be willing to let a few teens work at their stands? I'd be willing to train some of them on the farm and in the market."

Nettie appreciated Stephen taking over the suggestions. She was completely out of ideas. "That would be a new experience for them." Her lips quirked as she imagined the tough inner city teens doing chores on a farm.

"What's so funny?" Stephen asked.

"Can you see Aidan mucking out a stall?"

Stephen and Mrs. V both laughed.

With a grin, he said, "It'll definitely be a test of their courage."

"That's for sure." Nettie's spirits rose again. She loved how she and Stephen always seemed to be on the same wavelength.

"I like that idea, Stephen. Let's plan for that." She

wrote on her legal pad again. "I think I'll give each teen entrepreneur seed money to start a business."

Nettie's eyebrows arched. "No telling what that might be used for."

"Don't worry, Nettie," Mrs. Vandenberg assured her. "I won't give them cash. They can each have a certain amount of credit to order equipment and supplies."

"That would be wonderful." Nettie sighed. "How different my life would have been if I'd had a center like this or the warehouse."

"What would you have chosen to do?" Mrs. Vandenberg pinned Nettie with a soul-searching gaze, one that uncovered all her secrets. "It's never too late to reach your dreams."

Nettie had to answer honestly. "I wanted to be a beautician and cosmetician. I loved doing hair and makeup." She added a rueful smile. "I don't think I'd have many customers in the Amish community."

The twinkle in Stephen's eyes reminded her of another dream. One she'd never fulfill in the Amish community either—a man to love and marry.

She'd done too many things in her past the Amish considered unacceptable. Her heart had lightened as she told Stephen the truth about one of her secrets. The way he'd accepted everything without judgment had freed her from some of the shame. She might never tell her story to the world, but she'd just admitted some of it to Mrs. Vandenberg.

And she trusted Stephen to keep her secret. The downside of confessing about her past meant he now knew she wouldn't be a suitable partner. She'd made that clear. She was glad it hadn't affected his friendship.

Danke, Lord, for Stephen's listening ear and for his acceptance. And for Mrs. Vandenberg giving me this opportunity to help others.

Working at the center would alleviate some of the guilt Nettie had carried all her life. As a young teen she'd had no way to help her homies. Now, she could assist others caught in the trap she'd escaped.

If Mamm hadn't been Amish . . . If Mamm's sister hadn't been willing to take in a wayward teen . . . Where would I have ended up? Probably in jail. She'd been lucky that night. She'd gotten away, and no one had squealed. But sooner or later, if she'd stayed in the city, she'd have been caught.

"Nettie?" The gentle way Stephen whispered her name sent shivers down her spine.

"Sorry. I—I wasn't paying attention."

"It's a lot to take in." Mrs. Vandenberg gave her a sympathetic glance. "But we do need your expertise." She fired off a list of questions about professions that might interest gang members.

Before long, thanks to Nettie's answers, Mrs. Vandenberg had a long list of training ideas. "We probably can't fit all of these into the warehouse, but I'll talk with nearby community colleges and technical centers. We can provide transportation and tuition for off-site classes."

Mrs. Vandenberg finished making notes. "My new assistant will have plenty of calls to make tomorrow, but we've gotten a good start. If you think of any more, let me know."

Nettie stayed so absorbed in the possibilities they'd discussed, she barely noticed when Mrs. Vandenberg rose. "I'll leave you two alone to discuss things."

After all these years of feeling inadequate and unable to help her friends in the city, Nettie had just been given a gift. The chance to make amends. She hadn't been able to prevent anyone from going to prison, but maybe Mrs. V could get some of them out. And even better, Nettie now had a chance to help gang members start new lives, and she'd be able to prevent hundreds of children from making the mistakes she had.

They sat in silence for a while after Mrs. Vandenberg left.

"I don't want to disturb you," Stephen said. "I know you have a lot of other things to think about. But I'm so glad we're doing this."

The empathy in his tone touched Nettie's soul. He'd listened to her childhood woes and understood some of what she was going through with Gideon. Sharing that burden had lifted some of the weight dragging her down. She wished, though, that her city life had been the only confession she needed to make.

When Mrs. Vandenberg told Joline that her *daed* and Nettie were alone in the office, Joline couldn't believe it. Even worse, the two of them had the door shut. She barged into the room.

Daed and Sourpuss both jumped as the door banged against the wall behind them, but not before Joline had seen them gazing at each other with starry eyes.

She glared at both of them. "Where have you been? I've been looking all over for you. What if something had happened to your children?"

Nettie, her expression innocent, said sweetly, "We know we can trust you to take care of them."

Joline fumed. She'd made it clear she wanted to be in charge of her brothers and sisters, but she didn't like it thrown in her face.

Before she could speak, Nettie went on, "Katie's not as old or as mature as you, but she is used to watching the younger ones."

Nettie's rescue last week and her two gentle responses tonight made Joline ashamed of her outburst. But that only increased her irritation. "Katie can't see any of the children. She and Esther are in the library, reading. All the library shelves could smash down around them, and they'd never notice."

Nettie laughed. *Jah*, actually laughed.

"You're probably right. Katie gets very absorbed in her books. Esther probably does too. Good thing Abby is keeping an eye on Sadie, and Matthew's supervising the three younger boys."

Daed smiled at Joline. "We're lucky to have such responsible children."

Her own dad sticking up for Sourpuss?

Part of Joline warned her she was behaving like a drama queen and Daed would scold her later, but the other part—the part that worried Sourpuss wouldn't keep her promise—wanted to start trouble, big trouble. Anything to get rid of the fear snaking inside that warned Joline she'd lose Daed if she didn't keep him and Sourpuss apart.

But if Joline didn't act nicer, she'd be in for a lecture and additional punishment. She took a deep breath. "The center will be closing soon. We should leave."

"*Ach*, I didn't realize it was that late." Sourpuss stood.

Gut. Now to get her out of the room and away from Daed.

"We still have more than an hour," Daed said.

Joline crossed her arms. "But we have to get up early for chores and church tomorrow."

"That's true." Sourpuss seemed determined to be nice.

No matter what Joline did or said, Sourpuss came off sounding kind and caring.

Daed got up from his chair. "Joline, why don't you get Abby and Sadie? They might need to clean up painting supplies. Nettie and I can collect the boys and our two readers. We'll meet you in the lobby."

Fuming, Joline stomped off to find her sister. Not only hadn't she separated Daed and Sourpuss, now she had to go in the opposite direction, leaving them alone again.

After the tussle with Joline, Nettie helped Stephen herd the other children to Mrs. Vandenberg's van, grateful her own children were too sleepy to question her about rescuing Joline last Saturday. But as they prepared breakfast the next morning, Katie sidled up next to her.

"Mamm, what did Joline mean last night? Did you really save her?"

"*Jah.*"

"*Guder mariye.*" Nettie's mother-in-law sailed into the kitchen. "What can I do to help?"

"*Guder mariye*, Mammi." Katie kept her gaze fixed on Nettie's face.

I'll tell you later, Nettie mouthed.

Katie's lips drooped, but she didn't protest.

Much, much later, Nettie promised herself.

They stayed so busy with their usual morning jobs and getting ready for church, Katie had no time to question Nettie further.

But Nettie's relief lasted only until the singing ended. The first sermon topic, "Be sure your sin will find you out," made her squirm. She kept her eyes focused on the floor rather than on the minister. She'd hidden so much about her life. And her sins . . .

Opening up to Stephen yesterday had freed her from one burden. But telling one person was not the same as letting everyone know about her past. Years before Stephen arrived in Lancaster County, she'd confessed one of her sins in front of the church. Most people knew about it, but he didn't. Nobody knew the rest of that story, though. Was this God's warning that she needed to come clean?

Stephen sat across from Nettie in church. As if a heavy weight rested on her slumped shoulders, she kept her head bowed through all three sermons. Was she still worrying about her children going hungry the way she had?

Gideon preparing to date Fern had stirred all the old memories Nettie had recounted last night. If she hadn't been so upset, she might never have shared that pain with him or with anyone else. She'd have kept it trapped inside. He ached for her. She'd lived all these years hiding the childhood traumas that had left her with such a deep-seated fear of poverty.

Stephen was grateful he'd been there to listen to her, and he had only admiration for her courage and endurance.

Despite all she'd been through and the absence of supportive parents, she'd turned out to be a good mother. He appreciated her thoughtfulness to his children and her patience and kindness with Joline's snappishness and drama. She'd even risked her life to rescue his daughter.

He'd tossed and turned all night trying to think of a way to help Nettie. Other than praying for her, he didn't know what else to do. She'd never accept his monetary help. He'd be happy to pay her bills, but she'd refuse charity.

In the middle of the night, an idea had come to him. Had God planted it there? He'd been begging the Lord to show him a way to ease Nettie's concerns, to lift her burdens, to provide for her.

Marry her, a still, small voice repeated several times.

After a back-and-forth argument with himself, the impression grew stronger that this was God's will. By marrying Nettie, he could care for her and her children. She couldn't object to a husband providing for her.

Plenty of widows and widowers made marriages of convenience. Love could grow later. Actually, the more time Stephen spent with Nettie, the more he found himself falling for her. Whenever they were together, he discovered more qualities to treasure.

She didn't have feelings for him, but maybe those emotions would develop over time. She did trust him or she wouldn't have shared secrets she'd never told anyone else. Trust and mutual respect were good starting points for a relationship.

He could offer the financial support Nettie so desperately needed, and she might be the answer to his troubles with Joline. Perhaps that's what Mrs. Vandenberg had in mind. Would Nettie agree?

The idea had knocked around in his brain the rest of the night. Each time a possible objection arose, his logical mind countered it. The largest hurdles might be: Would Nettie consider him as a husband? Would her children like him? Would Nettie be willing to take on the care of five more children? If so, would his children like her?

The only way to find out the answers would be to ask her.

Stephen's throat closed. When the time came, would he be able to ask the most important question?

Chapter Twenty-Four

As Nettie gathered her children and herded them toward the buggy, Stephen followed her. She hoped he didn't plan to invite Katie for a second visit. Her daughter never wanted to go to the Lapps' house again. Maybe Esther could visit their house instead.

"Nettie, could I stop by later this afternoon to talk to you? It's very important."

Because she'd been expecting to fend off a request for her daughter to visit, she stood dumbfounded. Stephen wanted to talk to her?

They'd had a good conversation last night, but Nettie had disclosed way too much. She regretted confiding about her past. She'd kept it hidden from the Amish community since she'd been here. What had she been thinking to spill it to Stephen?

He clutched his suspenders as if he were nervous.

Nettie shouldn't keep him waiting for an answer. "All right." She hadn't meant to sound so off-putting. She tried again. "That would be fine."

"*Danke*. I'll see you then."

Rather than relaxing him, her response had only tightened his grip on his suspenders, making her wonder what he planned to talk about.

On the way home, she regretted agreeing. What would the neighbors say when they saw him come calling? What about Gideon, Caroline, and her in-laws? They might read something more into the visit. She could explain that she and Stephen needed to plan for an expansion to the center, but would everyone believe her?

After they arrived home, Nettie paced back and forth in the kitchen, trying to dispel her tension.

"Is something wrong?" Her mother-in-law, Elizabeth, came up behind Nettie, startling her.

"*Neh*," Nettie fibbed.

"Then why are you wearing out the floorboards?" Elizabeth's gentle smile showed she'd been teasing.

"Sorry." Nettie sank into the nearest chair at the table but twisted her apron with her fidgety fingers. She hoped Elizabeth wouldn't ask about the pacing.

Elizabeth passed Nettie and patted her on the shoulder. "When things bother you that much, it's better to be on your knees than on your feet."

Jah, she should be taking worries to the Lord. But Nettie didn't know how to pray about her attraction to Stephen or her concerns that others might misconstrue a relationship when that was an impossibility.

"It's a lovely day," Elizabeth said. "Caroline's playing volleyball with the youth before the singing, and Gideon's gone for a drive in the country."

Elizabeth didn't mention Gideon having company on

his ride, but with the way her eyes shone, Gideon had not gone alone. Nettie's in-laws adored Fern.

The reminder of the future marriage twisted Nettie into tighter knots than the ones she'd been crimping in her apron.

She barely heard her mother-in-law's suggestion. "Why don't we all go for a drive and have a picnic supper at the park? I'm sure the children would enjoy that."

"I, um, need to stay here. Someone's coming to—" *To what? To see me?* Elizabeth might misconstrue Stephen's purpose. Nettie settled on a neutral ending. "To visit."

Her mother-in-law's eyebrows rose. Nettie wanted to ignore the question on Elizabeth's face, but it would be better to allay her mother-in-law's suspicions.

"Just some business for Mrs. Vandenberg's new center. It's nothing special." Although Nettie wished it were. What would it be like to be courted by a man like Stephen?

"I see." Elizabeth's simple acceptance didn't match the curiosity in her eyes.

Nettie rose from the table. "The children would love to go to the park. Why don't I pack a picnic supper while you get ready to go?"

That would keep her hands busy at something other than wrinkling her apron, and maybe it might calm the fears of the future as well as her anxiety over Stephen's upcoming visit. And it would get all the witnesses out of the house, saving her from having to explain Stephen's presence.

A short while later, she waved goodbye to everyone as they headed off in the buggy. She had the house to herself. Grateful for the privacy, she compulsively straightened couch cushions and wall hangings, refolded afghans and quilts, aligned plates and cups in the cupboard.

Fifteen minutes later, Stephen knocked. When she opened the door, her heart, which had been hammering, beat twice as fast.

"Come in." Her breathy voice gave her away.

Stephen stepped inside, took off his straw hat, and rotated it in his hands. He looked as uneasy as she felt.

She motioned to the hooks near the door where he could hang his hat. He appeared reluctant to part with it, but he hung it up. Nettie could sympathize. Her apron still bore creases from her own jittery fingers.

After she led Stephen into the living room, he perched on the edge of a chair. Nettie took the rocker opposite him. For a long moment, neither of them spoke.

Finally, she broke the uncomfortable silence. "You have questions or ideas about the center?"

His blank look proved his mind had been somewhere else. "*Neh*. I, well . . ." He cleared his throat several times. "I had an idea . . . a question to ask you."

He'd thoroughly confused her. Whatever he planned to ask made him apprehensive. And that made her edgy.

In the darkness last night, marriage had seemed like the perfect solution. Now, with Nettie waiting for him to form a coherent sentence, Stephen had misgivings.

They hadn't known each other long and had little time to develop a relationship. She'd had no chance to get to know him and would consider him too forward.

Nettie stared at him expectantly, adding to his consternation. Such a pretty woman might not want to marry him. She already had four children. Would she be ready to take on five more?

"Maybe this isn't a good idea." Stephen started to stand. He'd made a foolish mistake.

"It's all right." Nettie's sweet voice soothed his agitation. "You can ask me anything you want. Or tell me your idea."

She'd think him crazy. But her gentle invitation had given him an opening. The worst she could say was *neh*. He definitely didn't want to hear that word from her lips. Her lovely lips.

Stephen forced his thoughts away from that and wiped his sweating palms on his pants legs. Usually, when you asked a woman to marry you, you started by telling her how much you loved her. Should he let her know he admired her? If only he'd planned a speech ahead of time.

Stephen had no choice. He plunged in. "Last night, when you told me you might not have a home, I wanted to do something to help."

Nettie's pinched face told him he'd begun this all wrong.

Before she could protest, he hurried on. "I know you won't accept charity and don't trust the church, but I thought maybe we could, um, get married."

"You want to marry me?"

She sounded incredulous. Almost as if she thought no man would be interested in her. Or she didn't believe he could possibly care for her.

"*Jah*, I do."

For a moment joy and relief washed across her face, then she turned her head away. "I don't think so," she said stiffly.

"It wouldn't be charity. We'd be helping each other.

A marriage of convenience for both of us. My children need a mother. Especially Joline. But the younger ones do too."

The shutters went down over her emotions. Then, she shook her head. "I couldn't do that."

"You don't like taking care of children?" That didn't seem to fit with her kindness to the children at the center. And she'd also risked her life to save Joline.

"I—I . . ."

"You could also work at the market stand if that would make you feel better."

Without looking at him, she only shook her head.

She obviously didn't have feelings for him like the ones he'd started developing for her. He'd hope in time . . . But that seemed to be impossible.

Nettie couldn't believe, after what Stephen had heard yesterday, he'd ever trust her to mother his children. In fact, she'd expected him to run the other way. But she had other secrets she hadn't shared. If he knew the whole truth, he'd never want to marry her.

"I know you don't have feelings for me, but we can make a good partnership at home, the market, and the center."

Stephen was wrong. Very wrong. She'd been fighting her attraction to him all along. At first, Nettie had labeled those feelings friendship . . . affection . . . caring. But she'd never been completely honest with herself. She even had romantic dreams of him at night, but during the day, she squashed those fantasies because of her unworthiness.

Keeping those emotions to herself while being around him every day would be excruciating. But she didn't have to worry about that. She couldn't marry him.

"I know this has come as a shock. Take your time to think it over. You can give me an answer when you're ready."

She was ready now. "*Danke* for your kind offer. But I—I can't." Those were some of the hardest words she'd ever said.

Her soul, her spirit, and her heart urged her to say *jah*. Her mind and conscience insisted on *neh*. She had too many things in her past she hadn't confessed to Stephen. Too many things he didn't know about her. Too many things that would make him run the other way.

"Why, Nettie?"

She couldn't face him, so she focused on her hands. With great effort, she kept them still. "I told you more about my past yesterday than I've ever told anyone. Even my husband and his family never knew. I left all that behind when I came here, and later when I joined the church, I confessed it to God."

"So it's over and forgiven."

Nettie shook her head. "I wouldn't be a suitable *mamm* for your children."

"Let me be the judge of that. In my mind, what's past is past. I admire you all the more for what you've made of your life since. I'm sure it wasn't easy."

Neh, it hadn't been. She couldn't believe Stephen had dismissed it all so easily. Maybe after he had time to think it over, he'd change his mind.

And she hadn't told him the things she'd done after she arrived in the Amish community.

* * *

Stephen leaned forward. How could he convince her he didn't hold her past against her? "If that's your only objection, I think you're a wonderful *mamm*. You love children, don't you?"

"Of course."

"I can tell. I've seen how good you are with my children—even Joline. And she can be a challenge. I have no doubt you'll do a great job of mothering."

"You wouldn't say that if you knew everything I've done since I came to Lancaster."

"If you want to tell me, I'll listen. And like last night, I'll keep it secret. But you don't have to. My offer to marry you still stands."

"Suppose I'm a serial killer?"

"I'll take that chance." He smiled. "I don't believe you are. And I meant what I said: Nothing will make me change my mind."

"You haven't heard what I've done."

He hoped this story wouldn't be as heart-wrenching as her previous one. She seemed to have more heartaches than one young girl should have to bear. "I'm listening." He kept his words soft and inviting, hoping it would encourage her to share.

Could she do this? Nettie wrung her hands in her lap. Some of her story was no secret. The whole church knew, but most had put it out of their minds long ago. None of them knew, though, what was in her heart back then.

"It's all right, Nettie. You don't have to tell me."

Part of her longed to confess it all, hoping he'd hear it in the same accepting manner he'd listened to her childhood stories yesterday. But her logical mind told her the truth would push Stephen further away.

"I don't want you to think . . ." Nettie stopped herself. She'd been about to say *I'm rejecting you.* She wanted him to realize the fault was with her, not him.

Stephen misread her hesitation. "I'm not going to judge you."

His caring brought tears to her eyes. He'd change his mind once he heard. Nettie recalled this time in her life with shame.

"A few months after I arrived here, I started baptismal classes."

Despite the shunning, Mamm had stayed Amish in her heart and her ways, and she'd begged Nettie to join the church. Nettie had obeyed, although she had reservations about becoming part of a community that had shunned her parents.

"Only my aunt and the bishop, who passed away last summer, knew about my family. They had no idea about the life I'd been living."

Stephen's eyes encouraged her to continue.

"I never felt good enough compared to the teens who were raised in the church. I related better to wild, rebellious teens than to the religious teens in the Amish community."

"God's given you a gift for that."

A gift? Nettie sat there stunned for a moment. Stephen considered that a gift?

"You don't look like you believe me." Stephen leaned forward as eagerly as he had last night. "Don't you think God allowed you to experience all that so you could help Mrs. Vandenberg with the center? Many times, you guided her to better decisions and ideas."

God had planned all of her childhood experiences so she'd be ready for this project? Nettic struggled to see her life from that point of view.

"You do see it, don't you, Nettie?"

Her *jah* came out hesitant and uncertain. Her whole world had just been flipped upside down and turned inside out. The kaleidoscope in her mind had twisted to shift all the pieces into a totally different pattern. If she accepted this new vision, she'd have to consider her past as a blessing rather than a curse.

Stephen believed it. Why couldn't she?

Nettie shook her head. She'd need time to change her old perspective. A brief glimpse of Stephen's perspective opened up new possibilities. Possibilities she wanted to explore.

First, though, she needed to tell Stephen the whole sordid story. No amount of kaleidoscope turning could alter the next few years of her life. Nettie rocked back and forth several times before beginning.

"I'm not proud of this. I, um, decided I wanted to marry for money." Nettie slid her finger around in aimless circles on the rocker arm. "While attending baptismal classes, I picked the boy in the community who seemed as if his family had the most money."

Now, Stephen would know what kind of person she'd

been. And still was. A woman whose main focus stayed fixed on money.

Stephen understood how her dread of poverty had led her to do that. Even now, years later, that same anxiety still paralyzed her. He wished he could take that anxiety from her, but even marrying her would provide temporary relief. Only God could remove such a deep-seated fear.

"I chose Thomas for security rather than love."

"That's understandable."

Again, Nettie stared at him as if he'd said something incomprehensible. For him, it only made sense. Last night as she'd recounted rooting through dumpsters and trash cans, desperation glimmered in her eyes. The same desperation Stephen had noted in the eyes of many of the women and children coming into the center.

"You were young and scared of being poor, Nettie."

"But that didn't make it right." She lowered her head. "If I hadn't come back to the Amish community and married Thomas, my children would have grown up in a neighborhood like the one around the center. I could have been one of those mothers standing in line to snatch up leftover produce or pick through donated clothes, hoping to find an outfit or shoes that fit my little ones. I never wanted my children to experience that."

That's exactly why he'd offered a marriage of convenience. "I don't want you to go through that again. That's why I asked you to—"

Nettie held up a hand. She seemed determined to convince him why he shouldn't marry her, but the more she talked, the more she convinced him he'd made the right decision.

"Thomas liked someone else, but I was determined to attract him."

Stephen couldn't imagine why anyone would prefer another girl to Nettie—one of the sweetest, most beautiful women he'd ever seen.

"I'd watched other girls in the city flirt so I knew how to do it. I hadn't done it myself. Mamm would never have let me date any of the boys I hung around with."

Thank the Lord for that. Where would Nettie have ended up if she had gone out with one of them? Gratitude for God's protection for this lovely young woman flowed from the depths of Stephen's soul.

"It didn't take me long to win Thomas over." *The wiles of the devil.* That's how Nettie thought of them now. At the time, she'd been proud of herself. "We sneaked out to be together even before we finished our baptismal classes."

Back then, breaking a rule like that after all she'd done in Harrisburg had seemed petty. Now, she understood why the community enforced it.

Stephen stayed silent, and Nettie debated about continuing. If she didn't, someone might mention it to Stephen. Better for the facts to come from her, even though it would cause him to look at her differently.

Nettie hesitated. She'd heard his brother Amos's judgment about sinning before marriage. Stephen would feel the same way.

Hanging her head, she made herself say, "We had to get married at seventeen."

Stephen responded in a loving, caring tone, "Other young couples have done the same. You confess before the church and get married. Then you put it behind you and move forward with your life."

He made it sound so simple. But it didn't always work that way. Sometimes those wounds festered and the poison inside built until . . .

"Nettie, what's wrong?"

Stephen's voice cut through the agony, the guilt, the self-blame.

"Thomas didn't put it behind him, and I can't." She had to admit the worst. "I'm the reason he committed suicide."

A swift intake of breath was Stephen's only response.

"Gideon and the family never blamed me." She rubbed her forehead. "But I knew the truth. I drove Thomas to it."

"*Ach*, Nettie, you can't blame yourself for someone else's decision. Many men and women are stuck in un-happy marriages or living with overwhelming burdens." Stephen reached for her hands, but she shook him off.

"Right before he went out to repair the barn roof, Thomas told me, he . . ." She dropped her head into her hands.

"Nettie?"

When she didn't look up, Stephen knelt beside her so he could look up at her. She wanted to squeeze her eyes shut to block out the compassion on his face, but the caring in his eyes mesmerized her.

"Listen to me." His words, low and urgent, revealed how deeply he believed in what he was saying. "You, of all

people, had plenty of reasons to"—he swallowed hard—
"to die."

Nettie longed to cover her ears, but he spoke the truth.
"Some days I thought about it when life seemed unbearable. I couldn't do that to Mamm."

"You could have, but you didn't. Don't you see? You
made the choice to live."

She almost hadn't. After two of her friends had been
shot—one on purpose, the other accidentally—within
weeks of each other and after Nettie had spent all weekend with hunger gnawing at her insides, she sat in her
room and stroked the side of her switchblade against her
arm. She had nothing left to live for.

"If you'd chosen to die, would you have blamed your
mamm?"

"Of course not."

"But she'd have blamed herself for failing you."

"*Neh*, it wouldn't have been her fault."

"And Thomas's death is not your fault."

Tears—cleansing tears—ran down Nettie's cheeks.
Stephen reached for her and cradled her in his arms.
She rested her head against his strong chest as floodwaters inside and out washed away another layer of guilt
and shame.

Stephen shouldn't be holding her like this. If anyone
saw them, he'd be disciplined by the church. But he
couldn't let her cry without comforting her. And, since
he'd been here, he hadn't seen anyone in her family.

Lord, please show me how to help her.

A quiet voice inside whispered, *Just love her.*

I do. Until he took her in his arms, he hadn't realized how much she meant to him. He wanted to care for her, protect her, cherish her for the rest of his life. But could he convince her to agree?

When Nettie lifted her damp face, the wetness in her eyes reflected a new softness, and the worry lines on her face had smoothed out. What a heavy burden she'd been carrying. And Stephen wanted to lift all of it for her.

Chapter Twenty-Five

Stephen loosened his arms from around her and returned to his chair, leaving Nettie aching for his touch.

Once he'd settled across from her again, he reassured her, "Nettie, nothing you've told me yesterday or today changes my mind. My offer still stands. A marriage of convenience will benefit both of us. Will you consider it?"

She longed to blurt out *jah* in answer to his question, but she couldn't.

No matter how much she'd like to marry him—for many different reasons—she didn't want to burden him. Supporting nine children would be a huge responsibility. Thomas had struggled under the financial weight of their family. Nettie vowed never to drive another man to suicide. Especially not one she cared about this deeply.

"Stephen, I can't marry you." Someone with her past wouldn't be a fit mother for his children. And she worried about their children going hungry.

"Please take some time to pray about it before giving me a final answer."

"I don't think—"

"Promise me you'll seek God's will. If it doesn't feel right to you after you've asked the Lord for direction, I'll accept your decision."

Nettie hadn't prayed about it. She doubted that would change her mind, but she should bring it to the Lord. "All right."

"Maybe we could talk about it after the school picnic this week? And if you feel God isn't leading you to marry me, I'd be happy to pay you to work at our market stand. That way, if you need to leave Gideon's stand, you could afford to support your children."

When he told her the pay, Nettie gasped. "I could never accept that much."

"Mrs. Vandenberg encouraged me to give employees a living wage."

"That's wonderful, except you'll put yourself out of business. Then, you and your employees will all have no money."

Stephen only smiled. "The business can afford it."

Perhaps his brother could, but Nettie had heard rumors about Stephen losing his business in New York before he moved here. He shouldn't be squandering money.

He couldn't even afford his own house. He lived with his brother. Where did Stephen plan to take his bride? To stay in Amos's house? How would Amos feel about five new people in the house?

Stephen had a good heart, but he didn't always plan ahead. She'd seen that when he climbed the ladder without— Nettie shied away from that incident. He might be doing the same thing here—jumping in to help without considering the consequences. As she had that first day they met, she might need to rein in his eagerness to assist others at his own expense.

He interrupted her musing. "I should go. I'll see you at the picnic. If that's not long enough to think it over and pray about it, I'll wait for as long as it takes for you to be sure of your answer."

"*Danke*," she choked out. That was another example of his kindness and generosity. His list of attributes went on and on. Nettie couldn't ask for more in a future husband.

Except for one important thing—financial stability.

As she closed the door behind him, Stephen read the answer in her eyes. She'd already decided *neh*. He hoped she'd pray about it, but maybe he'd misunderstood God's direction. He'd pray too. And he'd ask the Lord to help him accept her decision.

He drove home even more concerned about Nettie than when he'd arrived. She'd faced so many difficulties in life, and she condemned herself even for things she'd asked forgiveness for. He wished she could accept God's forgiveness and forgive herself. How could he convince her she was worthy of love?

The answer came clearly. *Pray for her*.

The whole way home, he prayed. And the rest of the evening, he begged the Lord to show Nettie her true worth and to open her heart to receive love.

Human love could never substitute for Divine love. Only God's love could overcome her feelings of inadequacy and give her the self-respect and self-worth she needed. But Stephen also vowed, if Nettie agreed to marry him, he'd do everything in his power to show her human love every day they had together.

Lord, if it's Your will for me to marry Nettie, please make me into a man who honors You and a husband who shows his wife the love Christ showed the church.

Nettie lay in bed that night for hours after the children had fallen asleep. She relived Stephen's arms around her. If she squeezed her eyes shut and imagined hard enough, she could almost re-create the tingling. But it was a poor substitute for the real touch, the real hug.

If she accepted his proposal, she'd be able to bask in that closeness anytime they were alone together as a married couple. Stephen had said he accepted her past, and he'd even reframed her city life. Had God given her that past experience to equip her to serve Him now?

Maybe all along, she should have been thanking the Lord. Instead of hiding her past, she should be sharing what she'd learned from it and how she'd turned her life around after she joined the church. At the thought of coming clean, of admitting what she'd done, Nettie's stomach churned.

Lord, if that's what You want me to do, I will. But You'll have to give me the courage.

She had something else to pray about.

Please also show me what You want me to do about Stephen's proposal.

The longer she waited, the surer she felt that the Lord

was directing her to say *jah*. But that couldn't be right, could it? Did God want her to go back into poverty?

Nettie shook her head. She couldn't do it. She'd never put her children through that. If she said *neh*, though, she'd face the same situation once Gideon and Fern married. But if she said *jah*, at least she wouldn't be alone.

Her thoughts whirling, Nettie fell asleep, uncertain what to do about her future.

As time dripped past, coming closer and closer to the school picnic, Nettie's anxiety increased. Torn between *jah* and *neh*, she still had no idea of what answer to give Stephen.

The morning of the school picnic, the children all woke early. Katie danced around the kitchen, making up songs about her first end-of-the-year picnic. And her brothers and Sadie shared her excitement. They'd be going too.

"Mammi," Lenny shrieked as Elizabeth entered the kitchen, "we're going to Katie's picnic!"

Elizabeth ruffled his hair. "I know." She looked over at Nettie. "Should I take the children to the park so you can help Gideon?"

Nettie, still mulling over her answer for Stephen, struggled to switch gears. *Focus on the picnic*, she warned herself. Then, she shook her head. *Neh*, that would only flood her mind and heart with more images of Stephen.

"You don't want me to take them? Are you sure?"

"What? *Jah*, I mean *neh*." Nettie was making no sense. "It would be a big help if you could drive them there. I need to go to the market to help Gideon get the food ready."

"I know." Elizabeth studied her worriedly. "Is something wrong?"

Depending on Nettie's decision today, it could be. Or it could be very, very right. She still hadn't chosen which path to take. Both had drawbacks.

And Nettie didn't trust the still, small voice inside urging her to go ahead. She feared it might be her own desires pushing her toward selfishness.

"Nettie?" Elizabeth's voice held a note of alarm.

"Sorry, I have something on my mind this morning." Something extremely important. Something that would determine the future of nine children and a man she cared about.

Gideon peeked into the kitchen. "Ready, Nettie?"

In a daze of dreams and fears, Nettie followed him to the buggy. Luckily, Gideon appeared equally as distracted. They prepped the chicken and salads in the deserted market, both lost in their own inner worlds.

By the time they arrived at the park, all the families had assembled. Because Gideon had donated the chicken and salad, other parents brought drinks, side dishes, and desserts to share. The park's picnic tables overflowed with baskets and coolers.

While several parents rushed over to help unload, Nettie checked to be sure her children had arrived safely. Then, she secretly searched out Stephen.

When their eyes met, her heart trilled a melodic *jah, jah, jah*. Her logical mind screeched the song to a halt. Setting out this bounty of food brought back all the times she'd gone hungry. She couldn't do that to Stephen's children.

Her eyes narrowed, Joline stood a few feet away from her *daed*. Sourpuss wasn't keeping her promise. Joline would have to keep them apart. But how?

Teacher Emily clapped her hands to get their attention. She warned the children to stay away from the woods and the creek. "Everyone needs to stay in sight of their parents. I want all of you scholars to keep an eye on the little ones. And have fun!"

The scholars—all but Joline—cheered. Many of the younger ones raced to the playground equipment. Matthew and his friends headed for the baseball game. No one noticed Joline hadn't joined them. She lifted her chin and pretended not to care.

Daed turned to her. "Aren't you going to play?"

"I have more important things to do," she said airily, hoping Daed wouldn't ask her what they were. And she also prayed he couldn't read the hurt she desperately tried to hide.

Nearby, one of the mothers balanced a squirming baby on her hip while she set out covered pitchers of water and lemonade.

Joline dashed over. "Would you like me to play with him?"

"*Ach*, would you?" The mother handed over her son and wiped her forehead.

Joline held out her arms to the small boy. "Want to play with that red ball over there?"

He squealed and bounced in her arms. She missed holding babies and little ones. Her brothers and sisters had grown too big to cuddle.

In a few minutes, she had a small circle of toddlers around her, clapping and laughing as she rolled the ball to them one at a time.

Teacher Emily passed by. Her eyebrows rose. "You're very good with the little ones, Joline."

"*Danke,*" Joline muttered. *I'm good with other things too*. She wished her teacher would notice those.

Grateful mothers led other young children over to Joline's circle. It filled the empty, lonely place in Joline's heart when the little boys or girls hugged her legs or begged to be held. She loved doing this but missed being part of a group.

Sadie stood some distance away, eyeing the red ball longingly.

"You want to join us?" Joline asked.

Taking a step back, Sadie shook her head. Joline pretended not to notice her and rolled the ball in Sadie's direction. Sadie bent to pick it up, then stopped and fixed wary eyes on Joline.

"You can play too," Joline told her.

Sadie bit her lip. She kicked the ball back into the circle. A squirrel darted past, and Sadie chased after it as it swished its tail and headed for the trees.

"Stay out of the woods, Sadie," Joline yelled after her and waited to be sure Sadie listened.

One of the toddlers tumbled and began to wail.

Joline bent to examine his scraped elbow. She carried him to the picnic table, wet a napkin, and cleaned off his arm. "It'll be all right," she assured him as she wiped away his tears.

After she applied a bandage, he sniffled and buried his head against her shoulder.

In the distance, some scholars and parents cheered for Matthew's home run. Joline longed to swing a bat and hear a satisfying smack as she sent the ball soaring high overhead, but none of the other scholars had seen her play. None of them even knew she could hit and run better than most of them.

She hugged the small boy close to ease some of that ache. Never before in her life had she been ignored or left out. Her heart had been scraped as raw as this little boy's elbow, but Joline had nobody to hold her or tell her it would be all right.

Stephen's pulse had tripped into overtime when Nettie arrived. At the look she'd given him, his spirits had soared. Then, she'd broken the connection. The wary, shuttered expression had returned. He hoped it only meant she wanted to keep their plans secret.

Crack! Matthew hit another homer. Stephen cheered along with several other parents watching. But after his son rounded the bases and slid into home plate, Stephen checked for Joline. She'd claimed she had other things to do, but the lost look in her eyes troubled him.

He smiled to see her surrounded by babies. That brought back memories of how she'd mothered her brothers and sisters. And at church in Mayville, little ones always clung to Joline's skirt even when her friends surrounded her.

Stephen frowned. After they'd arrived at the park, the other scholars crowded around Matthew and Ben, begging them to play baseball. Katie, who obviously had a loving heart like her beautiful mother, raced over to hug Esther. Abby ran to the swings to join two other girls, but Joline hung back. Nobody called to her or hurried to greet her.

In New York, the minute Joline exited the buggy, her friends swarmed around her, laughing and talking and making plans. Breathless with excitement, Joline had moved from playing baseball to chatting with a group of girls to caring for toddlers to watching over her siblings. Here, she'd done none of that.

Teacher Emily stood nearby. "Your children seem to be settling in well." She nodded toward the small circle of children surrounding Joline. "Your daughter has a gift for caring for little ones. She'll make a good mother."

Stephen agreed, but Joline's future didn't hold his attention as much as her present did. "Have you ever seen Joline play baseball?"

Teacher Emily shifted uncomfortably. "*Neh.* She, um, didn't have much recess time. I did explain that in the letter you never received."

"I see." A lot of things became clearer for Stephen. He'd suspected Joline had been having trouble adjusting, but he hadn't realized she'd made no friends at all. He needed to look into that.

Mrs. Vandenberg had been right about children being a priority. Lately, he'd been too busy buying pigs, helping Amos move, fixing up his house and his brother's, and tearing down the rotting wood of Amos's barn. Maybe he'd made a mistake in donating his free time to the center. And what about his proposal to Nettie? Was a marriage of convenience a wise idea?

The last time Nettie checked, all her children had been having fun. She joined several other mothers at the picnic tables to set out lunch. Then, they called everyone to eat.

Katie brought Esther with her. "She's going to sit with me, Mamm." They found a secluded spot at the farthest table as they chattered. Probably about books, Nettie guessed.

David and Lenny, who'd been at the baseball game, trailed Matthew and Ben into the pavilion. Instead of shooing the younger boys away, Matthew bent and helped them onto the bench beside him. Nettie shot him a grateful smile, and he returned it with one so like his *daed*'s it tugged at her heartstrings.

Joline ushered the toddlers she'd been playing with over to the tables to sit with their *mamms*. Then she stood there, looking forlorn. She surveyed the tables, spotting her siblings sitting with various friends. Even Abby had come to lunch with the two girls who'd been on the swings.

Nettie disliked seeing Joline left out. "Joline, want to help me put out the chicken and salads?"

Relief flashed across Joline's face. Once she realized who'd issued the invitation, the corners of her mouth turned down. But after a brief look around, probably to find someone else to sit with or talk to, she trudged over.

Sadie still hadn't come into the shelter. Nettie glanced around the park to find her youngest daughter. The last time she'd seen her, Sadie had been headed toward the group of young children Joline was tending.

"Where's Sadie?" Nettie asked.

Joline bristled. "I don't know. She ran after a squirrel." She waved toward the woods.

Nettie's heart stuttered to a stop. "I thought she was with you."

"She watched us, but she didn't join us."

"Did she go into the woods?"

"I don't think so. I told her not to."

"But you don't know?" Nettie's voice came out much too shrill.

Joline had her mouth open wide as if she intended to blast Nettie, but Stephen hurried over and set a hand on her shoulders.

He looked from one to the other. "Is everything all right?"

Joline's mouth snapped shut, and she compressed her lips.

Fighting back tears, Nettie answered, "Sadie's missing."

"She's not at any of the tables?" Stephen scanned the pavilion.

"*Neh.*"

Stephen pointed to a large group coming up from the baseball field and a smaller one near the slides. "Maybe she's with some of those children."

Nettie thanked him with her eyes. He must be right. She relaxed a little. But when both groups arrived, Sadie wasn't with either one. Her panic rose. Where was her little girl?

Stephen got everyone's attention. "Sadie Hartzler is missing."

People gasped and looked around. Some stood and checked the playground and baseball diamond.

"Who saw her last?" he asked.

Although she didn't want to accuse Joline, Nettie zeroed in on Joline, who paled, but Stephen didn't notice.

Joline couldn't believe it. *Nettie accusing me in front of everyone? That's so unfair. Why didn't she watch her own kid?*

While her *daed* divided people into search parties, Joline twisted out of his grasp and dashed toward the spot where she'd last seen Sadie.

No matter how Joline felt about Sourpuss, she couldn't let a little child get hurt. Even if she was Sourpuss's daughter.

Leaves and twigs crunched beneath Joline's feet as she stepped into the trees and thick underbrush. She froze at nearby rustling.

"Sadie?" she whispered. Then tried calling again louder.

A chipmunk darted from a pile of leaves.

Joline took a deep breath to calm her racing heart. Ordinarily, she would have followed the cute little animal to get a closer look, but she had a mission.

Lord, please help me to find Sadie. I should have watched to be sure she obeyed.

But the little boy had gotten hurt. Joline had to attend to him. Yet no matter how many excuses she made to herself, deep inside she felt guilty.

The deeper she moved into the woods, the closer together the trees grew. And the leaves blocked out more of the sun, making it darker and scarier. Sadie probably would be frightened. She wouldn't have gone this far.

Joline had almost convinced herself to turn around when, ahead of her on the path, someone whimpered.

"Sadie?" Joline called out.

The tiny cries grew louder.

"Where are you?" Joline headed in the direction of the noise, which was soon drowned out by the sound of rushing water.

"I'm lost." Sadie's fearful voice and her blubbering pinpointed her location.

Joline stepped through a grove of towering oaks into a clearing. Sadie sat beside a creek, hunched over on the ground, her face buried in her skirt.

"Sadie? Are you hurt?" Joline prayed not.

"*Neh.*" The little girl's skirt muffled her words. "I miss Mamm." She lifted her head, and her eyes grew big and round. She jumped to her feet.

"Everyone's looking for you." Joline held out her hand. "Come on, let me take you back to your *mamm.*"

Sadie trembled and backed away. "You're mean. You hurt Katie."

"I won't hurt you. I promise."

"*Neh.*" Sadie turned and dashed away. Straight toward the creek.

"That water's dangerous." Joline flew after her. Her hem caught on a bramble bush, jerking her to a stop.

Please, Lord, keep Sadie safe, she begged as she untangled her dress. Too impatient to unhook each barb,

Joline yanked at her skirt. With a loud rip, she tore herself free.

Ahead of her, Sadie stepped onto a flat rock in the creek. When she spotted Joline, she rushed to other stepping-stones, each one smaller and slipperier.

Joline stopped chasing her. She'd only scare Sadie farther out. If Sadie fell into the deeper part of the creek . . .

Lord, please show me how to rescue her.

The mean pranks Joline had played scrolled through her mind. Katie must have told her little sister. And Sadie believed her. How could Joline erase those from Sadie's mind?

The minister's sermon echoed in Joline's head. *Be sure your sins will find you out.* Hers had. And now they might be responsible for a small girl drowning.

Although he was a newcomer, Stephen took charge and set up search parties of three or four. He assigned them to different sections of the woods. "Stay together at all times," he warned. "If you find Sadie, yell or whistle."

Two mothers stayed behind to feed all the young children and keep them together while their parents and older siblings searched.

Stephen wanted to dash off after Joline, who shouldn't have gone into the woods alone. But first, he needed to talk to Nettie. "You should stay here until we get back."

"But I want to look for her."

"Someone needs to be here if Sadie wanders back."

When Nettie looked about to protest, Stephen added, "Trust me."

Those words sent sparks between them.

"I do," she whispered.

He read the deeper meaning in her eyes—she'd trust him now and till eternity. Stephen didn't want to leave her. He gripped her hands. "Hold that thought until we get back with Sadie."

Her eyes begged him to let her come. But he forced himself to turn and jog toward the trees.

Following Joline's trail proved easy. She'd trampled leaves and broken through underbrush. He had to find her, so he could search for Sadie. They couldn't have two missing children.

In the distance, the sound of rushing water slowed Stephen's steps. Ever since his childhood accident, he'd avoided creeks and streams. Memories of water closing over his head, choking him, churned his stomach even now.

"*Neh*, Sadie, don't." The fear in Joline's voice sliced through him.

He had to find them. Stephen raced toward the sound. He crashed into the clearing and froze. Sadie stood on a stone midstream, poised with one foot in the air, about to step onto a smaller rock almost covered with fast-flowing water.

His heart clenched. He struggled to breathe. Images of plummeting into the creek as a small boy paralyzed him. "*Neh!*" tore from his throat.

Joline whirled around. "Daed?" Her face a mask of relief, she begged, "Help Sadie. She won't let me—"

Splash! Sadie slid into the stream and under the water.

"*Ach!*" Joline's scream echoed through the trees.

Rising terror cemented Stephen to the marshy ground. He had to do something. But he stayed suspended in place. His muscles refused to move.

What was the matter with Daed? All the color had drained from his face, and he stood like a statue. For a split second, Joline wanted to run to him, but Sadie—

Joline spun and dashed toward the floundering girl. Sadie had grasped a thin, upright branch wedged between two rocks. It wouldn't hold for long. Water rose in a small tidal wave around her, tugging her backward.

Joline plunged into the icy stream. She tamped down her panic as the water rose to chest level. She couldn't swim. What if she and Sadie were both swept away?

Anchoring herself to a rock, Joline reached for Sadie. "Hold my hand," she ordered, extending her arm.

Sadie's wide, terrified eyes fixed on Joline.

"I won't hurt you," Joline promised. She prayed Sadie would believe her.

The twig snapped. Sadie flailed in the water. Her head went under. Joline gripped another closer rock. Cold water sloshed over her chin as she leaned out as far as she could and desperately grabbed for Sadie's hand and pulled her up.

Gasping and sputtering, Sadie let Joline draw her close. Sadie clung tight, wrapping her arms around Joline's neck in a stranglehold, choking off her breath. The current tugged on her sodden dress, dragging her down as water swirled and eddied around them. Water closed over her head.

We're going to drown. Dear Lord, I'm sorry.

Strong arms wrapped around them both. Joline relaxed her grip on the rock. Were these the loving arms of God?

Chapter Twenty-Six

As Joline thrashed and kicked, trying to hold Sadie's head above water, Stephen fought to suck air into his lungs. He had to move. He had to rescue them.

God, give me strength.

Fear for his daughter's safety overrode his own dread. He sprinted to the stream bank and waded in, ignoring the sickness somersaulting in his stomach, the terror constricting his lungs, the images floating past his eyes. He had to save his girls.

His boots slipped on the pebbly streambed. Several times, he slid, righting himself by pinwheeling his arms. Frigid water lapped at his chest as he reached out and scooped Joline and Sadie close.

Danke, *Lord.*

He lifted them both above the swiftly flowing water and turned to head back. The weight of the two girls and the strong current almost knocked him off balance several times. He picked his way along, carefully feeling around before placing each foot. If he lost his footing, they might all be carried downstream.

Please, God, help us to make it safely to shore.

Joline buried her face against his chest, murmuring, "I'm sorry, God. I'm sorry, Daed." Sadie untangled her arms from Joline's neck to snake them around Stephen's as he stumbled toward the grassy bank.

Cradling both girls close, he offered up a prayer of gratitude when his feet sank into the spongy ground beside the stream.

"Hang on tight, girls." His footing now secure, Stephen broke into a jog. He wanted to race back and ease Nettie's anxiety.

As soon as she spotted them, she came running toward them. "You found her!"

The joy on her face made Stephen long to sweep her into his arms too.

She studied him. "Are you all right? You look pale and—and . . ."

"I am now." Having Nettie studying him with concern sent his spirits soaring. And he'd faced a lifelong fear and won.

In many of his dreams, water had closed over his head, and he couldn't breathe. Today, he'd conquered that nightmare. And with Nettie by his side, he had the courage to face brand-new challenges.

Nettie broke their gaze to examine Sadie. She held out her arms, and Sadie wriggled out of Stephen's arms into her *mamm*'s.

"She's soaking wet, but she'll be fine," Stephen reassured her. "Neither of them were hurt."

Joline slid down to stand beside him, and she plastered herself against his side. Although it made it hard for him to move, he wanted to keep her close. He could have lost her and Sadie. To reassure himself she was still alive, he set a hand on her shoulder.

Nettie squeezed her daughter and kissed her until the little girl squirmed to get down. Once she did, Nettie's brow furrowed, and her relieved smile melted into sternness. "Sadie, you scared us. We didn't know where you were. Don't ever go off like that again."

Sadie ducked her head. "I'm sorry."

Then Nettie turned her attention back to Stephen. "What happened?"

He gave a brief account of Sadie slipping into the water. If they were going to get married, he needed to be truthful. "I—I froze at the sight of the creek. Joline jumped in first to rescue Sadie."

"*Ach*, Stephen! That had to be hard for you."

Nobody would ever know how difficult. Seeing Joline and Sadie being pulled under by the current and unable to take a step had been torture. But Nettie had an inkling of what he'd endured. He'd trusted her with his long-ago trauma. Like she'd trusted him with her past secrets.

And a short while ago, she'd given him her trust in a completely different matter—their future.

Joline stood beside her *daed*, shivering despite the bright sunshine. She'd almost died. If Daed hadn't shown up, she would have. Even worse, she'd have killed a little girl.

"*Ach*, Joline, thank you for finding Sadie and rescuing her." Nettie swooped toward Joline and pulled her close. Nettie didn't seem to care that Joline's dress was making her own clothes even wetter.

Tears burned behind Joline's eyes. It had been so long since she'd been hugged like that. Why did it have to be Sourpuss? Joline missed Mamm. Turning her face away, she blinked hard. An ache blossomed in her heart. If only she could be in Mamm's arms one more time. She'd never wriggle away the way Sadie did. She'd stay and soak up all the love.

For a short while, with her eyes shut, Joline pretended she was five again and in Mamm's arms. But that wasn't real. Standing rigid in Nettie's encircling arms, Joline wanted to correct everyone's misunderstanding. Sadie might have gotten hurt being in the woods alone, but she'd never have gone into the creek if Joline hadn't showed up. And if Joline hadn't hurt Sadie's sister.

Words pushed from the back of Joline's throat, but her chattering teeth wouldn't let them escape. She should tell everyone the truth and say she was sorry.

"You're cold." Nettie patted her shoulder. "I keep some old towels in the back of the buggy for accidents. I'll go get them for you and Sadie."

Daed stared after Nettie as she hurried to the parking lot. Then, he turned as if waking from a dream. "*Ach*, I forgot to signal everyone that Sadie had been found."

He put his fingers between his lips and whistled. One by one, search parties emerged from the woods.

People crowded around them, and Daed told the story several times. Each time he repeated it, the burning in Joline's stomach increased. How could she correct his mistake?

With all the kids from school crowded around, Joline couldn't say what needed to be said. For the first time, some of them looked at her with admiration.

Nettie returned with three towels. She wrapped one around Sadie's shoulders, tucking it carefully around her and holding her close afterward.

A hollow emptiness opened in Joline's chest. Mamm often did that.

Nettie turned to Joline and draped the towel over her shoulders. Then, Nettie smoothed it into place and followed it with a hug.

Joline gulped down the lump in her throat. Nettie would never have done that if she knew what happened.

When Nettie headed toward Daed with the last towel, Joline didn't let her out of sight. Nettie had better not give Daed the same treatment she'd given both of the girls. To Joline's relief, Nettie held out the towel.

"I have another one in the buggy if you need it."

The tender expression on Daed's face scared Joline.

"I'll be fine. *Danke* for this."

Nettie stood behind Sadie and smoothed some of her daughter's loose hairs into place.

Joline sucked in a breath, remembering the night she'd needed her hair fixed and Nettie had done the same thing. If she closed her eyes, Joline could almost feel the gentle fingers running through her hair. But she didn't want that touch to be Nettie's.

Sadie left her *mamm* and came running over to Joline and took her hand. "Sit with me." She pulled Joline toward a table near the food.

"Me too." Lenny raced after them, and David followed. He tried to pull himself up on the bench beside her. But he dangled over it, legs kicking. Joline reached over to lift him up. He snuggled close.

"I get the other side." David squeezed around behind

Joline and Sadie. He looked up at Joline with adoring eyes. "You found our sister."

Was everyone going to remind her of that?

Sadie thrust out her lower lip. "I want to sit by you."

"You can sit on my lap." After all, they both were already wet. Joline picked her up, and Sadie's smile pierced Joline's heart. "I'm sorry I scared you," Joline whispered.

"Not anymore." Sadie snuggled back with a sigh.

Teacher Emily stood at one end of the pavilion. "I'm glad Sadie is back with us. *Danke*, Joline, for finding her." The teacher looked as if she wanted to add a warning about Joline dashing off on her own.

Instead, she looked from one scholar to another. "I expect everyone to stay near their families. And remember, no woods or creek. We've had enough worries for one day." She ended with a broad smile. "Time to eat."

Everyone filled their plates, prayed, and chattered. A few girls came to sit across from Joline.

"You were really brave to go in the stream," one said.

"I'd be scared," said another. "That water's fast, and I can't swim."

"Neither can I." Joline took a big bite from a chicken leg. With her mouth full, she wouldn't have to talk. If she told them the truth, would they still sit with her?

"Really?" The girl's eyes widened.

Joline yearned for their friendship. But she wanted them to like her for herself, not because they believed a fake story about her.

She finished her meat. Then, she forced herself to tell the whole story. Taking a deep breath, she finished, "If I hadn't hurt Katie, Sadie never would have gone into the water."

"You shouldn't have done those things to Katie," the first girl said, "but you're still brave."

Sadie gave Joline a fierce hug. "You saved me."

Joline swallowed hard. She didn't deserve a hug or praise.

I almost got both of us killed.

Her throat had closed, so Joline did the only thing she could and wrapped her arms around Sadie.

Lenny and David leaned in and enveloped Joline and Sadie in a group hug. Joline's heart melted. Her own brothers and sisters were older. They weren't as affectionate as this anymore. She'd always loved carrying them around and holding them when they were small. She missed that.

Spending time today with the toddlers reminded Joline of how much she'd loved taking care of the little ones in Mayville. Earlier, she'd decided she needed to find some young children to care for. Maybe she had. And maybe she'd also found some school friends.

Nettie's heart, which had pounded out of control while Sadie was missing, went back to that furious pace as the picnic ended, and families headed home. By the time Gideon pulled in, almost everyone had left. Everyone except Stephen.

He and several other people helped load up all the things she and Gideon had brought from the market.

"I'll take these to the stand and then circle back for you and the children," Gideon said as he untied his horse.

"No need," Stephen said. "That's a long ride back here. We can drop the children and Nettie off." He waved toward Joline, who was pushing Lenny and Sadie on the swings. "They're having a good time together."

"That'd be great. *Danke*." From Gideon's broad smile, he intended to use his free time to go out with Fern.

That didn't pain Nettie quite as much as it had in the past, but it did bring up the old fears. She tried not to let them show.

And it reminded her that she needed to give Stephen an answer. Once he heard what she had to say, he might regret offering to drive her home.

Nettie sent David and Katie to chase the last few napkins blowing around the park.

Daed turned to Joline. "Nettie and I need to discuss something important. Could you take all the children over to the swings and slide?"

After what had happened today, Joline swallowed back her protest. She needed to make up for what she'd done. Besides, earlier this afternoon, she'd wished she could spend more time with small children. Now she had her chance.

Except she didn't like Daed talking to Nettie alone. His suppressed excitement made her wary.

He lowered his eyebrows, letting Joline know he expected her to obey. After his recent lecture, she'd been warned if she crossed the line again, she'd be punished.

"All right. Come on, everyone." She beckoned to her siblings. Sadie, Lenny, and David were already glued to Joline's side. Katie hung back, but Esther took her hand and pulled her toward the playground.

Nettie's appreciative smile made Joline sick inside.

She averted her eyes. *You wouldn't smile at me like that if you knew why Sadie fell into the creek.*

"Daed," Matthew asked, "can Ben and I play on the basketball court?"

"That's fine."

"We want to play too." David headed after them, with Lenny trailing behind.

"Sure." Matthew turned to wait for them.

Joline couldn't believe her brother would want to play with two little boys, but his smile seemed genuine.

Abby took one look at Esther and Katie whispering together, and then she pivoted on her heel and followed the boys.

Seeing Katie and Esther together triggered a different reaction in Joline. A heavy weight of guilt she needed to release.

With Sadie in tow, Joline approached the two girls. "Katie, can I talk to you?"

Katie stopped talking to Esther and stared at Joline suspiciously. Seeing Sadie so close to Joline, Katie frowned. "Be careful," she told her little sister.

"Joline's nice." Sadie reached for Joline's hand.

The small girl's hand in hers and her supportive words gave Joline the courage to speak. "I shouldn't have done those mean things to you," she croaked out. "Will you forgive me?"

Katie blinked several times and looked doubtful.

"She means it," Esther assured her.

"You're sure?" Katie asked her. When Esther nodded,

Katie bobbed her head up and down slightly in Joline's direction.

Not a strong sign of forgiveness. But Joline had done what she should. Besides, she'd been mad at Katie's *mamm*, not Katie.

Joline should also apologize to Nettie like Daed had told her, but she couldn't bring herself to do it.

Sadie tugged at Joline's still-damp skirt. "Will you push me on the swing?"

Joline nodded, preoccupied with watching Daed and Nettie. Behind the swings, she'd have a good view. She only wished she could hear what they were saying.

After Stephen sat across from her, Nettie's throat went dry. He sat patiently, waiting for her answer. How could she say *neh*, when all of her wanted to say *jah*?

But she couldn't deprive his children.

If she looked into his eyes, she'd never have the courage to turn him down, so she examined the gray weathered wood of the picnic table. She studied the cracks between the boards . . . the lines of the woodgrain . . . the gouges and graffiti . . .

Stephen didn't say a word. She wished he'd prompt her, push her into answering. But he stayed still. He left beginning the conversation up to her.

"Stephen?" Her voice cracked. She swallowed and started again. "I, um—" Nettie clenched her hands in her lap. "*Danke* for your kind offer." *Can I do this?* "But I must say"—she drew in a shaky breath—"*neh*."

"I see."

Those two words held such disappointment, Nettie darted a quick glance at him. He hadn't really wanted to marry her, had he? He'd said he'd be doing it for his children.

"I-I'd be happy to help with your children. Until . . . until you find them a *mamm*." Sharp pain shot through Nettie at that possibility.

"Nettie?"

The gentle, tender way he said her name made her eyes sting. She blinked back tears. What was she giving up by refusing his offer of marriage? He'd be a kind husband, and she cared about him. They had shared interests and—

"Can you tell me why?"

So many reasons. It was foolish to go into a marriage of convenience with someone you'd fallen for, but who saw you only as a business transaction. That was a recipe for heartbreak. But the gnawing of a hungry belly, the old memories of lack and shame and helplessness, those formed the biggest roadblock. She couldn't do that to any child. Not if she could prevent it.

She forced herself to tell him the truth. "I don't want to burden you or take money from your children."

"*Ach*, Nettie, I don't see you as a burden."

She had been before. First to Thomas, and now to Gideon. The thought of Stephen becoming overwhelmed like Thomas and— *Neh*, she couldn't bear it.

"Are you comparing me with your past?"

Nettie bit her lip.

"You are, aren't you?" His tone soft and soothing, Stephen added, "We can't go through life letting what happened in the past hold us back. We need to let go and trust God for the present and future."

"But what if it happens again?"

"Will worrying about it or being afraid to take chances on something new change anything?"

"It might." Not doing something could help her avoid it. But the truth of what Stephen was saying broke through her barriers. Worrying wouldn't change anything, and as Mamm always told her, it showed a lack of faith. Avoiding things also meant missing out on good opportunities.

"I've always believed time wasted worrying could be better spent praying and trying to solve the problem."

"You're right." But just because you prayed and looked for solutions, you didn't always succeed.

Nettie had begged God for many things throughout her childhood. She wanted Daed back, she wanted Mamm to make enough money to stay home at night, she wanted the rats and cockroaches not to run through the apartment, she wanted to find enough food in the school trash cans to fill her stomach all weekend, she wanted new shoes when hers had holes, she wanted protection from the gangs instead of being forced to join. God answered few of those prayers.

Even now, she prayed for things. She'd asked God for a happy marriage, for Gideon to keep supporting her children . . .

That desire burst from the depths of her soul. "I want safety and security for my children. I don't ever want them to experience any of the things I went through." And she didn't want Stephen's children to go hungry because their *daed* had more mouths to feed.

"Look, Nettie, I'd like to take care of you and the children. As much as I'd like to promise we'll never have financial hardships, I can never guarantee that."

She bowed her head and traced circles on the picnic tabletop with her fingertip. "I understand." He had a generous heart, but too many responsibilities already.

Nettie couldn't look him in the eye. Why had she fallen for a man who was unable to take care of her children? "You can't take on four more children and—" She'd almost said *a wife*.

But she wouldn't really be a wife, more like a business partner. A partner who'd drain money. She had to get away from here before she broke down. "I don't want nine children going hungry instead of four."

While she still had the strength, she pushed herself to her feet, holding on to the tabletop to steady herself. She had to walk away and not look back. She took the first step and prayed the next one would be easier.

"Wait, that's not what I meant. Gideon can't guarantee your children's safety and security either."

"He would have if . . . if it weren't for Fern. He promised." She sniffled. *Neh*, she wasn't going to cry, she couldn't cry. She turned her head to hide the moisture stinging her eyes.

"*Neh*, Nettie. Gideon could never do that. And neither can I." Stephen reached for her hand, the one still gripping the edge of the table, and the warmth of his fingers covering hers anchored her in place.

She'd endure another lifetime of pain to be with him, but she couldn't ask her children to do that. Never. And what about his children? They'd have to share what little they had. She'd never want to be responsible for his children going without what they needed. But to keep them from hardship and poverty, she had to give up the man she loved with all her heart.

Her throat clogged with tears, she choked out, "I can't do this, Stephen."

Stephen's brow furrowed. "Why, Nettie? Please help me to understand."

She squeezed her eyes shut against the pain on his face. "Because I don't want to be the reason your children go without."

"You wouldn't be the cause. We have no control over what happens. An accident, a fire, a death, any of these could sweep away money, love, or life. Only God has power over the circumstances we face, our future, and our children's futures."

Stephen's words stabbed her. All her life, she'd been looking for a savior outside herself. She'd wanted a human being to provide that security. She couldn't depend on her father. Then, she'd lost her husband. Gideon had fallen in love with Fern. And now Stephen had told her he couldn't promise to support her. Deep inside, she'd been wishing he'd promise her the security no one else had.

But he was right. No one could do that. No one but God.

That realization brought Nettie face-to-face with a truth she'd long avoided. Not only didn't she trust God to take care of her, she also blamed Him for her childhood misery.

"Nettie, I want to walk beside you every step of the way, to take care of you and the children, to keep you from hunger and want. But I'm only human. If God chooses to take me, to take my livelihood, my money, my worldly goods, even you—I'd be shattered, but I must keep believing whatever happens is His will."

Until she could believe that too, she wasn't ready for a relationship.

Chapter Twenty-Seven

Slipping her hands from under Stephen's, Nettie pulled away from that warmth and reassurance. Stephen would be a strong, steady rock during trouble. She could depend on him. But counting on a human wasn't the same as relying on God.

"I—I need some time alone."

She rushed off toward the trees. The sound of rushing water beckoned to her. Babbling brooks and crashing waterfalls soothed Nettie, unlike Stephen who feared them the way she dreaded poverty. Yet, today, he'd gone into the water to rescue her daughter.

He'd been paralyzed, but hadn't let his terror hold him back from moving ahead. Judging by his wet clothes, he must have plunged into deep water. And here she was, hesitating about taking a step forward.

What had Stephen said earlier? You can't let the past hold you back. He'd conquered his, but she was letting hers twist her inside out.

Nettie reached the riverbank and stepped out onto a large flat rock. She lowered herself onto the sun-warmed stone and closed her eyes, letting the rustling leaves, the splashing water, the singing birds wash away all the tension. Here, in the midst of nature, she sensed God's presence as never before.

If He had created all this, couldn't He care for her? Scripture verses scrolled through her mind. Not a sparrow falls . . . The hairs on your head are numbered . . . The lilies spin not . . .

The twittering birds brought another verse to mind: *Behold the fowls of the air: for they sow not, neither do they reap, nor gather into barns; yet your heavenly Father feedeth them.*

Wings flapped overhead. God feeds them.

In all the world, she was but a tiny speck. Yet He'd numbered the hairs on her head. How could that be?

Each reminder of God's goodness and bounty loosened a tight knot in her soul, unraveling the ball of doubt and opening her spirit to trust. To belief. To hope.

As Nettie walked off, Stephen regretted starting with the negative. Maybe he should have reassured her he'd take care of her forever. But they'd both lost spouses at a young age. Suppose they married and he died? She needed to prepare for that.

She also seemed concerned that the marriage might cause his children to go hungry. What was that all about?

Even if the business declined, they still had plenty of pigs and land for a vegetable garden. Why hadn't he pointed that out?

Deep inside, though, Stephen understood none of those things would allay Nettie's fears. Even reminding her the church would help if Gideon couldn't afford to support the children hadn't reassured her.

As Mrs. Vandenberg said, *Poverty leaves deep scars*. Stephen would give anything to erase those old memories, but only God could heal those wounds.

He bowed his head. *Lord, I'll do whatever You ask of me. Please show me how to help Nettie.*

"What's the matter, Daed?" Joline's voice behind him startled him.

Stephen had no answer for that question. Nettie had told him some of the things that bothered her, but he sensed something much deeper. He wished she'd shared her full internal battle. "I'm praying for Nettie. She has a big decision to make."

"Oh." Initially, Joline appeared concerned. Then her eyes blazed with suspicion.

Had she guessed what he and Nettie had been discussing? She'd find out soon if Nettie answered *jah*. But if she said *neh*, Stephen would rather deal with that disappointment alone. Disappointment? If she turned him down, it would be more than a disappointment. He'd be crushed.

Daed's acting all weird. Did he and Nettie have a fight?

Or . . .

Joline hoped the little hunch inside wasn't true. Had he asked Nettie—? Joline wouldn't go there.

If he had, it hadn't gone well. Nettie had run off. Maybe she was keeping her promise.

A small sliver of hope blossomed. If Nettie had told Daed *neh*, Joline wanted to hug her.

Well, not hug her. That brought to mind that awkward embrace. Joline pushed aside the yearning it brought up.

She'd wanted to tell Nettie *danke*. But Joline couldn't say why she was grateful.

"Are you watching the little ones?" Daed's question shattered Joline's fantasies.

He turned on the bench so he could check on everyone.

Why did he ask when he could see she wasn't? A spurt of anger rose in her chest. "Why is it always my job to look after everyone?"

Daed's automatic response popped out the way it always did. "Because you're the oldest. And watch your tone, young lady."

Joline gulped. He'd warned her twice already. What would the punishment be for that when they got home?

Then he faced her. "You know, it is a big responsibility. It might be better to share it."

Neh!! "I can do it. I don't mind doing it. You can trust me." Joline took off at a run. She definitely didn't want the kind of help Daed had in mind.

Nettie's heart slowly opened to the God she'd blamed for all her childhood misery. Her hardships paled in the light of Christ's sacrifice. After all He'd gone through for her, how could she hold on to her bitterness? She should follow His example.

When faced with death, He asked to avoid it, but He submitted and ended with *not my will, but Thine, be done*.

That should be her prayer.

With the calming sounds of nature surrounding her, Nettie bowed her head.

Heavenly Father, I've spent my whole life blaming You for my hardships and resenting the circumstances You put me in as a child, a teen, a wife, and even now. Please make me willing to accept whatever You have planned for the future.

For what seemed like ages, she wrestled with resistance. But finally, she surrendered and echoed the words of Christ, "*Not my will, but Thine, be done.*"

Cleansing tears coursed down her cheeks. Peace flooded her soul as she released everything in her past. When she finally lifted misty eyes to the world around her, the leaves appeared greener, the birdsong cheerier, and the water cleaner and clearer. Just like her heart.

Nettie's spirits rose so high she wondered if she were floating. Weightless. Unburdened. Her feet barely touched the ground.

Now she needed to give Stephen her answer.

Nettie's glowing face arrested Stephen's attention. He'd never seen her look so beautiful or at peace. The worry lines had smoothed out. Her lip curved upward in a smile. His heart thumped in his chest, and he couldn't form a coherent thought. All he could do was stare.

She settled across from him. Her face vibrant and alive, she leaned forward. "I've prayed . . ."

Stephen's insides clenched. From the joy on her face, she planned to accept. He held his breath.

"My past has been dragging me down and making me

fearful. And I've been blaming God for my problems in life. But I realized you're right. He did give me those experiences for a reason."

"Oh, Nettie, I'm so glad. You have a lot to give Mrs. Vandenberg's programs." Stephen's whole being rejoiced that Nettie could see her gifts. And he prayed assisting those in need would help her release old pain.

"Everyone in the Amish community says worrying is not trusting God, but until today, I've never believed it. You pointed out how foolish it is to worry. And you're right. All the worrying in the world won't change what's going to happen."

Stephen nodded. "So often the time we spend fretting could be put to better use looking for solutions."

"You're right. But I haven't been able to do that because I didn't trust God to work things out for good."

"Sometimes," Stephen tried to say this gently so she didn't think he was accusing her, "we don't see the good in our experiences until much later. Then we see God was directing us down a better path, but we keep fighting because we think we know what's best."

Nettie's smile lit up her face. "I thought about Jesus saying, *not my will, but Thine*, and I knew deep inside that I needed to do the same. Surrendering to God's will has brought me such peace."

"I'm so glad." All the sadness and conflicted feelings had been wiped from her usual expression. "You look, um"—he shouldn't say *beautiful* or *glowing*—"relaxed."

"I am. And now I know whatever happens with Gideon won't affect my future. I can trust Him to provide."

Did that mean she didn't want to accept the marriage

of convenience? Or was she saying she no longer worried about them getting married?

"Um, Nettie, did you pray about my offer?"

She lowered her eyes, but not before he noted a flicker of guilt. "*Neh*, I didn't. I needed to get right with God. I didn't think about—"

"It's all right. There's plenty of time. You took care of the most important thing in life."

"True. Getting rid of the fear means I can depend on God. I won't need to burden you. And I won't take away money you need to feed your children."

Earlier, she'd indicated she'd be the cause of his children to go hungry. "What do you mean? Why would getting married mean my children couldn't eat?"

"You explained you couldn't support us."

"*Ach*, Nettie." Stephen's laugh expressed his frustration with himself. "I've made a mess of this." He reached across and took her hand. "My children won't go hungry if I take on more mouths to feed."

She didn't look convinced.

"Even if the market business—which is doing quite well—were to fail, we might have to eat pork every night along with vegetables from the garden, but no one will starve."

"Don't the pigs belong to your brother? He might not want more responsibility."

Inwardly, Stephen groaned. Why had he done such a poor job of explaining his financial situation? She thought he couldn't take care of her and the children. And with her caring heart, she didn't want to force his family to go without.

"I bought the house, the property, and the pigs from Amos when I moved here."

Nettie blinked at him, as if uncertain whether to believe him. "But . . . but how? Everyone said your business shut down in New York."

Did she think he'd gone bankrupt? Not that he would ever do such a thing. He would work for as many years as it took to repay any money he owed.

"The market shut down, so, *jah*, my business closed. But I still had my home, my farm, and the pigs. I came here to take over the family home and business. Amos is expanding Lapp's Pastured Pork to another Lancaster County market and buying a house near his fiancée."

"But I thought . . ."

"What I said before was just to remind you that we don't know what the future holds. If you marry me, it's possible we could lose everything. I pray that won't happen, but we've both discovered life is full of unexpected changes."

"I know," she said softly, staring down at their entwined hands.

Nettie tried to rearrange her impressions of Stephen. She'd thought he'd been struggling and dependent on his brother. Instead, he sounded financially secure. Once, she would have jumped at the marriage proposal for that reason alone. Now, she no longer needed to grasp for that security. But where did that leave Stephen's proposal?

Maybe it had been best she hadn't known he could support her. If she'd accepted his proposal for that reason, she never would have faced her lack of faith. The Lord had led her down that path so she'd learn to put her trust in Him.

"Nettie?"

She didn't need to marry for security anymore, but what did she tell Stephen? He looked at her expectantly.

"Stephen, what happened at the creek today changed everything for me. I need to think about this and pray about God's will."

"Take as long as you need."

She already had strong feelings for Stephen, and the human part of her longed to say *jah*. Perhaps in time, he'd come to love her—if marrying him turned out to be God's will for her. But was this the direction God wanted her to go?

Chapter Twenty-Eight

For most of the night, Nettie tossed and turned. She prayed, but her human desires fought against full surrender. She couldn't honestly say, *Not my will, but Thine, be done*, about the marriage proposal yet. Too many other feelings and longings clouded her mind.

Questions bubbled up from inside of her, and she yearned to accept Stephen's offer.

As she had at the creek, she prayed to be willing to accept God's direction in her life. *And please, Lord, give me a sign to show me what You want me to do.*

After that prayer, she drifted off into a deep and peaceful sleep, determined that she would follow wherever He led her. The next morning, she woke with a strong resolve, ready for God to reveal her future path. The lightness of spirit she'd experienced ycsterday carried over into the morning, and Nettie couldn't stop smiling.

Gideon had been morose on the way to the market, and when Fern didn't show up to work, Nick called to him, "Why isn't Fern here? Did you two break up? That why you're moping around?"

Nettie stopped filling salad containers. She'd noticed

Gideon's depression on Saturday at suppertime. Was this God's sign? If Gideon and Fern were no longer together, Nettie and her children would still have a home.

If that possibility had arisen a few weeks ago, she would have been overjoyed. Today, it plunged her into unhappiness. Did God want her to give up Stephen?

Gideon still hadn't responded. With mechanical movements, he threaded chickens onto the spit.

Nick strolled over to Nettie. "From your face, I assume the answer is *yes*. Looks like you edged out the competition."

But Nettie didn't want to win. She'd told God she'd follow His leading, so she shouldn't rebel about going in that direction. Still, some of Nettie's joy leaked away.

"Hey, Gid."—Nick elbowed Gideon as he passed—"You gonna answer me?"

"Huh?" A blank look on his face, Gideon glanced at Nick.

"I asked why you're so down in the dumps." He shook his head. "Such a shame. Losing Fern'll be hard on all of us. At least, you have another woman who's thrilled to take Fern's place."

Nick had misread Nettie's joy, and though her inner peace stayed steady, her spirits dipped.

Gideon stared at Nick, confused. "I don't know if she's thrilled about it, but, *jah*, Sovilla will be here soon to take over for Fern."

"Sovilla?" Nick echoed the question Nettie wanted to ask.

"*Jah*, she'll be working at the bakery"—Gideon's sad eyes strayed to the bakery counters still draped with sheets—"until Fern gets back from South Carolina."

"South Carolina?" Nick planted his hands on his hips. "She just up and took a vacation without telling any of us?"

"It's not a vacation. She and Mrs. Vandenberg are going to see Fern's brother."

Their conversation was cut short when a cute brunette wearing a Midwest *kapp* showed up, pushing a cart full of baked goods. Gideon rushed to her rescue. Nettie hurried after him. They didn't have much time until the market opened.

All of them, even Nick, pitched in to unload the cookies and pastries. But of course, he couldn't resist his usual flirting. "So how come you Amish girls are all so pretty."

Sovilla's blush reached the roots of her hair.

"Leave her alone, Nick," Gideon growled. "I can't afford to lose a baker this week."

The market doors opened, and customers streamed in, sending them all scurrying back to their places. And once again, Nettie cheered up. Gideon and Fern were not breaking up. Why did that make her so happy?

"Hey, Stephen?" The maintenance man headed toward Stephen, waving a note. "Mrs. Vandenberg left a message for you. She's out of town, but she'd like to meet with you at the STAR center tomorrow evening."

"Thank you." Stephen took the note, which said the van would pick him and the children up at six thirty.

"I've been hearing great things about that center." With a quick wave, Martin shambled down the aisle. "I'm off to give the same message to Nettie."

So, Mrs. Vandenberg wanted to see him and Nettie? What did she want to talk about? She'd said to bring the children. That shouldn't be a problem. They loved being at the center.

He'd been hoping to give Nettie a little time, but he couldn't ignore Mrs. Vandenberg's summons. And, as he'd anticipated, the four younger children cheered. Joline struck her usual aloof pose, but just before she turned away, a hint of a smile appeared.

And the next evening, Joline jumped in the van first. Sadie was sitting next to Nettie, but as soon as Sadie spotted Joline, the little girl rushed from her seat.

"Sit with me," Sadie begged Joline, grabbing her hand and pulling her down onto the bench seat.

Stephen moved past his daughter to a seat behind Nettie so he could watch her without being detected. He enjoyed the whole ride, but he also used the time to pray for Nettie and her decision.

When they arrived at the center, Joline volunteered to take care of Sadie. Abby swiveled her head from Esther and Katie to Joline and Sadie.

As usual, Nettie sensed Abby's distress. "Did you want to do art again?"

Abby stared at the floor. "Not by myself," she muttered.

Joline surprised Stephen by walking over and putting an arm around Abby. "Sadie and I will go with you. Won't we, Sadie?" Joline smiled down at the little girl.

Sadie, who was clinging to Joline's hand, nodded.

"Looks like everyone's getting along like one big happy family." Mrs. Vandenberg smiled approvingly.

Stephen hoped her remark wouldn't upset Nettie. But Mrs. Vandenberg was right. Lenny and David tagged after the two older boys.

"Mamm, can we show you something in the library?"

Katie asked. "They have this big bookworm you can sit inside to read."

"Maybe later. I need to meet with Mrs. Vandenberg now."

"Oh, go ahead." Mrs. Vandenberg waved toward the girls. "I had that bookworm commissioned. It has twelve cubbyholes cut in the side to hold cushions. The kids seem to love it. I can talk to Stephen until you get back."

From the gleam in her eye, he suspected he'd be plied with questions until Nettie arrived. And he was right. After they reached Mrs. Vandenberg's office, she directed him to a new cushioned chair. Then she settled behind her desk, and the inquisition began.

"So, how's it going, Stephen? With Nettie, I mean. You did ask her to marry you, didn't you?"

He blinked. Did she have some kind of secret radar that picked up all his thoughts and actions? "*Jah*, I did offer her a marriage of convenience."

"And she hasn't answered yet, I'm guessing." At his nod, Mrs. Vandenberg pursed her lips. "Hmm. Maybe that's the problem. Most woman prefer declarations of love to business arrangements."

"But I couldn't." Were the feelings he had for Nettie love? Stephen had avoided that question.

"You don't love her?"

He hadn't said that. "I don't know."

"I think you do, but you're afraid to admit it."

Before he could reply, Nettie tapped at the door. She stuck her head in. "You wanted to see me?"

"I most certainly did." Mrs. Vandenberg motioned for her to come in. "Perfect timing. Stephen and I had just finished our little talk."

They had? As usual, Mrs. Vandenberg had gotten in the last word.

"Have a seat." She motioned Nettie to a soft cushioned chair.

Stephen couldn't help smiling. Mrs. Vandenberg had added another padded chair. She'd directed him to sit in one of them, but after her line of questioning, the wooden hot seat might have been more appropriate.

Nettie's gaze fell on the wooden chair that had been shoved to one side. Then she met Stephen's eyes and suppressed a giggle. He held back his laugh.

Stephen started to stand. "I'll leave you two to your conversation then."

"No, no." Mrs. Vandenberg waved him back to his seat. "I'll be talking to Nettie, but what we discuss might affect you."

Mrs. Vandenberg's raised eyebrows and—was that a wink?—puzzled him. Then his stomach twisted. Did she intend to force Nettie to answer him?

Ach! Mrs. Vandenberg knew how to talk people into things. He didn't want Nettie pushed into agreeing to something she didn't want to do. But Mrs. Vandenberg went in a totally different direction, stunning both him and Nettie.

"I've decided to hire a director to oversee the program for gang members." Mrs. Vandenberg fiddled with papers on her desk, then slid a thick sheaf toward Nettie. "I'd like your opinion on the scope of the program."

"Is it all right if I take it home to read?"

"Of course, but I'd like you to glance over the first page."

Nettie reached for the packet. She bent her head over

the typed lines and gasped. "This can't be right. You don't mean it."

Stephen wished he were close enough to read the paper.

"I most certainly do." Mrs. Vandenberg's crisp, no-nonsense answer brooked no argument. "Why don't you pass that to Stephen? Let's see what he thinks."

Dutifully, Nettie handed over the paper, but she protested, "Even if I do this, I can't accept that amount."

Stephen scanned the document. Mrs. Vandenberg planned to put Nettie in charge of the program and pay her a huge salary. If she made that much, she and her children would never have to worry about going hungry again. Even more importantly, Nettie was the best choice for the job.

Mrs. Vandenberg speared Nettie with a piercing gaze. One that made her shrivel.

I can't let Mrs. V talk me into this.

The whole idea overwhelmed Nettie. She had no experience.

"Remember what I said about paying people a living wage?"

"But this is way too much. If I accepted the job, I wouldn't take more than anyone else."

"You're right. I'll raise everyone's salary to match yours."

"*Neh*, I didn't mean—"

"You don't want other people to make more money?"

"*Neh*, *jah*, I mean . . ." Once again, Mrs. V had gotten Nettie all tangled up. *Jah*, she wanted other people to make that much money, but she didn't deserve it herself.

"You know, Nettie, I strongly believe that we get in life what we think we deserve. Maybe you need to raise your expectations."

How did Mrs. V always manage to answer Nettie's unspoken comments?

"But I don't have any experience."

"You do too." Steven's eyes blazed with an *I-believe-in-you* light. "You know more than both of us put together." He gestured toward Mrs. V and himself. "You had the best suggestions when we planned the center. And you were the one who came up with the idea for the gang members' center."

Mrs. Vandenberg beamed at him. "It sounds as if you'd like to see her do this, Stephen."

"Of course I would. Nettie would be perfect."

Her heart warmed. Stephen believed in her. The excitement in his expression convinced her he meant what he said. He thought she was perfect. Perfect for the job. But maybe not perfect for him. Perhaps his enthusiasm meant he'd found a way out of the marriage of convenience.

"Well." Mrs. Vandenberg leaned back in her chair. "That's one successful hurdle completed."

"Wait," Stephen said, "she hasn't agreed to take the position." He turned to face her. "Is that all right with you, Nettie? Is this something you want to do?"

Nettie's heart burned within her. She'd asked God for a sign, and He'd given her a powerful one. This job would allow her to turn her past into an asset; she could use those hardships to guide others past them.

And she'd be paying back her debt to friends on the street she couldn't save. Some had ended up in jail. Others had ended up dead. Managing the project for gang members would get many teens off the street and give them hope for the future.

"I forgot to mention," Mrs. Vandenberg said, "you'd only need to be here when the market is closed. It's a part-time job. I didn't want to interfere with your work at the stand or with your courtship."

Courtship? If Nettie took this job, she wouldn't have time for a relationship. She'd be here on her days off and most evenings. Was this God's answer to her question about whether or not she should marry Stephen? It certainly seemed to be.

Stephen tensed at the mention of courtship. Why had Mrs. Vandenberg brought that up? He'd told her Nettie hadn't answered him. A lovely shade of rose pink blossomed on Nettie's cheeks. And everything inside him wished she'd say *jah*. If she accepted Mrs. Vandenberg's offer, though, she'd no longer need his support.

Still, he wanted her to accept the job. She'd have a chance to use all her skills and turn her past into a positive force. Managing the project for gang members would get many teens off the street and give so many of them and their families hope for the future. She'd also cut back on street crimes, saving the lives of innocent victims. An opportunity like this took precedence over his offer.

Not that she couldn't do both. If she chose to marry him, it wouldn't be easy, but he'd do everything he could to support her in doing the job. But she no longer needed a marriage of convenience. She could turn him down because her children would be well provided for. The second outcome made his spirits plummet.

"Stephen?" Mrs. Vandenberg quirked an eyebrow. "You look lost in thought. Or love?"

Her teasing left Stephen with a blazing face and a question he couldn't answer aloud.

She put him out of his misery by sliding a second set of papers toward him. "What do you think of this?"

The second he glanced down, his own name caught his eye. What in the world? A contract like Nettie's? Except this one was for liaison between the new jobs center and the farmer's market.

"You want me to set up market partnerships for the gang members?" Stephen wanted to be sure he understood correctly.

Nettie sucked in a breath. "That would be wonderful."

"Exactly." Mrs. Vandenberg leaned forward. "Will you do it?"

"I'd be happy to do it, but not at this salary." A salary much higher than what he earned now.

"No problem. Nettie convinced me we need to raise everyone's pay to the same level."

"*Neh*, you misunderstood me. The only way I'll consider taking this job is if I can do it for free."

She blinked. "I wouldn't feel right not paying you."

"Those are my terms. Take it or leave it." He hoped he didn't sound too harsh, but he'd never accept money for helping people.

"I guess I have no choice, do I?" She sighed, but then brightened. "I'll agree to your terms if you'll do me one favor."

"Of course. I'd be happy to."

"Wonderful." She picked up her cane and pushed herself

shakily to her feet. "I'd like you to tell Nettie your true feelings on the marriage of convenience."

What? Stephen couldn't believe Mrs. Vandenberg said that in front of Nettie. He sat there tongue-tied as Mrs. Vandenberg tottered to the door.

One hand on the knob, she turned. "You know, Nettie, God doesn't always call us to walk a difficult path. Often, He give us the desires of our hearts."

Mrs. Vandenberg closed the door behind her with a snap. A snap that sent panic spiraling through Stephen. He had a sudden vision of the desire of *his* heart, but what should he say?

Chapter Twenty-Nine

The silence stretched between them as Stephen scrambled to find the words. Nettie looked at him curiously.

Then she said softly, "You want to back out of your offer? That's all right, Stephen." She rattled the papers in her lap. "You were kind to suggest it, but I'll be able to take care of myself and the children."

Neh, that wasn't what he wanted at all. But now she had no reason to marry him.

Mrs. Vandenberg wanted him to be honest. "I'd still like to marry you. I'd also like to see you take the job Mrs. Vandenberg offered. I'd do whatever I could to help you with that."

"*Ach*, Stephen, that's so . . ." Nettie appeared at a loss for words.

Her breathless voice and starry eyes gave him hope. Perhaps he should add that his feelings for her had grown. Mrs. Vandenberg had probably intended for him to confess his attraction to Nettie, his affection for her, his . . .

Mrs. Vandenberg had used the word *love*, but Stephen

hadn't had time to evaluate that yet. Or maybe he'd been avoiding facing his deeper emotions.

A troubled look crossed Nettie's face. "This all sounds so wonderful. Too good to be true." She patted the papers on her lap. "But I haven't prayed about any of it."

"Maybe we should do that now." He hadn't brought any of this to the Lord either.

He reached for Nettie's hand and enclosed it in his. Her shy smile sent sparks zinging through him. Maybe he should have waited to touch her. He meant only to show his encouragement for her decisions, but now he'd have trouble keeping his mind on spiritual things.

Dear Lord, please focus my concentration on You. I want to do Your will. Uplift Nettie as she does the same. Since I started praying about this, I've been feeling as if You've been leading me to marry Nettie. But if it isn't the direction I should go, please direct me in the right path. I want to do Your will.

He lifted his head. Perhaps he should have prayed about the job Mrs. Vandenberg had asked him to take. But as soon as he'd considered it, he had a strong sense he'd made the right choice. And his certainty over asking Nettie to marry him had been confirmed several times.

Nettie's head remained bowed. Her eyebrows had drawn together in earnestness. He admired this new side of Nettie even more than he'd been drawn to her courage in overcoming her past trials.

He sent another request heavenward. *Lord, please give Nettie clear answers to her questions. And help me to accept whatever guidance she receives from You.*

When she lifted her head, Nettie's eyes shone even

brighter than before. Could it be? Stephen hardly dared to believe she might be the answer to his dreams.

"I can't believe how good God is," Nettie exclaimed.

She still couldn't believe she'd been offered a job that would allow her to help gang members find hope. She could share her journey and her faith. And to be paid money for doing what she'd always longed to do, but had no way to make it happen.

Perhaps she, too, should offer to do it for free like Stephen. She'd have to depend on God for the money.

When she'd lowered her head for prayer, her hand tucked in Stephen's, it felt so right. The warmth and support flowing from his strong hand wrapped around hers made her yearn for a deeper connection. What if the two of them could pray like this daily? What if they could work on the program together? What if they could . . .

Nettie's excitement faltered. It didn't seem possible. But what if they could fall in love? What if they could add that eternal bond to their relationship?

Was Mrs. Vandenberg right? Did God want to fulfill the desires of her heart? If God had brought Stephen into her life, could He also give them an abiding love?

But how did she answer Stephen's request when she wanted more. So much more. She ducked her head unable to meet his gaze. She didn't want him to read the longing in her eyes.

"I—I feel like God wants me to agree to both you and Mrs. Vandenberg." That sounded so stiff and formal.

"You're sure?" Stephen sounded tense and on edge.

Did he want to take back his offer? But when she

looked up, the delight on his face filled her with joy. Maybe they did have a chance at love.

Stephen couldn't believe his ears. She'd said she'd marry him. His heart danced with excitement. He hoped, in time, their feelings for each other would grow.

"There's just one more thing," Nettie said hesitantly.

Stephen had weathered so many setbacks so far, he didn't want to face another obstacle. Not after she'd finally agreed.

"I promised I'd never marry you."

"What?" Stephen stared at her with disbelief in every line on his face. "When did you do that? And who did you promise?"

"Joline. The night she, umm, ran outside the center. Afterward, when I was brushing her hair, I told her she didn't have to worry about me marrying you because . . . because I never would."

"First of all, my daughter doesn't make marriage decisions for me. And second, what put it into either of your heads that I might ask you?"

Nettie shuffled her feet. That had been rather presumptuous. "I guess Joline worried about it from the time she saw us meeting with Mrs. Vandenberg. That might be why Joline disliked me."

"She was rude, and I'm so sorry. But she had no right to ask you for that promise."

Nettie hung her head. "I gave it willingly. I assumed you'd want nothing to do with me once you knew the truth about my life."

"You thought wrong." He softened his words with a gentle smile. "I admire you for all you've been through."

Nettie still couldn't believe it. But when she stared into his eyes, they reflected only honesty and caring. He meant it. She'd never thought she'd find a man to marry, one who'd know the whole truth about her past and still accept—her.

"I don't know what to tell Joline. I don't want to go back on my word. That's not a good way to start a family relationship."

"I'll take care of talking to Joline. It sounds as if she pressured you into making that statement."

"She didn't. I could tell she was afraid of losing you."

"Joline won't be losing me. She'll be gaining a *mamm*."

"Please don't be harsh with her," Nettie begged.

The corners of Stephen's mouth twitched. "Part of my problem with Joline is that I find it hard to discipline her. She's had so much to deal with since losing her *mamm* that whenever I should scold or punish her, I can't bring myself to do it."

"I can understand that. She really mothers the other children."

"And she's done most of the cooking. But after she ran away that night, I've tried to be stricter. And I needed to stop her rudeness and disrespect. Especially toward you."

"It's all right. I understand why she acts that way."

"Maybe once we're married, you can help me curb it."

Nettie wasn't so sure she'd be the right person for that. Her marrying Stephen would only increase Joline's anger. And Nettie had no idea how to change that.

* * *

"Since we believe this is God's will for us, should we set a date?" Stephen was eager to make this marriage of convenience official. "After the repairs on Amos's house are finished, he'll be moving out of our house. The Saturday after he moves will be the barn raising. What about the week after that?"

A frown creased Nettie's brow. "Barn raising? Will you be—"

"Don't worry. I'll stay on the ground." His fear of heights guaranteed that.

"You're sure?"

"I promise."

"All right. The Thursday after the barn raising."

Stephen couldn't tamp down his excitement. "I guess it's time to tell the children."

They rounded up everyone and headed to the office. Mrs. Vandenberg's eyes twinkled as the whole group passed.

"Congratulations," she called after them. "Look at the paper on my desk before you tell them."

Stephen shook his head. Mrs. Vandenberg was always one step—or even twenty steps—ahead of them. He met Nettie's eyes, and they both laughed.

When everyone had crowded into the room, he and Nettie checked the paper. When she saw the diagram, Nettie collapsed into Mrs. Vandenberg's chair and buried her face in her hands.

Stephen set a hand on her shoulder. "Are you all right?"

She shook her head. "How did she know? This was the main thing I worried about."

"She must have a direct connection with God. That's the only way she'd know all this."

He still couldn't believe it himself. The diagram showed the office Mrs. Vandenberg had under construction for Nettie and him. In addition to his-and-her desks beside each other, it had a huge play area for the children, a kitchen, and a dining room.

"I didn't know what we'd do about meals and spending time together," Nettie's voice came out low and shaky.

He'd wondered that too. "I guess God—through Mrs. Vandenberg—is providing for everything we need. It seems we're headed in the right direction."

Nettie lifted her head. "I asked God for a sign about my future." She laughed. "I didn't get a sign. I got a neon billboard like that one." She pointed to a sign blinking across the street, then patted the paper on the desk.

Stephen cleared his throat as she rose to stand beside him. And he made the announcement he wondered if he'd ever get a chance to make. "Nettie and I will be getting married."

The room broke into pandemonium.

Katie squealed and embraced Esther. "We're going to be sisters!" The two of them jumped up and down.

Abby scowled at them.

Esther extended a hand and pulled Abby into the circle. "All three of us will be sisters."

Joline sank into one of the comfy chairs, her expression sick. Sadie crawled onto Joline's lap. David and Lenny cheered at the top of their lungs and threw themselves at Matthew and Ben, who both looked surprised.

Then, Joline trained narrowed eyes on Nettie. "But you promised," she burst out.

Stephen jumped to Nettie's defense. "She intended to keep her word, but God led us both in a different direction. We're following Him rather than our own choices."

"So, you really don't want to marry each other?" Joline demanded.

Nettie appeared as discomfited as Stephen. He couldn't declare his feelings for her in public when he hadn't shared them with her in private. And he wasn't sure she'd welcome his change of heart.

He scrambled for an answer. "Um, of course we do. We want to do God's will."

Joline couldn't fight that. She ducked her head and mumbled, "But what about us?"

"I hope you'll all do your best to make this a happy family."

Not counting Joline, everyone but Abby seemed to be trying. Esther had her arms around both Abby and Katie, but Abby stood stiff and uncomfortable apart from Katie. Stephen hoped, in time, the three girls would become close. The older boys had their hands on David's and Lenny's shoulders. They seemed ready to embrace their roles as older brothers to the two smaller boys. Sadie sat on Joline's lap, looking thrilled.

"We did want to talk to you privately, Joline," Nettie said.

Joline screwed up her face, but after Stephen frowned at her, she smoothed out her features.

"The rest of you can all go back to your activities," Stephen told them. "Matthew, can you make sure everyone gets to the right rooms?"

Matthew straightened his shoulders. "*Jah*." He herded the others to the door.

"But I want to stay with Joline." Sadie wound her arms around Joline's neck.

"It's fine with me," Stephen said, "if your *mamm* agrees." Maybe Sadie would temper Joline's reactions.

Nettie's nod assured him he'd made the right decision. Now, they'd need to tackle one of their first challenges as a couple—Joline's attitude.

Joline sat there flabbergasted. After all her efforts, Daed had decided to marry Sourpuss. Except the name Sourpuss didn't fit anymore. Nettie's smile stretched so wide her cheeks must ache. Joline couldn't think of another nickname to fit someone who fake smiled like that.

Nettie turned her phony smile on Joline. "We're going to need a lot of help with meals and childcare. You've been doing it for your *daed*, so we'd like you to keep handling the same responsibilities after we marry."

Joline eyed her suspiciously. *She just wants to make me feel better.*

Daed reached for Nettie's hand. "We really do need you. Nettie will be taking a job at the center, so she'll have a lot of extra work."

"The center? After you're married?"

"That's right. She'll be in charge of the new program for gang members."

"Figures," Joline muttered. "But mothers should stay home with their children." Not that she needed a *mamm*. She was much too old. Well, maybe she did a little. But Nettie could never replace Joline's real *mamm*.

Sadie patted Joline's cheek. "You and Mamm can both take care of me."

That sweet gesture touched Joline, but she refused to show it. "We'll see," she murmured.

Daed cleared his throat. "Our family is going to be a bit different. Plenty of Amish mothers work in family businesses."

"*Jah*, but to work in the city for an *Englischer*?" Joline couldn't believe it.

"Like I said, it will be unusual. But Nettie and I both feel called by the Lord to work at the center."

"You're going to work here too?"

As Daed nodded, Nettie lifted a paper from the desktop and passed it to Joline. "Mrs. Vandenberg is building us a special office with more than enough room for all of you to play. She's even adding a kitchen and dining room, so we can have our meals together on the evenings we work."

"We won't be eating at home?"

"Some nights we will, but we can be together as a family at either table."

"That's why we need you, Joline. You're old enough to help with the work we'll be doing at the center, and you can also attend the classes. But we'll also need someone to watch the little ones."

It sounded as if Nettie wanted to push all her duties off on someone else. *Someone like me.* As much as taking care of little ones appealed to Joline, she didn't like the idea of Nettie not doing her share of the work.

Daed examined Joline's posture and expression. "We thought you'd like to keep the responsibilities you already have."

She did, but if she admitted that . . .

Why did Nettie always make everything so hard?

Joline wished they could go back to Mayville. Everything was easier there. And Daed would never have met Nettie.

"If taking care of the children or making meals is too much for you—"

Joline cut Nettie off with a wave of her hand. "It's not that. It's—it's . . ."

It's what? It's that everything has been turned upside down and inside out and nobody cares about me and we'll have to share our house with strangers and we won't even have a regular mamm *and I'll still be lonely and left out here because Daed will spend all his time with Nettie . . .*

Joline's thoughts whirled like a dog chasing its tail, going round and round, getting more and more tangled and knotted.

"This is new for all of us." Daed seemed sympathetic, but he couldn't really understand. "Why don't you take some time to get used to the idea? Then we can talk again. Nettie thought you'd like more responsibility than the others since you're the oldest, but we can divide the chores equally."

Inside, Joline seethed. They'd managed to put her in a bind.

If I say I want to stay in charge of things, I'll get stuck with all the work. But if I don't agree, Nettie will take over everything. It's so unfair.

Chapter Thirty

The weeks and months inched along slowly as Stephen waited for their wedding day. They had plenty to keep them occupied because he and Nettie had both begun working at the center as well as at the market.

He and Nettie spent plenty of time together trying to get the children comfortable with their blended family. And after a few sibling squabbles, they'd divided up the bedrooms, and Stephen fixed each room to accommodate the future occupants.

Joline had come around a little and even agreed to share a room with Sadie. But she still dragged her feet on accepting Nettie. The three younger girls had agreed to room together, and although the older boys preferred their own space, they'd given in to Lenny and David's pleading. The room now held two bunk beds, leaving one bedroom free for a nursery.

Amos had moved into his renovated home, and they'd closed the market stand today for the barn raising. Members of Amos's new church, all of Betty's family, and several people from the market, including Gideon and his *daed*, had come to help.

Stephen had peeked into the kitchen on the way to the backyard and was delighted to find Nettie had come too. Her eyes shone when she saw him, and they shared a special smile.

Though he wished he could stay around her, he hurried out to assemble bents. He stationed himself so he faced the kitchen windows as he worked. His heart tripped faster each time Nettie passed by or turned to check on him.

Betty's *daed*, Abe, chuckled, as he passed. "Ain't gonna get much work outta you and your brother today. You're more interested in what's going on inside the house." Abe mounted a nearby ladder.

Stephen vowed to fix his attention on the task at hand. He tried to limit his peeks, but it was hard. Whenever Nettie was nearby, he was always distracted.

He stationed himself on the ground, but he hadn't been there long when Abe called down, "Hey, Stephen, could you give us a hand up here?"

Nobody in Stephen's old church ever asked him to climb on a roof. He'd grown up there, so they all understood his fear of heights. He always worked on the ground, like now, nailing together bents or putting up siding.

"I need to finish this." He hoped if he delayed, they'd get someone else.

"Oh, go on." The older man next to Stephen gestured toward the roof. "We can find someone to take your place. We usually let the older workers do the jobs down here. You younger ones can scramble up and down ladders faster than us old folks."

"But I—"

"Get on with you. I'm sure you'd like to impress that pretty girl you have your eye on."

Heat suffused Stephen's face.

The man gave him a cheeky grin. "Thought so. She can see you much better up there." He jerked his thumb toward the roof.

Stephen followed Abe's pointing finger, and dread churned his stomach, each wave cresting higher, building to a tsunami that splashed burning acid into his mouth.

He swallowed hard to choke back the bile. "Nettie doesn't want me to work on the roof because . . ."

Merv rounded the corner of the barn, and Stephen trailed off. He didn't want Nettie's father-in-law to hear him blaming her.

"I can understand you not wanting to upset Nettie." Evidently, Merv had heard. "Thomas's accident was painful for all of us. But you can't let Nettie's fears keep you from working where you're needed."

Although Stephen had spoken the truth, Nettie wasn't the only reason he'd avoided climbing that ladder. It wasn't fair to hide behind her to avoid admitting his own cowardice. "It's not just that."

"Stephen, you coming?" someone yelled from the roof.

Merv clapped Stephen on the shoulder. "Go ahead. I'm headed to the house. I'll talk to Nettie."

The older man waited until Merv had moved out of hearing distance. "Thomas's accident was a terrible tragedy, but Nettie needs to learn to trust God."

The words stabbed Stephen. Since that childhood fall, he'd never moved beyond his boyhood terror. And, if he were honest, he'd hadn't faced those fears. Nettie wasn't the only one who needed to trust God.

"Hurry, Stephen, we need one more man up here."

Stephen's heart hammered so hard in his chest it

drowned out the sound of men pounding in nails. He placed one shaking leg on the first rung. This time he didn't have Nettie to grab the ladder if it tipped. He squeezed his eyes shut and reminded himself this ladder had been tied off.

Lord, please give me Your strength and courage.

When he'd climbed up to fix the farmer's market sign, he'd focused on the swaying wood above him so he wouldn't have to look down. Concentrating on the men working overhead, Stephen inched his way up the ladder.

But once he reached the roof, the ground below showed through the open rafters. He sucked in a breath. If he'd thought the tire swing and the farmer's market climb were bad, those seemed closer to the ground than this.

A lump rose in his throat, choking him, and his trembling increased. One slip, and he'd plunge much farther than he did as a child. And this time, he wouldn't land in water.

The back door of the house banged open. The man next to Stephen stared down at Nettie, who came charging from the house.

"Stephen!" Panic edged her voice.

Why had he climbed on the roof? He'd promised her twice he'd never . . . He'd broken that promise.

"Sorry, Stephen." Abe looked chagrined. "I should never have asked you to come up here. Amos told me about Nettie. I didn't remember."

Despite his dizziness, Stephen looked down at Nettie far below.

"Why don't you do some work on the ground?" Abe

suggested. "No point in upsetting her. Send someone else up, would you?"

"Nettie." Her father-in-law rushed out onto the back porch.

She ignored his call. "Stephen?" She stared up at him, her eyes welling with tears.

How could he do this to her after all she'd been through? "I'm coming down soon."

She shook her head. Her shoulders slumped, and her eyes burned over his betrayal.

This time, when her father-in-law called, she turned and ran in the opposite direction. Away from him. And away from Stephen.

Sick to her stomach, Nettie ran for her buggy. How could he have done this? With shaking hands, she hitched up the horse.

Before she finished, Stephen pounded toward her. "Nettie, wait, please."

She climbed in before he reached her and clucked to the horse to trot away. She'd been foolish to agree to marry him. What had she been thinking?

Thanks to Mrs. Vandenberg, I don't need a marriage of convenience. I can take care of myself. But why did that possibility make her so depressed?

Nettie refused to let herself answer that question. The answer didn't matter anymore. All that mattered was not having to watch another husband or almost-husband fall from a barn roof. She could never go through that again. Never.

Thundering hooves sounded behind her. Almost a blur

in the side mirror, a horse galloped toward her. Stephen's horse and buggy.

He'd gotten down from the roof safely. *Danke*, Lord! But she didn't want anything to do with him. She didn't want to talk to him or see him.

Nettie could urge her horse to go faster, but she didn't want to get in a buggy race. Besides, she knew who'd win.

After Stephen's foolhardiness on the roof, she didn't want to encourage recklessness on the road. She slowed her horse. Stephen would catch up to her, and she'd give him a piece of her mind.

She pulled onto the shoulder. He pulled in behind her and tied his horse to a signpost. Then, he jogged toward her. She turned her head away as he slid the passenger door open. She couldn't face him, or she might break down.

"Nettie, I'm sorry I scared you." If only he could go back and undo what he'd done.

When she didn't answer, he tried again. "I wish I hadn't done it. I never want to do anything to hurt or upset you."

"But you did."

"I didn't want to be up there, but they needed me. I was scared and shaking. I prayed the whole time."

"You looked so unsteady up there. I thought you were going to . . ." Nettie sucked in a shuddery breath. ". . . going to fall." She turned toward him, her eyes damp with unshed tears. "Do you have any idea how terrified I was?"

He could only imagine.

She squeezed her eyes shut. "I went through this already. I can't bear to lose someone I love."

Someone she loves? She loves me?

"Nettie, I promise I'll never do it again."

She shook her head violently. "*Neh*, I don't want to stop you. You must obey God and your conscience. I can't stand in your way. You need a different wife. One who can trust the Lord for your safety."

He put his arm around her and drew her toward him. "I don't want a different wife. I want you."

She stayed rigid in his arms. "Go back to the barn raising. They need you. I think we need to call off this marriage of convenience. I can't live with the uncertainty of building a life with someone who might die."

"We all die sometime. Only God knows when that will be. And how it will happen."

"That may be, but I don't want to marry someone who takes foolish risks."

"Nettie," he said gently, "hundreds of men participate in barn raisings all year long. Accidents rarely happen."

"But when they do . . ."

Logic wouldn't convince her. Her fears ran too deep. "Nettie, I—"

She held up a hand to stop him. "I can't do this. Just let me go home. I'm exhausted."

"Please, Nettie, won't you reconsider?"

"*Neh*." The flatness of the word signaled finality.

Her tone pierced straight through him. Her answer brooked no second chances. Perhaps if she had time to think about it, she'd change her mind.

"Take care of yourself," he said as he slid open the buggy door.

He walked slowly back to his own buggy. Had she really ended it for good? She'd said she loved him. But she'd been overwrought. Perhaps she hadn't meant it the

way he'd taken it. Either way, he had to find a way to win
her back somehow.

Joline couldn't stand it. After Daed returned from
chasing Nettie, he helped with the barn. He even climbed
the ladder twice to carry things up to the other workers.
She held her breath at his wobbly ascents.

Nettie hadn't come back with him. From her expression when she'd torn out of here, she'd never trust Daed
again. Maybe they'd call off the wedding.

Although part of her felt triumphant, Joline also squirmed
inside. She shouldn't be happy over Daed's misfortune.

After they returned home and cared for the pigs, Daed
slumped in a chair. Even after twilight fell, he didn't
bother to turn on the propane light. She rolled it from the
kitchen into the living room, but he waved a hand to keep
her from turning it on.

"*Danke*, but I'd rather be in the dark. I need to think."

The sadness in his eyes haunted Joline as she supervised her younger sisters getting ready for bed. After
everyone had been tucked in, she tiptoed downstairs.

"What's wrong, Daed?"

"Please go to bed, Joline." His voice sounded tired and
sadder than she'd ever heard.

"Is it Nettie?"

He put his head in his hands and groaned. "*Jah*. She
doesn't want to get married."

Joline's spirits danced for joy. But Daed looked so
broken. "I'm sorry," she said quietly.

"Are you really, Joline? I'd think you'd be glad. You
never wanted us together in the first place."

"Well . . . I don't want to see you unhappy."

"I see." Daed didn't lift his head or even glance her way.

Although Joline would never admit it aloud, she'd gotten attached to Sadie. Lenny and David were cute too, especially when they crawled onto her lap to hug her. Even Katie wasn't half bad. Esther would be crushed to find out Katie wasn't going to be her sister.

Other people besides Daed would be hurt. Nettie had a lot to answer for, and Joline planned to make sure she did.

She waited until after the church meal the next day. Nettie, looking as glum as Daed, still sat at the table after the other women went inside to clean up.

Joline charged over. Words popped out of her mouth before she stopped to think. "First, you broke your promise to me."

Nettie stared at her, confused.

"When you said you wouldn't marry my *daed*."

"I'm sorry."

Before Nettie had time to defend herself by saying she'd be keeping her word now, Joline hurried on. "Then you broke your promise to Daed."

A toxic mix of shame and sickness ate at Nettie's insides. "I know, but he . . ." How could she blame Stephen for going back on his word when she'd done it twice? And both were much bigger commitments. "You're right."

"And you're breaking your promise to God," Joline announced with triumph in her voice.

"God?" Nettie echoed weakly. They hadn't exchanged

wedding vows. Sadness washed over her at all she'd given up.

"You said marrying Daed was God's will. So you're going back on that too."

Nettie looked away from the fire burning in Joline's eyes. They'd told the children this marriage was God's will. If she backed out, what lesson would she be teaching them?

"Daed told us about your hus . . . um, your fear about people falling." Planting her hands on her hips, Joline laced into Nettie, "Did you even think about my *daed*? He's scared to death of heights, but he didn't let that stop him."

Nettie wished it had, but she couldn't say that. Not to Joline.

"Don't you think I was afraid when he climbed that ladder? He kept wobbling. I thought he was going to fall." Joline's anguished face showed she'd experienced the same terror as Nettie. "But I *prayed*."

Joline flounced off, leaving Nettie feeling gutted. Joline was right. Nettie should have prayed. Surrendering her future to the Lord meant little if she couldn't trust Him in everything.

Stephen paced the living room floor as Joline and Abby prepared a light supper on Sunday evening. He had no appetite. How could a house with five children feel so empty?

Every Sunday, including off-Sundays, nine children filled the house while he and Nettie made wedding plans or discussed the center. Today was the first time in weeks they hadn't all shared a meal together.

A knock at the door startled him. Stephen hadn't heard anyone approaching, but someone could have dropped a bomb, and he might not have noticed.

He'd rather not have company, but he couldn't be impolite. A neighbor might need help. But someone other than a neighbor stood on the porch. "Nettie?"

"Could we talk?" she asked.

He hoped she didn't plan to drive the knife in deeper. Maybe she'd want to have separate offices at work. Or she'd like him to give up the job so they wouldn't have to see each other at the center.

No matter what, he couldn't deny her request to talk. He pulled the door open wider.

She shook her head. "In private?"

How could he resist the pleading in her eyes? "What did you have in mind?"

"My—my buggy's here." Nettie gestured to her horse tied to a post.

He hadn't even heard the crunch of gravel when she'd pulled into the driveway.

"Could we go to the park?"

The park where they'd had the school picnic? That would bring back too many memories. But he followed her to the buggy, and they rode to the park in silence.

"I'd like to go to the creek to pray first. I know you don't like water. I won't be long." She gestured toward the picnic table where they'd sat last time.

"I'll go with you."

Stephen regretted his decision as they approached the rushing water. When they reached the bank, Nettie balanced on a smaller stepping-stone to reach a large flat rock in the stream.

He relived his own plunge and then Sadie slipping, splashing into the water. His whole body tensed as Nettie lowered herself onto the rock, and he prayed for her safety. Had she'd brought him here so he'd know how she felt when he'd climbed onto the roof?

Neh. Unlike him, Nettie was relaxed and peaceful. She closed her eyes and bowed her head. His heart ached at her beauty and her spirituality. She truly wanted to do God's will.

As her face scrunched tight and she seemed to be wrestling with something, he lifted her up to the Lord. When she finally opened her eyes and tilted her face heavenward, he sucked in a breath. Months ago when she'd emerged from the woods, she'd glowed. This time, she seemed lit from deep within.

Nettie basked in the sunshine and in God's grace. Clean and clear inside, she stepped lightly to the nearest stepping-stone and walked toward her future.

Once she reached the bank, the tense lines around Stephen's eyes smoothed out. She understood that apprehension, that dread. She'd experienced it when she'd seen him on the roof.

"I'm sorry to worry you," she said as she approached him. "I didn't intend to upset you. I just find this spot so peaceful and healing. The Lord spoke to me both times while I was here."

"I can tell."

"I'm sorry for what I said at the barn raising. I spoke out of fear. That's why I wanted to come here. I needed to get back to a place of trusting God in all things."

"So do I." He swallowed hard. "Being here at the water brings back memories of terror."

"I felt the same about you being on the roof. I've turned that over to God. I'm sure I'll still panic when you're up there, but I have to leave the outcome up to the Lord."

"I need to do the same—both for climbing roofs and for watching you crossing the stones in the creek. I have a feeling you'll be coming to this spot again."

She appreciated his understanding of her spiritual connection to this spot. "I hope to. It's a special place."

"Nettie, while you were out there"—he waved a hand toward the rocks—"did you also pray about God's will for us?"

She nodded. She certainly had. "I don't want a marriage of convenience." The last time she'd married for money. This time, she wanted to marry for love.

Stephen looked downcast. "I see." After a moment of silence, hope flared in his expression. "At Amos's house, you said you couldn't bear to lose someone you loved, did you mean—?"

She couldn't believe she'd blurted that out. Admitting the truth would take courage, but she had to be honest. "I meant you."

A slow smile spread across his face as her words dawned on him. He looked deep into her eyes, and the sparks that flew between them made her tingle.

* * *

Stephen couldn't believe it. When Nettie had run from him at the barn raising, he'd finally faced the truth. Losing her would be devastating. "I've fallen in love with you too." *Deeply and irrevocably.*

Her breath hitched in her throat, setting Stephen's pulse on fire. He reached for her hands. "I know you said you didn't want a marriage of convenience, but I do. And I want something more."

"So do I. But I never thought"—she lowered her eyes—"any man would marry me if I told the truth."

Hearing those words twisted Stephen's insides into a knot. "*Ach*, Nettie." His heart ached at all she'd endured.

She kept her head down. "I wanted to settle for a marriage of convenience and keep my past hidden."

"I'm so glad you didn't." Locking her secrets away had caused her to shut herself off from love. "Your past made you the wonderful person you are today. And it's given you a heart for the work at the center. It's also made you a wonderful, caring mother."

She shook her head as if she didn't believe him.

She'd been completely honest with him. He needed to do the same. "I was attracted to you when I suggested the marriage of convenience. But hearing everything you've been through made me fall in love with you."

"I—I can't believe it." She studied his face as if searching to be sure he meant it.

"It's the truth."

A tear trickled down her cheek. Stephen reached out and gently brushed it away. Then he wrapped his arms around her and cradled her close. She melted against him and rested her head against his chest. He longed to protect her from all future hurt.

"Nettie," he breathed out her name like a prayer, "will you marry me?"

She lifted shining eyes and met his. "If it will be a marriage of convenience—*and love.*"

"I promise it will be."

The joy on her face stole his breath away. When he could speak again, he murmured, "I'm so glad God gave me you." Then, he bent to claim the lips of the woman who'd be his bride in a few days. The woman who'd upended the marriage of convenience to capture his whole heart and soul.

Epilogue

Two years later . . .

As the sun peeked over the horizon, Lenny rushed into the kitchen, threw his arms around Stephen's legs, and hugged hard.

Stephen set a hand on his youngest son's shoulder and smiled down at him. "You look excited."

"*Jah.* Today's my first school picnic."

"*Neh*, it's not." Katie adopted a superior big-sister tone. "You've gone to picnics two times already."

"But they weren't *my* picnics. They were everybody else's." He waved a hand toward David tying the laces of his boots and Joline, who was supervising Sadie as she put a casserole in the oven.

Stephen smiled and ruffled his hair. "That's true. You weren't in school before."

Lenny shot a triumphant look at Katie. She laughed and finished setting the table.

"Better get your chores done so we're not late." Stephen smiled down at Lenny.

"*Jah*, come on," David called to him. "Matthew and Ben are already out in the barn."

"I'm coming, but where's Mamm?" Lenny bounced on his toes.

"Upstairs feeding the baby," Joline answered. "She'll be down soon."

Stephen still marveled at Joline's sweetness with her younger siblings. She happily taught them chores and took on more than her share of the work. She also fixed most of the meals when he and Nettie worked at the center. The kitchen Mrs. Vandenberg designed there had been a godsend.

The only thing that hurt Stephen's heart was Joline's referring to Nettie by her first name. He wanted to insist his daughter call Nettie *Mamm*, but Nettie had begged him to let it go, even though he could see how much it hurt her.

I don't want to force her. I'd rather she did it voluntarily, Nettie had said several times.

Stephen had agreed to do it her way, but he cringed every time Joline addressed Nettie. That thought fled from his mind when Nettie entered the kitchen carrying their newborn daughter.

His wife had grown more beautiful than when he'd married her, and his heart still quickened its pace whenever they were together. The thundering increased when she smiled at him. And seeing her holding the baby made his whole being overflow with love.

Nettie's eyes held a promise of quiet time together after they finished their hectic day. And Stephen clung to that promise. Raising ten children, caring for the pig farm and market stand, and supervising the center left little time for just the two of them. But Stephen was grateful they could work together all day, every day.

After beaming a quick flash of lovelight toward him, she turned her attention to Joline and Sadie. "*Danke* for fixing breakfast."

"I did it all by myself," Sadie said as she shut the oven door.

Nettie exchanged a conspiratorial smile with Joline. To Stephen's surprise, his daughter smiled back. One tiny step in the right direction.

As the day at the school picnic passed, Nettie still couldn't believe how her life had changed in the past two years. She had a wonderful husband who loved her and told her so every day. And they shared ten children now, with the addition of baby Hannah, asleep in her *daed*'s arms. Plus, they enjoyed working together at the market and the center.

Nettie and Stephen exchanged charged glances as they watched their children play. Her heart pitter-pattered every time she looked at him. And seeing him with their daughter cradled close made her chest ache with love. She'd never grow tired of sharing her life with this man who put God first and cared so deeply for his family.

Across the park, Joline smacked another home run high over the baseball diamond. Stephen broke into a proud smile as she raced for home plate.

Teacher Emily came up behind them. "She's quite a player."

"*Jah*, she is." Nettie was proud of her oldest daughter. After a rocky start, Joline had made friends at school and church, and now everyone begged to be on her team. But that wasn't the only improvement. Joline had been tested, and working with a tutor for dyslexia over the past two years had improved her reading.

"She's also doing well with her schoolwork." Teacher Emily beamed. "Quite a change from her first few weeks here."

"It certainly is," Stephen agreed.

Joline had also adjusted well to her responsibilities as a big sister to four—now five—new siblings. And she'd taken on a mentoring role to two younger inner-city girls at the center. But Joline had still not accepted Nettie as her *mamm*. Nettie hoped that would come in time.

As the picnic wound down, Nettie and a few other mothers sat in a shaded, private area to feed their babies. After Thomas's death, Nettie had avoided other young married women because she felt out of place and lonely. Now, she'd become the center of attention.

"Tell us more about the center," one of them urged, and Nettie obliged as she put Hannah over her shoulder and patted her back.

In the middle of one story, Sadie whooped and ran toward the parking lot. "My *onkel* and *aenti* are here," she yelled.

Nettie shifted Hannah into her arms and stood. What were Amos and Betty doing here? She hoped they hadn't come bringing bad news. Stephen intercepted her.

"Surprise," he whispered in her ear. "They're taking the children to the center so we can have some time alone."

Nettie laughed. "As alone as we can be with a two-month-old baby."

"Don't worry. I've taken care of that too."

As the rest of their children raced to greet Amos and Betty, Joline veered toward Nettie.

"Hannah's been fed," Stephen continued, "so she'll be fine for a few hours. And Joline promised to change her and take care of her."

Joline skidded to a stop in front of them and held out her arms. Nettie transferred Hannah to Joline, who supported the baby's head and cuddled her close. Joline beamed as she walked carefully toward Amos's buggy. Nettie had no doubt her little daughter would be safe with her big sister.

One by one, other buggies pulled out of the parking lot until only Stephen's remained.

As soon as they were alone, Stephen took Nettie's hand. "Let's go to the creek."

"You don't like water."

"But you do. You've been working so hard lately you deserve something special."

With her hand nestled in Stephen's, she approached the rushing water where she'd had some of her most profound spiritual experiences. Could her heart be any fuller?

She soon found out it could. Stephen encouraged her to sit on her special stone.

After she'd settled into place, he called, "Is there room for two on that rock?"

Startled, she studied his face. He was serious.

He squeezed his eyes shut for a moment, then picked his way across the small stepping-stone.

Nettie's happiness overflowed as he lowered himself beside her and put an arm around her. She laid a hand on his chest, hoping to calm his rapid breathing.

"Give me a second." Stephen closed his eyes, and after a minute or two, he took several deep breaths. Then he opened his eyes. "If you could turn your fears over to the Lord, I should be able to trust Him with this small one."

She laid her head against his chest. His heart still drummed in her ear, but his chest rose and fell more slowly. And then Stephen said the words that meant the most to her in the world.

"I love you so much, and I wanted to pray together in your special place."

They prayed aloud, each sharing what was on their hearts with God and each other.

Although the rushing water still bothered him, Stephen didn't want to leave. He could stay here forever with the woman he loved in his arms and God's heavenly presence surrounding them. But they needed to get to the center.

Hand in hand, they stepped from the stones, and when they reached the bank, Nettie turned to him. "*Danke* for doing this." She radiated joy.

"We should come here often." They could use more peace in their busy lives. "This park is special to me too, you know."

"It is?"

"Definitely. You said *jah* to me twice here." And he'd never forget either time. She'd said *jah* to a marriage of convenience and *jah* to a marriage of love. And they'd had both.

As they traveled to the center, they reminisced over the

past two years. So much had happened, and they'd grown deeper and deeper in love.

When they entered their private office/playroom/ nursery hand-in-hand, glowing from their time together with the Lord, Mrs. Vandenberg was rocking Hannah's cradle.

"Where's Joline?" Stephen asked.

"One of the little girls she mentors needed her. I told her to run along. I'm more than happy to watch this sweet baby. God has really blessed your family."

"*Jah*, He has," Nettie agreed.

"I love watching you two lovebirds." Mrs. Vandenberg's eyes sparkled. "I'll give you some time alone before the baby wakes up." She headed for the door. Just before she closed it behind her, she turned to Stephen. "Aren't you glad I suggested a marriage of convenience?" She clicked the door shut.

Nettie turned toward him with raised eyebrows. "She did?"

His cheeks turned ruddy. "Not exactly. She worried about you and asked me to take care of you. I came up with the idea of marriage. I wasn't sure you'd accept that, so I suggested a marriage of convenience."

"You wanted to marry me back then? You said you needed a mother for the children."

"I did, and I couldn't ask for a more wonderful *mamm*. You've been everything I longed for all of our children to have in a mother. But if I had to be honest . . ."

Once, Nettie would have braced herself, expecting to

hear something negative. But the two years she'd spent with Stephen had conditioned her to expect something positive. She leaned forward eagerly.

"I told myself I asked you because I felt sorry for you, but I denied the real reason. I'd already fallen for you. And fallen hard."

"You had?" Joy bubbled up and spilled out. She didn't need to be shy about confessing her own truth. "I had feelings for you back then too."

"Think how much time and heartache we could have saved if we'd been honest with each other."

Nettie sighed. "I never would have believed you. And because I was ashamed about my past, I couldn't accept anyone's love. God knew what He was doing—both with waiting and with sending you to me."

"And look what you've done with your past."

"That's thanks to you and God." If Stephen hadn't encouraged her to talk about it and accepted her just the way she was, she might not have taken the next step of taking it to God. And she never would have mentioned it in public.

Stephen shot her an admiring glance. "I love watching the gang members' faces when you share your past. Most of them look at us and roll their eyes, but when you start talking, their jaws drop. I think that encourages them to trust us."

Stephen was right. After hearing she'd once been in a gang, the newcomers to the entrepreneur program felt freer to confide about their own pasts. Now, rather than regretting her childhood, Nettie praised God. He was using her experiences to reach others and show them His love. The Lord had helped them turn around many lives.

In the past eighteen months, they'd trained and placed thirty former gang members, and fifty more from cities all over the state had joined the program. They'd already hired additional staff, and Mrs. Vandenberg was renovating buildings to provide student housing. The blighted area around the center had been transformed into a beacon of hope.

Stephen flicked the lock on the door. Wrapping his arms around Nettie, he drew her close and pressed his lips to hers.

The doorknob rattled, followed by a gentle tapping.

"Mrs. V? Daed?" Joline called softly through the door.

Reluctantly, they broke apart.

"I'll be right there, Joline." Stephen bent for one more quick kiss. Then he touched a finger to Nettie's lips. "Hold that thought. I'll be right back."

"You still consider this a marriage of convenience?" Nettie asked as he headed to the door.

He laughed. "And a marriage of love. And of children. And of service."

Joline burst through the door as soon as he unlocked it. "Is Mamm here? Sadie needs her."

Stephen caught Nettie's eye and quirked an eyebrow. He'd caught the slipup too. Joline had called her "Mamm."

"What's the matter?" Nettie asked.

"Sadie skinned her knee and won't stop crying for you. Matthew's carrying her. I came to get a bandage."

By the time Matthew arrived, Joline had helped Nettie get out the first aid kit. After a quick cleaning, a bandage, and a kiss and hug from both Nettie and Joline, Sadie skipped down the hall, holding Matthew's hand.

Nettie stopped Joline before she joined them. If it weren't for Joline, Nettie and Stephen couldn't have had that precious time together at the park. Her heart overflowing with gratitude for all Joline did to keep the family going, Nettie reached out and embraced her oldest daughter.

Joline stiffened in her arms. But when Nettie kissed her forehead, Joline blinked back tears.

Her throat tight, Nettie tried to put her appreciation into words. "*Danke*, Joline, for always being here for us. And for all your help with the children, with chores around the house, even here at the center. We couldn't do this without you."

"And *danke* for watching Hannah and the others so Nettie and I could stay at the park," Stephen added. "And for taking care of Sadie just now."

Nettie gave Joline another quick hug. "You're a very special girl."

Joline ducked her head, but she couldn't hide her smile. "*Danke*, Daed and Net . . . um, Mamm."

Stephen caught Nettie's eye and grinned from ear to ear. Joline had said it not once, but twice.

After she'd slipped out the door to rejoin her friends, Stephen relocked the door. "Now, where were we?"

Nettie rose on tiptoe and tapped a finger to her lips. "Right here."

Stephen gathered her into his arms again. "We are finally one complete and *wunderbar* family."

"*Jah*, we are." Peace and contentment flooded Nettie's soul.

"And I guess I got my marriage of convenience after all." His lips quirked. "Having you here with me is very convenient."

Then his eyes darkened with love and desire. He dipped his head and his lips met hers. And Nettie marveled at how God had transformed a marriage of convenience into an eternal bond of love. For all of them.